THE VAMPIRE'S BRIDE

A Gothic Romance

Brionna Paige McClendon

Book Cover Designed by Yanick Dionisio
Contact Artist on Facebook: ILIE'S ART STUFF

Visit my website at www.Facebook.com/brionnapaigebooks

Printed in the United States of America

ISBN-9781693417290

TABLE OF CONTENTS

CHAPTER ONE

The Choosing

THE VILLAGE WAS silent. As the days crept closer to *The Choosing*, a thick cloud seemed to form above the small village. Looming like a great shadow, syphoning the joy. Any happiness that once frolicked through the cobblestone streets was slaughtered in its tracks. The clouds had become thicker with each passing day, darker and darker they grew. As if nature itself were mourning the loss that was soon to come. Angst permeated the air. Nerves were rattled, fried to their core as the villagers bustled about. Whispered murmurs trailing along the wind like ghostly sighs.

Soon the village would be losing one of its people – a woman. And they prayed for the poor soul. For they would be taken away by the one monster this village feared. Count Dravmir. The vampire who resided in the gloomy castle nestled within the side of a mountain. The large rock formations cornering the village like a wall, a prison. But they had more freedom than the soon-to-be bride of the Count. Once in every generation, the monster left his castle to come and claim one of their own. And once she was stolen, she was never seen, nor heard from again. Not until she was returned to their gates as a lifeless corpse.

Hideously disfigured and mangled. Though the brides were not the only souls to fall victim to the Count's wrath. Many villagers went missing if they ventured too far from the village only to be found in a pile of mutilated limbs.

For decades, the brides would be found after a few months of their choosing. Their bodies dismembered like some savage animal had claimed them as their next meal. The village lived in fear of the Count. What could have angered him? What drove him to murder those poor, young women?

And no matter how many brides were returned to them as a cold corpse, the village never ceased offering the Count a new bride once the last one passed. For the village feared that if they kept a bride from the man, that they would summon his wrath. The vampire going on a ravenous rampage through their small village. Slaughtering any who dared step in his path or within his eyesight. The village elders deeming one life lost was better than every life. It had been several years since the last choosing, the anniversary of that very day creeping ever closer with each passing night.

"*Yelena.*" The grumbled voice of her sister drew her from her thoughts.

With a sigh, the young woman turned her gaze away from the foggy window, her finger had lazily traced patterns on it. The fog creeping back in and covering the doodles. Her sister lingered at the kitchen counter, chopping away at the fresh vegetables on the cutting board. The smell of cabbage and onions drifted lazily through the room as they boiled on the small stove, a hint of spices tantalizing the air. The small kitchen was illuminated by the old lanterns that dangled from the low ceiling. Gentle creaks echoed through the kitchen as the lanterns slightly swung on their hooks. Danna dipped her head beneath them as she flitted about the kitchen, gathering food or bowls. The kitchen was small but homey. The counters filling much of the space. Trinkets were clustered throughout the room and much of their home.

A dirtied old apron hung around Danna's waist, swishing around her as she moved about. Seeming as though she danced through the kitchen, light on her toes. A simple, brown gown draped down her petite frame, the sleeves rolled up to her elbows. There was a smearing of flour across her brow and cheeks, masking the scattering of dark freckles. The white powder contrasting against her light brown skin. Her dark tresses were pulled back into a low ponytail, a few strands dangling freely on either side of her round face. Her hair was like a cascade of liquid night, rippling down her back in thick curls.

The two sisters were a sharp contrast. Where her sister was level-headed, Yelena was the daydreamer. Often frolicking about within her own mind, spending her days gazing out their shop window. Her family knew that she wished for more than this simple life. More than helping bake foods and treats to sell to the village people. Though she was happy here with her sister, mother, and father, she wished to venture out. As if something were calling to her and she could not help but heed that call. That yearning. As if something out there waited for her but she had yet to find it. And perhaps, she never would.

Her sister arched a thick brow, her brown eyes seeming irritated but there was a slight grin upon her lips. "Daydreaming again?" She placed a floured hand on her hip, "Have you even heard a word I spoke?"

Yelena chuckled as she shrugged her shoulders, "Complaining about chopping onions?" She offered with a bat of her lashes.

Her elder sister released a sigh with a shake of her head, "Well yes, but I was talking to *you*. Or at least trying to, anyhow."

"Apologies, Danna. What were you talking about?"

Her sister's demeanor changed then, her gaze lowering back to the old cutting board. The knife slicing through the pile of onion pieces, dicing them. "I was talking about *The Choosing*." It seemed to pain her to rasp those words.

The look on her sister's face caused worry to stir in Yelena. As if a stone was setting in her depths. "What about it?"

Danna paused in her chopping, her eyes seeming to grow distant. Her brows knitting together. She took her bottom lip between her teeth. Her gaze seemed to drift but returned to the onions, as if unable to look at her sister. "The elders said that the Count will be coming soon."

Yelena watched her sister more closely now, turning her body away from the window and facing her. "We all know that, Danna. But why are *you* worried about it?"

Her sister opened her lips to speak but the creaking sound of the floorboards claimed both of their attentions. Standing in the small doorway of the kitchen, was their mother. A shorter woman with a heavy-set frame. Her skin a lighter shade than Danna's with hair of dark brown. Her elder sister favored their mother in looks, sharing the same rounded face. It was as if Danna were peering into a mirror that revealed her future, and the mirror in turn, showing their mother's past. Reminding her of her younger years, her youth.

Yelena had felt much like an outcast in her family when it came to appearance. Often wondering if there was somehow a mix up with her birth.

The Gods placing the wrong soul into her mother's womb. But her mother had assured her she had gotten her looks from her grandfather, though she had never met him. Passing away long before she was born. Yelena's skin was on the paler side. Her hair that of moonlight that spilled in soft waves from her head. Where her sister's was the dark sky, her hair was the stars that scattered against it. Yelena shared the same petite framing as her sister, though she was slightly shorter. Her face was angular, almost elven. Her lips pursed and full sitting beneath a straight nose. Her cheekbones sharp, as if the bones beneath her flesh had been chiseled and carved. And her eyes were crystalline, as if they were crystals crafted from the tender hands of the earth.

Her mother spared a quick glance to Danna before her brown eyes fell to her youngest daughter. She offered a smile that seemed forced. "Yelena, too busy daydreaming to help your sister with dinner?" She approached and gently ruffled the hair atop Yelena's head.

An embarrassed laugh escaped her, "Apologies mother, I believe I'm done now, I can offer a hand."

"Don't bother, Yelena. We don't need a repeat of last week's incident. Blood and onion soup doesn't sound too appetizing to me, personally." Danna teasingly grinned from the counter.

Yelena had allowed her gaze to drift toward the window as it always had, as if something drew her to it. Her eyes wandering through the streets, passed the gates, to the mountainside. Searching through the thick fog and trees for the castle that lurked within the shadows. She had begun to wonder if it even existed, as if it were nothing but an old folk tale told to children to scare them into never wandering into the forest. She had lost herself in such thoughts, that she cut into her thumb, nearly severing the small limb.

Danna had scolded her as she tended to the wound. Though she may have appeared angry, Yelena knew it was more worry than anything. Danna had always looked after her, taking care of her even when they were small children. Tending to the smallest of wounds or bruises. Danna wrapped a torn piece of fabric around her thumb once she cleaned the cut, tying the fabric tightly to keep pressure on it to halt the bleeding. Yelena flicked her gaze down to her hand and a pale scar met her gaze, stretching across her thumb. Gingerly, she traced a finger over the slight bump.

"Perhaps you're right, Danna. Yelena can take care of the clean up after dinner." Her mother said.

"*I'll* wash the knives." Her sister added.

The three laughed, the sound reverberating through the room, bouncing off the old wood. Moments like these were Yelena's favorite. Heartfelt and filled with laughter. Poking jabs at one another with good intent. Warmth permeated the air and caressed their souls. Oftentimes her father would join them, and their laughter could be heard echoing through the village. The clouds of despair unable to penetrate their wall of joy.

∞ ∞ ∞

Once they had finished dinner, the family had complimented Danna's cooking. Pressing swift kisses to her cheeks before parting from the kitchen. Their father patting his swollen belly as he waddled through the doorway. The man was short with pale skin. His head already bald. The two sisters shared a laugh as they watched the man hobble away with a full belly, their mother grinning with a shake of her head as she followed her husband. As promised, Danna cleaned the knives and anything with a pointed end. The two bent over the large sink cleaning the dishes from dinner.

For a long while, they cleaned in gentle silence. Yelena had allowed her gaze to drift to the small window above their sink. The pale-yellow curtains were drawn back from the rusted rod, allowing them to peer out into the darkening night. As she watched the writhing shadows, she couldn't help but think of dinner. Though it was lovely, and the conversations were nothing out of the ordinary, there was a sort of tension in the air. Almost threatening to choke them if they breathed too deeply. Perhaps her family was worried of *The Choosing*. For it crept ever closer with each passing night. Soon Count Dravmir would step foot into their village and claim his bride.

But her family had nothing to fear. They did not come from money or any sort of riches. They were a simple family with a simple home and namesake. The Count would not even bat an eye at Yelena or Danna. They would be safe, continue on about their lives as if nothing occurred. Danna would prepare their dinner in their small kitchen and Yelena would be less than helpful as always as she peered out the window. Yearning for a life that was far out of reach. Perhaps after the Count claimed his bride, that life wouldn't be so far...

Yelena had not realized the heavy stare of her sister's brown eyes until she tumbled forth from her inner thoughts. Danna met her gaze for a moment before dropping it, drying the knives she had cleaned. Yelena raised a brow but continued cleaning the last bowl. Grabbing a clean washcloth from a drawer, she began to dry the dishes. Danna put away the knives and wiped her damp hands on her apron. She stepped away and untied the knot, the apron falling from her waist as she hung it on a small hook on the post that stood in the center of the room.

"Goodnight, Ena."

Her hand stilled on the bowl she was drying, nearly dropping it. If she had been cleaning a knife, she surely would have severed her thumb this time. Her gaze flicked up from the dish, falling upon her sister that lingered at the doorway. Danna hadn't called her that since they were children. A childhood name that died once they grew into womanhood. Danna kept her back to her sister, her hands clenched together tightly.

"Danna? Is something wrong?"

Still, she stood in silence. Again, unable to look Yelena in the eyes. A pained express lacing through her features. Her lips parted as if to speak but she quickly sealed them. Without a parting word, she swept through the doorway and vanished. Leaving Yelena alone in the kitchen with nothing but the dishes to keep her company.

∞ ∞ ∞

Yelena had finished the chore and wandered upstairs, passing by the rooms of her parents and sister. The floorboards squeaking beneath her feet. Snores echoed from behind her parents closed door. Her father's snores rattled the wood framing of the house. With a shake of her head, she wondered how her mother could ever sleep. But she supposed after thirty years of marriage one could grow used to that sort of sound. Becoming a comfort, they couldn't sleep without and missing it when it was gone.

Yelena crept on silent feet though she doubted the creaking floorboards would wake her comatose father. As she drifted passed her sister's door, she found it open a crack. Peeking into the small room, she found the silhouette of her sister laid out on her bed. Her back turned to her. Those dark tresses splayed across her pillow. Yelena felt an ache within her heart. Why had Danna called her that? Was something truly wrong? What did her sister face that she felt she had to hide it from her?

Yelena assumed they were much closer than to keep secrets from one another. But it seemed as though she had been wrong in assuming so. Slightly wounded, she stepped away from the door and stepped into her own small room. The door clicked shut behind her quietly. Once Yelena dressed into her sleeping gown, she pulled back the thick quilt her mother had knitted for her and slid beneath its warmth. Nestling down into the bed, she laid on her side, her gaze wandering to the window. From her room, she could see passed their village to the great mountain range beyond. The fog growing thicker and darker as night plagued their world.

Tomorrow *The Choosing* would commence. Tomorrow, Count Dravmir would descend from his castle and whisk away one of the village women. Staking his claim on them. After tomorrow, all would be right with their world. Her family no longer having to dread those awful thoughts. For Danna and Yelena were safe from the Count's sight. Guilt swarmed her mind, stinging her heart like angry wasps. Though they were marked safe, someone else's daughter would not be so lucky. A family would soon be losing one of their own to the Count. Only to be returned to them in a pile of severed limbs once he deemed them useless or grew bored of them.

With a heavy mind and soul, Yelena's lids fluttered closed. Darkness encasing her mind as she wandered into the land of slumber. Her dreams were anything but sweet. For she found herself before the gates of the village. Her bare feet standing atop the cold cobblestones of the street. A chilling breeze whispered past, tousling her white tresses. Tugging them along the wind in wisps. A tremble rushed down the length of her spine, gooseflesh aroused along her arms. Wrapping them around herself, her gaze searched through the thick fog that had crept in from the forest.

The tendrils crawled toward Yelena, trailing across the tops of her feet like tantalizing caresses from frozen hands. Then, she felt it. A tug. Her gaze drifted back to the gates and there the fog lingered. A wall of grey shadows. Squinting her eyes, she could have sworn she saw a silhouette lurking behind the mist. And then, it moved. Stepping forth. Yelena found herself rooted to the ground, as if the tendrils bound themselves to her ankles and held her in place like earthly shackles. Yelena was forced to watch as the silhouette stepped forth from the fog. And a gasp parted her lips, her breath becoming a cloud within the air.

Before her stood Count Dravmir.

And he had come to claim her.

For she was his chosen bride.

∞ ∞ ∞

The Choosing had arrived. Sooner than the villagers had wished for. Soon the monster would come climbing down from his cave and claim the life of one of their own. Offering the poor soul to him as if they were nothing more than a pawn in their losing game. Even her family had grown gloomier, unable to hide their moods or forced expressions from her. Each of them hadn't bothered to meet her gaze, barely acknowledging her as if it pained them to do so. Their eyes squinting at her as if she were the sun, threatening to blind them.

Throughout the day, Yelena's mind was enraptured by the strange dream. Perhaps her parents worry had rubbed off on her. Her dreams giving their fears form. Senseless fear, senseless worry. Her eyes stared out the window, sitting before it as she did most of her days. Watching the villagers pass by on the streets. Hardly anyone spared a passing glance at one another, none murmuring even a simple greeting. It seemed as though a plague had cursed their village.

Yelena had been so captivated by the gloom of the people; she hardly noticed her father approaching. The older man taking a seat at the table beside her. The screeching of the chair legs against the floorboards snapped Yelena out of her haze. When she flicked her eyes to her father, she found his gaze did not meet with hers. Staring out the window much like she just had. His dark eyes watching each villager scurry along through the streets. There was a heaviness to his aura, making Yelena squirm in her chair at the discomfort she felt radiating from her father. His fear wreaking havoc within the air they breathed.

His eyes were so harsh Yelena felt as though whatever he felt was her blame. Reaching over, she placed her hand atop her father's clasped ones. The man blinked as if stepping forth from a fog, returning to the world. And yet, his eyes did not glance at her, only peering down upon her hand. A heavy sigh escaped her father as he shook his head. His shoulders slumping as if a burden had placed itself upon his shoulders.

"Father? What's wrong?" She asked.

He was silent for a moment before he spoke, "You know your mother and I love you greatly."

Yelena swallowed and nodded her head. Afraid to speak, waiting for some terrible news to befall her ears. When her father did not speak again, she said, "I know." She gently squeezed his hand, "I love you both."

There was a flicker within his gaze, as if her words had struck him. Causing pain to ache within his heart. Unfurling his hands, he grasped hers, squeezing them as if afraid to let go. As if he did, she would disappear. Yelena could have sworn she saw silver brim within his eyes but before she could question him, he gave her hand a gentle pat. Pushing his chair away from the table, he turned his back to her and left the kitchen. Leaving her alone in the small kitchen with an unspoken question lingering heavily within the air.

∞ ∞ ∞

As the sun crept across the sky, the brilliant blue fading into burnt orange, the villagers began to gather. The streets soon filled with every anxious soul. Many of the families had dressed up their daughters in pretty dresses, combing their hair. Hoping that the Count would take notice of their beauty and spare their lives, that she would not be returned to them as corpse.

The village elders had ordered every family with daughters of age, no older than twenty-five, to stand before the gates. Yelena and Danna followed behind their parents as they made their way through the crowded streets. Yelena did not miss the spared glances, the murmured whispers as they passed. As she tried to listen to the faint conversations, there was a warmth that enveloped her hand. Casting her gaze down, she found Danna had laced her fingers through hers. Clenching her sister's hand tightly but refusing to look upon her. Danna's face was stoic, set like stone. Any emotion she felt, was buried deep down. Even her eyes had become like steel.

Yelena tilted her head, trying to meet her sister's gaze, but Danna merely stared straight ahead. As if focusing on the back of their mother's head. Yelena's brows furrowed in worry as she turned away from her sister, clenching her hand tighter. She did not see the slight quiver in Danna's brow as her mask faltered for the slightest moment. Once they reached the gates, the village elders directed the families to stand along the sides, parents behind their daughters. So the Count could see them clearly. Not wishing for the man to spend too much time searching through the crowds, already eager to rid the village of his presence before he even arrived.

As Yelena and Danna stood before their parents, she felt gentle hands upon each of her shoulders as her parents grasped her. Their fingers curling into the fabric of her dress, fearing to let go. Danna still clung to her hand. Yelena wished she could ease their worries, to comfort them. But her words seemed to fall on deaf ears, unwilling to listen to sense. Preferring to cling to their fear as if it were some sort of safety to them, to their hearts. As if they prepared themselves to face the worst. So the blow would not hurt as badly.

Yelena made to face her parents, but gasps soon filled the air. Fearful sounds escaping the surrounding villagers. Her gaze darted back to the gates and there she found Count Dravmir. The man stepped through the thick fog as if he were part of it, as if it clung to his being. The tendrils traced along his broad shoulders tenderly, clinging to the man as if he were the source of their life. Behind him a wall of darkness erected as if he carried the night with him. Shadowing over his being and concealing the fading sun from gracing him with its rays. The shadows lingered above him until the moon had risen once the sun lay itself to rest. Yelena gaped at the sight of him – at the monster, the village feared. But he was no feral beast, he was a man. He towered above the elders as he stood before them, his presence menacing. As if he were a phantom coming to claim their lives.

The moonlight poured upon the man. His pallid skin seeming illuminated by it. From his head a curtain of raven colored hair spilled, there was a polished shine to it. It was parted down the middle and swept behind his broad shoulders. His face was angular, sharp. Yelena wondered if someone were to touch his cheeks if they would slice their fingertips. His lips were thin and pressed into a flatline. His nose was long and slender. His brows thick and dark above his feline eyes. Long lashes curtained over them with eyes that resembled the color of blood. They seemed to gleam beneath the silver light of the moon or perhaps they glowed from the blood that powered his body and soul as he feasted.

The man seemed to be crafted from stone. His features hardened like steel, as if the solemn, bored express he wore now was the only expression his face knew. The Count was handsome, perhaps the most handsome man she had ever laid eyes upon. She felt as though she had no right to gaze upon him, knowing she should not think that about the monster before them. No matter how human he may have seemed, she knew a beast lurked beneath that pale flesh. A beast that slaughtered one of their own every generation. And he had come for another.

The village elders each bowed before the man, "Welcome to our village, Count Dravmir."

Count Dravmir disregarded the bowing elders and stepped around them. Yelena watched as that glowing gaze swept through the crowd before him. His eyes drifting passed each young woman that stood before him, hardly even gazing at them. It was as if he knew what he searched for, and he was not finding it. Yelena's nerves slowly became unraveled as he made his way through the line of women swiftly. Perhaps he would not find his bride here and it pained her to wonder what would happen if he didn't. His gaze grew more irritated with each passing woman he glimpsed. Perhaps he was beginning to think the same.

That was until that red gaze fell upon Yelena.

And the world froze.

As if it held its breath.

Her mind had become stilled. Any thoughts that babbled through her head were silenced. The world faded away behind them. Becoming nothing but shadows that were forgotten. The only two souls that were left in the world were Dravmir and Yelena. Her mouth slightly gaped as she watched the Count slowly stride toward her. There was a prowess within each step he took, almost gliding across the earth. Her feet had been rooted into the very soil beneath her. But she paid it no mind, completely entranced by the man that stood before her. Yelena knew that any sensible person would have tried to flee, would have cried, and pled for their life. But it seemed as though the man had cast a spell on her. A hex that demanded she comply.

As if any will she had, had been eradicated.

Perhaps she would have tried to flee if she had any sense left. To turn tail and run as far away as she could from the man. But the monster would claim his prey. Aroused by the chase and hunt her down through the village. Striking any down that dared to step in his path. The Count would not return to his castle empty handed. Yelena was his claim, as he claimed the others before her.

That glowing gaze held hers for a heartbeat. And Yelena could have sworn to the Gods that there was a flicker of sorrow within those cursed irises. Pity. Pain. As if the monster before her was a man. A man with any emotion that lurked within his depths. Perhaps he was at some point in his life but from the stories she heard that man was long since gone. A beast stepping into his flesh and laying claim to the Count's body.

The man's lips moved as if he were speaking.

Perhaps he was.

Was he speaking to her?

His words had been lost to her ears as his spell unwound. Her mind returning in whirls of shrieks. The screaming seeming as though it echoed within the world around them. And when she finally returned to earth, she realized that it had. Yelena did not realize it, but she had stepped forth from her family to stand before the Count. Behind her, her mother wailed. Her father and Danna holding back the weeping woman. Broken sounds escaped her mother and it shattered Yelena's heart. Piercing it like an arrow through the chest. Yelena turned to face her grieving family. Crying out for the daughter they would soon lose. Only to be returned to them in a pile of bloody limbs. She could not help the burn that festered within her eyes as tears swelled, clawing to be set free.

Though part of her feared going with the Count, another part of her sighed with relief. For no other family would have to suffer this. At least not on this night. Not for another generation. Putting on a brave face for her family, she nodded her head. Telling them all would be well, to let her go. But looking into the eyes of her mother, father, and sister, it was hard to maintain her composure. Wishing for nothing more than to run to them and tackle them in her embrace. To return to their simple home and life. But that was over for Yelena. Her new home awaited in the shadows.

Her grave waited.

"It's okay." Her voice croaked, a broken sound. "I'll be okay." She tried to reassure her family, to reassure herself.

Her mother shook her head as she crumpled into her father's arms. Danna standing at her side and soothing her. The sisters never broke gazes. Words lingering unspoken within the air between them. The sound of light footsteps broke their trance as the village elders hesitantly approached, bowing their heads. One had stepped forth, a woman in her later years. Her deep brown skin was wrinkled with age, her eyes seeming to be cast in a haze. Clouds suffocated the once warm auburn of her eyes. She wobbled forth with her head bowed before the man.

"She is the next in the Vasiliev bloodline, Count Dravmir, and presumably the last." The elder spoke.

The Count hardly seemed to listen to the elder, his gaze fixated on Yelena.

Yelena raised a brow. That was not her family's name. What did this elder mean? How could she be the next in that bloodline? Her gaze slid back to her family and found the truth laid before her eyes. The answer she had been seeking all those years was set plainly before her; she was not their true daughter.

"How?" Her voice echoed across the crowd, hanging heavy above their heads.

Her family lowered their gazes, unable to meet her eyes. It was the elder who finally answered her, "You come from the line of the first bride of Count Dravmir." They spoke. "After your mother was... *found*," the elder shivered and stepped back from the man, "years ago, we placed you into your father's cousin's care."

"So where is my father? Why not place me in his care?"

The elder simply shook their head, "After your mother was claimed, he left the village."

He left you behind.

The words lingered unspoken.

Yelena returned her gaze to her family, the only mother and father she's ever known. How could they keep such a thing from her all those years? Even when she asked them? Yelena was not mad; she never would have been. Perhaps they wished to protect her from the truth for as long as they could. And they had. Gifting her a life of normalcy before she stepped out to meet her end. To be claimed by the Count. To be whisked away into another life. To live amongst monsters.

"We only wished to protect you." Her mother's shaken voice answered.

"We wanted to tell you, but we couldn't find it in ourselves." Her father added as he combed his fingers through his wife's hair.

Yelena's gaze drifted to her sister and she wondered how long she knew of this secret. If she's always known. Perhaps that was why she was always so protective over her, always tender with her.

For they all knew this day would come.

"I understand." Yelena rasped.

Truly, she did. Though her heart was laced in agony, she understood, for she would have done the same. Whispered footsteps greeted her ears and she faced the Count as he closed the distance between them. She faced the monster that had slaughtered her true mother. His gaze was harsh, making her feel so small before this man. Standing so much taller than her. His eyes flicked above her head to her grieving family before returning to meet her gaze.

"You may say your goodbyes." A velvety voice coated in shadows whispered into her ears. Like a dark and gentle caress.

Yelena whirled on her heel without a second thought spared and dashed toward her family with her arms wide. They collided together. Grasping ahold of one another, clinging desperately, never wishing to let go. Together they sobbed as they fell to their knees on the cobblestones. Yelena pressed her face into her mother's shoulder. Her tears wetting the gown she wore. On either side of her, Danna, and her father clung to her. Each of them weeping their agony into the world. Soon, their family would be torn apart. Yelena ripped away from their grasp and they would return home with one less soul. An empty room with no soul to claim it. An empty chair at the dinner table. It would be as though a phantom had lived amongst them. Drifting through the small home, filling the empty spaces with sorrow that tainted the air. Forever reminding them of the daughter they had lost.

Though Yelena wished to remain, she knew she had to leave, to fill her role and claim her duty. To face the Count and return with him as the women before her had, as her mother had. To face her fate with her chin held high. Drying her eyes, she slowly stood, her family following. Her mother's arms desperately clung to her like vices. Her father had to pry them from Yelena's waist and drag her back. Danna stood at her side and Yelena faced her. Her sister reached out and grasped her hands, gently squeezing them.

"I love you, Ena."

The name pained her heart, a lace of agony striking through it like lightning. "I love you too, Danna." She cast her gaze to her weeping parents, "And I love you."

Her mother's sobs were too much, choking on her own tears. Her father held her gaze and bowed his head. "And we love you, our daughter."

A crack trekked across her heart as she beheld her family. This would be the last she ever saw them. The last she would speak to them, hold them. This was goodbye. Until they met in the next world.

With one last squeeze and a heavy heart, Yelena dropped her sister's hands and turned her back to her family. Yelena approached the Count, but each step was forced, as if her feet were weighed down by burden. The man stood there waiting, emotionless. That stone cold face watching her movement as she stood before him.

"Thank you." She said to him.

The man nodded, "It is time." He offered his hand, "Come." The word was a command, demanding. There was no choice for Yelena.

Yelena's gaze slid down to his hand, pale and large. For a moment, she hesitated. Casting a glance behind her, she took in the entirety of her village. Of the people before her. The other families had not dressed their daughters in hopes of the Count sparing them, they had dressed them as if they were mourning. Attending Yelena's funeral. Tearing her gaze away from them, she reached for his hand. There was a slight tremble to her own hand as she slid it into his. And she found that his skin was not hard as stone, but a faint chill lingered upon his flesh. The Count closed his hand over her own and for a moment, she felt his thumb trace over her skin. As if offering the smallest amount of comfort.

The Count drew her closer, Yelena stumbling in her steps from the force and fell against his chest. Warmth flushed across her cheeks. As she tried to straighten herself and step back, strong but gentle arms wrapped around her. Keeping her against him. Tilting her head back she found that hard gaze bore down on her, feeling so small beneath him. So fragile within his stone embrace. There was no emotion on his face as he bent and swept her off her feet. A startled gasp escaped her as the world blurred for a moment. His movements quick.

"Let her go you monster!" Her mother wailed into the night.

Fear prickled her flesh as she turned her gaze to her family. Yelena prayed that the Count would not turn his murderous rampage against her family. Prayed that he would spare them, to forgive her mother's outburst. Surely, he had to understand. A mother was watching a man steal away their daughter. Knowing that she would only return to them dead. Slowly his glowing eyes slid toward her family and for a second, she feared the worst as his gaze settled on her weeping mother. Feared that he would lash out at them, that with a swift movement their blood would paint the cobblestones.

But the Count did nothing.

Only turning his back upon the village and approaching the gates.

As they stepped into the fog, her mother's cries followed behind them.

And Yelena's heart shattered.

CHAPTER TWO

A New Bride

YELENA WAS IN the arms of her mother's murderer as he carried her far away from the village she had called home. Once they drifted through the fog, it was only then that she allowed her façade to shatter. Silver tears wept from her eyes and trekked down her cheeks. The wind whispered passed them as the Count carried her through the forest. The breeze drying her tears and leaving gentle kisses upon her rosy cheeks as if to comfort her. Yelena could hardly bring herself to look at the man that had stolen her. His arms were solid around her small body, feeling so fragile against him. She knew he could squeeze the life from her, his arms that of stone, able to crush her in an instant. And yet, he carried her tentatively as if he feared clinging too tightly.

Yelena peered into his face, but his gaze was set ahead. His brows furrowed and his lips set into a flatline. His jaw seemed clenched. Behind them his raven hair trailed along the wind, like tendrils of wisping shadows. Yelena's gaze slid from his face to follow his gaze, just ahead of them, through the thick fog, she could make out the silhouette of a castle. Her new home. Mindlessly, her fingers curled into the thick fabric of the tunic Count Dravmir wore. His red gaze flicked down to her clenched hand but said nothing as he carried her to the castle. They lowered from the stars, the shadows releasing their hold upon the man as he lowered to the stairs that led to the grand doors.

Carefully he set her down and once her feet were securely on the ground, his hands left her. He stood off to the side. The man did not move, did not speak, allowing Yelena to take in her new surroundings. Her new home. The castle was immense. Fog crept around the structure, concealing it from wandering eyes. It towered almost as a high as the mountains it protruded from. Buttresses reached toward the two towers on either side of the castle. Spires raised atop them into wicked points. The dark stones the castle was crafted from hid it amongst the shadows, shielding it from wandering eyes. Yelena's gaze drifted toward the doors just ahead, waiting atop the darkened stairs. They were crafted from wood that was the deepest of browns. Attached to the wood – no it seemed like they *grew* from the wood – silver crept across the doors. Like wicked branches reclaiming the body that had been stolen, the tree that had been mutilated to craft those doors.

Resting above the doors, a large stained-glass window lingered. The panels of glass were tinted darkly, hardly able to peer through them. And she wondered if even the sunlight could penetrate it. To cast its golden light inside the Count's castle. But Yelena doubted the sun ever shone here. The fog thick and the clouds heavy within the sky, suffocating any light that dared shine through.

The Count took a step toward the stairs, casting a glance behind him at Yelena. He said nothing as he returned his gaze to the doors. Yelena approached him then and the two ventured up the stairs. The silent sounds of their shoes against the smoothed stone whispered through the silence. Count Dravmir walked at her side like a silent shadow. His hardened gaze focused on the doors, eager to return to his home. To step inside and vanish within the darkness where he belonged for the shadows were his home. Reaching a pale hand toward the doors, he forced them open. Loud groans escaped the doors as they slowly opened. Darkened tendrils wisped forth from inside, beckoning them within.

Welcoming the Count home.

Casting another spared glance at her, he stepped aside and motioned for Yelena to enter his home. Her home. For however how long she remained here. Until the Count deemed her useless and discarded of her as if she were nothing. Just as he had done to her true mother and the other women of their bloodline before them. Why was their namesake cursed? What had they ever done to bring the Count's rage upon them? Upon those who shared the smallest drop of blood as the first bride of his?

Her throat tightened, finding it impossible to swallow. Her fingers curled into the fabric of her dress, her knuckles turning pure white. Yelena had been brave for her parents and now that mask had fallen away as she stared at the monster and his lair. This was not her new home; this was her grave. Her final resting place. Sorrow crept into her heart and wrapped around the beating muscle. Yelena had never been able to leave her village, to glimpse upon the world. This was as far as she would travel. In some wicked sense, she had been given the gift to leave but never to return. It was as if the Gods found her suffering humorous. Giving her a gift that came with a wicked price.

Death.

"*Hurry.*" The word hissed impatiently from the Count's lips.

Yelena broke free of her tangled web of thoughts. Gathering up her shred of courage, she held her chin high and marched into the castle. She did not hear the Count follow behind her, only the sound of the doors thundering shut. The sound echoed throughout the vast castle and faded away. A shiver crept down her spine as she became aware of the monster that lurked behind her. Would he kill her here and now? Striking her down where she stood? The castle was utterly silent and yet Yelena could feel eyes upon her. Not the Count's. Her eyes searched through the thick shadows and she could have sworn she saw a flicker of movement. A flash of red gazes.

How many monsters resided within these stone walls?

Behind her, her ears tingled with the sound of a slight intake of breath. Her skin bristled. Finally, the man stepped from behind her, and a sigh of relief escaped her lips. Her shoulders slumping only slightly. Tonight, she would live. But what of tomorrow? Or the next the day? How numbered where her days truly? Only time would tell. Count Dravmir strode ahead, his hands clasped behind his back. His glowing eyes slid toward the brass railing that lingered above a dais. The shadows stirred once more as they met his gaze, as if leaving. Granting them privacy.

Yelena's eyes lingered there, searching above the railing. But nothing moved. Sliding her gaze down, she found two thrones situated atop the dais. A thick layer of dust coated them, as if they had not been sat upon in decades. One throne was crafted from the darkest marble. The other seeming to be crafted from moonstone, it was almost pearlescent. Was this the first bride's throne? Had they ruled side by side? Had her mother sat upon that very throne? Yelena began to wonder if the stories she had heard were wrong. Fabricated lies. But she remembered how this man before her had killed her birth mother. Her blood forever staining his hands as Yelena's soon would be.

The sudden sound of clapping startled her, a hand clenching above her racing heart. At once, flames blazed to life upon torches. The room was doused in a warm glow, allowing Yelena to see. Torches were lined through the room, attached to the tall pillars. Each one positioned before a doorway. The pillars towered high, smoothed down and polished. Crafted from black marble much like his throne. Above the pillars, the railing stretched around the rectangular room. The second floor loomed above their heads. Beneath her feet, a crimson carpet stretched from the doors and pooled beneath the thrones.

Count Dravmir turned to the side, his profile just as striking and angular. His eyes were settled upon one of the torches. The flames dancing within his eyes. "I have rules that I expect you to follow." His voice commanded the very air she breathed. Carrying throughout the room.

She arched a brow, "And what are these rules?"

His eyes seemed to narrow slightly, "Do not try to escape, your attempts will prove futile and fatal." It was then that his eyes slid to her as he fully faced Yelena.

The man took a step forth and she took one back. Count Dravmir stalked closer. Yelena backed away until she found herself against the doors. Flicking up her gaze, she found a monster looming above her. Those red eyes holding her in place. She sucked in a breath, her heart even seeming to halt for a moment. His gaze bore down into her soul, searching through her darkest depths. He leaned closer as her heart thundered. His nose mere inches from hers.

"My final rule," his voice was a rasped whisper, "*never* venture outside of these walls."

Yelena swallowed, "Why?" The word was trembled, and she hated how small her voice sounded.

He cocked his brow with a slight tilt of his head. Yelena watched as his raven hair spilled over his shoulder. "If you wish for an early death then be my guest." His gaze was piercing then, "If not, then I suggest you heed my warnings."

Yelena held his gaze, "Why? It seems death waits for me. When do you plan on slaughtering me like you did the others?"

Even she was taken aback by her words, buy her tone. Yelena was never one for confrontation. And here she stood before the Count, jabbing at the slumbering beast, tempting it to strike her. Dravmir blinked at her, as if he too, were shocked by her words. But he swiftly collected that cold, indifferent expression his face seemed to settle into so naturally. The man straightened himself and took a few steps back.

"My servants shall show you to your chambers." With those parting words, he turned on his heel and vanished through one of the many doorways in the grand room. Dismissing her as if she were nothing.

Yelena stared after him, her back still pressed against the doors. Her feet seeming reluctant to move, to take any more steps inside this prison. She had not realized it, but her hands were planted against the doors, her nails curling into wood. Taking in a breath, she peeled her fingers from the doors and took a step forth. Behind her, her freedom waited. She could feel its tug, its tempting call. But she knew she would hardly make it a step outside before the Count came to claim his runaway bride.

For a split second, Yelena had considered it. Her gaze drifting over her shoulder, gazing upon the tall doors behind her. If she did manage to sneak out before he noticed, how far could she get before he tracked her down? Chasing her through the fog and trees. Claiming his prey. Her body shivered at the thought of being tracked down as if she were an animal.

How many brides had tried to flee?

And how many had met their ends before they even saw the gates of their village?

Whispered voices echoed within the grand room, drawing Yelena's attention away from the doors. Standing before the railing, she saw three silhouettes. Their glowing gazes peering down upon her. Murmurs echoed hauntingly around them. And Yelena could have sworn she heard giggled laughter. The shadows then leapt over the railing and landed swiftly, quietly. Yelena caught sight of billowing dresses fluttering around their feet. The three seemed attached to one another, clinging closely. Their whispers became louder the closer they approached.

As the flames doused their light upon the silhouettes, Yelena found three women standing in the center of the room. Their beauty stole her breath. Were all immortal monsters this breathtaking? Perhaps they were. To lure in their prey, to have them within their grasp, and then steal their life. Each woman wore dresses of white. The fabric seeming almost sheer. The dresses tied behind their necks; a slit cut out in the fabric to expose their breasts just enough. Around their biceps black bands of metal clung, sheer bits of fabric fluttered down from them. Billowing behind the women as they strolled forth in waves of satin along the air. Their slender legs slipped forth from the dresses, slits racing up the sides. Yelena noticed that the same bands around their arms, adorned their ankles.

The woman to the left was curvy, her breasts and hips full, her stomach plump. Her skin was dark and beautifully smooth, appearing almost like a painting. As if an artist had created her flesh with gentle strokes of their brush. Her onyx hair was thick with tight curls that brushed down to her shoulders. Yelena noticed beneath the woman's thick brows, glowing eyes just like the Count's could be found. Each of the women had those eyes. Bloodlust dancing within their red irises as they stared at Yelena. The woman held her gaze and a slight but tight smile caressed her full lips. As if she were offering some sort of comfort, conveying to Yelena that all would be well.

But would it?

The woman in the center towered above the other two. Her body slim and feline. There was a prowess about her. Her eyes were narrowed upon Yelena and a wicked grin curved at the corners of her thin lips. She arched a fine, fiery brow. A scattering of freckles dusted across her pale skin, over the bridge of her nose and stretching to her slim cheeks. From her head spilled fiery tresses that rippled passed her waist, untamed and wild. The woman traced her pale fingers over her bottom lip, her sharpened nails pricking into her own flesh. Yelena could see within the woman's eyes a thirst for blood. For *her* blood.

The third woman stood to the right. Her skin a light brown, reminding Yelena of her sister. Her midnight hair was cropped short and straight. Parted down the center and framing either side of her face, reaching slightly passed her jawline. Her cheeks were round, and her chin pointed. Thin dark brows framed atop her feline eyes. The woman lowered her gaze, angling her head down. As if she could hardly bring herself to meet Yelena's gaze. She seemed to cling to the fiery woman in the middle, her hands wrapped around the woman's bicep and forearm.

They stepped forward, "What's this? Has the Count gifted us with a new plaything?" The fiery woman purred.

Panic seized her then. Would she truly meet her end so soon?

But the woman to her left swatted her arm, a stern look crossing those cursed eyes. "Drezca, don't frighten the poor thing."

The woman smirked, "Nothing wrong with having a *little* fun, Daria."

The third woman remained silent as they crept closer. Yelena dared not move, knowing she would never out run these monsters. She did not wish to tempt their hunger, their wish for a hunt. So, she remained rooted to the ground like a tree. Her skin bristled as the women broke apart and began to stalk around her. Gentle breaths of air whispered through her pale tresses as the monsters familiarized themselves with her scent.

"So, this is Count Dravmir's new bride." Drezca rasped with laughter dancing in her voice.

Almost in mockery.

"She's just like the others." The silent woman whispered; her voice so faint Yelena had to strain her ears to listen.

"You know the brides come from the bloodline of the first, Danika." Daria spoke.

There was a tug on her hair as Drezca toyed with a strand of it. Wrapping the white strand around her slender finger. "I do wonder why he bothers with mortals."

Pain laced through Yelena's scalp as the woman yanked on her hair. Feeling as a few strands were torn free. Yelena winced at the pain but kept her lips sealed, swallowing the shouted cry that bubbled up in her throat.

"They're so fragile, like glass." The woman's words hissed.

"*Drezca.*"

Daria was nothing more than a blur of shadows to Yelena's eyes as she stormed toward the woman, snatching her hand from Yelena's hair. "We have rules too, Drezca, unless you have forgotten."

The fiery woman narrowed her eyes upon Daria but said nothing more. Turning her back to the woman, she faced Yelena and offered a chilling smile.

"Apologies, it has been too long since a mortal has graced this castle. Forgive me." But her tone was anything but apologetic. Whirling on her heel, she said, "Follow us to your chambers and please do try and keep up."

As Drezca vanished into the shadows, hardly waiting for Yelena, she began to wonder if the monster who murdered the women of her bloodline was not the Count. Whispered footfalls approached Yelena and she knew that Daria and Danika only did it for her benefit. Knowing they could walk so quietly their prey was none the wiser. Neither of them had made the slightest sound earlier when they first made their appearance.

Daria stood before her and offered a smile that seemed forced, "Come."

Yelena nodded her head and followed behind the two women. Danika reached out and claimed Daria's hand. Like a child clinging to their mother, afraid to let go. They kept an even pace, so Yelena could follow easily without rushing after them. It was more than Drezca offered, disappearing from the room before Yelena could even take a step. The two led her toward the right side of the grand room between a set of pillars. A tall, arched doorway was nested into the wall. The carpet flowing into the shadows that waited. Daria released Danika's hand for a moment as she clapped her own together. Again, flames ignited upon torches. Fires crackled down the hall, chasing away the slithering darkness. And Yelena wondered if the shadows were given voice if they would shriek at the invading light.

Their footfalls whispered through the silence of the castle. Before her, Daria had claimed Danika's hand once more as the women strolled ahead. Yelena could not help but watch their dynamic, their demeanor. Daria had seemed stern with Drezca but with Danika, she was tender. As if she could allow her barriers to fall around the other woman. Danika seemed to act the same with both Drezca and Daria. Clinging to them in fear that they would vanish as soon as her fingers left them.

As they wandered through the halls, Yelena cast her gaze to the walls. Large canvas paintings hung upon the stones. Many were depictions of the Count. Standing against a crimson background with that same scowl painted upon his face. Others were of the Count's brides. Each of them sharing the same face with slight differences marking them. Some had beauty marks either beneath their eyes or above their lips. Others had long tresses while some had them cropped short. Some of them wore soft expressions, simple smiles upon their pale lips. Others had mournful looks within their eyes, though they beamed. They were painted with tender hands. Delicate strokes giving them form, granting them life upon canvas where they would be immortalized. Never forgotten even as death had claimed them.

Yelena could not help but wonder why the Count kept their portraits. Would they not be a constant reminder of the women he had murdered? Was it guilt that kept those paintings nailed to the stone walls? Or did they serve as trophies? The longer she looked at them, she began to think that second option was a false assumption. If they were a trophy, why were they painted so beautifully? So calm? There was not a trace of fear within their crystalline eyes. As if they had come to trust the Count that had stolen them and sentenced them to death. Yelena wondered if she would come to trust the monster that had relished in her mother's blood.

It seemed these women had.

Or perhaps they had no other choice, trapped within these walls until their final days.

Yelena passed by another portrait, hardly paying it any mind knowing that the woman looked the same as the others before and after her. But as she strolled passed, she felt a tug. Something pulling her back. Halting in her tracks, she cast a glance over her shoulder upon the portrait. Yelena found it was the last one in the hall before the end doorway. Hardly paying attention to the monsters ahead of her, she traced back to that portrait. She stared into those familiar eyes for they were hers, in another time. The woman's face was more rounded than her own, her white tresses barely swept down to her collarbones. Wisps of bangs dangled across her brow. Her smile was warm and welcoming. As if telling Yelena all would be well. As if the woman could truly see her.

Silent footsteps approached her as the women stood at her side. And still, Yelena could not face them. Her attention fully upon the portrait as it claimed her. "This was Count Dravmir's last bride." Daria spoke gently.

Your mother.

The words lingered unspoken.

Yelena had not noticed but her hands slightly trembled as she mourned a mother, she had never been given the chance to know. Lifting her hand, she reached for the portrait. Neither of the monsters had tried to stop her. Allowing this moment. Gently, her fingertips traced over her birth mother's soft face. The gentle brush strokes in the paint bumped against her fingers. Yelena was tender as she touched the portrait, afraid that the paint would peel and chip beneath her hand.

A sense of sorrow embraced her heart. Warmth stirred and prickled behind her eyes. All her life she lived her days never knowing of this woman. The one who brought her into this world. She mourned the mother she never knew. Mourned the time that had been stolen from them. She wondered what her life would have been like had the Count never claimed her. Yelena loved and appreciated the mother that raised her. She was forever grateful for being given the chance to be raised with a mother's love.

But was it so selfish to wish it had been her birth mother that had raised her?

To have her love?

Perhaps in a sense Yelena had her love.

But she would never truly know it.

"What is lost is never forgotten." Danika's voice was a whispered caress of comfort. Each word echoing hauntingly down the hall.

Yelena nodded her head and swallowed the tears that burned behind her eyes, choking them down. Her hand slid down from the portrait. As she made to turn, a gasp escaped her. Danika stood closer, her gaze holding Yelena in place. Her face was unreadable, a stoic look settled over her like a mask. The woman lifted her arm and Yelena stilled, holding her breath, as the monster reached for her. Gooseflesh rose along her skin as Danika pressed the tip of her finger against the center of her chest. A bite of cold nipped at her warm flesh.

"Here." Her voice whispered.

Here is where your mother can be found.

Yelena bowed her head, "Thank you."

Danika dipped her head and her finger fell away from her chest. Taking a step back, she joined Daria's side once more. Her fingers entwining through the woman's. A word was not shared between them as they made their way through the hall and through another doorway. Yelena had halted at the threshold, stealing one last glance upon the portraits. Feeling their eyes watching her go. She could not help but wonder when her portrait would grace these walls. And wondered what the woman that came after her would feel as she stared upon the painting.

If there would be any women after, presumably the last of her bloodline.

What bloodline would be cursed after hers ran dry?

With a sigh, Yelena stepped through the doorway.

Turning her back to the long-lost brides.

∞ ∞ ∞

Daria and Danika had led Yelena up a set of stairs and found themselves within another hall. Again, portraits lined the walls. These appeared older, the paint faded and chipping on some. This was the line of the first brides. The latest ones continued down the stairs. Yelena felt their watchful gazes as they drifted through the hall. A sense of sorrow permeated the air here. The women in the portraits not as welcoming as the others. Though they smiled there was a sadness about them. In the way their shoulders seemed hunched. Yelena thought back to the last brides, some seemed genuinely happy, radiating from their frames. And the others seemed as though burden gripped them.

She wondered why some were happy and others were sad.

Many questions swarmed within her mind. The tales she had heard did not quite gift her an answer. If anything, she had more questions now more than ever. Who was Count Dravmir?

And what truly happened to his brides?

Daria and Danika stopped at the end of the hall before a set of grand double doors. Grasping the silver, elongated handles, she forced them open. Quiet groans escaped the aged wood as they revealed the massive room. Yelena's gaze fell instantly upon the fiery monster draped across a velvet couch. The back of it dipping low and vanishing. Her elbow was propped atop the only armrest. Laying on her side with one leg stretched out and her other knee draped over it. She grinned at them, tapping her fingers upon her hips. A lioness sat before them, eyeing her prey. Yelena's nerves bristled at the sight of Drezca. She had not been warm in her welcome. Yelena's scalp aching as if to remind her.

"You mortals trudge in your steps."

"Or perhaps you're too impatient." Yelena grumbled.

Again, she found herself startled. Allowing her thoughts to take form upon her lips. Had coming to this castle already changed her? Or was it the thought of her impending death that made her careless? No longer worried of her mortality as she waited for the monsters to strike her down where she stood.

Drezca arched a brow, seeming... *impressed.* Her smirk grew into a feral-ness. Yelena had begun a game she would never win. "This mortal has a tongue on her." She swung her legs over the couch and slowly stood. With a prowess in her step, she strode toward Yelena. "Perhaps I'll have to cut it out."

"*Drezca.*" Daria hissed again, "Leave. I'm tired of needlessly reminding you to be on your best behavior."

Drezca smiled, "I never promised I'd be good, Daria."

Daria jabbed a finger to the doors, "*Out.*"

With a heavy sigh and roll of her eyes, the fiery monster strolled from the room. Her fingertips trailing through Yelena's hair. She felt the slightest tug, but the strands remained where they grew. Drezca toyed with her. Reminding Yelena that she was useless against them. That with a swift move, Drezca could kill her before she ever realized it.

Yelena was a mortal living amongst the immortal.

Tsk. Tsk. Daria stared after the woman, shaking her head. "I do apologize for her," a sigh then, "I know she'd never truly apologize." Daria cast her gaze to Yelena and offered a sincere smile, "She may seem awful, and believe me, most days she is. But there's a heart beneath it all."

Yelena raised a brow as she crossed her arms over her chest, "I do find that hard to believe."

Laughter sounded from the woman, "I know, oftentimes I forget myself."

Danika remained in silence; her eyes settled on Yelena.

"Now, this is your chamber." Daria waved a hand toward the large expanse of space before them.

Yelena could hardly believe the sight. At her home in the village, her room was slightly bigger than the small living space in the front of their home. Her bed filling much of the room with a simple stand beside it. Now, she stood in a chamber that was larger than her family's home. The house would fit inside these walls with empty space surrounding it. She was in disbelief such a massive room was hers. Hers for however long she breathed.

The floors were a polished blackened marble, the castle seeming to be born from it. A plush, crimson carpet covered much of the hard floor. Behind the couch that Drezca had been lounged on, a set of glass doors lurked. Crimson drapes dangled on either side of them. Yelena saw a balcony that stretched forth from the doors, railing edging around it. The silver light of the moon streamed into the room. Here, the windows were not darkened. Allowing the twinkling light of the stars to shine within. Though the sun rarely graced their world, the clouds separated just enough at night to allow the moon to bless the world.

Yelena dragged her gaze away and flicked it to the left wall. There, a fireplace could be found. The mouth of it standing a head taller than her. The hearth extended forth. The mantel above the sleeping fireplace was bare of any trinkets. Her gaze slid up the wall, staring at the bareness. There was a faint outline of dust. Squinting her eyes, she realized it was in the shape of a frame. What portrait had hung there? And why had it been removed?

Daria approached a set of doors a foot away from the fireplace, Danika trailing at her side. "Here is your closet."

Opening the doors, she revealed another large room. Dresses spilled in beautiful fabrics toward the floor as they swept against it. There were two sets of rails on either wall, reaching toward the high ceiling. Yelena guessed these would have belonged to the former brides. The top rows belonging to the firsts.

The fabric seemed old, yellowed. Left behind forgotten and untouched. This room becoming a tomb of lost souls.

"If you wish to reach the ones on top, feel free to ask one of us or a servant to fetch them for you."

Servants? She had not seen anyone other than the Count and the three women. Perhaps they were hidden in other parts of the castle.

Daria closed the doors and strode across the room to another set. These were grand like the doors that led into this chamber. Pulling them open, Yelena's mouth gaped. Before her eyes laid a grand bed that filled much of the room. It sat atop a dais, four stairs leading up to it. The red carpet spilling into the room and stretching up the stairs. Black metal posts rose from each corner of the bed, rods stretching from one to the other. Velvet, crimson curtains draped down either side of the bed, sweeping across the floor. Her gaze slid toward the headboard. It was crafted from the same metal, mimicking the look of vines. Spiraling and curling outwards. Sculpted roses were scattered across the headboard, seeming almost as if they grew from the dark metal. Upon the bed, black sheets of silk covered the large bed. Red pillows were rested against the metal vines.

"And here you can find the bath and chamber pot." Daria walked toward the far-right wall and opened a small door. "Servants will come and fill your bath and clean the chamber pot."

Yelena was in disbelief. This was her life now. Her remaining days spent in luxury. Pampered like an old dog that would be leaving this world behind it. Yelena was never one for materialistic desires, but she could not help the slight excitement that bubbled within. And for a moment, she could hardly wait to tell her sister.

And then, she faltered.

Her smile fading.

Danna would never know. For Yelena could never leave.

Never see her family again.

It was truly settling in now. Threatening to suffocate her.

Pain ruptured her heart, clenching a fist upon her chest. Her body had begun to tremble as tears swelled within her eyes. A gasp escaped her lips as the dam burst, warmth flowing down her cheeks. Her family was lost to her. Never again would she watch her sister dance about the kitchen as she prepared dinner, pestering Yelena and her wandering mind. Never again would she laugh at the table with her parents, dining on the meal her sister prepared.

It was gone.

The memories seeming so distant now. As if years had passed since she arrived at the castle. She shuddered to think how her coming death would shatter her family. How her mother would fall to her knees and scream out her name. How her father would try his best to console his wife but his tears choking him. How her sister would stand there in silence, trying to keep her composure for their parents. But her façade would slowly crumble around her as she shattered completely.

How could Yelena enjoy such trivial things while her family mourned the loss of their daughter? How could she bring herself to face each day with her chin held high knowing she would never see her family again? How selfish could she be? Finding pleasure in these things, marveling at her new life as if she were not dying within the coming days or weeks.

Perhaps that was better, to find some sort of happiness instead of drowning in pits of despair. To not give in to their poisoned calls. Yelena would continue on, for as long as she could. If not for herself then for her family. For the woman that came after her. Hoping to stall long enough so the woman could live a life of happiness. To be able to free herself from the shackles of home and see the world.

But she could not save every bride from the Count.

That caused a burden she could never free herself from to weigh on her shoulders. A burden each woman in her bloodline has faced and carried through the decades – since the first bride.

Would this cycle ever end?

When Yelena finally stumbled forth from her haze, she felt strong arms gripping her shoulders, keeping her steady. Blinking through the fog, the world became clear. On either side of her stood Danika and Daria. There was worry written within their glowing eyes as they stared at her. As if waiting for Yelena to black out at any second. Massaging her temples, she gathered her thoughts and took in a steadying breath.

"Thank you." She rasped.

Daria nodded with a smile, "Of course."

Without warning, Daria and Danika snapped their heads toward the entrance of the chamber. Yelena followed their gaze and found the Count standing at the threshold. Those cold eyes met hers instantly. His gaze drifted down to the hands that clung to her shoulders. Swiftly, they fell away as the women moved aside. Danika found Daria's hand, attached to the woman's side. The two bowed their heads to the Count. He acknowledged them with a simple nod before returning his gaze to Yelena.

"Leave us." His voice echoed through the room.

Before Yelena could blink, the two had fled the chambers. Vanishing on a breath of shadows. Leaving silence in their wake. The faint sound of the doors to the main room closing found Yelena's ears. Now, it was only the Count and her alone within the room. The man towering heads taller than her. His hands clasped behind his back.

"Do you find the room suiting enough?" He asked.

Yelena nodded, "Yes, thank you."

His gaze slid from hers toward the windows across the room, silver light pouring within and flooding across the bedsheets. "I have come to ask you something the brides before you have been asked."

Her interest was piqued. "What is it?"

Immediately those glowing eyes found hers once more, "Do you wish to be changed into an immortal?"

Yelena faltered. Blinking at the man as if he had gone mad. Changed. *Immortal.* Those words buzzed through her mind. "Pardon?"

"Do you wish to be changed into an immortal?" He asked again.

He would so easily offer such a thing? She had only just arrived and now he presented her with this. Could Yelena find it in herself to shed her mortal flesh and step into the skin of a monster? She cast her gaze down into her hands.

Hands that held Danna's. Hands that had embraced her parents. Skin that was warm and soft. Fragile and mortal. Her fingers curled into the palms of her hands. If she rejected his offer, would he kill her here and now?

Meeting his gaze, she had decided.

"No."

The word hung within the air between them.

So heavy one could reach out and pluck it from the wind.

The Count's face was hard to read. Was he truly such an emotionless being? His gaze never strayed from hers. With a subtle nod of his head, he finally spoke, "Alright."

Yelena took in a breath, relief washing over her.

"But I shall come each night and ask the same."

She arched a brow with a tilt of her head, "Why?"

Count Dravmir turned to the side, dismissing her. "Perhaps you'll learn before you meet your end." There was such a coldness to his tone that her body shuddered.

With those parting words, the Count strode across the room and vanished through the doors. Their groans echoing within the room.

CHAPTER THREE

A Portrait

EXHAUSTION HAD FINALLY claimed her. Her body becoming sluggish as her mind grew weary. The events of the day had chased at her heels, nipping at her as she fled. But they leapt and claimed their prey. Yelena was hardly able to keep her eyes open. She trudged through the large, lonely room to the wardrobe. Stepping inside, her eyes flicked toward each of the dresses. All of them were unique to the former bride who wore them. Though she could spend an entire day gazing upon the marvelous gowns, she needed sleep.

Finding a rack of sleeping gowns, Yelena tugged the first one she found from its hanger. Leaving the wardrobe, she began to peel her dress from her body, allowing it to crumple to the ground at her feet. The one piece of her life she had brought with her to the castle. A piece of the village, of her family. Turning her back to it, she slipped into the silky gown. It caressed her bare skin like cool water as it flooded down her legs and pooled at her feet. A river of silk streamed behind her as Yelena returned to the bedroom, closing the doors behind her. Stepping up the few stairs, she lingered at the foot of the vast bed. Her fingertips grazing the dark sheets.

Yelena had never wished for such finery. Never knew that deep within, she had yearned for this sort of life. She was grateful for all her parents had given her. Had found comfort within her ordinary life. Pain laced through her chest, for this was the first night since Danna had taken the role of cooking their meals that Yelena had missed dinner. Never again would her tongue tingle with the spices Danna dashed into their soups. Never again would she watch her sister dance about humming to herself as she chopped vegetables. Though Yelena had not eaten since morning, her stomach did not howl. Her gut twisted into knots.

Brushing away those thoughts, Yelena climbed onto the plush bed, falling into the mattress as if it were a cloud. The bed released a sigh as if it had been waiting far too long for a body to grace it. Yelena slid beneath the sheets and lay on her side, slipping a hand beneath her cheek. Her gaze drifted toward the vast wall of windows. Her eyes searching through the stars as if they could provide her any solace. Whispering the answers, she desperately needed, into her ears.

But whatever she searched for was long out of reach.

Her freedom stolen before she had ever been given the chance to grasp it.

As her lids closed, a lone tear rolled down her cheek and fell upon her pillow.

∞ ∞ ∞

"Ena!" Her sister's voice shrilled her name. "Ena! Hello? Are you listening to me?" Danna waved her small, brown hand before Yelena's dazed eyes.

Yelena blinked, returning to their world. She offered a sheepish smile, "O-Of course I was!"

Danna arched a brow as she crossed her arms over her chest, "Really? Then what was I saying?"

Yelena lowered her gaze as she fiddled with her fingers. "Uh... that you were excited about what momma was cooking tonight?"

A sigh escaped her older sister, "I said that five minutes ago, Ena." There was a slight whine to her voice, frustration coating her words.

"Sorry, sissy. What were you talking about?"

"Are you going to listen this time or wander off again?"

Yelena crossed her fingers over her heart, "I promise I'll listen this time!"

A sigh escaped Danna as she shook her head, "I was saying that when I'm older I want to have my own bakery. Could you imagine it, Ena? Oh, I can already see it!" There was a wistfulness to her tone as she clapped her hands together and twirled on the tips of her bare feet.

Dust wafted into the air from the dirt as Danna whirled about behind their home. Winter had slowly crept into their world, claiming the life from the grass and trees. A gentle breeze swept passed them, tousling her sister's dark tresses. Rippling along the wind in dark curls.

Yelena giggled. Danna had been helping their mother cook dinner for the past year now, expressing interest in preparing their meals. Their mother was more than hesitant to let her young daughter cook alone. Worried she may slip and slice her finger or mix the wrong spices and make something horrid. But Yelena could see a grown version of Danna drifting about her own kitchen, preparing foods of all sorts. Humming a wordless tune as she chopped away at vegetables and meats.

"What do you want to do when you're older, Ena?" Danna asked.

Though her sister knew what she wanted, Yelena did not. Her only interest seemed to lay in escaping their village within her mind. Wandering within worlds of her own making. Leaving this place far behind her and venturing out to find something magical.

Yelena merely skipped ahead of her sister, "See the world!" She beamed.

There was a dampness upon her cheeks as Yelena stirred from the dream. Trying desperately to cling to it, to remain within the memory. Knowing that when she woke, she would be in the Count's castle. Never again to wake in her own bed. Her eyes slowly flicked open and found a grey morning sky. The clouds thickening to swallow the sun's light. Forbidding it from stepping foot into this land. A land ruled by monsters that lurked within the shadows of this world. Yelena could not help but wonder if the Count was forged from the darkness. The shadows lingering just beneath his pale flesh. Writhing like serpents.

With a sigh, she tossed away the bed sheets and scooted across the large mattress. There was a slight chill within the room. The marble floor nipped at her bare feet as she wandered from the carpeted path. Yelena rubbed her hands on her arms trying to warm herself. Though there was a lingering chill, she felt a brush of warmth lazily drifting through the air. Approaching the doors to the bedroom, there was a gust of warmth that crept forth from beneath the doors and caressed her toes. Forcing them open, her ears were filled with the sounds of a steadily crackling fire. Warmth embraced Yelena eagerly as she stepped into the main room. Approaching the hearth, she stretched out her arms and warmed her chilled fingers. The heat of the flames licked against her flesh, chasing away the lingering cold.

As her body warmed, a thought had flickered across her mind. *Who had lit the fire?* Yelena had not done so before she slept. Perhaps Daria or Danika had come into the chamber and lit it for her, knowing that her mortal flesh would freeze within the night. As if her thoughts were spoken aloud, there was a knocking upon her doors. Daria and Danika swiftly stepped into the chamber. There was no hint of the fiery monster with them. Yelena relaxed as she breathed out. Her scalp and hair were safe, for now.

Before Yelena could greet them, a hiss escaped the women and they cowered within the darkest corner they could find. Perplexed by their sudden outburst, she followed their gazes. And there she found that her bedroom doors were open, allowing the pale light of the day to filter within. Though the sun had been suffocated, some of its light lingered. Yelena flicked her gaze to the women, their eyes narrowed upon the lone beam of light. Hurrying to the doors, she pulled them close, sealing out the day.

Facing the women, she found them straightening themselves. Daria offered an apologetic smile, "The sun is not too kind to creatures such as us." She spoke.

Yelena nodded, "I didn't know, I'm sorry. I'll be more careful next time."

Daria waved her hand in the air, "No need for apologies. Now, we come on behalf of the Count."

Her skin bristled at the mention of the man, "Why?"

"He wishes for us to ready you. Your portrait shall be painted today."

Yelena blinked. "So soon? I've only just arrived."

"He has a portrait made of each bride." She answered.

Yelena's brows knitted together, "Why?"

A sorrowful smile caressed Daria's lips, "To remember them."

Daria did not say anything more, spinning on her heel and approaching the closet. Danika lingered close at the woman's side as they stepped into the wardrobe, sifting through the dresses. After a few passing moments, Daria returned with a dress. Yelena's gaze drifted down to the fabric that dangled from the hanger. It was simple yet beautiful. The neckline and sleeves would cut straight across her chest, leaving her shoulders bare. The bodice of the dress was crafted from the deepest black she had ever seen. The sleeves were short and puffed out in white ruffles. Pointed blackened ends feathered out from the cuffs of the sleeves like thorns. The skirt of the dress billowed out thickly in waves of midnight satin.

"Do you like it?" Daria asked.

Yelena could hardly place into words how much she *loved* it. "I do." She whispered.

Daria smiled, "Good. I thought it would best suit you." The woman became nothing but a blurred whisper of shadows as she crossed the space that separated them within a breath, startling Yelena slightly. She reached out and gently reached for Yelena's hair, "The sleeves reminded me of your hair."

There was such a tenderness to her tone, in the way she caressed the strand of hair between her fingers before letting it spill through the spaces of them. The hair falling back into place. Yelena did not miss the faint flicker of sorrow within the woman's red eyes. Did the brides before Yelena pass through her thoughts? Remembering the white tresses that their bloodline shared and knowing what would soon become of the mortal woman.

Daria took in a breath and plastered on a smile, "Alright, let's get you ready."

Yelena seated herself on the furthest end of the couch were the back faded down and vanished. Danika stood behind her and combed her hair silently. The brush gently unknotting the tangles in her tresses. The tender tugs caused gooseflesh to creep along her scalp and down her arms. Yelena could feel herself relaxing from the gentle movements, reminding her of when her mother combed her wild hair as a child. Tangled and matted from a day of running through the town with her sister. Those memories seemed so long ago now. As if a lifetime had passed. But that was another lifetime ago. Forever far out of her reach as she wandered throughout this new life. Living amongst monsters.

Yelena cast her gaze to Daria, the woman stood before the crackling flames. The fire dancing against her red irises. The woman seemed lost within her own thoughts. Drifting about within another world.

"Why didn't Drezca come?" Yelena asked.

Daria blinked as if she had been in a haze, "Count Dravmir needed to discuss something with her." Her voice was slightly monotone as if half of her still lingered within her own world.

Yelena wondered what the Count needed to discuss with the woman.

∞ ∞ ∞

The Count stood before his throne. His glowing gaze cast down upon it. It seemed to mock him as it stared back. Dust had encased it like an old quilt. Dravmir had not taken a seat upon this throne in decades. Not since his first bride...

The shadows whispered as Drezca swept into the room. The Count did not bother looking at her, his gaze fixated on the throne before him. "Daria told me what you did to my bride." His tone was dry as he spoke.

Again, the shadows whispered, and he could feel her presence lurking just behind him at the base of the dais. "Daria should keep her nose where it belongs. I was simply having a little fun, no harm done."

Dravmir scoffed. "No harm done." He repeated with sarcasm dripping from his lips. "Why must I remind you with each bride, do not scare them?"

"Why does it matter what I do to her? She'll be dead soon anyways. She's a... *mortal.*" The word hissed from her lips. "She's nothing."

His brow twinged, growing annoyed with the woman. "Drezca, my word still stands. Need I remind you I'm your Count."

There was a heartbeat of silence that trailed behind his words before the woman spoke again, "You don't care for the mortal so why care what I do with her?"

A sigh escaped the Count, "I might not particularly care for her," He turned his head to the side, casting a narrowed glance upon Drezca, "But if I find you have harmed her again, you will not enjoy what I have in mind for you. My *final* warning."

Drezca's face was pinched in frustration, her thin lips pressed together. But she bowed her head before the Count. "Of course." The words hissed from her mouth.

∞ ∞ ∞

Once Daria and Danika had deemed Yelena suiting enough, the two women led her forth from the chambers and into the shadows of the castle. As the doors closed behind her, Yelena felt a tug back to the room. To the roaring fire and dim sunlight. Reminding her that not all was dark within this world. That there was light even in the darkest of places. Turning away from the doors, she trailed behind the women. She mindlessly followed them through the long stretches of halls and stairs. Her eyes flicking about each portrait or carved statue. Gargoyles could be found nested in the highest corners of the halls. Like stone guardians, silently protecting from the shadows. A shudder trembled along her spine as her gaze met with one of the gargoyles and she could have sworn, it looked back.

Daria and Danika led Yelena through the grand entry room. Yelena's eyes slid toward the balcony above, as if searching for Drezca to be leaned over the railing. Taunting her with a venomous smile. But there was no sign of the woman, at least not to her mortal eyes. And for a moment, her gaze slid toward the doors. Just beyond them was her freedom, waiting for her to take that leap. To take the chance and flee the shadows of this castle. But Yelena was no fool. Though the women before her treated her with kindness, she knew if the Count ordered them to hunt her down, they would. And they would not be merciful.

They strode across the center of the room and passed through another arched doorway. Turning to the left they strolled down another long stretch of hallway. Yelena wondered how many halls and rooms were here. Wondered if she would ever get to explore each one before her untimely demise. Before she realized it, they had made several more turns down each hall and ended up before two doors that loomed feet above them. Daria stepped forth and rasped her knuckles against the dark, aged wood. A silent moment passed, the world seeming to still around them before an answer came.

"Come in." The Count's voice echoed from the other side.

Daria pulled open the doors and stepped aside, Danika following her movements. A grand room was laid out before them. Circular and wide with a staircase that wound up one side of the walls. She realized this was one the towers in front of the castle. The windows here had thick midnight drapes hung over them from the ceiling and sweeping across the marble floor. The front curve of the wall seemed to be crafted entirely of glass. Standing in the center of the room, was the Count. Dressed in such simple clothes Yelena found herself taken aback. His raven hair was pulled back from his face. Wisps of strands dangled on either side of his angular cheeks. A cream blouse billowed loosely from his body, tucked into black leather pants. The sleeves were rolled up to his elbows, exposing the length of his pale skin. A white apron was securely tied around his narrow waist. His glowing gaze met with hers instantly and she found it hard to look away.

Beside him was a blank canvas nested against an easel. Hardly a foot away from it sat a lone chair. Carved from deep, cherry wood and polished. The arms had an elegant curve to them and velvet cushioning atop them for her to comfortably rest her arms. The back and seat of the chair were lined with the same crimson cushioning.

She had not been told that the Count would be the one to paint her portrait.

Yelena steeled herself and kept her chin high. Taking a step forth, she halted at the threshold. Her eyes meeting with Daria's. The woman waved a hand at her, encouraging her to go. Taking in a breath, Yelena entered the room, the doors were swiftly closed behind her. The Count watched her every step like a hawk. Extending his arm, he gestured toward the chair, urging her to take a seat. Yelena strolled toward it and situated herself down on the cushion.

"How would you like me to pose?" She asked.

His face was indifferent, "However you wish." And he stepped toward the easel.

Beneath the canvas there was a long tray attached to the easel beneath it. There were rows of small paint jars, their lids gone. A glass vase held various brushes, some thick and others seeming as though they only had three hairs. Beside the vase was a jar of water and a paint-stained washcloth. His slender fingers plucked a brush and dipped it into one of the paints. His red eyes settled upon Yelena, waiting for her to situate herself. Awkwardly she shifted about before resting her elbow on an arm of the chair. Draping her other arm into her lap and clasping her hands together. Straightening her spine, she was ready.

The Count merely nodded his head and shifted his gaze back to the blank easel. As he lifted his hand, it blurred. Yelena gaped at the man. Watching the bleary movements. She was astonished at how *fast* he painted. All the while the

Count's face remained void of any emotions. His gaze fixated upon the canvas. Yelena had caught the few times he had spared a glance at her before returning to the portrait. She wondered how paint did not splatter about, sprinkling on the ground and spraying the man. But she could not find even the faintest of specks. These immortal monsters were perfect in almost every aspect it seemed. And Yelena found herself in awe of the Count. And perhaps a bit envious. Feeling like such a fool. Any soul with enough sense would know to *fear* these monsters. But it appeared that they were more mortal than Yelena believed. That there was more to them than just bloodlust. That perhaps, their hearts still beat with mortality though their bodies were immortalized.

The Count's hand stilled as his gaze swept back to her. Silently, he set down his brush and approached her. Yelena stiffened as the Count vanished behind the chair. A cold chill swept over her body. She sucked in a breath as cold fingers grazed her bare shoulder, sweeping her white tresses back. Allowing them to fall over her shoulder and down the length of her back. That small, tentative touch sent a tremor along her spine. His fingers traced over the edge of her shoulder; his touch so slight she could have sworn she imagined it. Without saying a word, the Count returned to the easel and continued painting. Yelena hoped that the warmth she felt within her cheeks did not stain her skin.

The moments swept by them as Yelena watched his blurred movements. Dipping his brushes into the paints before swirling them within the darkened water of the jar. His hand had finally stilled as he set down his brush. Taking a step back, the Count admired the portrait before him. Yelena could hardly sit still, eager to see the painting. The Count took notice of her fidgety movements and motioned to her with his hand. Leaping from the chair, she rounded the easel and stopped. Her eyes grew wide as a light gasp escaped her. It was as if she were staring into a mirror. The portrait was almost too perfect. The skin of her face was smoothed, no sign of brush strokes to be found. Her hair in the painting seemed so much silkier than in reality. The Count had painted a soft smile on her pink lips. Her crystalline eyes staring back at her like brilliant jewels. Yelena had to fight the urge to reach and feel the painted canvas beneath her fingertips.

"What do you think?" His dark voice rasped behind her.

"It's beautiful." She whispered, awestricken.

"Good." The Count stepped around her and untied the apron from his waist, hanging it on the back of the easel. "I shall fetch Daria; she'll show you back to your chambers." So soon, he had dismissed her.

His tone left a bitter chill against her skin.

Would she spend the rest of her days treated as if she were the scum beneath his polished shoes? As if every breath she stole irritated the Count. Her mere presence nothing more than a nuisance he would soon rid himself from.

Count Dravmir opened the doors to the room and turned halfway to face Yelena, waiting for her to leave. Lifting her chin, she strolled toward him and did not bother giving him a passing glance, brushing passed the Count as if he were nothing. Treating him how he had been treating her since the moment she stepped into this cursed place. If it irked him, she would never know. But she would take pride in the fact she stood up for herself, even if it was in the smallest of ways.

A small victory.

And she would revel in it for as long as she could. For death was creeping upon her. It was almost a shock that she left the room, thinking the Count would strike her down for such an offense before she could get another foot passed him. Instead, the doors quietly sealed behind her. The Count locking himself inside with her portrait. Perhaps he would ruin it as some sort of punishment. Movement in the shadows before her broke her free of her own thoughts. Three figures lurked toward her, Daria, Danika, and Drezca. The woman met her gaze instantly and a feral grin grew at the corners of her thin lips. Though Yelena had disgraced the Count, she found her bravery faltering staring back at the lioness before her.

Daria stepped forth from the group and offered a warm smile, "Come I shall escort you to your chambers."

Yelena was thankful that only Daria would be taking her back, leaving Drezca far behind them as they vanished from the hall. Their walk was spent in silence, Yelena's heavy footfalls echoed through the vast castle. Once they reached the doors to her chamber, Daria spun to face her. "A servant shall bring your meals to you. I shall send for one after I leave here. Do you have any requests?"

Yelena wanted to say, *my sister's onion and cabbage soup.* But she knew she would never taste it again. And any other soup made by a different set of hands would never taste like Danna's soup. It simply would not be the same. Would not be right. A silent sigh escaped her, "Surprise me."

Daria nodded and faced the doors, forcing them open. The sound of a steadily crackling fire greeted their ears. Warmth spilled forth from the chamber and swept by them. A thought flickered in her mind as she cast her gaze to the woman at her side. "Daria, did you light the fire while I slept?"

But she shook her head, "It wasn't me. Now, I shall go tell the servants to prepare your food." Then, Daria had become nothing more than a shadow as she vanished.

Yelena entered her chambers and closed the doors. Her gaze flicked toward that roaring fire. She approached its warmth and thawed the Count's chill that clung to her skin like a curse. As Yelena watched the dancing flames, she could not help but wonder who had lit the fire. Surely the Count had not done it. Did he truly care enough to ensure she didn't freeze to death in her sleep? As if he cared at all if she were cold. Perhaps he wished to be the one to kill her, to claim her life. Yelena cursed the man. If his face was not crafted from stone, he would be so much easier to read. To gauge how much longer she had left. Perhaps after her little stunt tonight, she did not have much time left.

∞ ∞ ∞

Yelena had not realized how much time had passed. She busied herself with undressing from the gown and slipping into something much cozier. A nightgown that was crafted from cream colored velvet, much warmer than the first gown she wore. Her fingers separated her hair and wove the white tresses into a long braid and swept it over her shoulder. The rumbled sound of her stomach crying out in hunger brought her back from her thoughts. Clawing her way through the maze.

Then, as if to answer her howling stomach, there was a knocking upon her doors. Yelena leapt from the couch eagerly, ready to fill her belly. Turning the handles, she flung open the doors and her excitement died. As did her hunger as fear crept into its place. Its icy claws sinking into her flesh as it embraced her being. Standing before her was no servant, but a monster. Drezca smiled, as if she could taste the fear permeating from Yelena's being.

"Where's Daria and Danika?" She forced the words out with mock bravery.

Those glowing eyes slid down the length of her being before meeting her gaze again, "Not here." Drezca purred. "I've come to speak with you alone, Yelena."

"About what?"

A slight chuckle sounded from the woman, the sound silvery and musical. A pouted expression settled on her features, "Unfortunately, I have been warned against harming you."

Yelena's shoulders slouched with relief.

But Drezca grinned wildly, "But I do enjoy playing my little games. And ours, mortal, has just begun."

"What have I done to you, Drezca?"

"Oh, come now, it's only a little bit of fun."

"For you." Yelena glared.

"Of course."

Gooseflesh crept along her arms as fear had claimed her entirely, staring into the face of the beast before her. Yelena could hardly breathe, hardly move. She was rooted to the floor. She was thankful for the silent footsteps that approached as a servant rounded the doors. A small and short woman held a silver tray within her hands with dishes covered in silver domes. She cast her glowing gaze to Drezca and bowed her head immediately before the woman. Drezca seemed to revel in this, smirking down upon the trembling servant.

"Eat well, Yelena." She flicked her tongue across the sharpened teeth that lurked within her mouth.

Once Drezca vanished, the servant approached Yelena. But Yelena's gaze was fixed on the writhing shadows. Waiting for the lioness to pounce from the darkness and claim her.

"My lady, are you alright?" The servant asked.

Finally, Yelena tore her gaze away and nodded. "I am, thank you."

∞ ∞ ∞

The savory scent of the food drifted lazily through the room. The gentle sizzles hissed against Yelena's ears. She set the silver tray down on the small table before the couch. Three silver domes lingered atop each plate. There was a glass pitcher of crisp water along with a wine glass. Reaching for the first lid, she slipped her finger through the loop and lifted. Beneath the dome, a bowl of sliced, steamed potatoes waited. Flakes of dark and red seasoning were scattered atop them, streams of butter trickled down the sides of the potatoes.

Her mouth watered as she breathed in the spices, able to taste them from their mere scent.

And for a fleeting moment, guilt swelled in her being. This was not her sister's cooking. Her delicate hands had not chopped those potatoes, did not dance about the kitchen as she dashed sprinkles of spices atop them. Pouring simmering butter over them like a glaze. How could Yelena eat anything that was not prepared by Danna? How could she sit in this vast, lonely room and dine on such fine foods? No longer would there be laughter echoing around untamed as she ate, no longer would there be those familiar conversations at the dinner table. Now, it was only Yelena. Sitting alone before the fire with not a soul to keep her company.

She was alone.

Completely,

And utterly,

alone.

Shoving those thoughts to the back of her mind, she unveiled the other courses of her dinner. Buttered, toasted biscuits lingered beneath the smallest lid. And a bowl of potato and carrot soup beneath the other. With a saddened sigh, Yelena grabbed the lone spoon and ate. Each bite was like ash in her mouth. Once the food touched her tongue, she could taste the savory-ness, but it faded quickly as guilt gripped her. Stealing away her sense of taste as if it were some sort of punishment. How dare she enjoy food that was not made by her sister?

How dare she.

Yelena ate in silence with only the crackle of the flames to keep her company.

∞　∞　∞

Before long, Yelena's belly was swollen. Food piled up to her throat and she found it hard to swallow. Releasing a breath, she leaned back into the couch, curling her legs in front of her, resting her knees against the armrest. Yelena's gaze drifted toward the flames, watching them dance. The embers burned through the logs hungrily, feeding their starvation. Soon the wood would be devoured entirely and nothing, but blackened ash would remain.

Knock. Knock.

Yelena startled, her heart leaping into her throat. "Yes?"

"It's Count Dravmir." His voice rumbled on the other side of the doors.

"Come in."

One of the doors opened and the Count stepped inside. Dravmir wore a simple, black tunic with trousers that matched. His polished shoes clicked against the marble floor until he strode across the thick carpeting. His raven hair spilled down his back, two thick strands framing either side of his face. Those glowing eyes were narrowed upon Yelena as he came to a halt a foot away from the table that separated them. She sat up straighter in his presence, waiting for him to speak. Yelena had an idea of what he came here to say or ask.

"You know why I come." His voice was like liquid velvet that settled over her skin, a lingering chill remaining behind.

She simply nodded.

"Do you wish to be changed into an immortal?"

And Yelena's answer remained the same. "No."

She did not wish to shed her mortal flesh, did not wish to become a monster crafted from stone, void of any emotion. She did not wish for that curse.

The Count merely nodded, "Alright. Goodnight."

With those parting words, he turned on his heel and swiftly left the room, closing the doors behind him. Yelena had stared at the doors, he left just as quickly as he arrived. She waited as if he would walk into her room again. Explain why he bothered himself with asking Yelena the same question and would continue to do so each night, even knowing her answer. Was he expecting her to change her mind? Did the Count wish for her to join him? To be a monster to rule at his side, craving the blood of innocents?

She shook her head, banishing those thoughts.

Yelena would never accept such a curse.

Never.

CHAPTER FOUR

A Dress for the Bride

Y ELENA HAD DREAMED of her family. She had run toward them, toward the village. Somehow, she had fled the castle, trekked through the shadows of the forest, and returned home. Her heart swelled, brimming with so many emotions as she passed through the village gates. Soon, she would be in the arms of her family. Soon she would sit at the dinner table and eat her sister's food. All would be well. She would be home.

When she burst through the door and dashed through the short hall to the kitchen, there she found her family sitting at the table. Eating away at the dinner Danna had prepared. Murmured conversation filled the air as they conversed. Yelena lingered at the doorway, tears swelling in her eyes as she watched them. She made to take a step toward them but stopped herself. Yelena could not join them. They had mourned her loss and now wished to recover, to go on about their days as their wounds healed. How selfish could she be? How could she run to them and reopen their scabbed wounds? The Count would surely find her and steal her away. Her family having to begin the grieving process all over again.

Yelena could not bring herself to do that to them. No matter how desperately she wished to fling her arms around them. To return to her old room, to lay upon her stiff, small bed. She wished for that simple life, finding herself missing it. Longing for it. All those years she spent within her own head running far away from the village. Wishing for some grand adventure. She had taken so much for granted without ever realizing the fate that waited for her.

With a heavy heart, Yelena retreated into the shadows. The tendrils reaching out and embracing her body. Turning her back to her family, Yelena fled through the village. Her tears overflowing and burning down her cheeks. As if punishing her for being so foolish, so selfish. The gates sped passed her as she dashed through them without a single glance back. Leaving her home behind her for the second time. Never to see it or her family again. They were gone to her.

She ran and ran until she stood before the looming castle. Where her fate waited for her. Where death lingered in the darkness waiting to strike. Yelena could hardly muster the strength to keep her chin high. Her steps becoming sluggish and heavy. Burden and regret threatened to crush her, bearing down so heavily on her shoulders she thought she would fall to the ground. Her legs burned with each raised step as she traversed the stairs, they seemed to be never ending. Growing higher and higher. When she finally reached the doors, she grasped for them, her fingertips grazing the old wood.

Before she stepped within, fear prickled her spine. Unease had settled within Yelena's depths. Gooseflesh crawled across her arms. Her back burned as if someone or something were watching her. Her hand had begun to tremble as it lingered against the door. Swallowing down her fear, she turned a glance over her shoulder. At first Yelena could only see the writhing shadows that lurked within the trees. The fog had trekked across the ground, misting it. Yelena waited, watching. Feeling as if she had gone mad. As she made to face the doors, a growl rumbled behind her.

∞ ∞ ∞

The strange dream had plagued Yelena's mind during the hours of the day. Spending her time locked within her chambers, watching as the dim sunlight faded away. Waiting for the night to claim the world. Yelena feared venturing outside of her room. Though her curiosity pled for her to venture through the grand halls of the castle, fear held her back. Drezca would surely be waiting and watching for Yelena to be alone. No Daria or the Count to protect her from the lioness. Yelena hated being such a coward, but she was a mere mortal. What chance did she stand against the woman?

None.

So, she took her defeat and waited till Daria and Danika came to her chamber. Assuming they would. As Yelena stood before the wall of windows in her bedroom, her hand drifted toward her neck. Her fingers brushed over the smooth skin of her throat and for a fleeting moment, Yelena wondered what it would be like to be turned into one of them. If she had accepted the Count's offer, she would not have to fear Drezca. She would have the strength to claim her ground. Yelena's hand fell away as she shook the thought from her mind. Toss away her mortality so she can hold her own against a monster? A monster who has had years – perhaps decades even – to sharpen their strength and turn it into a blade. Yelena did not know the first thing about fighting. Her life was forfeit no matter which way she looked. Yelena would do good to accept that.

Knock. Knock. "Yelena, it's Daria and Danika. May we come in?"

"Yes."

The doors opened and the two women strode into the room. Danika tightly grasped ahold of Daria's hand. Daria offered a warm smile in greeting, "We have been asked by the Count to take you for your measurements."

Yelena's brows knitted together. "Measurements?"

"Each bride is fitted with their own dress."

Yelena's gaze slid toward the wardrobe; would her dress soon join the others? Left forgotten in this room to gather dust and fade. Yelena would not even be a memory within these walls. She would be another lost soul. Nothing more and nothing less to the Count. Her portrait would crumble away into dust as the paint aged and her face would no longer be recognizable.

Yelena would be nothing.

With a sigh, she followed the two women and could not help but wonder where the third lurked? Did Drezca watch them from the shadows, waiting for the perfect moment to strike? The only comfort Yelena would take with her in death would be that Drezca could no longer torment her. As they strode through the halls, Yelena cast her gaze to the portraits of the brides. Her eyes meeting with those of her mother's. A pain laced through her heart. Not being able to bear it, she cast her eyes away from the portrait toward the opposite wall.

Then, she halted.

Adjacent from her mother's portrait was Yelena's. Hung upon the wall and smiling back at her. So soon her painting graced these halls. Did that mean her death would come next? Was the Count having her fitted for a dress she would wear when he stole her life? As if it were some sort of cruel ceremony. Perhaps it was. After the Count killed her, would Daria, Danika, and Drezca leap upon her corpse and drink the very blood from her veins? Yelena knew Drezca would be more than eager to do so. An image flickered within her mind, of the fiery haired woman partaking of Yelena's blood, crouched over her lifeless body. A shiver crept down her spine and she shook the thought away, quickly catching up with Daria and Danika.

They arrived at the doors of the second tower of the castle. Daria stepped forth and rasped her knuckles against the polished wood. Heartbeats passed before a voice summoned them within. Pushing the doors open, Yelena was greeted by the sight of another circular shaped room. The vast wall of windows were revealed, the drapes pushed aside allowing the full view of the night to be seen. The faint silver light of the moon and stars filtered through in thin beams. Specks of dust lazily drifted about, illuminated only when they touched the light.

Her gaze drifted to take in the rest of the room. A plum-colored carpet filled the room, covering the darkened flooring. Candelabras were mounted into the stone walls. Flames flickered atop the candles, bathing the room in warmth from all around. Above their heads a vast chandelier hung. Crafted from what seemed to be pure silver with clear crystals that dangled from chains between each loop from one candle to the next. There was lightness to this space, an airy and warm feeling as if life could be found here amongst the immortal souls.

To the left of the room, a large three paneled mirror stood. Framed in golden filigree that delicately wrapped around the mirrors like vines. Roses were sculpted in the gold, smoothed so beautifully they appeared real. As if you could brush your fingertips against the petals and feel their silkiness. A short pedestal was set before it. Covered in a dark velvet fabric and flat across the top, giving a flat surface for one to stand on while they got their measurements taken.

In the center of the room there was a small black velvet couch with a table before it. To the right of the room there were two large wardrobes. Their doors were open revealing the various dresses and tunics that dangled from their hangers. Against the right wall closest to the doors was a shelf that reached high to the ceiling with bundles of different assortments of fabrics. And there, hovering within the air at the highest shelf, was a woman.

The dress she wore was pure as snow. The skirt of it was crafted from nothing but piles of ruffles. The bodice was cinched in tightly, her breasts nearly bursting from the gown. The sleeves puffed out on her shoulders and slimmed down around her arms. Her skin was a shade deeper than Yelena's. Chocolate tresses fell in bouncy curls down to her waist. Her glowing eyes fell upon them instantly and a wide smile followed by a shriek escaped the woman. Eagerly she lowered before them and fell into a swift bow.

"It is such a pleasure to finally meet the Count's bride!" There was such a radiance about the woman, spilling out into the world like a warm embrace. She clasped her hands before her chest, "I am Charlotte, it is truly an honor."

Yelena could not help but smile, "I'm Yelena, the pleasure is likewise."

Those red eyes sparkled, "Ah, you honor me!"

Daria took a step forth, "I'm sure I can leave Yelena in your care now?"

Eagerly Charlotte nodded, "Yes, yes!"

"Don't overwhelm the poor dear." Daria raised a brow.

Charlotte waved the woman off, "Of course not! Come, come. Let us get your measurements!" Excitedly, she grabbed Yelena's hand and led her toward the mirrors. "Now, you stand up here. Oh, would you like a steady hand up?"

Yelena shook her head as she gathered her skirt, "No, but thank you." And stepped up onto the pedestal.

Daria and Danika lingered by the doors, "When you're finished there will be a hot meal waiting for you. Do you have any requests?"

"Surprise me." Yelena answered.

Daria smiled and nodded her head. The women turned on their heels and vanished from the room. Leaving Yelena alone with Charlotte. Turning her gaze to the woman she found her back at the wall of fabrics. Her arms already full of bundles of varying colors. The woman had a skip in her step as she trotted over to Yelena, dumping the bundles onto the couch, and plucking one forth. A fabric of lilac was wrapped around a white board. There was slight shimmer to it, a silky sheen. Charlotte approached Yelena and held the fabric up to her.

"What do you think? *I* think it suits your hair and skin."

Yelena admitted it was a beautiful color, but her gaze slipped passed the woman to the couch where several more bundles waited. "It is beautiful."

Charlotte had followed her gaze, her eyes widening as if in horror. "Oh, we certainly would not pick the *first* fabric I showed you! I have plenty to choose from and we have plenty of time!"

Yelena's smile faltered. Did she have time, though? Surely Charlotte did, but Yelena's was limited. Charlotte was too busy with the fabrics to take notice of the slight change in Yelena. The woman skipped back to the couch and rested the bundle against the back of it. Charlotte gingerly flipped through the bundles of varying fabrics. Yelena noticed she had selected quite a few pastel-colored ones. Compared to the rest of the castle this room seemed to truly breathe with life. As if Charlotte still desperately clung to the shred of mortality that lingered within her soul. Refusing to let go. Though she could never bask in the warmth of the sun again, she found a way to capture its warmth and trap it within these walls. In her soul.

Charlotte skipped between Yelena and the couch for several passing minutes, holding up different colored fabrics to Yelena. Time had passed and Yelena hardly noticed, craving this sort of warmth. This seemingly utterly normal interaction. Yelena had nearly forgotten that she was in the presence of a monster. Only being reminded when she looked in those glowing red irises. The way the woman beamed or how her eyes twinkled whenever she selected a color, she thought suited Yelena caused something to swell in her chest. An ache for familiarity. Memories flickered in the recesses of her mind. Of days her mother would make her stand on the small table in their living room, gently swatting her legs as she skipped on her feet, unable to stand still for even a second. Laughter would fill the room and with it, warmth. The memory was so vivid she could have sworn she heard her mother's laughter echoing in the room like a phantom.

Something wet trickled down Yelena's cheek. Reaching up, her fingers brushed across her cheek coming back damp with her tears. The droplets glistening on the tips of her fingers. Charlotte had faced her again with another fabric and her eyes widened, a gasp escaping her. Hurriedly, she tossed the bundle back to the couch and vanished from sight, becoming a blur of shadows before returning. A silken handkerchief was in her grasp as she approached Yelena.

"There, there." She spoke gently as she dabbed at the tears. "I didn't think the colors were *that* atrocious."

A burst of laughter escaped Yelena, the warmth returning to her.

Charlotte offered a tender smile, "There you go."

"Thank you, Charlotte."

"Of course, dear. May I ask, what troubled you? Was it something I said? Or were the colors that terrible?" She gave a pouted look with a huff.

Yelena shook her head, "The fabrics are wonderful." Her gaze lowered, "I just miss..." She chewed her bottom lip, afraid that if she spoke those words out loud, the tears would return.

Charlotte nodded, understanding. Her gaze drifted toward the windows, peering out into the writhing shadows the night offered. Those red eyes growing distant. "I miss it too." There was sorrow that clung to her every word. A wistfulness in her tone as she yearned for the mortality she lost. "I decorated this room in my sister and mother's favorite colors." She gestured to the plum rug, "My mother." Her gaze drifted back to the couch and a smile touched her lips though it never reached her eyes. "My sister. Though some would argue black is not a color."

"It is a mixture of all colors, so would that not make it a color on its own?" Yelena offered.

Charlotte's gaze drifted back to the woman standing on the pedestal, a line of silver brimming in her eyes. "My sister used to say those exact words. You remind me of her."

All Yelena could offer was the comfort of a smile that spoke with understanding.

The conversation faded away into the shadows as Charlotte returned to the fabrics. It was not much longer till they found a color that suited Yelena. A deep plum that reflected the carpet of the room. Charlotte then wound the thin measuring tape around Yelena's body. Taking notes on each number that went with each part of her being. Charlotte's touch was so gentle Yelena hardly felt her fingers graze her body. Working gingerly and quickly.

As Yelena watched the woman work, another thought snuck into her mind. Perhaps this was not a dress for a ceremony of her death. Perhaps it was in a way. As she watched Charlotte flitter about, Yelena wondered if this dress that the woman would be stitching would be for her funeral. Long after the Count stole her life, would her corpse be decorated in the beautiful gown? And then left before the gates of their village like a shattered porcelain doll.

"Alright, all done." Charlotte stepped back and laced the tape measure over her neck like a scarf. "I'll fetch Daria for you."

With a parting smile, the woman vanished from sight, the doors silently groaning as she left. A couple minutes passed by before Charlotte returned with Daria, Danika, and to Yelena's dismay, Drezca. As she stepped down from the pedestal, Daria offered an apologetic smile. Charlotte bowed her head to the women before shooing them out. Insisting that she needed complete and utter silence to complete the dress. The sound of the doors slamming behind them resounded through the empty halls, concealing the warmth within the room. Its lingering tendrils hardly grasping Yelena. And the further they strode into the cold dark of the castle; the tendrils lost their grip and fell away. Retreating to the warm room.

Yelena kept a distance between the lioness and herself, gluing herself to Daria's side. Danika standing at the woman's other side, Drezca strolled along beside Danika. The woman had looped her arm through Drezca's elbow, clinging to her. Yelena could not help her wandering gaze, drifting toward the pair. Yelena thought perhaps they were lovers but a closer look at them revealed to her that was not the case. Danika clung to Drezca like a child, lost and wandering the world. Desperately holding tightly to their mother in fear of losing them in the vast world. Danika's gaze drifted toward Yelena as if she sensed her too heavy eyes. Shame flustered her cheeks as she cast her gaze ahead, knowing it was not in her right to pry into their lives.

But a curious mind could not be helped.

∞ ∞ ∞

When they returned to Yelena's chambers, a servant waited within. A man stood before the table; a silver tray held within his grasp. The man bowed his head in greeting as they swept into the room. Daria, Danika, and Drezca lingered at the doors. Yelena approached the servant, he nodded his head to the couch, waiting for her to take a seat. Nestling herself down onto the cushions, he set the tray on the table before her.

"Your meal, Lady Yelena." His voice rasped with nervousness, trying to keep his voice calm in her presence.

She smiled warmly to the man, "Thank you."

He bowed his head, "Of course." Then he hurriedly left the room behind. The three women staring after him.

Daria closed the doors and the women lingered there, watching as Yelena removed the silver domes from the platters. The smell of cabbage soup wafted into the air as wisps of steam rose from the bowl. Her hand stilled within the air, still holding the lid. Her gaze stared into the soup and it stared back, mocking her. Pain laced through Yelena's heart and her grip tightened. She wondered what Danna was making back home for dinner. If her family now ate in painful silence. Their eyes locked on their food, never lifting their gazes, afraid their eyes might drift toward the empty chair.

Or perhaps they went about their days as if Yelena had never existed. Forcing their pain down into their depths. Never truly coming to terms with it and facing the beast. Allowing it to slowly tear them apart from the inside out. Plastering fake smiles upon their faces and forcing conversations while they ate. How long until they broke? Until they looked down at their plates of food and hurtled them across the kitchen, the plate shattering, and the food splattering. Crumpling down on the floor and wailing their pain into the world.

"Yelena?" Daria's voice was a faint echo within her mind, drawing her forth. "Is it not to your liking? I can send for another tray."

Yelena blinked as if coming out of a trance. Shaking her head, she forced a smile, "No, no! There's no need. It's lovely. It's just... I love cabbage soup." And she left it at that.

Daria nodded and Yelena devoured the meal. Each bite tasted traitorously upon her tongue, simmering down her throat, and rampaging in her stomach, twisting it into knots. She drank a glass of cool water, hoping to wash away the burns that were left behind, but it too, festered like an open wound.

"Daria?"

The woman stood before the crackling fire. "Yes?"

"Is there anything to do here? Must I be locked away in here until I greet my death?"

A scoffed laugh sounded from across the room. Daria narrowed her gaze on Drezca, but the woman merely winked. A sigh escaped Daria and she returned her eyes to Yelena, "I shall speak with the Count and see if we can have something arranged for you."

Hope fluttered to life in her chest, as if a butterfly had been locked away inside her. Slowly unfurling its wings as it woke. "May I visit the village? Visit my family?" There was an eagerness to her tone, a hopefulness that poured from her being and coated the air.

Daria's eyes darkened, a troubled look crossing her face as she pinched her lips together. Not wishing to dim the light in Yelena's eyes. Not wishing to steal this hope from her. But Yelena was no fool, seeing the clear answer within the woman's red gaze. Her smile faded and her shoulders weighed down.

"I'm sorry," Daria spoke gently, "One day, you will understand."

"*If* she lives long enough." Drezca remarked from the corner.

A hiss escaped Daria and Drezca rolled her eyes. Meeting Yelena's gaze again, she offered a reassuring smile, "I shall speak with him now. Come along you two. *Especially* you, Drezca."

Drezca pushed off the wall and sauntered behind Daria and Danika. Before she left, she cast a glance over her shoulder. Flashing a smile to Yelena and then, two of her teeth lengthened into sharpened points. A startled gasp escaped her and Drezca laughed as she closed the doors.

∞ ∞ ∞

The throne room was draped in silence so thick it was almost suffocating. The shadows writhed as if they too, were choking on it. Daria strode into the room, her feet silently whispering across the floor, shattering the silence to appease her own ears. Her gaze drifted toward the thrones and a dark silhouette loomed before them. As if a phantom haunted these halls. And in a sense, it did. Dravmir lingered before the dust incased thrones. His body a tensed statue, crafted from the harshest of stones. He stood there every day; the marble molded to his feet. Staring at those thrones as punishment, tormenting himself during his waking moments when his nightmares could release their rage upon him.

Daria lingered at the bottom of the dais. "Yelena thinks she is locked away within her chambers. Do not keep her caged like an animal, Dravmir."

Moments of silence passed before a sigh escaped the Count. "She cannot leave." His head turned to the side, staring toward the wall as if he could see through the stones and into the forest beyond the castle. "This you know."

"I know but take her *somewhere.* Anywhere in the castle. Don't let her wither away locked in that chamber. Don't kill her soul." Daria paused, watching the side of the Count's face. There was the slightest flicker within his eye, and she knew she had broken through to him. "Take her to the rose garden, I believe she will love it. It would be good for her and for you, Dravmir."

The front of his brow slightly drew upward, an exhausted and pained expression grasped ahold of his face. "I don't get close to the brides. Not after what happened before."

Daria nodded, her heart aching in remembrance. "I know but I think it would be good for you both. You don't always have to be so cold, Dravmir, so locked within yourself. Open up to her. Companionship is not something to be feared."

Dravmir finally met her gaze, fully facing her. "If I befriend her, it will only make it harder in the end."

The small crack she formed in his barrier had filled. A sigh escaped Daria. As she turned to leave, she said, "Think on it, Dravmir."

And then, she was gone.

∞ ∞ ∞

The silk bedgown pooled at her feet, her toes poking out from the fabric. The warmth of the fire licked at them, chasing away the cold. She wiggled her toes, stretching them, savoring the heat against the bare skin of her feet and arms. The palms of her hands were filled with heat as if she reached into the flames and cradled them. Yelena relaxed as she sat before the fire, allowing her mind to rest for the moment. Knowing that if she drifted too far into her memories, they would only shatter her. As she began to lull into the world of dreams, hardly stepping a toe into the land, a flash of white flickered before her closed lids. Her eyes snapped open as thunder roared above the castle like a mighty beast. Casting her gaze to the glass doors, rivulets of droplets raced down the glass. The gentle patter of the rain against the pane echoed within the chamber like a hushed melody. It was not yet cold enough to freeze the droplets and cast the land in a snowy blanket.

Yelena stood and approached the doors. Her fingertips pressed against the cool glass; fog traced around her hand as her warmth met with the chill of the storm. Grasping the handles, she turned them and opened the doors, welcoming the rain. The wind swept into the room, brushing her white hair over her shoulders. It left a chill as it embraced her being. Yelena took a step forth into the storm. The rain was gentle as it pattered down upon the world, trickling over her head, and dampening her tresses. Yelena approached the railing and braced her elbows against it. Closing her eyes, she tilted her head back and basked in the rain. A faint smile twitched at the corners of her lips.

Memories stirred but they were welcomed. Yelena embraced them as they emerged from the crevices of her mind. Reminiscing on days and nights from her childhood. When Danna and Yelena would sneak out onto the roof and bask in the rain, allowing it to drench them entirely. And though their mother would often scold them while she combed through their tangled and wet tresses, she never stopped them. Allowing them to be children and partaking in the beauty of the world, becoming one with nature. Gifting them memories they would cherish as they grew older. Their bodies wrinkling with time, aging like fine wine.

A sudden wave of sadness washed over her. Yelena's gaze drifted down to her hands. Never would they know age. Growing wrinkled and crooked as time warped them. She would never see her face slightly sag and crows' feet grow from the corners of her eyes. Yelena would never see her parents in their olden years. She would not grow old with her sister by her side. Yelena would only know her youth, mourning the loss of her aged years before she ever could greet them. And though Yelena never fancied the idea of having children, she often danced with the thought of finding love. Something like a storybook romance.

But again, that had been stolen from her.

Grieving the loss of a life she never was given the chance to know.

With a sigh, Yelena pushed away from the railing and returned to the room.

∞ ∞ ∞

The night was restless. The storm raging and howling against Dravmir's ears like a feral beast starving to death. The wind whipped his raven tresses about, tangling them but the Count paid it no mind. His thoughts had enraptured him entirely as he strolled outside the castle. The walls had felt as though they were closing in around him, threatening to crush him. Dravmir needed a breath of fresh air. Needed to clear his mind and silence the thoughts that rampaged through his head. Daria's words crept in through the cracks, whispering between his ears no matter how forcefully he pushed them back, they always broke through. His mind was tormenting him, forgoing venturing to Yelena's room to ask her that pointless question, he wandered out. Though he knew the answer she would give, that each bride gave him, a small selfish part of him wished she would say,

Yes.

His mind drifted toward the empty thrones. A Countess had not sat upon that throne in so long Dravmir feared that if any tried to take a seat on it, it would crumble to ash beneath them. Though Dravmir tried he could never forget *her.* The first and only bride to take their seat upon that throne. But then she met her demise, her blood painted the earth, and it eagerly drank it in. The Count shook his head vigorously, banishing those thoughts and memories. He did not wish to think of the thrones, to think of *her.* He had no right; her death was his burden to bear. As were the other brides.

He was a monster and nothing more.

Dravmir came to halt and tilted his head back to bask in the mist of the rain, clearing his mind. As his gaze drifted toward the dark and storming sky, his eyes flicked to the balcony of a room. A room where a certain bride could be found. But she was not hidden behind the walls, there she stood in the rain. Allowing it to soak her being, paying it little mind. Dravmir drifted further into the shadows of the trees, concealing himself from sight. Though he knew better than to linger, he could not take his eyes away from the woman. There Yelena stood. An agonizing, torturous reminder of his former brides. All of them stood there, molded together into one soul. One vessel.

There was a look of mourning on her face, wearing it like a mask, but it did not linger too long. A phantom of a smile caressed her lips, a hollow movement that did not reach her eyes, not truly. There was a glimmer there, but it was faint. As if a fond memory had played before her eyes. And then, her smile faltered. Her eyes opening as her gaze drifted down to her hands. The look of sorrow on Yelena's face stirred something in Dravmir but he slaughtered it before it could breathe with life. With a sigh, the young woman retreated into her chambers and closed the doors. Dravmir could not help but wonder, what had crossed her mind?

What memory could cause joy and sorrow wrapped together in one?

His gaze lingered on the balcony as he stepped forth from the shadows. As he stood there, Daria's voice whispered into his mind again.

"You don't always have to be so cold, Dravmir, so locked within yourself. Open up to her. Companionship is not something to be feared."

A sigh escaped him as he decided,

he would take her to the rose garden.

CHAPTER FIVE

Rose Pricked

YELENA FOUND THAT she could no longer find solace within the recesses of her mind. Her dreams were nothing but her memories. Her mother and father's laughter echoing about her mind. As if she were right there with them. The smell of cooking foods and boiling soups filtered through her nose. Her mouth began to water as she tasted the air upon her tongue. Danna's voice scolded her for daydreaming as she always had but laughter soon followed. Yelena had woken with tears staining her satin pillow and her heart aching.

The day crept passed, the storm still lingering. Yelena stood before the windows in her rooms, watching as the rain poured in sheets upon the world. Thunder rumbled lazily across the grey clouds; faint strikes of lighting ignited the world in a flash of light before fading away. Turning on her heel, Yelena left the storm behind her and readied herself for the day. Wishing to occupy her mind and hands, to keep herself busy somehow before she went mad trapped within these stone walls. Perhaps that is what became of the other brides, driven to insanity leaving the Count with no other choice than to kill them.

Offering them some sort of peace though he was the one to bring the sickness upon them.

Yelena did not know how long she sat on the couch, watching the crackling flames until there was a knocking upon her doors. Straightening herself, she called out, "Come in."

She had been hoping to see Daria but instead, a true monster lingered in her doorway, draped against one of the doors. Drezca was leaned against the wood, her hand curled around the knob while the other rested upon her hip. Her smile widened as she watched fear flicker within Yelena's eyes.

"Charlotte has summoned for you. It seems she isn't aware of our little game otherwise I doubt she would have asked me to fetch you." Drezca winked.

Yelena swallowed her fear and steeled her eyes, straightening her spine. "I don't fear you; you cannot harm me."

Something sparked in the woman's eyes, her grin turning feral. "Ah, but I think you forget words can be just as venomous as actions. You'll soon learn that little mortal." Her gaze narrowed, "Daria may have a soft spot for you mortals, but I do not."

A shadow appeared behind the woman, "Drezca." It called out in a silent voice.

A sigh escaped her as she slouched her shoulders, "Again, my fun has been ruined."

Danika stepped forth; her hands tightly clutched together. "You know Daria would not be happy."

Drezca smiled, "What she doesn't know won't hurt her, Danika."

Danika's gaze drifted toward Yelena, "I shall take her."

Yelena's body sagged in relief, allowing herself to breathe. Praying to whatever Gods were watching over her for sending Danika.

"My fun always gets spoiled." Drezca walked past Danika before tossing a wink over her shoulder at Yelena and vanished into the shadows.

Danika lingered at the threshold, "Come, Charlotte is waiting."

Yelena nodded and hurriedly left the room, following behind the woman. Their walk was spent in silence as they strolled through the halls. Danika kept a steady pace, allowing Yelena to keep up with her easily.

"Thank you, for taking me to Charlotte."

Danika nodded her head without looking at Yelena.

"May I ask, why does she hate me so? Have I done something to offend her?"

Danika was silent for a moment, her eyes growing distant. "No." She finally spoke. "Drezca is tormented."

"By what?"

Danika halted in her steps for a moment, her gaze meeting with Yelena's. "Are you not tormented by something?"

Yelena blinked at the sudden question.

Danika gazed ahead, "We are all tormented."

And the conversation fell into silence.

As they continued in silence, Yelena could not help but wonder what tormented these women? Was it the Count? But they did not seem to fear him. They did not cower when he was near. What have these women witnessed?

What have they survived? Yelena hoped she lived long enough to learn their stories, even Drezca's.

∞ ∞ ∞

Charlotte was nearly bursting at the seams with excitement as she ushered Yelena to the pedestal, urging her up. The woman sped across the room toward one of the wardrobes and plucked a dress from it. With a bright smile, she faced Yelena and approached her, holding up the finished dress.

"Well, what do you think? Beautiful is it not? My talent often takes me by surprise sometimes." She puffed out her chest with pride.

The dress was sewn from that beautiful plum colored fabric. Yelena was stunned at how quickly Charlotte had finished the dress. Something so intricate would take any mortal *weeks* to finish. The sleeves were made of sheer fabric that tapered into points. Rounded, clear crystals were scattered about the sleeves, catching the golden light of the flames in the room, and twinkling with life. The neckline of the dress was heart-shaped, the sleeves would rest below her shoulders. There was scalloped trimming that traced across the heart of the neckline. The bodice dipped into a V and the skirt spilled from it. The first layer was crafted from the same fabric of the sleeves with crystals sewn into it. Beneath that layer, a darker shade of plum satin could be found.

Yelena's mouth gaped as she stared at the dress. Words were stolen from her.

Charlotte seemed to lose her confidence, "Oh," she said, "You hate it. I should have known! I am terribly sorry; I will work immediately on another dress!"

Yelena quickly shook her head, "No, no! The dress is *gorgeous!* You did a wonderful job. I love it, truly."

Charlotte beamed; warmth flooded through the room from her being. "Ah, you bless me, truly! Come, come! Let's get you into the dress!"

Charlotte gestured across the room to some dressing panels and handed Yelena the dress. The woman ushered Yelena excitedly to the panels. She vanished behind them and hung the dress over one of the panels and began to undress. Slinging her gown over another panel, she grabbed the new dress and slipped into it. It fit her perfectly as if it were a second skin. The skirt swished on her legs and whispered across the floor as she stepped from behind the panels.

Charlotte gasped, clapping her hands together excitedly. "Oh! You look beautiful! Come, come!"

Charlotte grasped ahold of Yelena's hand and nearly dragged her to the mirrors. The woman placed a hand over Yelena's eyes and helped her onto the pedestal. And when her hand fell away, Yelena took in the reflection before her. She could hardly believe the reflection. Yelena had thought the first dress she wore when Dravmir had painted her portrait was stunning, but *this* was something plucked from the pages of a fairytale. Stolen from some princess now one dress short.

"Charlotte..." She was lost for words.

A giddy squeal escaped the woman, "Ah, just beautiful! It fits you perfectly! No need for adjustments. I am a master of my craft."

"That you are, Charlotte. Thank you so much."

"Of course. Here." She offered a hand to help Yelena down.

Once Yelena had stepped down, there was a knocking upon the doors. "Come in!" Charlotte called out.

The doors groaned and Daria stepped forth. Her glowing gaze landed upon Yelena instantly. A tender smile formed on her lips. "You look beautiful, Yelena. You should wear that dress tonight."

Yelena's smile faltered, her heart stopping in her chest.

Had her death arrived?

She was dressed for the occasion and now her time had come.

But Daria continued, "The Count wishes to take you somewhere special. He will like the dress," she winked, "I promise."

As Yelena followed Daria from the room, her mind drifted. Why had the Count all of the sudden taken an interest in her? Wishing to take her to some place special. It was odd. From the cold behavior he has displayed since she first arrived; Yelena did not expect this. And she did not know what to anticipate for tonight. Her stomach twisted into knots but something else stirred, as if butterfly wings brushed against her insides.

∞ ∞ ∞

Daria's fingers gently combed through her hair as she readied Yelena for her evening with the Count. She had parted it down the middle, gathering a portion of it and twisting it behind her ears, winding it to the back of her head where she pinned it. Wisps of white strands framed either side of her face. Daria swept her hair behind her shoulder, leaving one bare and the other covered in her hair.

"Daria?"

"Yes?"

Yelena chewed on her lip, "Why does the Count wish to see me tonight?"

"He wishes to open up to you, the best he can, anyhow."

"Why bother? He will kill me soon enough."

Her hands stilled in Yelena's hair. "One day, you'll understand."

But Yelena doubted she would. She wished they would tell her instead of dancing around it, afraid of broaching the subject. So, Yelena allowed their conversation to sputter and die out like an old flame. Not even an ember remained.

"Alright," Daria gently patted Yelena's shoulders, "All done."

"Thank you, Daria."

The woman stepped around her. For a moment, she did not speak. Only studying Yelena's face as if it were the last, she would ever see it. Though that was not true, her portrait would always linger as a reminder. Daria reached out and gently brushed the smallest strand of hair behind Yelena's ear. "Of course." Then, her hand fell away. "I shall fetch him."

With those parting words, Daria was nothing but a blur of shadows, leaving silence trailing behind her.

∞ ∞ ∞

Yelena nervously paced about the chamber. The sound of her silk shoes whispered through the silence. She picked at her nails as she chewed her lip. Her mind racing with a dozen thoughts. Was the Count going to rid himself of her tonight? Or would he dine on her flesh slowly, torturously? Drinking of her blood, feeling the warmth of it trickle down his throat. Drezca's smile flashed before her eyes, of pointed teeth eager to plunge into her flesh.

A shiver trembled down her spine.

Knock. Knock.

Yelena nearly burst from her skin, clutching a hand above her heart. Taking in a breath, she tried to steady her thundering heart and trembling body. Smoothing out her dress, Yelena strode toward the doors with a straight spine. Wrapping her fingers around the knobs, she took in a breath and pulled them open. A light breeze swept past as the doors flung open and standing before her, was Count Dravmir. The man wore a simple, midnight tunic. His raven hair freely falling behind him like liquid night.

Yelena's hands fell to her sides as she held the Count's gaze. His eyes widened for a moment, as if shock overcame him. Slowly, his gaze slid down, taking in the plum dress she wore. Eyeing each and every detail sewn into the fabric. His eyes slid back to meet with hers and even the Count seemed at a loss for words. Stunned as if he truly saw her for the first time. Dravmir gathered his composure and clasped his hands behind his back.

"Charlotte did a good job." He finally said, "The dress... suits you."

It seemed as though he wished to say more but left it at that.

The Count stepped aside, "Come."

And Yelena followed.

The Count gave no indication as to where he was taking her. Yelena kept pace at his side. She noticed he had slowed in his steps so that she could join him. They made their way through halls that never seemed to end. Turning down doorways left and right until finally, they stopped. Before them was a set of doors much like the entrance ones. The Count approached them and forced the doors open, flattening his large hands against the aged wood and pushing. With a groan, they swung open and unveiled a sight that Yelena could hardly believe. Count Dravmir had stepped aside, allowing her to step out on the stone stairs. With wide eyes and mouth agape, she stood before him, unaware of his watchful gaze.

Before Yelena was a vast garden of roses. Around the edges were hedges so tall she could hardly see over them. A cobblestone path led from the stairs and broke into separate paths, winding through the large garden. Along the pathways, rose bushes bloomed. Her eyes followed down the path straight before her and found a fountain further ahead with benches seated around it. The gentle sounds of splashing water filled the air. The songs of frogs drifted into her ears, their croaks echoing off into the night. Around the garden Yelena noticed tall marble pillars. Green vines wrapped around their bodies as nature embraced them. Faint golden flickers ignited the night as fireflies fluttered about the breeze. The scene before her was magical. Yelena wondered if she were dreaming, if she had dozed off while waiting for the Count to come for her.

But it was real.

"It's... beautiful..." She could hardly find her words.

Dravmir stood at her side but Yelena could not find it in herself to meet his gaze. As if this place had hexed her. "Come."

And she followed again.

As they strolled along the path, Yelena's gaze drifted toward the blooming roses. There was a slight ache in her heart for winter was coming soon and these beautiful flowers would wither from this world. Their brilliant crimson color fading into a mudded brown. Their petals becoming brittle and breaking away with the gentlest gust of wind. Crumbling into ash that danced along the air. The two walked around the fountain, her eyes wandering down into the clear water to find golden fish swimming about. Their tails splashing at the surface. Lily pads lazily drifted about atop the water, many of them had frogs resting upon them as they croaked their chorus into the night.

Yelena trailed her fingertips across the edge of the smooth marble fountain as they strolled passed. Beside her, the Count remained in solemn silence. She watched as he walked, and she could not help but notice the slight change in his demeanor. The Count seemed more... relaxed here. Perhaps the garden was his place of sanctuary where he could escape into a world and free himself of his mind. To come here and simply *be.* Yelena could see herself spending hours perhaps even days lost within this garden. Losing herself to the serenity this place offered. Listening to the songs of the frogs, trailing her fingertips over the silky petals of the flowers.

Yelena stole a glance at the man beside her and she became all too aware of the small distance between them. Her skin bristled and there was a slight tremor to her hands. Clasping them together, she squeezed her fingers to steady their shaking. "Why did you bring me here?" She finally broke the silence.

Disturbing the serenity.

The Count stopped.

And Yelena did the same.

His brows furrowed as if he searched for an appropriate answer. She watched as his throat bobbed. That glowing gaze never drifted toward her. "Daria suggested I bring you here. That you might like it."

Yelena did not know what she was hoping for. That maybe, the Count had a heart nested somewhere within his stone body. But she had been wrong. He did not bring her here of his own accord. But she was thankful that Daria had suggested this and that he had listened. The Count brought her here when he did not have too and for that, she was thankful. For one night of freedom from that chamber and feel something other than the dread that loomed over her like a grey cloud.

"She was right." Yelena finally said. "I love it."

The Count merely nodded his head.

They strolled ahead, passing by more rose bushes. Yelena could not help herself. She came to a stop before one, not watching to see if the Count had stopped too or if he continued along. Mindlessly, Yelena reached toward a rose and brushed her fingertips across its petals. They brushed against her skin like smooth silk, cool to the touch and a tad damp from the morning rain. Leaning down, she closed her eyes and sniffed the flower. Filling her nose with its floral scent, a smile caressing her lips. When she opened her eyes, she cast her gaze to the side and found the Count beside her. He was so close their bodies nearly touched. His gaze bore down on her, as if he tried to read down into the deepest pits of her soul.

Yelena was eager to put space between them, wondering what had caused him to act in such a way. She fumbled a step back and her fingers brushed passed the petals of the rose and to the stem. A breath escaped her lips as her fingertips caught on the thorns, tearing at her skin. Yanking her hand back she found droplets of crimson forming on two of her fingers. They beaded up and rolled down the slender length of her pale skin. Again, the Count closed the distance between them. Her hands brushed against the velvety fabric of his tunic. His gaze was focused on her fingers, his brows slightly upturned as if... as if he *worried* for her. Then, the Count lifted his hands to cradle hers. His touch was tentative, as he caressed her wrist. One of his hands held the back of hers while his fingers traced up the other side of her hand.

There was conflict within his irises. Tempted by the blood that poured from her fresh wounds. As if he could hear its sweet, alluring call. Beckoning to him. Pleading for him to have a taste. To feast. Dravmir fought against that desire that stirred within his depths. But he was losing that fight. His carefully built exterior was slowly coming undone. His façade crumbling away and turning to ash upon the wind. Count Dravmir gave in to that temptation and lifted her hand gently to his mouth. Yelena's breath hitched as his lips traced against the tips of her fingers. And she found that his skin was soft to the touch. That it was not sharp, and it did not slice her like she had once thought when she first lay eyes on him.

The Count closed his eyes and took in a breath, breathing in the scent of her blood. It was the purest of smells to him. Tantalizing, mocking almost. The scent of life clung to her fragile, mortal flesh. Pale and pink with blood that ran through her veins just beneath the soft surface. And so easily, it had been broken. The mere prick of a thorn spilling that sweet substance into the world.

Dravmir had fought and he had lost.

His lips kissed the swelling crimson droplets from her fingertips. The taste of copper lingered upon his tongue. Yelena's blood smeared across his thin lips, painting them as he had painted her not long ago. His hold on her hand stiffened as he slowly brought himself back to his senses. Cursing the blood's tempting melody, falling victim to it as he always had. And always would. Slowly, his eyes flicked open and found Yelena staring back at him. Within her eyes, he found so much fear. And looking further, he found acceptance. The woman had braced herself for death, ready to greet to it. Thinking that he would kill her within this garden, drain her of her life surrounded by the roses that had doomed her.

With a shake of his head, he dropped her hands as if she were something unclean. The Count's composure was gone as he took a few trembling steps back, holding out his hands. He desperately tried to reclaim control over his being, to silence that deep desire within to pounce on the prey before him and claim his prize. His nostrils flared as her scent tainted the air. Tempting him once more. Dravmir fought against every instinct that woke within him. Forcing down that thirst and building his façade once more.

When he finally opened his eyes, Yelena flinched at the coldness she found within those cursed irises. There was disgust written across his eyes. There was such a sudden change within the man. Yelena had thought that tonight, she would find that beneath that hard exterior there was a man deep within. But she had been wrong, she knew that now. Her gaze drifted down to find that her blood still stained his pale lips. And she was reminded that the Count was a monster who feasted on the flesh of innocents. Who drank his fill of blood from every bride that ever stepped foot inside his castle.

And soon, he would claim Yelena's blood.

Her life.

The Count regained his composure and without saying a word, he vanished within a dance of shadows. Fleeing away into the darkness of the night where the tendrils waited for him, embracing him. Yelena stared after him, at the empty space where he had stood. Her legs trembled and gave out beneath her, falling to the stones below. A broken sound escaped her as the fear she had been drowning surfaced and sank its wicked claws into her. Ripping Yelena's soul apart as she wept. Her fingers still bled, her life dripping into the world and staining the stones below her in crimson.

Taking in a shuddering breath, Yelena had decided, it was time.

Time to leave this place and return home,

to her family.

∞ ∞ ∞

A thousand curses swarmed his mind as if angry wasps had swept into his ears. A fiery agony scorched him from within, burning through his every pore. Dravmir fled, vanishing from the garden. His last sight before the shadows swallowed him was of Yelena's face and the utter fear within her eyes. The Count banished her from his mind but as he bit his lip, he tasted the sweetness of her blood. Lingering like a cursed stain. Reminding him of the monster he was, that he would always be. Dravmir had returned to the confines of the castle, standing before the thrones as if they had drawn him here. He hated them. They were nothing more than cruel reminders. Mocking him for the deaths that burdened his shoulders.

Dravmir did not understand why he had allowed himself to lose his composure, to defy the distance between them. But when he saw Yelena halt before that rosebush, he could not help his curiosity. The woman had a softness to her features, the fear he had once found on her face when he was near had vanished. There was a tenderness to her now as she reached out and gently caressed the rose, as if forgetting of the monster that stood close. Her guard lowering. She once kept a wary eye on him as if he would pounce at any moment, but now, she had forgotten of the Count. The Count watched her fingertips trace over the silky petals. And then, she had closed her eyes and leaned forth. Taking in the scent of the blooming flower. The Count had been drawn to her. To the serenity he found on the woman's face, that leaked from her being and danced along the air. He wished to drink it in, to understand such peace. Around the woman, fireflies flickered their lights, illuminating Yelena in a golden halo.

Yelena was the sun in this dark world.

The light in that dreadful castle.

She cast away the shadows and brought warmth back to this cold place.

Before the Count could realize what, he had done or why he had done it, he closed the distance between them. All he wished was to bask in her light and warmth. To feel the sun against his cold, immortal flesh without fear of burning in its light. His body nearly pressed against hers, but his eyes were transfixed on her face, as if the woman had cast a spell over him. Yelena's eyes flicked open, and her gaze drifted to his and the fear crept back in. Remembering the monster that had captured her. She backed away from him, her hand trailing away from the rose. And before he could give a warning, her fingers had been rose pricked. Yelena snatched her hand from the flower and his eyes were drawn to the brilliant crimson that began to swell on her pale skin. Staining it in red, the scent permeated the air.

Dravmir had lost control. His perfectly sculpted façade crumbled before his and Yelena's eyes. His hand reached out and grasped ahold of her hands. His touch was gentle, feeling the supple softness of her skin. Warm against the cold of his own. He could feel her blood racing through her veins, her heartbeat echoing within her wrist. His slender fingers traced up the side of her hand. All he could hear in this moment was the call of her blood. Its sweet melody singing out to him and he could no longer resist. Bringing her weeping fingers to his lips, he kissed her wounds. And the coppery sweetness of her tantalized his tongue. When his gaze found hers, the world came crashing down on him. Dropping her hands, he backed away from her and fled like a coward.

For he was.

Footsteps whispered into the room. The Count did not move, his gaze remained on the thrones. The lithe sound of the footfalls whispered of Drezca's presence. "Did you finally rid this castle of that mortal?" Drezca sniffed the air, "I can smell fresh blood."

Dravmir's eyes narrowed, "No." His voice was dry and hollow.

There was a whispered snarl that echoed through the room. "Do you not think it best to rid yourself of her now? Before you grow attached to such a fragile, weak thing?"

A vein feathered in the Count's jaw as he clenched it. "You are dismissed, Drezca." There was a warning in his voice.

Silence lingered for a moment before the woman finally spoke, "As you wish, Count."

And then, she was gone.

∞ ∞ ∞

It was not long before Daria and Danika had found Yelena. Following the scent of her blood they found her in the garden. The woman seemed stunned, her fingers bleeding leaving crimson droplets raining down on the cobblestones. The two women led Yelena back to her chambers and tended to her wounds. The bleeding had slowed. Yelena watched as Daria cleaned the blood, cleansing the small pricks. There seemed to be no indication that the smell or sight of her blood bothered the woman as it had Dravmir. But if she watched the woman close enough, she saw faint flickers of temptation within her eyes.

"There you go, dear. All done." Daria smiled and patted the top of Yelena's hand.

"Thank you, Daria."

"Of course." The woman stood from the couch and gathered the dirtied washcloth, "Dravmir meant no harm, Yelena, I assure you."

Her brows pinched together, "Pardon?"

Daria did not meet her gaze, drifting toward Danika that lingered by the doors. The scent of Yelena's blood called to her and she wished to put distance between them. "He never meant to scare you. It's... hard for him. The smell of it. It's harder for most."

Yelena sighed, "Why does it matter if he never meant to scare me? Won't he rid himself of me soon like he did with the former brides? None of this makes sense to me, Daria."

The woman bit her lips as her grip tightened on the cloth, "You'll-"

"Understand someday. I know." Yelena interrupted. "Why can't anyone explain it to me? Please, Daria." She pled.

The woman approached the doors, "It is not for me to tell. That is for the Count. I'll have a servant bring you dinner." With those parting words, Danika and Daria swiftly left. Seeming eager to be far away from the blood tainted air that surrounded Yelena.

∞ ∞ ∞

As promised, a servant came to her chambers and delivered dinner. Yelena thanked them and closed the doors. She lingered for a moment, waiting until she thought the servant was far enough away. Hurrying to the table, she dumped the warm tray of food on it, forgotten. She did not bother changing from her dress, not wishing to waste even a precious second. Yelena rushed to the bedroom, thrusting open the doors and stormed inside like a mad woman. Grabbing the sheets, Yelena yanked them off the bed, the sheets of silk piled at her feet. Stretching them across the floor, she began to tie the ends of the sheets together making a rope. Bundling them within her arms, she dashed into the main chamber and out onto the balcony, closing the doors behind her. Tying one end of the makeshift rope, she hurtled the other end over the balcony. Grasping the sheet, she gave it a strong pull, making sure it was secure enough to hold her weight.

Yelena took in a breath, readying herself. Hiking a leg over the edge of the railing, she grabbed ahold of the sheet and planted the tips of her toes on the edge of the balcony. There was a slight tremble in her hands as her confidence wavered. Refusing to look below, Yelena began her descent. Her arms burned, not used to such exertion, carrying her body weight. Making her way down, fear crept into her being. What would happen if the Count or the others found her before she could escape? Would they kill her? Punish her for the attempted escape?

Finally, her feet brushed against the ground.

And Yelena was free.

She did not look back as she dashed into the writhing shadows.

She was free.

She was going home.

Yelena nearly burst; tears prickled behind her eyes as a smile widened on her face. Soon, she would be in the arms of her family.

She was going home.

$$\infty \quad \infty \quad \infty$$

Dravmir paced through the halls, hidden within the shadows, cloaking his being in them. Not wishing for his servants or the others to see him. To question the tormented look writhing on his face. Dravmir knew Daria would be looking for him, question what had transpired in the garden. The Count should have known better, should have never asked Yelena to come with him. He was a fool to delude himself into thinking there was a trace of mortality lingering within him. Buried in the deep recesses of his soul – if he had one.

But Daria's words had persuaded him.

"Don't kill her soul."

Echoed within his mind.

And then, a face appeared within the mist. Before his eyes, a woman stepped forth. Yelena. The scene replayed in his mind. Of her soft face twisting into fear, her eyes growing wide as her body trembled. And then, there came the blood. Dravmir shook his head, banishing her yet again from his thoughts. But she lingered, stubbornly. When he tumbled from his thoughts and returned to the world, the Count found himself standing outside the doors of Yelena's chamber. The shadows around him fell away as he stepped forth. His hand reaching out and tracing down the wood. Feeling the polished bumps and knots within the door. His fingers lingered on one of the handles. Dravmir battled with himself, should he go in or leave? Yelena perhaps never wished to see his face again. But could he truly leave it at that between them?

A sigh escaped him. Dravmir knew what he needed to do. Knew he had to apologize. Not for him, but for the fear he had caused the woman. He tightened his grip on the handle and raised his other to knock. His knuckles rasped against the door. Silent moments passed and nothing answered him. Dravmir knocked again, more urgently. And still, there was no voice to call out to him. Turning the handle, he opened the door and peered inside the chamber. The main room was empty of any soul. He sniffed at the air; the smell of blood tinged it, but it was fading. As was Yelena's scent. His eyes fell upon the table and found the tray of food, untouched.

Yelena was gone.

"No."

The Count whirled around and vanished into the shadows, chasing after his runaway bride.

CHAPTER SIX

Withering

YELENA DID NOT think of the repercussions of her actions. If she were going to die, she wanted to see her family one last time. To tell them how much she loved them, how grateful she was for their love and care all those years. She wanted to feel their warmth a final time as they embraced. Yelena wanted a proper goodbye without the watchful eyes of the village and the heavy gaze of the Count. She could not leave her family with that sort of memory. That could not be their last memory of their daughter. Watching her get ripped away from them, never to see her again.

Yelena's feet beat against the dying earth, pushing her further. Her lungs burning as she ran. Her legs aching but she no longer cared. Her only thought was getting to the village. Before her eyes, she could see her family, their images urging her onward. The forest grew ever darker, as if the shadows from the castle chased after Yelena, drenching the world around her in a dark maze. But she pushed on, fueled by her desire to return home. As Yelena ran, a prickle rippled down her spine. The snap of a branch echoed through the silence of the night. She did not stop, running faster. Then, a rumbled growl filled the air, and she was reminded of her dream.

As fear nipped at her heels, Yelena forced her legs faster, ignoring their burning pleas. She would not stop now, not when she was so close. Before her, through the thick, dead branches of the trees, she could make out the shape of the gates. The village. Tears trickled down her cheeks as a desperate laugh escaped her. She was going home.

Home.

As the gates became clear, the trees separating, and a clear path formed, Yelena dashed toward them. Toward the hope that dangled before her eyes. Tears fell to the ground beneath her, her smile wide and untamed. Yelena could picture her little home now, in her mind. She could see her family waiting at the door, arms open, waiting.

Waiting for their daughter to return them.

And soon, she would.

As Yelena burst through the darkness of the forest, something plummeted from the sky. A shadowy silhouette blocked her view of the gates. Icy dread settled into Yelena's veins as the Count took a step toward her. Her lips crashed into a frown; her hope syphoned from the core of her being. A tremble rattled her bones as her body shook, taking uneasy steps back into the shadows. Yelena had been so close and yet so far. Just behind the Count was her village, her home, *her family.*

If only she had been fast enough...

"You foolish woman." A snarl hissed from the man, "What were my rules? Did you wish for death?"

Yelena merely stared at the man before her. Was that her punishment? Death? For fleeing the confines of that castle, wishing to return to her family. She shook her head, "No." She choked back the new set of tears that burned behind her eyes, "I wanted to go *home.*"

For a moment, those glowing eyes seemed to soften. The rage that once scorched them faltered. A snap sounded behind Yelena and his gaze narrowed, darting around, peering through the shadows that writhed behind her. The Count prowled closer to her, a frantic look within his eyes. His hands made to reach for her, but Yelena shook her head, taking another step back.

Fear flashed through his eyes.

"Yelena." His voice warned.

"Please," Tears swelled within her eyes, "I want to see my family. Please..."

But her pleas fell on deaf ears.

The Count was a blur and then Yelena's feet left the earth. He scooped her into his arms and snatched her away from her home. The wind whipped through her white tresses, blurring her vision as she looked back at the village. Growing ever smaller the further they traveled, venturing deeper into the depths of the forest. And Yelena could have sworn, she saw her old home. Nestled within the center of the village. Her body trembled as the tears unleashed themselves, burning down her cheeks in waves of despair.

The Count gently squeezed her body, as if offering some sort of comfort. But she did not want his comfort for he was the one keeping her prisoner. Dangling the keys of her freedom before her eyes and snatching them away as she reached out, smothering her hope as he pocketed the keys.

They landed before the doors of the castle, the Count pushed them open and hurriedly stepped inside, closing the doors behind them. Sealing them within. Gently, he placed Yelena on her feet, his hand lingering on her lower back for a moment before falling away. She stood before him, consumed by her grief. Tears stained her rose tinged cheeks. The whites surrounding her eyes streaked with red. And within her gaze, the Count found a searing hatred boiling inside the woman.

Yelena's fingers curled into her palms, her nails piercing the soft flesh. How foolish could she have been? Did she truly think she would escape this place? Did she truly think the Count would not have hunt her down? What was she thinking? If Yelena had truly made it to the village, returned home, what monster would she have unleashed upon those people? The Count surely would have come to reclaim what was his but slaughter any who stepped into his path as punishment. Making her witness every death, knowing each one would burden her shoulders.

That sliver of hope, that small seedling, within her soul had withered. The hope she had nurtured, tended to its every need, and desperately clung to it, had died. Buried beneath the dirt in its own grave. The Count had taken that from her. Taken her home and family from her. Yelena had nothing.

She was alone.

A spark ignited within her chest, her agony igniting and shattering from its cage. It rampaged through her veins as liquid fire spilled into her being. A crack formed within her heart, the ache lacing through her chest as if an arrow had pierced her. Yelena closed her eyes and a shriek escaped her. Her agony filling the air as it echoed from her lips. And then, she lashed out. Her fists pounded against the Count's stone chest. She struck him again and again. Beating out her pain, wishing to inflict it upon the man so he knew how she felt. Wishing to hurt him as he hurt her, to take away his hope and stomp on it. To reach inside his chest and vanquish his heart if he had one.

But she was a mere mortal.

The Count merely stood there, his hands by his sides as Yelena struck him. He did not move, hardly phased by her outburst. She planted the palms of her hands against his chest and *shoved.* At first, the Count did not move, as if he did not feel her weak attempts. So, she shoved again. This time, he slightly moved as if by some chance Yelena had mustered up enough strength to the move the statue before her.

"I was almost home!" Her voice rang out in the room. *"Almost to my family!"*

Then, her shoulders began to tremble, and she stopped shoving. Her fingers curling into the fabric of his tunic. "And then you took me from them. You stole me." A lone tear rolled down her cheek, "And soon, you will kill me." She tightened her grip on his tunic, wishing to tear the fabric, "You are cruel, Dravmir. You are a monster. For only a monster would trap a maiden and keep her prisoner, smothering any shred of hope that dares linger in her soul. You've done it to the brides before me and will do it to the ones who come after."

Her words hung within the air above their heads.

"You're right."

Silence crept into the room on silent paws, draping its tail around them as it purred.

Yelena blinked.

"You're right." Dravmir said again, his voice rasped.

There was an anguished look in those red eyes as his façade cracked.

Gently, the Count wrapped his slender fingers around her wrists, holding them for a moment, before releasing her hold on his tunic and dropping her hands. The man stepped away from her and stepped into the darkness of the room and vanished. Leaving Yelena standing there alone, her eyes wide, lingering on the spot where Dravmir stood only a moment ago.

Yelena wrapped her arms around herself and crumpled to the floor, curling in on herself and wept her sorrows into the world. Not caring if any of the servants saw or heard her. Not caring if Drezca stalked toward her, ready to claim her prey. Yelena lay there on the cold stones and cried until darkness crept into her mind and she tumbled down into a black abyss.

∞ ∞ ∞

The air was cool, the evening warm with the lingering remnants of the summer sun fading from the world. A gust of wind whispered through the trees, shaking the leaves, rustling them in song. In the distance, a bubbling creek could be heard. Birds cried out their melodies as they retreated to their homes for the night. Opening her eyes, Yelena watched the setting sun. The sky transforming in hues of burnt oranges. Deep reds and pinks danced along the horizon like waves rising onto the shore, gently crashing against the sky. The final rays of the day glimmered through the darkness that rolled in, as if crying out for mercy. But the shadows swallowed the sun entire, banishing its light.

The roof creaked as another soul climbed onto it. Danna nestled herself down next to Yelena, propping back on the palms of her hands and stretching out her legs. "Figured I would find you up here lost in your own head." She teased.

A smile found itself on Yelena's lips, "Where else would I be?"

Danna brought her knees to her chest, wrapping her arms around them. "I wonder what it's like up there." Her voice sounded wistful, "I bet you conjure up beautiful worlds." Danna rested her head against a knee and reached out to her sister, tapping Yelena's temple with her finger, "When can I visit them?"

A sigh escaped Yelena, "When I learn such a spell that will allow one to walk through my mind."

A chuckle escaped Danna as she shook her head. "Come on, daydreamer, dinner is waiting. And I rather like my food hot instead of cold."

The two adolescent girls crawled back into the home through the window. Yelena slid it down and latched it into place. Her eyes lingering upon the forest that stretched beyond the gates, searching through the arms of the trees. Searching for a world that was far more beautiful than the ones locked away in her mind.

∞ ∞ ∞

Days had passed. Yelena's dreams filled with warm memories, of days she yearned to return to. Where the warmth lingered but with each day, grew colder as it faded away. She reached out desperately, wishing to clutch that warmth and cradle it close. Nursing it with her body heat, dreadfully aware that soon winter would grace her soul. Steal away any warmth and hope that dared linger, withering her like the flowers in spring. Each day, she could feel the ice webbing through her being. Stretching through her veins and reaching toward her heart.

Yelena dug within herself, planting the small seedling of warmth – of *hope* – and covered the hole. Patting the soil gently with her hands. Yelena could not surrender to that despair. Could not revel within the darkness any longer. Days had passed her by as she locked herself within her mind. She did not wander within worlds of her own making, she trapped herself within her memories. A bystander as she watched her family and her past self laugh and dine together. Nothing was amiss, no doom lingering beyond the horizon. It was simply them in those cherished moments. And she would keep them safely locked within her heart, tucked away.

Until the day came where Yelena no longer needed to clutch tightly to those memories. For Yelena was not planning on living the remainder of her days trapped within these castle walls. Though her first attempt was futile she would not allow that to dissuade her. Yelena yearned to see her family, if only for a moment. She *needed* to see them. To tell them she was not angry at them for hiding her heritage from her. She could not die without a true goodbye, she refused. And she refused to allow them to sit in their home thinking that their daughter held any hatred or anger toward them.

Knock. Knock.

"It's Daria, I've brought you dinner."

The door opened without Yelena calling for the woman to come in. Daria had forgone waiting days ago. Wishing to ensure that she was still within her chambers and she had proper meals each night. Yelena had not seen a servant since she had been back, Daria taking to bringing her meals. The woman slid into the room on swift feet and closed the doors behind her. Approaching the table, her glowing gaze fell upon the untouched tray of food that lingered from early this morning. Yelena could not bring herself to meet Daria's gaze, knowing what she would find. Worry, sorrow. Things she wished not to see. Wanting to stay within her memories for another moment longer. To linger within the warmth of them. The phantom echo of her family's laughter whispered through her mind. Daria set the fresh tray down and gathered the old one.

Yelena's gaze kept focused on the crackling flames before her with her chin propped atop her hand as she leaned her side into the arm of the couch. Her memories began to drift away, returning to the safety of her heart. The last face she saw was her mother's, the one who raised her all her life. Her smiling face fading away as Yelena locked her within her heart.

"What was she like?"

Yelena's voice echoed through the room.

The first she's spoken since she shouted at the Count, cursing his existence.

Daria halted at the door, "Who?"

Yelena's eyes lingered on those dancing flames, "My mother."

Daria was silent for a moment, her gaze searching Yelena's face. She resembled her mother, so much so that it was near painful to gaze upon her.

Every bride was a mosaic of the women who came before them. Their faces morphed into one. A sigh escaped Daria as she cast her gaze down upon the silver domes on the tray. "You remind me of her." She finally said. "She often wandered these halls, wishing to see every nook and cranny, leaving nothing undiscovered." Her hands tightened on the tray, "The rose garden was her favorite place to venture to."

At those words, Yelena tore her gaze from the flames and slid her eyes to Daria. "Did you know her well?"

Daria offered a sad smile, "Not as well as I would have liked." Her brows creased together, and she cast her gaze down, "I shall return this to the kitchens." And the woman vanished through the doors, leaving hardly a whisper behind.

Yelena's gaze settled upon the fresh tray of food and again, she could not bring herself to lift those domes. Her stomach did not even wish to indulge in foods that were not of her sister's making. With a sigh, she returned her gaze to the flames. And in the depths of her mind, her memories came forth.

∞ ∞ ∞

Daria swiftly made her way through the halls, ready to dump the tray and leave it forgotten, until she crossed paths with a servant. Handing it over to them, she vanished into the writhing shadows, searching for the Count. But she always knew where she could find him, where he would always be, brooding his eternity away. Tormenting himself.

Daria stepped into the throne room and there he stood. With a solemn shake of her head, she approached and halted before the steps. "Dravmir." Her voice was gentle, "She is withering, as are you."

His shoulders tensed at the mention of his bride.

"Dravmir, speak with her. Spend time with her."

"You know what happened the last time we..." His voice trailed off, shaking his head. Banishing those forsaken memories. The taste of her blood tainted his tongue.

"Why don't you tell her the truth?" Daria's voice was desperate, pleading to the man before her. "Help her to understand instead of leaving her blind."

Dravmir was silent. And for a moment, Daria believed her words had finally gotten through to him, penetrating that thick skull. Slightly, he turned his head, the side of his face glancing over his shoulder. But his glowing eye did not look at Daria, only peering down at the floor. A lone strand of raven hair fell over his face, curtaining his cheek.

"It's better if she hates me."

Those words settled into the stones of the castle.

Dravmir turned his face away and returned his gaze to the dust incased thrones.

Daria lowered her head in defeat and stepped away from the dais. She lingered at the doorway, her hand resting against the cold stones. "Dravmir, you know you can save this one. You could have saved the others and I know that knowledge kills you from the inside out. But this one, you can save if you only tell her the truth. Please..."

Was her last desperate attempt to reach the man.

When an answer did not come, Daria left.

Time passed and another knock came to her door. Danika had come to keep her company, taking Daria's place as they took turns watching over Yelena. Danika's gentle presence was welcomed, as was Daria's. But Danika was more of the quiet sort, allowing Yelena to drift far away without disrupting her imagined worlds and yanking her down from the clouds. Perhaps that was why they exchanged shifts, Danika allowed her mind to wander, and Daria was the one to ground her in reality when Yelena was gone far too long.

Today, Yelena decided she no longer wished to drift about her mind. Today, there was a place she wished to go. A place that gave her a small connection to the woman who had birthed her into this world. Though she was not given the chance to know the woman, going to the garden would give Yelena a small piece of her mother's soul. No matter how small a piece it may be, she would cling to it. Yelena dawned a simple cream-colored gown with a black overlay that laced together in the front like a corset. The black sides fluttered down either side of the cream skirt. The sleeves of the dress were long and clung to her arms, they tapered off into delicate points that rested atop the backs of her hands. Sweeping her hair over one shoulder, she wove the white strands together in a thick braid that swept past her waist.

Facing Danika, she asked, "May we go to the rose garden?"

Danika blinked, as if shocked that Yelena had acknowledged her. Nodding her head, she approached the doors. "Of course."

And Yelena followed the woman out.

The two strolled along through the castle, draped in silence as it trailed in their footsteps. Yelena's eyes met each gaze of every bride that hung from the walls. A sense of dread pooled in her soul the longer she held each gaze. Knowing each bride that stared back at her was gone from this world. Their souls taken far too soon, never truly able to experience life in all its beautiful agony. To feel love and loss and embrace each emotion, every turmoil. Yelena's heart weighed heavily in her chest; such was the burdens she bore.

When they stood before the doors that led to the garden, Yelena held her breath, her chest aching. Danika approached them and grasped ahold of the handles, pulling them open she unveiled the night and the garden before them. Yelena took a step out of the doors and lingered on the first step. Her eyes searched about the garden, taking in every budding rose. Watching as the fireflies ignited the night in warm, flickering orbs of gold. Chasing away the shadows that lurked within the corners of the garden. The sound of the frogs singing their melodies mingled through the air, dancing with the gentle splashing from the fountain as the fish slapped their tails above the surface of the water.

Looking at the garden before her, Yelena could almost envision her mother wandering along the paths, taking each curving one, venturing further and deeper into the garden. It was almost as if her spirit lingered here, appearing like a translucent silhouette, and flitting about. Drifting from one rosebush to the next, tracing her ghostly fingers across the silky petals, humming to herself. Yelena could see her white tresses floating about the air as if she were submerged in water. She watched as the phantom of her mother vanished behind a bush and did not emerge on the other side.

Quietly, Danika and Yelena descended the stairs and entered the garden. Their whispered footfalls mingled with the other sounds the garden created, joining the melody. As they strolled, Yelena reached for the rose but snatched her hand back remembering what occurred the last time she touched the flowers. Clutching her hand to her chest, she kept her gaze ahead, searching for her mother's ghost but found no remnants of her lingering in their world.

Casting her gaze down, she glanced upon her hand. The pricks on her fingers had healed, the scabs falling away, revealing the pale skin that lingered beneath them. Nothing remained from that night except for the memory that oftentimes waited for her in her dreams. Only Yelena's mind had twisted it, conjuring something wicked. The Count would lunge at her and pierce her neck with those sharpened teeth, relishing in the taste of her blood and screams. And no matter how much she thrashed against his hold, it never wavered. Clutching to her tightly until he drained every drop of blood that lingered in her veins. Leaving a lifeless corpse laying limp within his arms. And Yelena was no more.

"Danika?"

"Yes?"

"May I ask you something?"

The woman nodded her head.

Yelena halted in her steps, allowing her eyes to drift toward the roses before them. "Can you tell me what the Count is hiding from me?" Daria wouldn't tell her, but Yelena hoped that perhaps Danika would.

The woman's gaze drifted toward Yelena. "That is not my story to tell."

Disappointment weighed on her shoulders as she let out a sigh.

Danika shifted on her feet as she took a step closer to the roses. Reaching out a hand, she traced her fingers over the petals tentatively. "But I can tell you mine."

Yelena flicked her gaze to the woman, eyes wide. She had wished to learn these women's stories, but she never thought Danika would be the first to offer her own. "I would love to hear it."

The woman nodded her head, keeping her gaze on the rose. Yelena watched as the woman's eyes had grown distant. Burrowing within herself and digging up memories, disrupting the soil they slumbered in. "I come from the village." She began, her voice hardly a whispered breath. "Many, many years ago."

Yelena kept her lips sealed, daring not to interrupt the woman.

"I had three sisters." The smallest smile quirked at the corners of her lips. The only emotion Yelena had ever seen on the woman's face. Then, her eyes darkened, the glow fading. "We lived with our father; he was not a kind man. Our mother had passed away, he always claimed it was sickness, but we knew better." There was a bitterness to her tone. "A day came where my two other sisters and I found the body of the third."

There was a quiver to her lips.

"She was laid on the floor of her room, her clothes..." Danika steeled her gaze then and straightened her spine. "She had fought back. She was always the strongest of us. Our father left her for us burry. It took us all day to dig her grave and lay her body to rest. I'll never forget her face before we begun piling the dirt atop her. She seemed so at peace, as if she were in a deep slumber." Her fingers curled over the fragile petals of a rose. "I could not bear to return to that home. So, I fled into the forest. When night came, he found me. I fell before the Count's feet, pleading to him to change me. I had heard the tales of him, and I knew he could give me the weapon I needed for revenge – for my freedom."

Yelena's heart formed another crack. How could a father do that to his own daughter? How vile could a man truly be? She pictured her own father within her mind, gentle and loving. Yelena had wished Danika had been born into their family, to know the tenderness of a father's love.

"I enacted my revenge; my sister could truly rest in peace. My other sisters no longer having to suffer beneath his hand." There was a gleam in the woman's eyes, as if seeing the memory play before her eyes, reliving her father's final moments. The gleam faded and her face became stoic once more, settling into a mask it knew well. Keeping her emotions locked within her heart. "I did not extend this..." she gazed down into her hands, "to my sisters. I wished for them to live out their mortal lives, to have families of their own. I had given up mine so that they may live. So that they would not have to suffer because of that man again."

Silver welled within the woman's eyes, but it did not spill over as she cast her gaze to the dark sky above. "I did not see them again after that day. I did not wish for them to remember me as this. I wished for them to remember the woman I once was, the laughter we shared. I wanted them to have untainted memories of me. I did not even say goodbye."

Danika finally met Yelena's eyes, her gaze tracing over the tears that streamed down Yelena's cheeks. "I did not tell you this to upset you." She spoke gently. "I told you so that you know the Count is not as monstrous as you think him to be. He gave me this gift to avenge my sister and took me into his home."

Yelena wiped at the tears on her cheeks, "Thank you, for sharing your story, Danika." She entwined her fingers, "But if the Count is not a monster, then what happened to the other brides?"

Danika retreated into herself and turned away from Yelena. "Come."

Yelena wished she could take back her words and swallow them. As she followed behind the woman, she had a new admiration for Danika. It takes a special sort of strength to endure what she had. To give up one's mortality in exchange for becoming the very weapon one needed to enact their revenge. To turn your back on your family to let them live their remainder of their mortal years in peace. Their memories of your mortal years were all that was left of the soul that had been forever changed – cursed.

But perhaps, it was not a curse.

Perhaps, it was a gift.

As they returned to her chambers, she felt the prickling sensation of guilt swell in her stomach. For Yelena had another plan blooming in her mind. She was going to see her family again if it were the last thing, she ever did.

∞ ∞ ∞

A few hours had passed, spent in silence. Danika had walked her to her chamber and excused herself. Yelena had changed from her dress to a bedgown. There were several different ones, each showing which generation of brides they came from. This one was long sleeved crafted from silk. There was lace detailing stitched into the gown, fluttering across her breasts in delicate waves. The middle of the dress was crafted from the same lace with flowers designed into the pattern, stretching over Yelena's ribs, and exposing her pale skin. The silk fabric solidified above her bellybutton and spilled down to pool around her feet. The sleeves were loose and rippled down like silken waves to her calves, tapering up to reveal her hands. Her white tresses were freed from the captivity of the braid and streamed around her, curtaining either side of her face.

A knock rasped upon her doors and Daria had entered with a tray of food. The woman smiled in greeting and set the tray before Yelena. The scent of the fresh food wafted into the air and tantalized her tongue. Her stomach howled as if it finally wished to indulge itself. Giving in to its needs, Yelena removed the domes and dug into the food. As she ate, Daria lingered before the fireplace. The flames danced within her red irises, her face unreadable.

As Yelena finished her dinner, Daria had finally spoke. "Danika told me she shared her story with you."

Yelena patted a handkerchief at the corners of her lips as she nodded her head, "She did." Pain laced through her heart as she remembered Danika's tale.

Daria nodded, "She does not share that story with just anyone."

"Why did she tell me? We hardly know one another."

"You remind Danika of her."

Her.

"My mother?"

"They were close. Danika is like the Count in some ways. She often keeps a distance from the brides, but your mother was a tender woman, her love poured from every pore of her being. She often talked about you, Yelena. You were just a babe and yet she spoke of you as if you had been in her life all her years. As if she still held you each and every day."

Yelena wished she could burrow deeper into her memories, to find any fragments of her mother's face. Not just the portrait. She had seen her mother before but through the eyes of a newborn. Whatever image lingered of her mother would be blurred by the years, forgotten within the recesses of her mind. Guilt wound around her heart like a thorny rose. Prickling the beating muscle until it wept. How could she forget the woman who birthed her into this world?

How selfish could Yelena truly be?

A gentle hand tilted her chin up and she found herself staring into eyes of red. "Stop that nonsense." Daria spoke, "I see the guilt in your eyes."

Yelena bit her lip, trying to stop the trembling as the tears formed. "I saw her face once before. How could I forget it? What sort of daughter forgets their mother's face?"

"Yelena," Daria gently stroked a tear away, "You were a babe, there is nothing to be guilty of. As the years go by, memories fade, but they are never truly forgotten." Her hand fell from Yelena's chin and traced down her chest to rest above her beating heart. "Here they can be found when the mind has forgotten them, the heart always remembers."

Yelena choked back her tears and nodded her head, "Thank you..." Her voice was rasped.

The woman smiled tenderly, "Of course, dear."

When Daria left, it burned a hole in Yelena's chest. Perhaps she should stay here in this castle. Perhaps she shouldn't flee into the forest. But her family's faces surfaced in her mind, reminding Yelena why she wished to leave.

She needed to see them.

She clutched a hand above her heart.

Here they would always remain, but she was not yet ready for their faces to become blurred within her mind. Not yet ready to lock them in her heart forever.

Not yet.

CHAPTER SEVEN

A Garden Wall

THE DAYS BLURRED together, the nights melding into shadows. Yelena plotted her escape each waking moment, oftentimes dreaming of it. She could scale down from her balcony again, but she thought that the Count may have a servant watching her from the shadows, lurking just outside. She even foolishly considered walking out the entrance doors but again, servants could be lurking or perhaps a certain lioness...

Then the day came.

Yelena had decided on her escape. She was no fool, she knew the Count would eventually find her, that she would not live with her family in their small home again. But all Yelena wanted was to see them, to hold them. She had been spending her time in the rose garden, often accompanied by Daria or Danika. Drezca would appear before being shooed away by Daria. Each night, Yelena was escorted to the garden, the women would stroll with her. As the nights passed, they had taken to waiting at the doors until she was ready to go back. And then, they had stopped watching her all together, growing a trust in Yelena. Thinking she had given up on her foolish attempts at escaping. But they had been wrong.

Part of Yelena felt terrible for betraying their trust, but she would do anything to see her family again.

If only for a moment.

Even if it meant angering the Count.

∞ ∞ ∞

The night was the same as any other. Daria brought dinner for Yelena and she eagerly ate but not too fast, not wishing to arouse suspicion. Once she was full, she dressed in a simple gown. A long black dress with a white overdress. Yelena slipped her arms through the thick straps and clasped the three, brass buttons in the front. The skirt of the overdress split in two and fluttered down her sides, leaving the black skirt unveiled in the front. Parting her hair down the middle, Yelena fashioned it into two braids and tied black ribbons at the ends.

Once she was dressed, they headed toward the garden. Fear swelled within her belly, churning her stomach. Yelena regretted eating as much as she had for now, she feared she would retch it up on the polished floors of the castle. She swallowed it down and kept her chin high, though her hands trembled. She laced her fingers together and strolled along as if nothing were amiss. Daria kept a steady pace at her side, leading Yelena along the same path they traveled each night. When the doors that led to the garden were before them, all Yelena could see was the smiling faces of her family etched into the wood.

Waiting.

I'm coming.

Daria pushed open the doors and stepped aside, "Knock when you're ready to come in and I'll be here waiting."

Yelena nodded and took that step out into the night. She halted for a moment, "Thank you, Daria."

"Of course." And the doors closed with a quiet groan.

Taking in a breath, Yelena descended the stairs and entered the garden. It was such a beautiful sight, Yelena understood why her mother favored this place. There was a serenity within the air, intoxicating as she breathed it, her lungs expanding with it. She wandered about, waiting until she thought Daria was no longer listening. Yelena ventured further, strolling deeper along the winding paths. The rose bushes creating a maze that grew tall all around her. A fortress crafted from nature, coaxed by the earth that gave them life.

She had come to a stop before a bush, unable to resist the call of the sweet roses. Reaching out, she traced her fingers over the petals. Yelena remembered that night, where the flower had pricked her fingers and her blood spilled. The Count had been so gentle as he caressed her hands but that glow within his eyes revealed the temptation her blood posed to the man. Dravmir had been unable to resist the call of her blood and stolen a taste. Yelena had not seen him since that night.

"Well, well, look what I found." A voice purred behind her.

Yelena whirled around and found herself faced with the lioness. Drezca smirked as she placed a hand on the curve of her hip. "What? Aren't you happy to see me, little mortal?"

She steeled her gaze, "Not particularly, Drezca."

"What a shame, I only came to play our game."

"I don't want to play."

Drezca grinned and took a predatory step closer, "I did not ask." The woman flicked her gaze to the rose Yelena had touched, her eyes tracing down to her hand, lingering upon her fingers. "Your blood spilled here once." Her gaze found Yelena's once more and her grin widened into something feral, "and it can spill again."

Though the icy prickle of fear traced its hand along her spine, Yelena held her chin high, matching the woman's gaze. "The Count would not be too pleased with you, Drezca."

"Now, now, don't be a spoiled sport." She reached out and toyed with the end of a black ribbon, "Our game has hardly begun, don't ruin our fun before it begins, Yelena."

She tugged on the braid, not enough to cause pain, but enough to give a warning. With a chuckled laugh, Drezca turned on her heel and vanished from the garden, leaving Yelena alone with the roses. Weaving her fingers together, she steadied the tremble within them, and turned her back to the castle, continuing her stroll along the paths.

Yelena walked until she reached the end of the garden, a wall of hedges looming tall before her. Casting a glance over her shoulder, she searched the shadows for any movement and found nothing. The darkness looking back, watching the peculiar woman, waiting to see what transpired within her mind. Taking in a breath, Yelena faced the hedges with determination and reached out. Her fingers dug through the thick green and found the branches beneath.

She began her ascension.

She plunged her feet into the hedge and climbed ever higher. Her heart beat thundered against her ears, her arms began to tingle and burn. Her breath coming out in huffs. The skin of her hands was scraped and scratched, her dress catching to the hedge, but she ignored it all. Pushing herself to go faster. The faces of her family burned within her mind, urging her on.

And then, she reached the top.

With a triumphant smile, she descended the hedge and leapt to the ground. Her feet hit the ground hard, her bones aching from the impact, but she ignored the aches and dashed off into the forest. The trees raced past her, their boney branches reaching out and grasping at her braids. Her scalp was sore as the trees tugged at her hair, threatening to rip it from her head. It was as if they had tried to stop her, but Yelena pushed forward.

Just one more time...

That was all she asked for; just one more time to hold them.

To say a proper goodbye, then she could die at peace.

But only then would she gladly accept her fate.

The darkness writhed around Yelena. Stretching across the small dirt path, the wisping tendrils reached toward her, caressing her ankles and feet. Sending cold trembles rattling her body. All around the night grew ever darker, blackness settling across the land. Not even the faint light of the moon and stars penetrated the thick clouds that covered the skies. It felt as though she were racing through a dark abyss. Would this be what waited for her when death greeted her?

Darkness and nothing more?

Was this to be her afterlife?

To spend eternity in the cold shadows?

Yelena shook those twisted thoughts from her mind, unraveling their wicked vines. No. That would not be her afterlife. Yelena would frolic through the distant lands she had always spent her days imagining. She would swim in vast oceans and soar through vast skies. Only in death would she truly see the world. But that was not where her focus needed to be. Her goal now was to reach her family. And even if she failed again, she would not stop. Not until the Count stole her life. Yelena would fight till the end to see them again. She would never stop. Not until the Count stopped her heart.

Snap.

Yelena faltered.

Her eyes darted around, searching through the dancing shadows. At first, there was nothing but the trees, until something dashed through the darkness. A flash of red against the inky black. A growl rumbled along the wind, chasing after Yelena. Fear wound itself around her heart, squeezing the thundering muscle, strangling it within its grip. Panic seized Yelena's mind. Was this the Count? His true form? Something more monstrous than her mind could ever conjure chased after her. It toyed with her for Yelena knew the monster could capture her easily, could outrun her.

But instead, it played with her fear, prodding at it. Arousing the panic in her being, enjoying the helplessness that swelled within her crystalline eyes. The monster kept a steady stride with her. The silhouette of the creature raced through the shadows between the trees, the only things separating Yelena from it. Those red eyes never strayed from the woman, watching her feet beat against the earth. Her tangled braids trailing behind her, the ribbons at the ends of them coming undone and flapping against the wind.

Yelena dared to flick her gaze ahead, taking her eyes off the monster. Her eyes widened; the path was coming to an end. The trees halting as an opening spilled out. And there, within the night, the gates of the village stood. Yelena was so close; she was nearly home. But the huffing breaths of the monster drew back her attention. Those red eyes flashed in the shadows and then, the creature vanished. Engulfed by the night. Gooseflesh prickled along her arms as silence returned. Yelena feared slowing down her pace but feared reaching the end of the path all the same. Knowing that the monster lurked nearby, waiting for her to step into the opening, to emerge from the trees.

As the path began to narrow and the forest retreated, a shadow stepped forth. A hulking beast that blocked the sight of the gates. Yelena's feet halted, her heart roaring against its cage as she locked gazes with the creature before her. It stood almost as tall as the village gates; blackened fur spurted from its body. It stood like a man with the head of a wolf. Its limbs human in appearance mixed with the blood of a wolf. Its feet were that of a wolf but more monstrous in appearance as claws jutted forth from its flesh. Its hands that of a man hung loose at its sides. Its cold, red eyes held hers. Behind it, a bushy tail steadily swayed. As if it were the hands of a clock ticking her time away.

Tick-tock.

Tick-tock.

For death knocked.

The beast flatted its pointed ears against its skull. A low growl escaped it as it bared sharpened teeth, flicking its tongue across them. The creature was hungry, and it was prepared to feast. For its meal stood before it. Yelena could hardly think, and she did not know if she breathed. Her body had become stone, rooted into the earth, unable to move. To flee.

Was this why the Count forbade her from leaving the castle?

Yelena had learned too late.

A snarl escaped the beast as it lunged.

$$\infty \quad \infty \quad \infty$$

Daria and Danika searched the entirety of the gardens. Panic taking ahold of their minds. Drezca merely watched the women, watching as they searched through the bushes, wandering along each path. They hurried past Drezca in a blur of shadows, racing to Yelena's chambers, only they would not find the mortal there. She was long gone from this castle. Drezca had watched the woman's pathetic climb over the hedge. She admired the mortal's determination, but she was a fool all the same. Pushing away from the doors, Drezca wandered to the throne room where the Count could always be found. Wasting his time away staring upon dust encased chairs. She swept into the room on silent feet, a triumphant grin upon her lips. The mortal would no longer taint these walls with her weakness. She was nothing but wasted space, poisoning the air with her mortality. Her fragility.

Drezca knew that Daria would come soon to deliver the news, but she wished to be the one to inform the Count of his runaway bride. Drezca halted at the stairs and stared upon the man's broad back. "It seems as though your little pet has fled again, Dravmir."

The air whispered as the Count whirled to face her, a wild look within his glowing eyes. *"What?"*

Drezca lowered her head so he would not see the pleased look within her eyes. "She cannot be found, my Count. Her scent led us to the gardens."

A growl reverberated through the room. The walls trembled and Drezca found herself cowering, for none wished to face the Count's wrath. His face was contorted in rage and... *worry*. A snarl twisted Drezca's lips. But the Count had not taken notice. No longer aware of her presence as his mind was engulfed by fear. And then, as if to taunt his panic, a scream resounded through the night.

"Yelena!"

Drezca was brushed aside as the Count became nothing but a blur of shadows as he stormed through the room. Chasing after his bride. The doors thundered against the stones of the castle as Dravmir forced his way through them, nearly shattering the wood and ripping it from its hinges. Drezca stared after the man, rage simmering beneath her flesh.

∞ ∞ ∞

Yelena's lips parted and her voice ripped free from her throat. It echoed within her ears and shrieked through the forest, fading along the wind as it carried through the trees. When she forced open her eyes, the world had slowed. The beast had lunged at her, its mouth wide. Bloodlust danced wickedly through its glowing eyes. Streams of drool webbed from one sharpened tooth to the next. Its tongue lulled from its mouth, eager to taste of Yelena's supple flesh. To feel the warmth of her blood flowing down its throat.

This is how she would die, in the belly of the beast. Before she was taken as the Count's bride, Yelena always envisioned herself passing away in her sleep when old age became her. After she lived a life of adventure she would finally be allowed to rest. But her dreams were vanquished before her eyes as the beast lunged toward its prey, ready to claim her.

As the beast drew closer, the distance between them fading, another shadow leapt from the trees. Yelena watched as the dark silhouette collided with the creature. A yelp escaping it as the two were sent tumbling to the ground, rolling along the path. The silhouette had become clear to her, she watched as the Count tangled with the beast. Viscous snarls escaped them as they bared their lethal teeth at one another. They thrashed against each other and vanished into the trees. Snarls and growls erupted from the darkness of the forest. Man, and beast battling within the shadows. Yelena watched the blackness, searching for the two monsters but found no movement. Her mortal eyes unable to pierce through the veil of night.

Then, the air rattled with an agonizing howl. Of a beast crippling in pain. Silence followed soon after, an eeriness draping around the forest. Even the wind had settled its whispers, as if it too, were watching. Waiting for something or someone to emerge from the shadows. Yelena clenched her hands above her heart, anxiety gnawing away at her bit by bit as her eyes searched passed the trees. There was a slight movement, her heart leapt into her throat. The silhouette stepped forth, victorious. No sign of the beast followed the man, left alone to the shadows to die.

It was then that the clouds parted, and a silver stream of moonlight poured down, illuminating the Count as he stepped forth from the arms of the trees. His raven hair was astray, tangled. Strands of it fell over his face like a mask, shielding himself from Yelena's watchful eyes. His red tunic was torn, the shoulder of his right sleeve was so torn it clung on by only a few threads. The Count came to a halt a breath away from Yelena, his red eyes settling upon her. His gaze flicked across every inch of her face, trailing down her neck to her body. As if he were searching for any injuries, worried the beast may have hurt her.

"You are a terrible listener." His voice grumbled but there was a sense of relief coating his words. "And foolish."

Yelena found her words, her throat loosening. "I want the truth, Dravmir. No more hiding."

The Count opened his mouth to speak but howls reverberated throughout the forest. Dravmir cast his gaze around them, searching the shadows. "We must leave. *Now.*"

The urgency in his voice told her that more beasts were coming, thirsty for death. The Count closed the distance between them and swiftly took her into his strong arms. She stole a glance behind them at the sleeping village. Again, her family had been just within reach, but they passed through her fingers. Yelena began to doubt she would ever see them again, their smiling faces. Never feel their warmth as they embraced or hear their laughter. Casting her gaze down to the earth that raced below, she caught flashes of glowing eyes staring up at them. Shadows raced below, chasing after the two as they soared through the shadows above the treetops.

And perhaps it was best Yelena did not reach her family tonight. Did not open those gates for she would have brought death upon the village and those she held dear. Her fingers curled into the fabric of the Count's tunic. The man did not speak, only cradling her closer as they soared through the stars.

The Count lowered before the doors of the castle, setting Yelena on her feet. His hand lingered on her back as she wobbled. Her body ached from the trembles it suffered tonight from the fear that leached away at her being, the panic that had torn its claws into her flesh. Once he was sure she would not tumble down the stairs, he opened one of the doors and stepped aside. Yelena brushed passed him but halted at the threshold, casting a glance over her shoulder. She searched the shadows for glowing eyes, looking for beasts that may be watching, but her mortal eyes found nothing amiss in the darkness.

Facing the doorway, she stepped through. The Count followed in her steps and closed the door behind them. Its groan echoed through the silent room. Yelena felt the Count looming behind her, her skin prickling as if a phantom lurked over her shoulder. Taking a few steps further into the throne room, she turned on her heel to face the man. The Count lingered before the doors, masked in the shadows, his glowing eyes reflected from the darkness.

She lowered her eyes, "I only wished to see my family."

The Count did not speak, only watching her.

"Is that why," she gestured toward the doors, "your rule was to never leave the castle?"

He nodded.

"What was that?"

"A werewolf."

His words hung stagnant in the air between them as Yelena's mind processed the fact. There were more creatures, other than the Count, that lurked within this world, that roamed through the forest. That other bloodthirsty creatures waited in the night to feast, eager to bathe in blood.

"Will I never be able to see my family again?"

A weary sigh escaped the Count, "I once let a bride visit her family, many times. Her family no longer had to mourn the loss of their daughter. But one day, she ventured to the village alone." He paused, as if it pained him to tell this tale. Yelena could not read his face, her mortal eyes squinting to see passed the shadows. "The werewolves had found her before I could. Her family had to begin their mourning again. Their healed wounds torn open."

"You don't wish for my family to have hope only for it to be taken from them." She rasped.

Again, he nodded.

"Is that why you asked if I wished to be changed into an immortal? So I could protect myself?"

"Yes."

Footsteps whispered through the room as the Count stepped forth from the shadows. He halted before her, and she met his gaze. "I trust you won't do something so foolish again." Though his words sounded harsh, there was a tenderness to his eyes now. Tossing away his mask for a moment, revealing the face beneath the stone façade.

Yelena swallowed and nodded her head.

The Count stepped around her and made for an arched doorway. Yelena turned and spoke out to him, "Thank you for saving me, Dravmir."

The man halted in the doorway, lingering for a moment, before stepping through.

∞ ∞ ∞

Daria and Danika had swept into the throne room. Relieved looks washed across their faces. Daria had brought Yelena into a strong embrace, her arms like stone around her mortal body. The woman was careful not to squeeze too hard but just enough to assure herself that Yelena was alive. That she had returned safe and unscathed. Once Daria's arms had fallen away, Yelena followed the two women back to her chambers.

A servant had waited by the doors with a tray of food. Danika took it from their hands and dismissed them. The man scurried away into the shadows without a spared glance at Yelena. Daria opened the doors and they stepped into the room. The warmth of the crackling flames embraced Yelena's body. Chasing away the chill from the night, soothing the gooseflesh that lingered on her arms. Yelena approached the fireplace, bathing in the warmth the flames offered. Closing her eyes, she allowed the truth to settle into her. Etching into her bones.

Werewolves prowled this world.

And perhaps, the Count was not as monstrous as she once believed.

He had saved her not only once, but twice.

Yelena remembered her first attempt of escape. How his eyes darted around in a panic, searching the shadows behind Yelena. Seeing things that were cloaked to her mortal eyes. The Count could have let those beasts feast on her mortal flesh, gnawing on her brittle bones. But he had chosen to leave the safety of his castle to go find her. It seemed as though Yelena had much to learn about the mythical world around her and a Count that shared his home with her. Though she had gotten one truth from him, there were many more questions that were left unanswered. What truly happened to the former brides? And why does he steal them away from the safety of their village and bring them into a life of peril? Knowing that those beasts prowled through the woods, hungry for blood and flesh.

Why?

The sound of the tray being gently set on the table stirred Yelena from her thoughts. Stepping away from the warmth of the fire, she seated herself on the couch and removed the domed lids from the food. Steam wisped into the air like tantalizing tendrils, beckoning her to indulge in the warmth of the foods. Before her was a bowl of potato and celery soup and a loaf of bread with butter drizzled over the top. Her stomach howled, impatient to be filled. Grabbing the spoon, Yelena began her meal. She felt Daria and Danika's gazes upon her, watching as she ate. She knew they wanted to know what happened. If the Count had finally unveiled the truth if Yelena truly understood. When she finished her meal, she met their gazes. And whatever spoke from her eyes, caused Daria's own to widen ever so slightly.

"He finally told you." Her voice rasped.

Yelena nodded her head, "He told me why I was never allowed to leave the castle. That there are werewolves out there."

There was a flicker of disappointment within the woman's eyes. "That was all he said?"

"Yes."

A sigh escaped the woman. "I suppose in a way, I should be proud of him for at least opening some of the truth to you. That in itself is a small victory." Daria approached the couch and reached toward Yelena. Gently, she tilted her chin up with her finger, those glowing eyes peering down into her own. "He may not realize it, but he has opened himself to you, no matter how small it may be. He has not told a bride that truth in many years, Yelena. Now is your chance to understand the Count."

Understand him? How would she break through the walls of his barrier? It had taken Yelena nearly losing her life for him to finally tell her some portion of the truth. With a sigh, she nodded her head and Daria offered a comforting smile.

"Alright, I shall go fetch a servant to fill your bath. I'm sure after tonight, you'd wish to relax in a soothing bath."

Yelena's muscles groaned in agreement. "That sounds lovely."

Daria's hand fell from her chin and the two women approached the doors. As Yelena watched them leave, she called out to them. "I'm sorry for deceiving you."

The women halted and peered over their shoulders. There was no trace of resentment to be found within their red irises. "It's alright, dear." And with those parting words, they closed the doors, leaving Yelena alone with only the crackling flames to keep her company.

∞ ∞ ∞

Daria informed a servant to fetch hot water for Yelena's bath, knowing she would wish to soothe her aches and mind. The servant hurried along, preparing the water, and mixing lavender scents into it to ease Yelena's mind, to help her sleep. Daria continued along, searching for the Count. But she never had to search too long. Standing in the doorway, she watched the lone silhouette. Wishing he would cease this foolish torment. To forgive himself but it has been decades and Daria had once believed he never would. But after tonight, she had hope. A spark of it igniting. He had finally told Yelena part of the truth and that was more than she could have ever hoped for. She only prayed he would not stop, that he would not erect a thicker barrier around his heart.

She approached him, "You told her." Her voice echoed loudly within the silence. When the Count did not speak, she said, "Yelena's a clever one isn't she? Earned our trust enough to make us a believe she wouldn't flee. And then she climbed a hedge." There was a slight chuckle as she spoke, "Though clever, I doubt she'll try to leave again because she knows the truth. Part of it."

The man stood there like a statue, unmoving, never speaking, only listening.

"Now is your chance, Dravmir, to open up to her. So, she can fully understand the man that you are and the monster you are not. You have removed part of her blindfold, do not slide it back over her eyes." Her voice lowered into desperation, "Help her to *see*."

"How can I help her to see when I have been blinded by my own fears all these years, Daria?" The Count cast a glance over his shoulder, *"How?"* His voice pled.

"Only you know how, Dravmir." Daria placed a hand above her heart. "Here."

His eyes slid down to her hand, lingering there for a moment before facing the thrones once more. "I need some privacy."

Daria's hand fell from her chest as she nodded her head, "Of course."

∞ ∞ ∞

As promised, a servant came and filled the bath. Steam wisped atop the water, the scent of lavender lazily drifted about the room, permeating the air. Yelena closed her eyes and breathed in the smell, filling her lungs with it. The servant left, closing the door behind them. Yelena allowed her dress to slide down her body and pile around her ankles. The air had a lingering cold to it, the floor nipping at her bare feet. Lifting a leg, she dipped her toes into the water, testing the heat. It was perfect.

As Yelena lowered herself into the bath, a moan escaped her lips as she relaxed her body, leaning back into the water. Her muscles loosened, the aches in them fading away as warmth seeped through her flesh and caressed her bones. Yelena closed her eyes for a moment, allowing her thoughts to quieten. To rest her mind. But when the darkness was all, she could see, glowing eyes peered at her from the shadows. With a gasp, Yelena's eyes snapped open. Sitting up, she wrapped her arms around her knees, hugging them close to her breasts. Her white tresses curtained either side of her face, cascading down into the water, wisping about the surface, rippling like gentle waves.

All around, the steam danced like serpents, circling Yelena. She traced a finger in the air, separating the wisps, creating another stream. Her mind began to drift, racing with thoughts. Curiosity eating away at her brain. Daria told her to understand the Count. But how could she when the man had erected walls so thick between them Yelena could hardly crack the stones? How could she when they towered so high, she could not scale them?

How could Yelena melt a frozen heart?

CHAPTER EIGHT

Understanding

"**Y**ELENA, COME DOWN THIS INSTANT!" *Her mother's voice shrilled through the air. Watching as her daughter climbed to the highest branch of a tree and seated herself upon it, dangling her little legs in the air. Kicking them back and forth. Danna had raced inside; terrified Yelena would tumble to an untimely death. "Yelena!" She shouted again.*

But the little girl's mind had drifted far away. Gazing out across the village and toward the vast mountain range just beyond the forest. Yelena imagined herself floating atop a cloud, allowing it to lead her to lands far away. To lead her on fantastical adventures one could only imagine. Birds fluttered around her, chirping their lovely songs into her ears. Butterflies landed within her tresses; some brushed their delicate wings against her cheeks in gentle kisses. Tickling her skin causing giggled laughter to sound from the young girl.

"YELENA!"

Her mother's voice finally shattered her daydream. It faded away from her eyes as their world crept back in. The dazzling pastels of the sky deepened into a blue. The clouds drifted away from her and returned to their spots amongst the sky. The sun radiated its golden light upon Yelena, bathing her in its warmth. Casting her gaze below, she found her mother standing at the trunk of the tree, hands placed upon her hips. Though there was a scowl on her face, Yelena could see the worry in her mother's eyes. Beside her, Danna stood, hands clasped above her chest. Her sister had been too scared to climb higher than the second branch, crying after Yelena to come down. And when her sister didn't listen, Danna ran inside to tattle to their mother.

"Sorry momma..."

A sigh escaped the woman as she shook her head, "Just, come down, Yelena. Please."

As she began her descent, a deep, hearty laugh filled the air. Yelena glanced down to find her father approaching, hands on his belly and a warm smile on his face. He stood next to his wife and placed a gentle hand on her shoulder. "Now, now, dear. Yelena is a skilled climber. No need to fret. Besides, I'll always be here to catch her if she falls." Her father glanced up at her.

"Promise?" Yelena asked.

He winked, "Always."

With a smile, Yelena scaled down the tree and made it to the second branch. Her father stepped closer and opened his arms to her, "Jump, my little climber."

And then, she leapt into the air.

A startled gasp escaped her mother and sister as they watched the little girl plummet through the air. But as her father promised, he had caught her. A huff of breath escaping the man as Yelena slammed into his waiting arms. He staggered back but quickly regained his footing. The two laughed, the joyous sound reverberated through the world around them. Warmth radiated from their beings. Her father set her down on her feet but the two held one another's hands. Together, the family strolled inside their home where a warm dinner waited for them.

∞ ∞ ∞

When Yelena woke from her dream, there was a hollowness within her chest. She yearned more than anything to see her family again. The Count had said he let a bride in the past visit her family perhaps he would allow her to visit. Though she doubted he would be warm to the idea. Yelena would need to thaw the icy man if she wished to her family again. Hardening her resolve, she tossed away the blankets and flung her legs over the side of the bed. Today Yelena would begin her quest at earning the Count's trust.

To understand.

Daria and Danika brought food, setting the tray on the table while Yelena readied for the night. Slowly she was growing accustomed to the nocturnal life, hardly waking before the sun set below the horizon. Yelena ran a brush through her tangled hair, combing out the knots. Sweeping her hair over her shoulders, it rippled down her back in white waves. She chose a simple dress, crafted from thick midnight velvet. Though the flames kept her chambers warm, the rest of the castle was tinged with a trace of eternal winter. The neckline of the dress cut across her chest and rounded to her shoulders. The skirt whispered across the floor as she made toward the couch, her stomach howling to feast in the food that waited for it.

As Yelena reached for a silver dome, Daria spoke, "Why did you not try to escape during the day?"

Her hand stilled in the air above the dome. Yelena slid her gaze toward the woman that stood before the fire, her gaze locking with one of red. "Pardon?"

Daria turned her eyes back to flames, "I've been wondering, curious. Why only try to escape at night?"

Yelena lowered her gaze to the dome before her, her reflection looking back at her distorted. "I didn't wish for you to get hurt if the Count sent you after me." Yelena remembered how the women backed away from the sunlight, cowering in the darkest corner.

"That is very kind of you, Yelena." Daria said.

"Would he have sent you after me?"

"No."

Yelena nodded and removed the silver dome. Seasoned chopped potatoes waited for her, steaming in a bowl. Now that Yelena knew they would not go after her if she were to leave during the sunlight hours, it tempted her mind. Though it was enticing, she would not try to escape again. The wolves still lurked within the forest, waiting for her to flee. Ready to tear their sharpened teeth into her flesh. And once they were finished with Yelena, they would leave her mangled body before the gates of the village. A shiver rattled her body at the thought of her family seeing their daughter in such a state. Their last memory of Yelena as a hardly recognizable corpse.

Banishing the thought from her mind, Yelena grabbed the fork and speared a potato slice. While she ate, her eyes drifted from Danika to Daria. Curiosity stirred awake as she wondered what these women meant to the Count. They did not fear the man and when Daria spoke of him, there was such a tenderness to her voice. But sorrow crept into the woman's eyes.

"Daria? What are you three to the Count?"

Silence settled around them and Yelena regretted asking.

Her gaze fell back to the food before her, "I'm sorry. I shouldn't have…"

"No, no. It's alright." Daria stepped away from the fireplace and seated herself on the other end of the couch. Danika moved closer to the two. "We are the Count's confidents and guards when needed. He trusts us to offer our honest guidance should he seek it."

Yelena's brows knitted together, "Then why does he take brides? If he has each of you and trusts in you, then why? He seemed to despise my mere existence since the moment he saw me. I don't understand."

Daria bit her lip, her brows turning upward as if she wished she could tell Yelena everything. But she shook her head, "Only the Count can tell you the entire truth."

"But why can't you?" She was impatient, stubborn. All she wanted was to stop being lied too, for the truth to longer be hidden.

"Because that is the Count's story." Daria's eyes slid to Danika.

And Yelena understood.

For another soul's story was not Daria's to share.

Steeling her gaze, she said, "I wish to speak with him."

The halls were silent until their footsteps disturbed it. Echoing through the castle as if phantoms wandered about. The shadows writhed in the corners and in the highest points of the ceiling, reaching down and caressing the white strands of hair that rippled from Yelena's head. She noticed that the torches that lined along the walls had dimmed, their flames settling into slumber. Clapping resounded through the hall, bouncing off the walls, as Daria clapped her hands together. The flames blazed with a new life, crackling and roaring. Warmth and golden light spilled over them as they strolled along. As Yelena watched the dancing flames, she knew that there was much she had to learn when it came to these creatures she now lived with.

Daria and Danika halted before a doorway, the women stepping to either side, opening a path for Yelena. Daria smiled, nodding her head encouragingly as she gestured for Yelena to go ahead. Settling her face into a mask of calm, Yelena clasped her hands together, straightened her spine, and stepped forth. It was time to face the Count, to uncover the truth, and see passed the monster he wore as a mask. To untie its ribbons and free him from the façade he crafted.

The throne room radiated with a gentle warmth. All around the torches had been ignited. The crackles of the fires kept the silence at bay. Yelena passed two pillars and emerged into the grand room and standing before the thrones was the Count. His back faced to her; his hands clasped behind him. Swallowing the small prickle of fear that bubbled in Yelena's throat, she approached the man. The flames on either side of him, attached to the pillars next to the dais, drenched him in both shadow and light. A golden halo surrounded him, but his silhouette was nothing but darkness.

"What brings you here?" His velvety voice echoed through the room.

Yelena studied his posture, so frigid and tense. Yelena could almost feel the bitter chill that coated the man. She wondered what thoughts murmured through his mind. "To know the truth."

A scoff, "Which one?"

How many secrets did the Count keep buried within?

"Why do you take brides?"

"I don't."

The room stilled.

Even the cries of the crackling flames had been silenced, as if they held their breath, watching and waiting. Afraid yet enticed to see what would transpire.

Yelena blinked, "You do. You steal them from the village, just like you stole me."

The man's shoulders slumped ever so slightly, a light and weary breath escaped him. "The village elders offer them to me." He cast a glance over his shoulder, a red eye flashing in the darkness. "As they offered you to me."

For a moment, her strength wavered. Her face contorting as Yelena tried to understand; understand that her own village had offered her as if she were a lamb up for slaughter. Her mind had become a whirlwind of thoughts. Had her family known this horrible truth? Known her entire life as they raised her? How could the elders give her over as if she were nothing, something to dispose of so easily? Yelena supposed one life was a worthy trade for every life in the village. But that did not make the pain lessen.

The Count faced her then, his eyes seeming to study her. Tracing over the confused and hurt expression that tortured her face. "They offer brides after the former one has passed." He continued, "The killings that the villagers – that *you* – believe are my doing, are not."

Werewolves. The truth glowed in his eyes.

The mysterious disappearance of villagers always nagged Yelena's mind. Oftentimes the village elders would act as though that soul had never existed, other times they would lay blame upon the Count. Warning the villagers to never venture outside the gates at night. Many villagers did not heed those warnings. Young couples would sneak out into the forest, wishing for a bit of adventure and a night filled with passion only to be met with their untimely demise. Men would take late trips to stream to gather fresh water never to return with only a bucket left behind and a corpse to be found days later. Within, Yelena always knew there was something more. The truth buried deep within the ground, waiting to be unearthed.

The Count's gaze slid toward a fiery torch, as if needing to look anywhere else other than her tormented face. The betrayal that lay bare in her eyes. "The village elders believe if they offer me a beautiful bride that I'll cease my murderous rampage."

Yelena collected herself, "Why have you not told the elders this? Why take a bride, why take them away from their homes?"

"I have tried to reason with them, to tell them to cease offering brides." And for a moment, those red eyes softened. A tortured look twisting his handsome, chiseled features. "I tried not to take a bride once, but the elders sent the woman into the forest, alone." His voice lowered into a whisper, "I found her, but it was too late."

The Count's mask had cracked, his guilt seeping through the thin opening. Yelena saw the agony in his gaze, the flames reflecting in his irises as if revealing the torment inside the man. The fires of guilt eating away at him as if his soul were the timber that kept the flames alive.

Yelena knew this was her only chance before he erected those cold barriers again to get as much of the truth out of him as possible. Before he shut her out entirely. "How did the wolves kill the other brides?"

"It seems you all are born with an innate sense to return to your families. Harboring such strong affection for them that you cannot bear to be apart from them. It is both your greatest gift and your curse. Each bride before you fell victim to it, driven mad by the desire to return home, to their family. That is how each bride has died."

That is how you will die.

Lingered unspoken.

"It has already lay its claim on you, Yelena. I can only hope that you will not be so foolish to listen to its call again." Though his words sounded harsh, Yelena now understood it was his fear speaking.

"All I wish is to see them again." Her voice sounded so small.

The Count did not speak, finally tearing his gaze away from the fire of the torch. His red eyes found hers, holding her in place. "The wolves wait in the forest to hunt you down like a deer."

The Count slowly descended the stairs of the dais. Yelena wished to move, to back away, but her feet had been molded to the ground. Her heart quickened its beat, thumping against the cage in her chest. The man stopped before her, standing heads taller. His gaze weighed down on Yelena and yet, she did not shrink beneath him. Something shifted in his irises as he studied her face. Raising a hand, he absentmindedly reached out and grasped a strand of white hair. Twirling it around his finger, seeming so lost in thought. As if he were in another time, another place. Yelena had sucked in her breath, not daring to move, and she could not help but wonder what transpired in the Count's mind.

Who did he see before him?

Because Yelena knew he did not see her.

The Count blinked, tumbling free from the memories that enraptured him. The cold mask slid over his face once more as he released her hair. The strand fluttered down and swept to her chest. He stepped away from her, retreating to the thrones and the shadows. Without a parting word, the Count turned his back to her and cloaked himself in darkness. Yelena stood there, staring at the empty space where the Count once stood. Her hair tingled as if it reminisced of the man caressing it around his slender finger.

Tonight, Yelena found a glimmer of hope. She had seen the man that was trapped inside, saw past the façade of the monster he portrayed.

There was hope.

Slowly, she was beginning to understand.

∞ ∞ ∞

When Yelena left the throne room, Daria and Danika waited for her in the hall. Neither of them spoke, having heard the entirety of the conversation shared between them. As they trekked back to her chambers, Yelena's gaze wandered toward the portraits of the brides. Their eyes watching as she strolled past and she could have sworn, she saw something flicker within the women's eyes. Pity entangled with envy. Pity for the woman that would soon join them but envy that Yelena breathed while they rotted in the earth.

Again, she found herself coming to a stop before her mother's portrait. Reaching out, her fingers brushed over the smoothed texture of her mother's painted cheeks. There was tinge of rose to her pale skin. As if she were supple with life. Now that Yelena knew the truth of the brides' demises, it caused her soul to ache. Knowing the sort of end her mother faced. Being mauled to death by a beast, its teeth and claws shredding the woman apart bit by bit. The picture was too gruesome for Yelena, shaking her head she banished the thought from her mind, her hand falling away from her mother's portrait.

Soft footsteps approached as Daria stood at her side. "I'm sorry for your loss, Yelena." The woman spoke gently.

Her gaze remained on the painting, "Why didn't she choose to be immortal? If it could have saved her life, then why?"

"Many of the brides did not know the truth, your mother was one of them. But the few who did know, did not wish for such a curse. Did not wish to carry the burden an immortal soul could be."

Yelena's gaze slid to Daria, but the woman did not meet her eyes. "Do you regret it?"

There was a slight tug at the corner of her lips. "There are days when I wish I could feel the sun against my skin again, to bask in its warmth without fear of burning in it. But there are days when I am profoundly grateful for this life. I have a family here in this castle, a home."

"Do you miss them? Your mortal family?"

"If I could recall my mortal memories, perhaps."

"You don't remember?"

Daria shook her head with a light sigh, "Dravmir had found me, all I remember was pain and pleading for it to end. Instead of killing me, he changed me. We suspect I was trying to cross the stream but slipped on the rocks as I skipped atop them, bashing my head. There was enough strength left in me to get to the land. I remember laying on my back, sputtering up the water that trickled into my lungs. My skull throbbed; I could feel my pulse beating against my head. That is all I can recall of my mortal life – my death."

Yelena's heart wept at Daria's tale. How any inklings of her mortal memories had been eradicated from her mind. From such a simple slip, all had been lost to her. Never again to know her mother's face, her father's. To recall moments that had now been lost to time. It would destroy Yelena knowing she had lost something so precious. She would spend her days trying to recall even a shred of a memory, of a voice or blurred face. Yelena would drive herself to madness digging so deep into her thoughts she would become lost within the darkness.

Danika stood at the woman's side, reaching out and grasping ahold of Daria's hand. "But I have been given the chance to know a family in this life and I would not trade it for anything." Daria said.

Yelena's heart warmed. There was such an immense love within Daria's eyes. Happiness. Though she had lost her mortal years, she had gained a new life and family. In death, she lived. And Yelena could not help but wonder what her path looked like. Before her there was a fork in the road, two paths laid out. One to her mortal life and the other that led to immortality, should she choose it. Yelena hesitated, her eyes shifting between each path. But for now, she would walk the one of mortality. Not yet ready to shed her mortal flesh. Undecided if everlasting life was the true course of her uncharted future.

But one never knew what waited for them.

$$\infty \quad \infty \quad \infty$$

Later that night, after Daria and Danika departed Yelena's chambers, she readied herself for bed. Weaving her hair together in a braid and dawning a simple sleeping gown. Yelena nestled down into the silky sheets of her bed. It felt as though hours had passed, sleep evading her no matter how far out she reached for it. It slipped through the spaces of her fingers, fleeing far away. Yelena tossed and turned as frustration gripped her. With a defeated sigh, she tossed away her bedsheets and swung her legs over the edge of the bed. Her mind was far too restless. Demanding answers. Casting a glance over her shoulder toward the wall of windows, she glimpsed the forest that lay beyond the perimeter of the castle. She wondered if werewolves were looking back at her.

Casting her gaze away from the windows, she stood. Yelena drifted through her chambers and stood before the doors. Her hands itched as she fought her thoughts. Reason told her to stay within her chambers. But her curious side was cunning, and it swayed her. Yelena wished to see more of this castle. To explore its mass and transverse through its long halls and step inside its many rooms. If she were to stay here, she wanted to know her new home. Taking in a breath, she grasped one of the doorknobs and turned it. The door opened a crack with a silent creak. Yelena poked her head between the space and peered into the hall. Silence greeted her ears and darkness welcomed her eyes. There was a lone torch ignited against the wall opposite her room. Left ablaze for her mortal eyes.

Yelena slipped through the crack and closed the door behind her quietly. With careful steps, she wandered through the halls like a phantom. Her sleeping gown trailing behind her in a river of white, whispering across the floor. Her braid steadily thumped against her back as she walked, hands clasped together. She strolled through the familiar hall until she reached the portraits of the brides. Darkness coated the walls, concealing their dead gazes from her. Yelena wondered if their ghosts roamed these halls. Trapped for an eternity in this castle, cursed to live their afterlife watching each bride after them suffer the same fate. Yelena's skin bristled at the thought.

Would she share the same fate?

Steeling her heart, she continued on, banishing the thought. She strode toward a familiar doorway that led into the grand throne room. She swept through it, aiming for the doorway just across from her. She wondered what that side of the castle had in store for her. What lingered within those halls and chambers? She wished to unearth the ancient secrets that stowed away within the stones and marble. With excitement bubbling in her stomach, she nearly dashed across the room. She had gotten halfway when a sudden thread of unease wound its way through her. Yelena halted in the center of the room. Gooseflesh prickled along her arms and her heart began to thump viciously against its cage.

A heavy gaze weighed down on her. Yelena flicked her eyes toward the banisters, searching through the shadows to find the slightest of movement. She caught only a flicker, so fast she believed her mind had conjured it from fear. Until it moved again, and a chilling laugh followed it. The sudden sound of clapping caused the torches within the room to ignite in blazing flames. And crouched atop the railing above Yelena, was Drezca. The fiery lioness had a wildness within her red eyes, a wicked smirk curled upon her thin lips. Flicking out her tongue, she traced it over her elongated fangs. It sent a shiver down the length of Yelena's spine, but she keep her face stoic.

With a wink, Drezca vanished into the shadows. Yelena's eyes widened as she searched the room. The only trace of the woman was the gentle rustle of the air. Laughter echoed within the room and Yelena whirled around to find the woman balanced on her feet atop another railing. Her white gown spilled down her body, the sleeves rested atop her shoulders but split down the seams and rippled in separate currents down her arms. Her fiery tresses curled and swept down to her waist in a river of flames. The woman lifted one foot and dangled it in the air, balancing perfectly on her other. With a grin, she leapt and landed smoothly on the ground, two feet from Yelena. Within a blur of shadows, Drezca closed that distance quickly. Now a breath away from her face.

Drezca reached out and grasped a loose strand of white hair, twirling it around her slender finger. "What do you want?" Yelena gritted out.

The woman's smile widened as she dropped the strand. "Just to remind you."

"Of what?"

Drezca flashed her fangs before vanishing. Yelena blinked at the woman's sudden disappearance. And then fear claimed her when a whisper of air stirred behind her. She clenched her hands so tightly her nails nearly pierced her flesh. Fingers brushed away the hair that covered Yelena's ear, gently tracing down the length of her neck. She held her breath when sharp nails trailed over her skin. Cool air brushed against the lobe of her ear, lips nearly kissing her skin.

"That you won't last in our world, little bride." Drezca purred into her ear. "None of you have." Laughter danced in her voice as she smiled against Yelena's ear.

"You cannot hurt me, Drezca." Yelena reminded her.

"Oh, I may not, but the wolves do not heed to the Count's ruling." Breath brushed against Yelena's neck as Drezca's lips grazed her skin. "Soon, you will join the others."

"No, I won't." Yelena snapped.

But Drezca laughed against her throat, "The foolish will of mortals is truly admirable."

Yelena had grown tired of these games. Drezca wished to strike fear into Yelena, to make her scurry back to her chambers like a mouse and hide within until fate greeted her. But Yelena refused. Though she was mortal, she would not bow down to the lioness behind her.

"*Drezca.*" A deep voice resounded through the room.

Yelena and Drezca grew still at the sound of the Count's commanding voice.

Relief washed over Yelena as the woman backed away, her mouth leaving her throat. Drezca brushed passed her and bowed her head to the Count. He stood there with shadows writhing around him, wisping as if they were ready to strike. His crimson eyes glowed as they narrowed upon the woman before him.

"What did I tell you, Drezca?" The words growled from his lips.

"Count, I was merely speaking with her. I never would have bitten her."

His lips were a flatline. "Leave us."

Drezca wasted no time as she vanished into the darkness; leaving the two alone. The Count's gaze did not follow the woman as she left the room, those glowing eyes falling upon Yelena. His gaze sliding down to her neck as if to reassure himself that Drezca had not pierced Yelena's flesh with her fangs and drank of her blood.

When his eyes found hers again, he said, "Come, I'll escort you back to your chambers." He turned on his heel and made for the doorway.

Yelena made to take a step but cast a glance behind her. She had wanted to venture around the castle, but it seemed that she couldn't even do that. With a defeated sign, she followed the Count from the throne room. Silence surrounded them as they strolled through the halls. Yelena watched the man's back, walking so stiffly yet so fluidly all at once. There was assurance with each step he took but there was lingering doubt that weighed his shoulders.

When they reached her chamber, he opened one of the doors and stepped aside. Yelena stepped over the threshold and halted. "Thank you." She spoke.

The Count loomed before her. His gaze drifted passed Yelena and toward the fireplace. The logs were no longer being devoured by crackling flames. Orange embers glowed upon them, pulsing like a heartbeat. Lifting his hands, he clapped them together and a fire roared to life upon the logs. Yelena watched the flames dance atop the logs, awed.

"I never believed such things existed; magic." Her voice was hushed as she stared into the fire, unsure if the Count still stood at her doors.

There was a long moment of silence that settled between them, Yelena believing that the Count had finally vanished leaving her alone, speaking to the empty air. But his voice shattered the silence.

"Our magic is mundane."

Yelena met his gaze, "How so?"

His eyes drifted toward the fire, the flames dancing within his crimson irises. "We are of the dead so we can only summon things that hold no soul." With a flick of his wrist, the flames stoked with life, blazing.

Yelena was enrapture watching the Count work his magic. It was nothing of what she dreamed in her fantasy worlds. It did not glimmer. Gave no indication that magic was being worked until it was done. "Fire seems to breathe." The flames seemed to exhale as they brushed forth from the hearth before retreating.

"Though the logs feed the flames and they eagerly devour it, they hold no soul. Shadows. Air. Things that *seem* alive but are nothing more than empty vessels – like vampires."

Like me.

Lingered unspoken.

The Count believed himself an empty vessel. Soulless. Once, Yelena would have believed that, once thought it. But looking into his eyes now, told her otherwise. There was a soul there, buried deep within the man as if it were in a shallow grave, a withered garden surrounding it. He only had to unearth his soul and tend to the garden within, nourishing it. But clouds had settled within him as his turmoil turned into a storm.

"Goodnight, Yelena." With that, the Count turned his back to her and vanished down the hall.

Watching him go, a thought flickered in her mind. "Did you light the fire in my room that first night?"

Before the shadows had swallowed him entirely, he halted. Half his silhouette devoured by the darkness. He stood in silence for a moment, his back facing her.

"Yes."

And then, the Count was gone.

CHAPTER NINE

The Belly of the Beast

THE DAY HAD vanished beneath the haze of grey clouds. Yelena had slept during the sunlight hours, only waking once the moon graced their world. As the shadows stirred, so did Yelena. She woke from the warmth of her dreams, faint tendrils of it clung to her flesh as if the dreams weren't quite ready to leave her. Reluctant to be banished to the recesses of her mind, wishing to linger in this world like phantoms. When Yelena's eyes fluttered open, the dreams had vanished. Her family retreating into the depths of her mind where they would remain until Yelena tumbled into the world of dreams once more.

Tossing away the warmth of her bedsheets, Yelena swung her legs over the side of the bed. With a yawn, she stood, stretching out her still sleeping limbs. Though Yelena had got plenty of sleep, there was a heaviness beneath her eyes. Tugging on them. Yelena made to brush her stray hair from her face when her fingers snagged in her tresses. Her sleep had been restless, her hair a tangled mess from tossing and turning. As if she wished to fight back her memories, wished to force them into a chamber deep within her mind and lock them away.

As if the memories were becoming too much for Yelena to bear. Seeing the faces of her family causing an ache to swell in her heart, running a thread so deep into the muscle it caused her agony each time it beat.

As Yelena readied for the day, a servant had brought her food. It was odd since Daria and Danika had been bringing her food. The servant set the tray on the table, bowed their head, and left the chamber. The doors groaned and clicked shut, leaving Yelena alone with only the crackling flames to keep her company. Her gaze drifted toward the tray of silver domes. Perhaps the women wished to give her space, allowing her to breathe on her own and clear her thoughts. But as she sat there, loneliness crept in. Yelena was not used to being alone. She was always in the company of her family even if she often wandered off into her own daydreams, there was always someone with her.

Coming to this castle, Yelena never thought of the loneliness that waited for her. The coldness that lurked within these stone walls, always lingering no matter how brightly the fire burned. And little did she know of the monsters that lurked within the forest just beyond this castle, prowling through the shadows. Yelena was not prepared for the world she found herself tumbling into. That the Count was not the monster responsible for the deaths of so many brides. That her own village elders offered them as if they were cattle up for slaughter. The world she knew unraveled before her eyes with each truth revealed. Her body shuddered as she wondered what other truths waited for her.

Once Yelena ate, she shoved those thoughts from her mind and stepped toward the doors. An uneasy feeling settled in the pit of her stomach as she grasped ahold of the knobs. A memory flickered in her mind, of Drezca's sharpened teeth grazing the delicate skin of her neck. Shaking her head, she banished that memory and opened the doors, stepping into the darkened halls. The shadows writhed in the deepest corners, dancing like serpents as they watched Yelena stroll passed them. Golden light trickled into the darkness from the torches that blazed upon the walls. Warmth brushed against her as she walked through the halls. Descending the stairs, Yelena found herself amongst the portraits of the past brides. Her eyes drifted toward her portrait, lingering for only a breath before flicking her gaze to her mother's.

An ache thumped within Yelena's heart each time she met her mother's gaze. The woman smiled at her as if she could see the young woman that stood before the portrait. Yelena was drawn to it again, reaching out for her mother's face and tracing her fingers over the smoothness of the aged paint. There was an emptiness within her heart that would never be filled. A yearning that would never be satisfied. Unable to look at the portrait a moment longer, Yelena tore her gaze away from her mother's face. No longer wishing to bear the pain that riddled her heart each time she stole a glance at that painting.

As Yelena turned, her heart leapt into her throat. Before her stood the Count. Looming like a shadow, those glowing eyes fixed on her. As her heart calmed, Yelena straightened herself. "It isn't too polite scaring people, you know?"

The Count merely arched a brow at her. "I greeted you, but it seems as though you are hard of hearing."

Yelena blinked at him. Perhaps she had been too lost within her maze of thoughts. She crossed her arms over her chest, "Do you find pleasure in insulting me?"

A breath escaped the Count as his gaze drifted from hers, to the portrait behind her. Something shifted within his eyes then as he beheld the face of Yelena's mother – his former bride. Yelena followed his gaze back to the painting, stealing a glance at the others that hung upon the dark walls. A question that had been burning in her mind since she first saw these portraits escaped her lips.

"Why do you paint them?"

His gaze never wavered from the painting, "To remember them."

"Why are some of them depicted happily and others painted with sorrow?" Yelena's gaze sifted through the portraits, there was lightness to some of the women's eyes and a darkness in others. Some smiled and others seemed forced, hardly able to hold up the corners of their lips.

The Count opened his mouth to speak but an ear-piercing scream shattered the air around them. Panic seized her heart. Darkness stirred within her stomach; pain ruptured within her heart. That scream sounded all too familiar to her ears. A memory awakening in her mind, of her sister squealing at the sight of a rabid dog. Yelena shook her head. Banishing the wicked thoughts that dashed through her mind. Had the werewolves torn through the village? Devouring every soul, they found.

"Dravmir..." Yelena forced his name from her throat as it threatened to close, swelling up with fear.

That red gaze narrowed and held her place. *"Stay. Here."* The words hissed from his lips.

The shadows began to form around the man, the tendrils grasping at his clothes. Before he vanished, Yelena reached out and grasped ahold of his tunic, her fingers curling into the fabric, threatening to shred it. If it was her sister out there, then Yelena was going with him. Damn those monsters that lurked. Yelena needed to see her sister.

"Take me with you, *now.*"

A snarl of annoyance curled on the Count's lips, but he did not argue. They were wasting precious time. Gathering Yelena in his arms, the shadows engulfed them and carried them from the castle on a current of darkness. The waves rippling through the air and crashing through the doors, bursting them open as they raced out into the night.

∞ ∞ ∞

Darkness surrounded them. The branches of the trees seeming like crooked hands reaching out for them as they sped past. The wind roared against Yelena's ears, tossing, and tangling her hair. Her hands clutched tighter to Dravmir's tunic as another scream rattled the earth. Her heart leapt into her throat, threatening to choke her.

We're coming Danna. We're coming...

Though fear crept in and whispered into her ears that they would find a corpse waiting for them. That Danna would be found within the belly of a beast. The shadows seemed to quicken their pace, carrying them further and faster through the forest. The Count's hold on Yelena tightened as they burst through the trees, following the sound of her sister's screams. They came upon the trail that led toward the village and when they reached the end, they found a hulking beast standing over her sister. The woman had fallen to the ground but clutched a kitchen knife in her trembling hands, aiming it at the beast. Yelena's lips parted to cry out for her sister but Dravmir tightened his hold on her. Sealing her lips, the Count swept down from the stars and swiftly placed Yelena on her feet behind a tree. His gaze met hers for a moment, those red eyes narrowing.

Stay.

His eyes said before he vanished and lunged at the beast. Yelena stood behind the tree, her nails curling into the bark until the wood splintered beneath her nails. Fear seized her heart as the werewolf lifted its muscled arm into the air, clawed hand ready to claim the life from her sister. A scream formed on her lips as time seemed to slow around them. The Count became nothing more than a blur of shadows as he raced toward the beast. His raven hair becoming darkened tendrils upon the wind. Yelena's eyes watched as he reached out for the beast and his hand penetrated through its flesh.

A howl resounded through the night. The werewolf attempted to flee from the Count, thrashing around, but it was too late. For Dravmir wrapped his fingers around the beast's heart and pulled. Another agonizing howl escaped the creature as the Count tore the beating muscle from the beast's chest. The werewolf fell to its knees and toppled over upon the earth. The Count stood above the corpse with the beast's heart held in his palm. Crimson stained his pale skin as it trickled from between his fingers, raining down upon the ground. Danna sat before him, the knife still held in the air, a tremble coursing down her arms as she beheld the bloody Count before her.

Shock had overcome Yelena. Staring at the Count that loomed above the corpse at his feet. A heart grasped within his hand. A beast slain by a monster. Again, Yelena felt fear lacing through her chest. The picture of the Count plunging his hand into the beast and claiming its heart would forever ingrain itself in her memories. Perhaps it would visit Yelena in her dreams. As if hearing her thoughts, the Count cast that crimson gaze over his shoulder upon her. Their eyes held and the fear she felt faded from this world. Dravmir had slain a beast, saving her sister's life. For that, Yelena would forever be within his debt.

Yelena stepped from behind the tree and rushed to her sister, *"Danna!"*

Her sister's dark gaze tore from the Count and beheld Yelena rushing toward her. Relief relaxed her arms as she dropped the knife, a smile widening upon her lips as silver begun to line her eyes. Before Danna could stand, Yelena tackled her sister in her embrace, sending the two tumbling down to the earth. Paying no mind to the corpse of the werewolf or the Count that lingered behind them. Their laughter echoed around untamed as tears wept from their eyes, holding tightly to one another. Yelena nestled her face into the nape of her sister's neck. Her thick hair smelling of spices, reminding Yelena of home. Of the meals Danna prepared with tender hands.

Moving from atop her sister, the two raised onto their knees before each other. Yelena reached out and held her sister's face in her hands, feeling the warmth of her skin against her palms. Danna was alive. She was safe. A sigh escaped her smiling lips. "Are you alright?"

Danna nodded, "I am." Her gaze flicked to the man that lingered in the shadows. "He saved me." She said, a questioning tone in her voice. "What was that creature?"

Yelena chewed on her bottom lip, "A werewolf. Now, why were you out here, Danna?"

Shock flickered in her sister's widened eyes for a moment, her mind trying to comprehend the truth. Her gaze drifted toward the massive corpse behind her sister, the truth laid out plainly before her eyes. Danna slid her gaze back to Yelena and sorrow revealed itself in her eyes. "We miss you, Ena." Danna's lips began to tremble as she lowered her blearing eyes, shaking her head. "I-I had to see you again. I wanted to bring you home." A forced laugh escaped her as her gaze fell to the knife that lay on the ground. "I brought our sharpest knife, but I doubt it would have done much against that *thing.*"

Yelena's heart broke and she wrapped Danna in her embrace. "Never do something like that again. I almost..." The words choked in her throat, "I almost lost my sister." Yelena pulled back, leaving her hands on Danna's shoulders, "Mom and dad lost one daughter, they don't need to lose another."

Danna's hands grasped her wrists, "They haven't lost you." Her grip tightened, "You're still here."

Yelena's family had been waiting for their daughter to turn up at those gates as nothing but a broken corpse. Yelena nodded, "I'm still here." To reassure her sister that she truly was, that this was no dream. To reassure herself that Danna had not fallen victim to that beast. *"We're still here."*

Danna's gaze drifted to the Count, "He won't let you come home, will he?"

Yelena cast a glance over her shoulder and found that red gaze upon her. She remembered what he had said. Why he did not wish for brides to visit their families. If he had failed in protecting her, then her family would have to grieve once more. To have their hearts broken twice over. Yelena yearned to see her family again, for them to be together, but she did not wish to fracture their mending hearts.

"Not now." Yelena said. "Not yet."

Yelena would see them again; she knew it in her soul.

Danna simply nodded.

Yelena stood and helped her sister off the ground, grabbing the old kitchen knife. Fond memories swam about her mind, the scar on her thumb tingling. "I think it best this return with you. We both know how I am when it comes to sharp things."

With a saddened laugh, Danna took the knife from her hands. "I'll keep it safe for you in case you happen to find yourself missing it."

Yelena nodded her head and faced the Count. The man refused to step forth into the moonlight. To reveal the blood that stained him. Choosing to remain hidden from their wandering gazes. Yelena faced her sister once more, "Go on," she nodded her head toward the gates, "Go home."

Heartache laced through her sister's eyes. "We'll be waiting."

Yelena watched as Danna reluctantly faced the gates and hurried toward them. They opened a crack and before she stepped through, she cast one last glance upon her sister before vanishing behind the gates. The silent groan of the gates caused her to flinch. As if they had struck her. The village reminding her that the elders had handed Yelena's life over as if it were nothing. Out casting her from the place she called home. Yelena did not know how long she stood there until she heard the softened sound of approaching footfalls. The Count's presence loomed behind her like a shadow.

Settling her face into a stoic expression, she faced the man. Her eyes widened slightly at the sight of him. One side of his face had a splattering of blood, his one arm coated in crimson. His hand dangled at his side as ruby droplets fell from his fingertips. He stood there, unmoving. His red eyes staring deep into her own. Reading the emotions that stirred within her irises, searching for any sign of fear, of disgust. But there was none to be found. Yelena stood before him, unafraid. Something shifted within his gaze as he watched her.

"You saved my sister." Her voice broke the silence. "Thank you."

The Count's head tilted, "Why didn't you return with her?"

"Would you have let me if I choose too?"

He held her gaze as he said, "Yes."

"But the elders would send me out, wouldn't they?"

The man did not answer, silence coating his lips.

So easily, Dravmir had freed her. And yet, something whispered to her. A voice stirring about within her mind. Yelena couldn't leave, not yet. For so long, she had stared out her bedroom window to the forest that lay beyond the gates. To the castle that loomed within the shadows. Perhaps this was the adventure she had been seeking. The future that had been laid out before her. Yelena would walk its path to wherever it led her.

And right now, it was leading her to the Count.

Dravmir saw the decision in her eyes and closed the distance between them. Not a word was shared between them as he scooped her into his arms and the shadows swallowed them.

∞　∞　∞

Yelena had not spoken a word during their return to the castle. Her gaze staring off into the forest, toward the village. Danna had ventured out into the night with a kitchen knife to rescue her sister. Yelena had nearly witnessed Danna's death by the hands of a beast. The fear that swelled in her belly was something she never wished to face again. Yelena yearned to go home with her sister, but the elders would cast her out again once they caught word of her return. Force her to walk through those gates alone and face the beasts that lurked within the shadows. The truth caused pain to web through her heart. That the village elders who she had trusted her entire life, had offered her to the Count. Had given the brides that came before her over to him. The elders believed him a monster and so eagerly they had given their people over to him.

When they landed before the doors, the Count set her down and opened the doors. Yelena swept inside with Dravmir following in her steps. The groans of the wood echoed through the quiet room. The Count's presence behind her was thick, like a shadow threatening to suffocate her. Yelena did not face him, her gaze drifting toward the lone thrones that resided on the far side of the room. She couldn't help but wonder how long it's been since a bride sat upon one of the thrones. Long it sat unused, gathering dust, becoming a relic. Her feet had grown a mind of their own, her eyes fixated on the lone throne beside the dark one. If Dravmir followed, he made not a sound, merely watching Yelena drift across the room.

Ascending the few steps, Yelena stood before the pearlescent throne. Her hand reaching out and her heart stilled. Delicately her fingers traced over the arm of the throne. The stone and marble it was crafted from was cool beneath her touch. Her fingertips tracing patterns in the thick layers of dust. A shiver tingled down her spine as the Count's presence closed in behind her.

"Can you answer my question from earlier?" Her voice was loud amongst the silence.

Before the screams of her sister reached the castle, Yelena and Dravmir had been in the hall surrounded by the faces of the previous brides. Their unseeing eyes watching them. Yelena wondered why so many brides seemed joyful and others holding sorrow deep within their hearts. A weary breath whispered behind her. Gentle footsteps echoed in the room as the Count stood at her side. His red gaze fixated on the throne before Yelena. She turned her gaze to his and found that his mask had lowered, and agony filled his face. There was such a heaviness in his eyes it caused her chest to ache. Guilt and regret eating its way through the man.

"After the first bride," he began, "I treated the others that came after coldly, dismissively. As the years passed, I found companionship in some. Some brides touched my heart and filled it warmth that I thought would never return." His brows furrowed, a tightness clenching his jaw. "And once they were murdered, I killed that warmth. Suffocating it so I wouldn't have to bear that pain. And so, the cycle would begin again."

Yelena felt the urge to reach out and offer him comfort. The pure agony in his gaze was enough to brew tears in her eyes. "What happened to the first bride?"

His eyes narrowed on the throne, "Killed by those *beasts.*" The word hissed viciously from his lips.

Yelena wished to know more of the brides, of the souls that had been lost to this world. Wished to understand the Count, to thaw that frozen heart. "What was she like?" Her voice was a gentle whisper.

It was then, that the faintest smile quirked at the corners of his thin lips. A softness lightening the harshness of his eyes. Yelena could see a flicker of warmth kindling within the Count as he remembered his first bride. The love within his gaze was undeniable. "I loved her." He spoke, his tone sincere and rasped. "And she loved a monster such as I. Her soul was like the summer sun and I didn't find myself burning in her radiance. Instead, I basked in the warmth of her rays."

A small smile filled Yelena's lips. She had never seen the Count look so vulnerable. It yanked at her heartstrings, pulling her toward the man. But that warmth within his eyes sputtered and died out like an old flame. That viciousness returning.

"The night I was to turn her, those beasts stole my bride from me." A vein in his neck feathered. "I remember her. I remember *all* of their faces. They are forever stained in my memory. Their mangled bodies burned into my mind as a reminder how I had failed them." It was then that his gaze found hers, "How I will fail you."

Yelena held her breath as Dravmir reached out for her. His fingers gently grasping a strand of her pale hair. The ache within his gaze cried out to her. Already the Count was feeling guilt for Yelena's death. As if she had passed from this world and she nothing but a phantom before him now. Here to torment him until the end of eternity.

"You won't fail me." She spoke.

His eyes did not find hers, "But I will."

And his hand fell away.

$$\infty \quad \infty \quad \infty$$

Yelena remained at the thrones. The Count had vanished into the shadows, leaving her alone. Her gaze lingered where Dravmir had been standing, staring at the emptiness. With a sigh, she stole a parting glance at the thrones and stepped down from the dais. Yelena drifted through the halls absentmindedly, her mind wandering far away, allowing her feet to guide her being. The faces of the past brides emerged from the depths of her mind. But their faces were twisted and contorted into pure agony. Screams were frozen upon their gaping mouths. Their throats torn apart, spilling their blood into her thoughts. Crimson waves pooling and crashing against the shadows that writhed within the depths of Yelena's mind.

A horrid thought drifted through her mind as her own face emerged from the crimson waves. Her lips parted and her eyes wide with terror. Blood spilled from her throat. Her white tresses were stained in red, the ends of them soaking up her blood. Yelena dared to allow her mind to wander to such darkness. Would she face the same death as the brides before her had? Was that truly her fate? The fate of each woman of her bloodline. Was there truly no escaping it? No fleeing from that sort of demise? Yelena shook her head, banishing her tormented face from her thoughts. The crimson waves crept back and vanished into the crevices of her mind. Yelena steeled her resolve. No, she would not face that end. She would break the cycle.

"Yelena?" A familiar voice broke through her dark web of thoughts.

Coming back to the world, she found Daria standing before her. "Yes? Sorry I was a bit lost in my own head."

"It's quite alright." Those red eyes seemed to search Yelena's face. "I've been looking for both you and Dravmir for some time. Him, I cannot find. Did something happen?"

Yelena knitted her fingers together. "We heard a scream." She began, the memory playing before her eyes. "We followed it and found my sister at the mercy of a werewolf. Dravmir saved her and she went home."

Daria tilted her head to the side, "Are you alright, dear?"

She nodded, "I am. It was... it was nice to see my sister again." Yelena forced a smile.

Daria's brow pinched together, "May I ask, why was she out in the forest?"

"She went out to find me, to bring me home." Yelena paused, chewing her lip, "Dravmir asked me why I didn't go back with her."

Daria's brow arched, her eyes widening slightly.

"I believe my place is here. To break this cycle of the brides. I don't know how I'm going to stop it, but I will."

The woman smiled, "A courageous soul you are, Yelena." Daria stepped aside, "Come, dinner is waiting for you in your chambers."

Yelena fell into step beside Daria as they made their way through the halls. Once they reached her chamber, Yelena spoke, "Dravmir told me of the first bride."

Daria's hands stilled on the knobs of the doors, casting a glance over her shoulder. "He did?"

Yelena nodded, "He told me he loved her and how the werewolves killed her before Dravmir could change her."

Daria blinked as if in disbelief, "He truly is opening himself to you, Yelena. In time, I hope you can know the man within just as I do." Then, Daria pushed open the doors.

Once Yelena dressed into a sleeping gown, she nestled down on the couch and began to devour the meal that waited for her. All the while, Daria lingered before the crackling flames, her gaze transfixed on the burning fire. Seeming so lost in thought, drifting to times that have long since passed.

"The Count loved her immensely." She spoke, breaking the silence but her gaze remained on the flames. "And she loved him just the same. The first bride had chosen to become one of us, to spend eternity with Dravmir."

Yelena had halted, her fork becoming still in her hand as she listened.

"I remember the night that she was supposed to be changed. She had ventured from the castle, we assumed she wished to visit her family before she shed her mortal flesh." Daria shook her head as a sigh escaped her, "We heard the screams, but we were too late. Dravmir has not been the same since then." Those red eyes drifted toward Yelena, the flames reflecting in her irises. "I can see that warmth returning to him, slowly. You are waking something in him that has been dormant for far too long. His heart regaining its beat. I can see flickers of the man he once was, and it gives me hope that he will return to us."

Daria stepped away from the flames, retreating toward the doors. "Enjoy your dinner, Yelena, and sweet dreams." With a parting smile, Daria swept from the room, leaving Yelena alone with only the flames to keep her company.

The Count had drifted through the darkest halls of the castle, ones that had been lost and forgotten to time. Torches rested unlit against the walls, dust coated the air, sweeping across the floor and grasping the walls. Dravmir's mind wandered back to the forest. Of a beast standing tall above a frightened woman, her hands trembling as they clutched a knife. Death had permeated the air, tasting like ash upon his tongue as he breathed it in. Behind him, his bride's heart thundered against its cage, roaring within his sensitive ears.

Dravmir rushed at the beast's unguarded back, the werewolf none the wiser of the monster that crept toward it. As it raised its arm into the air, Dravmir lunged, his fist plunging through the beast's back, using every ounce of his immortal strength. A howl filled the air as Dravmir wrapped his fingers around the werewolf's heart, feeling as it frantically beat against his palm. Dravmir had allowed the monster that resided within the pits of his soul to awaken. A snarl curled on his lips as he bared his fangs. With a swift pull, Dravmir had claimed the beast's heart, its blood sputtering from the wound and painting the Count in its life. Staining his soul forevermore. For a moment, his gaze met with Yelena's sister's. And there within her eyes he found so much fear. That she would be the next victim.

He had watched as Yelena stepped forth toward her sister. How pure joy escaped the two women as they wrapped themselves in each other's embraces. Their laughter like music that danced along the air. The relief that poured from their beings was tantalizing. Nearly mocking as Dravmir inhaled its scent, never to know such joy. When Yelena's sister returned to the village, Yelena had remained where she stood. Watching her sister slip through the gates. Dravmir found it curious how Yelena did not try to flee, did not chase after her sister.

Yelena turned and faced him. Dravmir braced himself for the disgust he would soon find on her face. Knowing how monstrous he appeared, he waited to see that disgust, that fear swelling within her eyes. But when their gazes met, it was not fear that he had found. Yelena did not cower at the sight of him, did not retreat. She stood before him, taking in the sight of him. Of the blood that stained his face, his arm. Watching as rivulets of crimson poured from the tips of his fingers.

When they returned to the castle, Yelena had wandered toward the thrones. Dravmir watched her every step, curious. Silently, he followed behind her. Watching as her pale fingers reached out and tenderly traced over the arm of the throne before her. And for a moment, he imagined her seated upon that throne. Claiming it as hers as he sat beside her. The Count banished that thought from his mind. A bride has refused that throne for decades, none sitting upon it after the first.

Yelena's voice whispered through his mind as she spoke. Telling him how he wouldn't fail her. Placing so much trust within him. But Dravmir knew, that no matter how hard he tried, he would fail her. As he failed the others. This was his curse, to watch each of his brides perish in gruesome deaths. Cursed with the guilt that he did not save them, that he was not quick enough. Always a second too late before death swept in and claimed his brides.

And soon, it would claim Yelena.

When he tore himself from the gloom of his thoughts, he found himself before the thrones. As always, his wander led him to this cursed room. To those cursed thrones. Always mocking him, always reminding him that a bride shall never again sit upon them. Dravmir wished to vanquish those cursed thrones. To turn them into nothing but dust beneath his polished shoes. But he could not bring himself to destroy them. To destroy the throne his first bride sat upon. Dravmir always saw her there before him, sitting upon that throne as if she had never left. Her phantom trapped within these cursed walls. Oftentimes he reached for her, but she would fade away at his fingertips.

"*Annika...*" Her name rasped from his lips.

Dravmir never forgot it, as he would never forget her.

Or the others.

"Dravmir." Daria's voice shattered the image of Annika on the throne. "When will you cease this?"

A weary sigh escaped him, "This is my punishment."

"To burn in such guilt? Such regret? To allow the fires to consume you till nothing remains of your soul but ash?"

"I have found shelter burning in my own guilts and regret."

Daria took a step closer, "You will burn yourself till there is nothing left to burn, Dravmir."

"Is there a reason you've come here?" Dravmir brushed aside the conversation.

"You told Yelena of Annika." Daria watched as his shoulders tensed, "You have begun to open yourself to her, Dravmir."

The Count faced her then, red eyes harsh but burning in agony. "And I shall regret it – as I always do."

Daria matched his gaze, "Yelena wished to break this cycle, but she cannot do it alone. Open your heart to her and she will do the same."

Something flickered within his gaze, but it vanished, "She will die as the others have." And he turned his back to Daria.

"Dravmir..."

"You are dismissed, Daria."

With those words, the woman vanished from the room, leaving the Count to burn in his guilt. Allowing it to consume his soul entire. He burned until only a small ember remained.

CHAPTER TEN

Blood and Warmth

NIGHTMARES PLAGUED YELENA'S mind. Tormenting her and laughing while she cried, while she screamed and pled for it to end. Yelena tossed and turned, wrestling her bedsheets while she fought to escape the clutches of the nightmare. Growls rumbled through the fog in her mind. Snarls filling the emptiness. Yelena found herself in the forest. The trees tall and menacing as they towered above her, their branches like crooked hands reaching down at her. A scream rattled her ears and her heart leapt into her throat. Yelena took off into the forest, traveling through the thick fog. When she broke through the arms of the trees, she found her sister in the clutches of a beast.

Her sister's gaze found hers, Danna's eyes widening as her lips parted in a scream. Yelena did not stop, running at the beast. But the faster she ran, the further the beast and her sister grew. As if the earth expanded between them. No matter how fast Yelena ran, she never reached them. She watched as the werewolf parted its mouth, its sharp teeth gleaming before it snapped them around Danna's head. Crimson burst around its mouth and poured down her sister's mangled neck. A broken sound tore from Yelena's throat. Her scream rattling the earth beneath her and the trees trembled at the agonizing wail. Danna's body became limp in the beast's arms. When it opened its mouth, Yelena could not tear her gaze away from the sight before her. All that remained of her sister's head was the mangled emptiness above her neck. Sickness churned in her stomach and she heaved on the foggy ground. Her throat burned and tears shed from her eyes.

When Yelena lifted her head, the werewolf's gaze had found hers. The beast dropped her sister's corpse as if it were nothing and approached Yelena. Her body had been paralyzed by fear. Becoming a statue as she watched the beast waltz toward her with a prowl in its steps. When it stood over her, she tilted her head back and met its gaze. The beast lifted its arm and when it swung, Yelena closed her eyes and braced herself as death came for her.

As the werewolf's claws tore into her body, Yelena was freed from the clutches of the nightmare. Her eyes snapped open as she jolted in bed. Her heart thundered against her chest and roared in her ears. A cold sweat had dampened her body, her hands trembling as she reached for her throat, finding it smooth, unmarred. Relief washed through Yelena and calmed her racing heart. Shaking away the lingering remnants of the dream, she tossed away the sheets and stretched out her sore limbs. Her legs and arms ached as she stood. Casting a glance at the bed, she noticed that the pillows had been tossed across the room. One of the sheets had cascaded to the ground in a pool of fabric. The rest of the bed was wrinkled from her restless slumber.

Stepping out of her room, she found Danika before the table. Atop it a tray of food waited. Though the smell of the food was tantalizing to her tastebuds,

Yelena's stomach couldn't bear the smallest crumb. The dream left her stomach uneasy, and she did not wish to tempt it further. "Danika, can you ask a servant to ready the bath for me, please?"

Danika's gaze studied her. The way Yelena held herself as if fearing she would crumble. The woman nodded, "Of course."

The woman swiftly left the room and returned almost instantly with two servants. A man and a woman. The two bowed their heads to Yelena, who was now seated on the couch before the warmth of the fire. They disappeared into her chambers, readying her bath. Yelena ached to relax her tensed muscles and mind. To submerge herself in the warmth and lose herself to the world if only for a moment. To swim into realms of her own making and become lost within their depths. To dance amongst their storming waves.

The servants finished preparing her bath, Yelena thanked them before they left the room. Danika lingered before the fire as Yelena made her way to the bath, almost hearing it call out to her, leaving her food untouched. Quickly undressing herself, Yelena lifted her foot over the lip of the tub and dipped her toe in. The water was perfect. Yelena eased herself into the tub, steam dancing around her in smoky tendrils. Closing her eyes, she leaned against the back of the tub. Her lungs filled with the scent of honey and cinnamon. Her aching limbs slowly were soothed by the warmth of the water.

Holding her breath, Yelena submerged herself into the water and the world became silent. It was as if she had been transported to another world or lingered between this world and the next. Floating in the emptiness between them, becoming a phantom herself. All around her, there was warmth and it embraced her. Comforting her mind and soothing her aches, reaching down into her soul. But as she found comfort there, within the depths of her mind, something wicked stirred. Opening her eyes, Yelena found herself in a bath of blood. Her lips parted as a silent scream escaped her lips. Bubbles blurred her vision and she jolted up in the bath, swallowing the air. The water was clear once more, but the warmth was slowly leaving it as the cold crept in.

Running her hands over her hair, she smoothed it down against her head and stood from the water. Trickles of it cascaded down her being. Grabbing a towel, she dried herself and dressed once more. When she returned to the main chamber of her room, she found Danika still standing before the crackling fire. Her gaze drifted down to the untouched tray of food. Danika halfway turned as Yelena seated herself on the couch and lifted the largest dome, revealing eggs and bacon waiting for her on a plate.

"I can send for fresh food." She spoke.

Yelena shook her head, "This is alright, no sense in wasting it."

Danika nodded as Yelena began to eat. "What happened?" The woman asked.

Yelena's hand stilled, her gaze remaining on her plate. She hadn't realized that Danika would have heard her scream. "Bad dream." Yelena said, a shiver coursing down her spine.

Danika nodded before returning her gaze to the flames. "I have those often."

Yelena could venture a guess at what sort of nightmares plagued the woman. She could hardly believe a person could be so vile, especially a father. Yelena quickly lost her appetite and pushed her tray away, unable to take another bite.

"I'm sorry..."

"You should not apologize for things that are not your blame to carry." Danika said. "My father saw the justice he deserved. I have healed from the scar he left on my soul. All that is left is lingering memories that show themselves in my dreams." Danika's gaze slid to Yelena, "Do you wish to talk about it?"

Yelena hardly felt she had any place to speak of what troubled her mind. It seemed so small compared to what Danika had to face. Absentmindedly, she had wrapped her arms around herself as the image of her sister at the mercy of that werewolf flickered before her eyes.

"One's pain is not less than another's." Danika said, drawing Yelena's attention. "Do not compare pain."

Yelena dropped her gaze as she shook her head, "I almost watched my sister..." she took in a breath, "she almost died before my eyes. I can't free myself from that scene. If Dravmir hadn't have gone to her, she would be..." Yelena couldn't bring herself to say it. Afraid to speak it into existence.

"I understand." She spoke. "I lost one sister to a monster and the others to old age. I would not wish that sort of pain upon anyone." Danika's hands seemed to tighten as she held them. Something shifted in her stoic face, her eyes became a storm of turmoil. Turning her back to Yelena, she strode toward the doors, "I shall fetch Daria." With that, Danika left.

∞ ∞ ∞

Guilt gripped Yelena as she combed through the tangles of her hair. That look on Danika's face haunted her thoughts. The silent creaks of the doors stirred Yelena from her thoughts. Daria entered with a welcoming smile. The woman clasped her hands before her as she approached Yelena.

Before she could speak, Daria said, "Danika needs some time. Do not blame yourself, you did nothing. Though our aches are decades – centuries – old, they still haunt us from time to time."

A sigh escaped Yelena as she lowered the brush, shaking her head. "I–"

Daria closed the distance between them and gently tilted Yelena's chin up with her finger, "Shush, now. Everything is alright, don't go worrying that pretty head of yours."

Yelena offered the smallest smile.

Daria returned the gesture and lowered her hand. "Now, I'll take the tray back to the kitchens, if you're finished."

Yelena nodded; she doubted her appetite would return any time soon.

Gathering the tray, Daria swiftly left the room. Yelena set the brush down and stood from the vanity, unable to look upon her reflection. Tonight, she would venture through the castle. She would not allow Drezca to scare her into hiding in her chambers. There was much of this castle that Yelena wished to see, and she would see it all. She would venture through every unknown hall and slip inside every untouched room. She would soon know this castle like the back of her own hand. Slipping her feet into silk shoes, Yelena ventured forth with her chin high.

The halls were silent, not a whisper of a soul to be found. No phantoms lingering within the corners. The gentle crackles of the torches were the only lingering whispers to be heard. Yelena strode through the doorway, passing by the portraits without a spared glance, and found herself in the throne room. She halted in the center and allowed her gaze to drift toward the dais. Toward the aged thrones. There they sat, alone. Left to decay in the shadows. Blanketed in decades of dust. Even though layers of the passing years covered them, their beauty shone through.

As Yelena freed her gaze from them, she felt the watchful eyes of another upon her. Gooseflesh prickled along her arms. Her eyes flicked above to the balconies, searching for a fiery haired monster to be watching but found nothing. Her gaze drifted down to the tall, marble pillars and there she found a dark silhouette standing between them. It stepped forth and the glowing eyes of the Count found hers instantly. The soft click of his heels against the floor echoed through the room as he approached her. Yelena dared not move, holding his gaze as he stood before her.

The memory of yesterday stirred in Yelena's thoughts and her eyes drifted toward his cheek. His pale skin showing no traces of the blood that had once stained it. Once splattered across his cheek in a twisted painting, as if his flesh were the canvas. Yelena stole a step closer to him and he did not move, those glowing eyes watching her. Yelena did not know what overcame her, but she had reached out to Dravmir. Her fingertips brushed against his cold skin and she could have sworn he stiffened beneath her touch. But he did not move, his gaze becoming curious. Many questions had rampaged through her mind, wishing to unearth the truths that had been hidden. Yelena had once thought the Count had claimed the life from his brides' veins, drowning himself in their blood. But she had learned he was not the monster she once thought him to be. Though a question still burned in her mind.

"Do you drink blood?"

The question had hung heavy within the air between them. Yelena had thought he would not answer until the velvety sound of his voice rasped against her ears. "No, but it is a constant craving. To monsters such as us, we crave it for it holds the very essence of life."

Yelena's brow furrowed. "You don't need it to survive?"

Dravmir's gaze traced down her jawline to her neck, as if he could see the veins beneath her flesh. See the blood coursing through them. "Think of it as a craving. A sweet pastry. You don't need it, but you *want* it."

"Are you craving it now?" Her voice was hardly a whisper.

Those red eyes flashed to hers. "A monster is always craving."

Yelena's palm formed over his cheek. Dravmir's hand slid up to hers and pressed against it. For a moment, she watched as the walls between them cracked. The Count pressed into the warmth of her palm, their gazes never wavering. His fingers traced down to her wrist, gently grasping it as he pulled it away. Yelena held her breath as the Count brought her wrist to his mouth. His lips traced over the smoothness of her skin before feathering a kiss against her wrist.

Dravmir's eyes closed as his lips lingered upon her skin. He felt as her pulse thundered at his mere touch. The murmur of the blood in her veins sang sweetly into his ears, tempting him to steal a bite. To drink. He could feel the rush of her blood against his hand, flowing beneath that delicate layer of flesh. When he opened his eyes once more, he found Yelena watching him. There was no fear, no disgust, no resentment. Just pure curiosity. As if she were trying to unravel every truth and secret, he kept stowed away.

Perhaps, she would.

And Dravmir would allow her to unravel him entirely.

Until there was nothing left.

"You are no monster." She spoke unwavering.

He released his hold on her hand and took a step back. "I am."

She took a step closer, "A monster would not have saved my sister." Another step, "A monster would not have saved me twice over. You are no monster." She repeated.

Dravmir closed the small distance between them. Yelena blinked, nearly stumbling back but he reached out for her. His hand grasping her waist, steadying her. Freeing it from her hip, he traced his fingers down the length of her arm and he felt as she shivered beneath his cold touch. His fingers wound around her wrist and lifted it between them. Turning it over, he brought it to his lips once more. Holding her gaze, he bared his fangs to her. And to his surprise, she did not startle at the sight of them. Arching a brow, he traced the pointed ends of them against that delicate skin. Yelena watched him but her face had become unreadable. Concealing her emotions deep within.

Dravmir spoke against her wrist, "If I wanted, I could pierce your flesh now and drink your blood. I could drink every drop from your veins and there would be no stopping me."

She matched his gaze, "But you won't."

And Yelena was right.

He would never harm her.

She steeled her gaze, "You wish to frighten me away, but I see through that façade, Dravmir. You wish for the world to believe you a monster, but I do not see a monster before me."

Dravmir tilted his head, "Then what do you see?"

It was then the slightest emotion spilled from her as her eyes softened. "A man drowning in his aches. Suffocating in his regrets. Dying in his guilt. Burning in his agony."

Dravmir hated her for how she saw through his charade. So easily she could read him, and he despised it. He dropped her hands and stepped back into the shadows, "The man you're searching for is dead."

And the Count was gone.

Yelena stood alone in the throne room with the lingering touch of the Count burning against her wrist.

$$\infty \quad \infty \quad \infty$$

The castle was silent. Yelena was unable to bear it any longer. Her feet led her through the halls. Her footsteps echoed loudly against her ears. All was quiet as if no other souls lived amongst these cold walls. But Yelena knew the immortals lurked within the shadows, perhaps watching her every move. Brushing aside the chill that lingered, Yelena made her way toward one of the towers. Toward that room that brimmed with warmth and life. Toward Charlotte. Yelena had found spending time with that woman cleared any worry from her mind. Able to release herself from the fear that gripped her. Fear that she may never see her family again. Never feel the warmth of her mother and father's embrace. With Charlotte, Yelena felt at home within those walls. Within the warmth of the sun that Charlotte had managed to trap within the castle without burning in its light.

It did not take her long to find the room, standing before the grand doors. Rasping her knuckles against the wood, a voice called out almost instantly. "Come in!" Charlotte trilled.

With a smile, Yelena stepped into the chamber. Into that warmth. The doors quietly shut behind her as she basked in the golden glow of the room. Her eyes flicked to the tall ceiling above as if searching for the sun. Across the room, Charlotte could be found surrounded by bundles and heaps of fabrics. Colors of all sorts spilling out like an ocean. A wide smile found itself on the woman's face as she waved Yelena over.

"Ah, Yelena, come, come! What brings you to my chamber? Need another dress? Did the other not really satisfy you? I can assure you I will make a dress you'll truly love!"

A light chuckle escaped Yelena as she shook her head, "I love the dress, Charlotte, truly. Though I must admit it may need some tending to on the hem, since my first escape attempt." Guilt swam in her being, swelling like rising waves.

Charlotte waved a hand in the air, "Oh that'll be an easy and quick fix. Nothing to be worried about. I'll have Drezca or someone fetch it for me."

Yelena's skin bristled at the mention of the woman.

Charlotte straightened herself and stepped out of the pile of fabrics, smoothing out the wrinkles in her dress. "Now, what brings you to me, then?"

Yelena's gaze drifted toward the wall of windows. The curtains pulled back, revealing the lurking night beyond the castle. Mindlessly, she strode toward the windows. Her gaze searching through the shadows that writhed between the wicked branches of the trees. Her hand pressed against the cool glass. Fog danced around her fingers as her warmth seeped onto the glass. Yelena waited, watching. Searching for any movement within the darkness. Searching for a flash of a watching gaze but found nothing. Her mortal eyes blind to the supernatural world.

"Don't you worry about them breaking through the glass?" Yelena asked, flashes of horrific pictures flared within her mind. Of those werewolves crashing into the castle and slaughtering every soul trapped within these walls.

Charlotte joined Yelena's side at the window. When she cast her gaze to the woman, she found the warmth within those red eyes was gone. Replaced by a coldness that lurked deep within. The woman reached out and traced a finger along the pane of one of the squared windows. "They are lined in silver."

Yelena's brow furrowed, not quite understanding.

Charlotte turned her gaze to her and offered a sad sort of smile, "Silver is deadly to them as sunlight is to us." There was a yearning within her voice. A want to bask in the sun's golden halo but would never again know its warmth. A wistful sigh escaped the woman, "Oftentimes I go to the roof and watch the sun rise. I tend to press my luck, waiting till the last second before retreating into the shadows. For a moment, I'm able to glimpse the rising sun. Able to watch the sky churn from that turbulent grey and gloom and burst to life in hues of oranges and reds, chasing away the darkness."

Charlotte's face glowed with that warmth she imagined in her mind. As if she had trapped a piece of the sun within her soul before she shed her mortal flesh. But even though she glowed, there was a darkness in her eyes. A yearning that shall never be fulfilled. A sorrow that shall never free its weight from her heart. The woman blinked as if pulling herself from the recesses of her mind.

Painting a smile on her lips, she faced Yelena. "Would you feel more at ease if I shut the curtains?"

Yelena shook her head, "No, that's alright." She turned her back to the dark forest and faced the warmth of the room. "I hope I'm not intruding. I just wanted to be in some warmth." A light laugh escaped her, "That probably sounds silly."

"Not at all! Being within this room gives me a sense of mortality. As if I could dare bask in the sun once more." Charlotte flitted toward the pile of fabrics, sorting them into piles. "You may come here as often as you wish, my doors are always open to you, Yelena."

"Thank you, Charlotte."

The woman beamed, dousing Yelena in her warmth. "Of course."

∞ ∞ ∞

Yelena had not known that hours had passed her by, not until the Count came knocking upon the doors. The steady beats against the wood disturbed Yelena from her daydreams, dragging her back to the world and darkness that waited. Even Charlotte had been startled, lost within her fabrics, organizing them by color. She hurried toward the doors, dancing along the shadows that writhed at her feet. Yelena wondered where the shadows had been hiding within such a vibrant room, even the corners held warmth within their grasp. When the doors opened, the Count stood at the threshold. His gaze drifted passed Charlotte and found Yelena's. As their gazes held, Dravmir's shoulders slightly slumped, as if a weight had been lifted from them. For a moment, a memory from earlier flashed before her eyes and her wrist prickled with a lingering chill, warmth flushed her cheeks.

"Daria said you were not in your chambers. We've been searching for you, dinner waits."

She had not missed that he said, *we.* There was worry in his eyes no matter how hard he steeled his gaze; she found the layers of fear hidden beneath his cold façade. Had Dravmir thought Yelena attempted another escape? Had he envisioned his bride fleeing into the forest with death chasing at her heels? Whether the Count realized it or not, the ice that had formed around his soul, around his heart, was thawing. Whether he realized it or not, he had slowly begun to care for Yelena.

Without a word shared between them, Yelena stood from the couch, uncurling her knees, feeling the stiffness ache in her numb limbs. She gave Charlotte a parting smile and stood before the Count, crossing over the threshold. Quietly, the doors closed behind her and it was only them within the shadows. The Count held her eyes for only moment before breaking away from her gaze as if it were too heavy to bear. Turning away from her, he began his stroll down the hall with Yelena walking by his side. Their lips remained silent, their eyes ahead. Around them the shadows writhed within the darkest corners, chased away by the light of the flames from the torches.

Yelena cast a sideward glance at the man. He walked with his chin high, and hands clasped behind his back. Each step he took was with confidence. As always, his face was hardened like stone and she wondered what it looked like beneath the weight of that mask. She wished to reach out and untie its ribbons and reveal the man within. She only saw a small glimpse of him, but she knew he was there. That Dravmir was no monster. That he was capable of *feeling.* Of loving. The emotions were bare on his face when he spoke of his first bride, Annika. He said her name with such tenderness, but pain creased his brow. As if he had to force the name from his lips, his guilt wrapping around his throat as if he believed he had no right to even mutter her name.

When Dravmir cast those red eyes upon her, she quickly averted her gaze. Glancing past him to the windows that lined along the walls. The dim light of the moon poured into the castle, dousing it a silver glow. Yelena couldn't help but wonder if those beasts prowled through the trees, waiting and watching for one of them to leave the confines of the castle. To step into the night tempting death.

"Why do the werewolves kill your brides?"

Her voice echoed down the hall as they came to a halt. The Count faltering at her question but quickly composed himself. He followed her gaze to the window, peering past the thick fog and shadows as if he could see the werewolves prowling the forest. As if the beasts stared back.

"It's the natural way of things." He finally spoke. "Think of a snake and mouse." His gaze slid back to hers, "The snake slowly squeezes the life from the small creature before claiming its meal. The snake is the predator and the mouse the prey."

"Then what are the werewolves? What are you?"

"Predators who share the same territory fighting for dominance."

"Is there no hope for peace between your kinds?"

Dravmir faced ahead, "No."

And with that, he continued along.

∞ ∞ ∞

As promised, there was dinner waiting for Yelena in her chambers. Her stomach growled as she breathed in the enticing scent. Daria and Danika were there to greet her when the Count swiftly vanished, closing the doors behind Yelena. Seating herself on the couch, she scooted the tray toward her and lifted the silver domes. Steam danced within the air as it exploded in a cloud before her eyes, restless from being trapped. Before her a bowl of creamy potato soup waited. Bits of shredded cheese melted across the top, sinking into the depths of the soup. Eagerly, Yelena grabbed a roll and dipped into the soup. A sigh escaped her as the savory food tantalized her tongue.

Yelena stirred the lingering remnants of the soup lazily with a spoon. Her stomach swollen and aching. Her gaze drifted toward the two women who stood before the fire, murmuring amongst themselves. Their voices so quiet Yelena strained her ears to listen but couldn't decipher their words. "Daria? Danika?"

At the call of their names, they turned their gazes to her. "Yes?"

Yelena's gaze drifted back to the soup, "I wish to know Dravmir. To understand him a bit better. To know his interests."

Daria offered a smile, "You know one of his interests already."

A memory conjured within her mind. Of her first night within these walls. How the Count had painted her portrait. The feel of his fingertips grazing the skin of her bare shoulder as he swept her tresses behind her. Yelena remembered how perfectly he had captured her likeness. As if she had peered into a mirror and not a canvas.

"Ask him about his paintings." She continued, "That is something he holds dearest to his heart."

Yelena nodded; plan set in her mind.

She would understand the Count.

She would unmask the man he kept locked within and bring him forth into the world. And she begun to wonder if the Count would wish to understand her.

And would she let him?

∞ ∞ ∞

The Count was a predictable man, to the point it was nearly painful. As always, he lingered before the empty thrones with only dust sitting upon them. The air hung heavy with gloom, dampening any life that dared linger, suffocating it as the shadows crept in. They writhed around Dravmir, echoing the turmoil within his soul. The man was unaware of the watchful soul behind him, their steps so silent they fell deafly upon his sensitive ears.

"She wishes to know you." Danika rasped, startling the Count.

His shoulders tensed but he did not face the woman.

Danika continued, "And you wish to know her, too."

She paused, waiting for him to speak and when he didn't, she continued, "Get to know one another, Dravmir." The words were edged with finality. There was no arguing them, no arguing with her.

For a long moment, her words dangled within the air between them. Mocking him, taunting him. Whenever Danika spoke, he knew the words were needed to be heard. Though Daria would allow him to dismiss her, to turn away her advice, and give him space to think it over, Danika would not be so easily deterred. She stood strong, unnerving, until Dravmir listened. She would stand there till the end of time until he gave in. The Count knew he had to work, to do his part in breaking this vicious cycle. And it had to begin with him breaking his cold façade. To shatter the ice around his heart.

And so, he would take that first step.

But the shards of broken ice that thawed from his heart fell and pierced his soul. His shoulders weighed down as a sigh escaped him, "It is my curse to love each bride and watch them die." He faced Danika, her face unreadable as always. "I will see her tomorrow."

With those parting words, he left the room.

CHAPTER ELEVEN

Sunlight Graces a Monster

THE WARMTH OF the sun embraced Yelena's skin in a blanket of comfort. A gentle caress. She leaned her head back, basking in those golden rays. Her skin absorbing the sunlight and allowing it to touch her soul. Filling her with warmth until it swam just beneath the surface. She leaned back on her hands on the roof of their family home. The shingles were hot from the summer sun, but it didn't bother her. Above Yelena was the vast, endless sky. Like an ocean adrift above their world. The clouds the foaming waves. Yelena had heard stories about oceans and the grand ships that set sail across them. In her daydreams were the only places she could stand before the sea, feel the tickle of the waves lap against her ankles as they crashed ashore.

Beyond the fence of their village, through the forest, lay a grand ocean. The river the villagers gathered their water from, was filled by it. Yelena had pled to her parents to take her to the ocean, wishing to swim with the fish. But they had forbade her from ever leaving the safety of their village. But it never ceased her yearning. Spending her days gazing toward the horizon searching for the sea.

The roof creaked as her sister crawled atop it, settling down next to Yelena. "Daydreaming as always, I see." Danna teased.

Yelena's gaze remained distant as she asked, "What do you think the ocean looks like?"

To Yelena's mind it was a shimmering shade of turquoise, the waves growing darker further down into its depths until there was nothing but darkness. The foam as white as freshly fallen snow as it lapped against the sandy shore.

Danna followed her sister's gaze and gave a slight shrug, "Like water?"

A snort escaped Yelena as she nudged her sister's ribs, "Come on, Danna! Be serious. Tell me, what do you think it looks like?"

Her sister's brow furrowed as she thought, chewing her bottom lip. "I'm not sure, I've never seen an ocean." She flicked that dark gaze to Yelena, "What does it look like to you?"

A wistful smile caressed her lips as a light sigh escaped her, "Beautiful."

Danna shook her head with a laugh, "Come on, lunch is waiting."

∞ ∞ ∞

When Yelena stirred from the dream of a memory, she found a faint, golden glow pouring through the windows. A light warmth had filled her room, acting as another blanket. Sitting up, she rubbed the tiredness from her eyes. There was a weight beneath them, knowing she had only gotten a few hours of sleep. Instead of laying down, Yelena tossed away the sheets and stretched out her aching limbs. It had been too long since she last basked in the sunlight. Though most days it never penetrated those dark clouds, other days it prevailed. Today, it was waging war against the gloom, both sides coming at a standstill, allowing a shred of the sun's light to pour onto their cold world.

Yelena had missed the warmth the sun offered, and she stepped toward the windows, drawn to it, as if it beckoned to her. Reaching out, she pressed her palm to the glass and found faint tendrils of warmth lingering. Closing her eyes, she absorbed that light and warmth. Filling her soul to the brim with it until it spilled over. When she opened her eyes again, she found that the warmth did not ignite her in quite the same way as it once had. That she had grown accustomed to the night and the silver light of the moon. That shadows had slithered in her soul and taken root, laying beneath blankets of warmth. Her hand fell from the window and she turned her back to the sun.

Yelena had tried to claim sleep, but it would not have her. The quiet loneliness of her chambers had become too much, and she found herself venturing forth into the darkness of the castle. Not realizing that the shadows had slowly became her comfort. Yelena ventured through the hall, silence greeting her at every turn. There was not a soul to be found, even the shadows seeming to be dormant. Fear crept into the back of her mind, whispering into her ears. A fiery haired woman danced through her thoughts, her wicked laughter echoing through Yelena's head. Shaking her head, she vanished Drezca from her thoughts.

Yelena slipped through the doorway and found herself in the throne room once more. She stole a glance toward the lonely thrones. She pictured the Count and his first bride, Annika, seated upon them. Their hands clasped with love in their eyes. The image made her chest ache and she cast her gaze away, unable to bear it a moment longer. Her eyes traced across the room toward the doors and the stained window above. Though it was daylight, the sun did not pierce through the darkness of the pane. Forbidding it from entering these walls.

As she stood there, mind drifting, a prickling sensation crept along her arms. Someone was watching her. Holding a breath, she slowly turned her head, waiting to meet the eyes of the lioness that prowled this castle. Across the throne room, lingering in a doorway, a silhouette stared back. Red eyes glowed from the depths of the shadows, watching her. Slowly, the figure stepped forth and the Count freed himself from the darkness. Yelena took notice of his hair and clothes. The loose blouse he wore was rumpled as were the trousers he wore. His raven hair was slightly mussed, gathered in a low ponytail. Had the Count had trouble sleeping as well?

"Good morning." His voice was rasped and groveled, as if he had just woken.

She was surprised that immortal beings slept but she supposed they needed sleep too, to escape into a land of dreams and free themselves from their curse. But from the look on the Count's face, Yelena knew his sleep had been restless.

"Good morning."

The Count stepped forth, keeping a distance from her. She saw as he seemed to battle with himself. His eyes a whirlwind of emotions. "What has you wandering the castle this early?"

Yelena shrugged and turned her gaze back to the dark window, "I couldn't go back to sleep. Though I could ask you the same, I didn't truly know if you immortal beings slept or not."

Soft footsteps echoed though the room as Dravmir closed the distance between them. But when Yelena glanced at him, she found his gaze settled on the window above the doors. A darkness had settled across his features, a coldness permeated the air around him, chilling Yelena.

"It is all we have left of our mortality." It was then that pain feathered across his face. "When we sleep, we can escape into our own minds and feel what is was like to be mortal. To feel the sun, though it hates us."

Before she could speak, the Count drifted toward the doors and slowly rose into the air as the shadows gathered at his feet, carrying him. Yelena watched as he hovered before the stained window. And before she could blink, the sound of shattering glass filled the air. It rained down on the floor as the Count drifted to the ground, evading the lone beam of sunlight that slipped into the castle. Dravmir held her gaze as he closed the distance between them. Yelena dared not move. Her heart steadily hammering against its cage. The Count stalked to the side, standing before the beam of light that separated them.

A gasp escaped her lips as Dravmir stepped forth.

The beam an inch from touching his cheek.

His eyes studied her, flicking from her widened eyes to her parted lips as a silent protest lingered upon them unspoken. It was clear within her eyes that Yelena feared for him, feared of what would become of him if he stepped into the sun's blessing light. Yelena cared. Whether she realized it in this moment or not.

The Count's voice was hardly a whisper as he spoke, agony clinging to his every word. "How can you care for a monster such as I?"

Yelena blinked. His question burning a hole through her chest. She had come to care for him, in some manner. He had saved her, saved her sister. And that had caused a slight warmth in her heart that ignited near the Count. Yelena saw through his mask to the lonely man beneath. To the agony and guilt that tormented his soul.

"Because I see no monster before me." The words a whispered caress to Dravmir's ears.

The grief on his face twisted into flickers of rage. Not toward Yelena, but toward himself. For allowing her to care for him, for a monster. She was doomed just as the other brides to fall victim to Death's cruel blade. Cursed. *He* was cursed, he was the curse. Every bride would greet death and he would be left with their broken bodies burned into his memories, haunting him for all eternity. Dravmir should have been colder, more distant. He should never have listened to Daria and Danika. He should have left Yelena alone, should have never came close to her. Because now, he had cursed her. There was only one thought in his mind, one thing he could do to cause Yelena to flee. To never come close to him again.

Dravmir took another step forth.

A gasp echoed through the throne room.

And his cheek blazed.

The sun eating away at his immortal flesh. Burning his sins.

Dravmir did not flinch away from the pain, endearing it. Though a scream built in his throat, wishing to rip free from his silent lips. He wanted Yelena to fear him. To see the monster that he was. He wanted her to flee, while she had the chance. He was a fool to think he could protect her. But he knew the inevitable. That the elders would disgrace her from the village, seeing her as cursed touched. The elders thinking Dravmir would come and slaughter them all for harboring his runaway bride. But he never would. Fear would be the death of Yelena, her people bringing death upon her from their own fear. Love would be the death of Dravmir. He could feel it slowly kindling in his soul and he wished to extinguish that flame. But no matter how hard he tried, embers of it remained.

Dravmir waited for Yelena to run. To scream. To name him a beast. But she stood before him. There was fear in her eyes but not of him, of the sunlight that burned him. She took a step closer, her hands reaching out as if to push Dravmir away from the light, but he moved back before her fingers could ever touch him. He did not understand why this woman before him had come to care, even in the slightest of ways for him. For all the coldness he had greeted her with, what had made her come to care for him?

"I'm a monster." He repeated. Almost more for himself than for her. "Nothing more and nothing less." His teeth gritted as his jaw clenched, "I am undeserving of love and incapable of giving it."

The words were meant to scare her away, but Yelena was stubborn. Seeing through the lie. She stole a step forth, lightly shaking her head. "You are not incapable of it." She spoke, "You loved your first bride. You loved them all – cared for them all. Otherwise, their portraits would not be hung on the walls. The paintings speak volumes of your love, Dravmir."

And finally, Count Dravmir shattered.

He fell to his knees before her and hung his head. As if his immortal body could no longer bear the weight of his burdens and guilt. "I'm a monster." His voice broke.

Yelena knelt before him and reached out, this time, he did not move away from her touch as the warmth of her palms embraced his cheeks, lifting his head. It was then their gazes held. Truly peering into one another's eyes, peering down into the souls within. Reading every ache and woe that riddled them.

Dravmir's eyes were fathomless seas of sorrow as he lay them bare to her. Decades upon decades of unending heartache. She had once believed his eyes were cursed – perhaps they were. Cursed with such pain that she could barely stand it, but neither could she look away. The Count had finally lowered that cold, indifferent mask and revealed the man beneath. He was no monster, but a man plagued with regret. Guilt gnawing away at him until so little remained of the man he once was. His heart becoming nothing but a heavy burden he must bear until the end of his days. And Yelena found herself foolishly wishing she could reach out and take hold of some of his burden. Shouldering it and relieving his heart for a moment, to allow the man to breathe and heal without looking as though it pained him each time, he filled his lungs.

When the Count looked into Yelena's eyes, truly peered into them, he saw endless oceans from worlds far beyond their reach, locked within the confines of her mind. He often wondered what lurked within the recesses of her thoughts. Wishing to steal a glance upon the worlds she conjured. As he looked into the rippling waves of her irises, he was able to see a window of what she imagined. Dravmir had stolen glances upon her, seeing as she drifted far away to the distant lands. He had once done the very same in his mortal years; he knew that look all too well. But Yelena was a world all on her own. The earth orbiting around her, the sun and moon at her beckoning call. Her eyes were like lolling waves, pushing and pulling against the shore. Beckoning to him, luring him forth. Pulling him in before retreating back into the sea. There was no denying that there was some earthly force drawing them together and when they touched, it pulled them apart. Or perhaps they both were at fault. Pulling back from one another before they came too close.

Or perhaps the blame lay with him.

Dravmir feared of losing her, another bride.

He could not bear the pain any longer, each bride that was taken slowly chipped away at his soul till only a small piece remained. And when Death comes for Yelena, she would take with her that final piece.

And so, Dravmir retreated.

Always the coward.

Always allowing the fear to consume him.

Gently he grasped ahold of her wrists, lingering for a moment before taking her hands away from his face and stood. Sliding that mask over his face once more. Without a parting word, the Count vanished, leaving Yelena alone in the silent throne room.

∞ ∞ ∞

The mortal finally stood from the ground and trudged back to their chambers, vanishing through the darkened doorway. Heat simmered beneath Drezca's immortal flesh. A snarl curling on her lips as her nails scraped down the pillar, leaving scars in the polished marble. Hatred had bred within her soul, creating something far more dangerous than the monster she was. For years, Drezca had tried to penetrate the Count's barriers, searching for any crack or crevice she could slip through. But he had forbidden her from climbing over his walls. Keeping her locked out. But he had fallen to his knees for that *mortal.*

With a snarl on her lips, the lioness crept back into the shadows.

∞ ∞ ∞

Yelena had felt like a fool sitting on the ground. Her eyes lingering on the empty air where the Count had vanished. His touch still lingered on her skin, icy and warm all at once as it prickled. But the sting from his rejection lingered a moment longer, overcoming the warmth. Though she understood why he preferred to keep his distance, she longed to know him. She saw fragments of the man within, wishing to piece them together until the puzzle was completed and the true Dravmir finally stood before her.

With a sigh, she finally stood and made her way back to her chambers. Exhaustion was beginning to cloud her thoughts, her eyes growing weary. She tumbled through the doors and fell onto the bed, curling beneath the sheets. Yelena hardly remembered closing her eyes before sleep laid its claim on her and dragged her into the land of dreams. When she walked into the world, she found her mind had brought her to the Count. There the man stood, waiting for her, bathed in sunlight. But he did not burn beneath its rays. The man smiled at her, looking so odd on his usually cold face. There was a warmth that touched those cursed eyes as he beheld her. Dravmir offered his hand to her and Yelena happily took it.

Yelena did not know how long she slept. Stirring forth from her dreams, she found the faded silver light of the moon greeting her when she woke. A yawn escaped her lips as she rubbed the sleep from her eyes. Part of her mind still lingered within her dream, running through the tall grass that swayed in the wind like rippling waves, hand in hand with Dravmir. There was such a warmth to his face that she had not known him capable of, it touched her though she knew it was dream. Tossing away the sheets, she swept into the main chamber and found Daria and Danika waiting within, a tray of food waiting for Yelena sat on the table. Daria greeted her with a smile and Danika inclined her head. As Yelena nestled down to eat, her gaze wandered back to the women.

"I haven't seen Drezca as of late." Yelena said. Though she did not care for the woman, she had thought it odd that she hadn't crossed paths with her.

Daria and Danika exchanged looks, an unspoken conversation passing between. "We haven't seen her much ourselves." Daria said. "She often vanishes from time to time, wishing for some time alone, outside of these walls." She offered a smile, "It's nothing to worry yourself over, Yelena."

And yet, Yelena could not help the uneasy feeling that crept over her shoulders. Shrugging it off, she poked her fork into the yolk of the eggs on her plate. Watching as the yellow liquid pooled around the sausage links. As her mind begun to wander, it drifted toward the Count. "Have you seen Dravmir tonight?"

Daria flicked her gaze to Yelena, but the woman did not meet her eyes. "Only in passing. His mind seems to be captivated, more so than usual." A slight smile grew on her lips, "I do wander why that is."

Yelena's mind drifted to the moment they shared in the throne room. How Dravmir had shattered the window and stood in the light of the sun. Yelena would never forget how his immortal flesh had burnt. It did not melt or burn like mortal skin, instead it seemed to crumble. Burning like parchment, darkening at the edges as the flames ate away at the man. Dravmir had stood unflinching but she saw the agony in his eyes crying out to her and she wished to shove him from that light. Unable to bear his pain any longer. But as she stepped forth, he retreated. She remembered how he fell to his knees, seeming so defeated. She remembered that look in his eyes as their gazes locked, unable to tear their eyes from each other. Reading down into the burdens that their souls carried.

Again, her mind wandered to that dream. Where Dravmir could be freed of his guilts and regrets. How he had smiled so warmly at her, how he basked in the light of the sun without fear of burning in it. Though she knew it was not her duty, she wished to thaw his heart. To bring light into his soul once more. Yelena wished to *know* Dravmir. Cracks had webbed through the icy barriers and she could cast a glimpse upon the man trapped within the Count. She wished for nothing more than to reach through the crevices, take his hand, and guide him out. To bring him into her warmth.

Yelena did not meet Daria's gaze as she spoke, "I wonder as well." And ate a bite of the eggs.

∞ ∞ ∞

Daria left Yelena's chambers, Danika remaining to keep the woman company. She drifted through the halls and rounded into the throne room. There, as always, was Dravmir, lurking before the lonely thrones. Her steps whispered through the room, announcing her arrival. The Count did not face her, remaining as still as a statue. Daria came to a halt before the dais.

"Something happened between you and Yelena." She said, her voice loud amongst the silence.

Dravmir's shoulders tensed ever so slightly, "It was nothing."

Daria arched a brow, "The fact you acknowledge that *something* occurred, tells me it was not simply nothing."

Silence settled between them, but Daria did not leave, simply waiting.

Finally, he spoke, "There's so much fear." His voice was hardly a whisper. "I cannot endure another loss, Daria." He hung his head, shaking it. "I cannot love another bride. For when they love me in return, they die. My love is a curse, a poison. I do not wish to bring that fate upon Yelena. I cannot."

"Dravmir," Daria's voice was tender, "When shall you see that your love, that *you*, are no curse?"

A harsh laugh barked from his lips, "Don't you find it too coincidental that each bride I've loved died shortly after?"

"That does not mean it was a curse. Those beasts stole your brides from you. Not your love, *them.*"

At the mention of the werewolves, the Count's body tensed. Hatred brewing and awakening from its dormant slumber as each bride drifted across his mind. Their broken bodies mocking him. Their screams taunting him.

His fault.

His fault.

His fault.

"It's better this way, Daria."

"Dravmir..."

"Please," he pled, "don't push this matter further."

A sigh escaped the woman, "Yelena cares for you, whether you wish it or not. She cares. And you care for her."

When Dravmir did not speak, Daria turned on her heel and left him to wallow in his sorrows.

∞ ∞ ∞

As the night grew darker, Yelena had tired of being trapped within her chambers. She had paced around for an hour, stepped out onto the balcony, and basked in the dim silver light of the moon, sat before the comfort of the roaring fire. But she had grown tired of these walls, feeling as though they were closing in, suffocating her. She needed out, needed to roam, to breathe. To clear her mind and venture into a world of her own making. Leaving her chambers behind her, Yelena strolled through the halls, turning corners she hadn't yet turned. Venturing further and deeper into the maze of halls.

Yelena found that her daydreams had shifted. No longer did the sun rise into her violet skies. Shadows had crept into her seas of turquoise grass. The moon had taken the sun's place, bathing its silver light upon Yelena as she wandered through the grass that reached up to her hands as if to entwine between her fingers and never let go. And though the change had shocked her, she found that she enjoyed it. Walking beneath a sky of stars and counting each constellation she found, mapping them within her mind.

As Yelena slowly left her world of dreams, she found herself in an unfamiliar hall. The shadows seemed thicker here, reaching down from the high ceiling and sweeping across the crown of her head. No paintings could be found hung upon the walls, no windows. There was nothing. But she felt the weight of eyes upon her. Squinting her eyes through the darkness, she found a glowing red gaze staring back. For a moment, fear crept into her throat, threatening to choke her. Had she crossed paths with Drezca? Was the lioness finally going to claim her prey? But as the figure stepped forth, relief washed through Yelena as the Count stood before her.

But as she looked into his eyes, there was a harshness to them. As if the ice that encased his heart had frozen him from the inside out. Yelena nearly flinched at his stare as if the ice had bitten her. Those red eyes studied her. Dravmir stood like stone before her, unmoving. Hardly seeming alive. Something had cracked in the man, had withered and died, in the time they were apart. Yelena wandered what had happened in those mere hours since their shared moment. Why had he grown so cold?

"Dravmir?" Yelena stepped toward him.

His eyes narrowed as he stepped just out of reach of her touch. "What brings you to my side of the castle?" Even his voice had darkened. Not a hint of warmth could be found in his words.

Yelena snatched her hand back and straightened her spine. Hardening her gaze, she said, "I was exploring the castle."

The Count merely regarded her. Without speaking, he stepped around her. The shadows that writhed around him brushed against Yelena. The tendrils gently coiled around her arm and fingers, tugging her. As if pleading to her to follow the Count. To not allow them to leave that coldness between them. Steeling her gaze and closing her hands into fists, she whirled around and followed the path of writhing shadows. Their wisping hands guiding the way to Dravmir. The man had already vanished from her eyes, but Yelena would not allow him to push her away, not anymore. He had given her glimpses of the man he could be, that he was. And Yelena was determined to bring him out. Her feet beat against the hard floor, the sounds thundering through the long and empty halls. Her heart hammered against her chest, heavy breaths escaped her lips, but she did not stop. Not until she reached him.

Finally, the trail of shadows ended, and the Count once more stood before her. His back facing her as he stood upon a lone balcony. Yelena did not know what part of the castle she was in, but she did not care. She followed the long, crimson carpet toward the glass doors. The curtains that hung over them were opened slightly, revealing Dravmir upon the balcony. His head was tilted back as he basked in the silver light of the moon, gazing upon the stars above that seemed to gaze back. Standing there, so alone, Yelena's heart ached. Though his back was faced to her, she could picture the agony that lay bare on his face. The way his shoulders slumped as if he could no longer carry his burdens. The way his hands gripped the railing. There was no denying that Dravmir was shredding his soul apart, allowing his guilt to eat away at him till there was nothing left.

Grasping the handles of the doors, she pulled them open. The Count's shoulders tensed as she approached him, but he did not move. Did not face her. Yelena reached out and placed a gentle hand upon his back, "Dravmir..." Her voice rasped his name. She felt him tense again beneath her touch.

But the Count remained silent. Never facing her.

Yelena's fingers curled into the fabric of his midnight tunic. "Dravmir." She tried again, her voice pleading to the man within. *"Please."*

And still, he remained unmoving.

Her hand formed into a fist, gathering a bundle of the fabric into her palm, "Don't shut me out, not again. I've seen glimpses of the man you are, Dravmir. You are no monster. So, I beg you, please do not push me away." Yelena had thought she had finally broken through the barriers to the man within, but she found several more waiting for her, mocking her.

But Yelena could not see the tormented look that twisted his face. How his mask had completely and utterly fallen to the earth below and agony writhed in his eyes. Dravmir's soul was immensely sore, wishing for a cure. Wishing for anything that would cease the pain that claimed his heart each and every night of his immortal existence. Wishing for something to bring it to an end. To bring him to an end.

Anything.

Dravmir's grip tightened on the railing, nearly shattering it. "Leave." His voice commanded, forcing that word from his throat, grating against his teeth.

But the Count knew Yelena was stubborn and there she remained. The warmth of her delicate hand radiating against that one spot on his back. Her fingers twisting into the fabric of his tunic, threatening to rip it. There was a slight tremble growing within her hand. Her frustration building and bubbling beneath the surface. Anger gnawing away at her.

"You gave me the slightest piece of hope, dangling it before my eyes like I'm some starved animal, and snatched it back. You gave me a glimpse of the man inside you before you locked him away again. Before you tossed away the key, sealing me out." She yanked at his tunic, wishing he would face her. But he remained unmoved. Heat simmered behind her eyes, threatening to spill down her cheeks in steaming streams. "Let him out, Dravmir, I beg you."

Yelena waited. Hoping that he would face her.

When he didn't, Yelena could no longer stand it. With both hands, she grasped ahold of his tunic and *tugged.* Not caring if her mortal strength was futile against the Count. Not caring if she tore the fabric. Yelena wanted him to face her. No more hiding, no more concealing.

"Let him out!" Her voice cracked as the dam burst and hot tears spilled down her face. Her frustration had grasped ahold of her and poured out into the world. "I know he's there, Dravmir. So please, *let me in.*"

And then, he faced her.

The Count whirled around and gently grasped her wrists as her hands tore free from his tunic. Her crystalline eyes widened as she glanced up at him and she found that Dravmir had tossed away that cruel mask and lay himself bare before her. And finally, she saw the man within. All his fears, all his sorrows, there before her eyes. The agony that he felt was so immense that it broke Yelena's heart gazing into his eyes. His brows were pinched but his eyes were yearning. Pleading for Yelena to go, to leave. But she there she remained. Dravmir wished to be left alone to wither in his turmoil, to fall into its darkened pits, but Yelena reached out a hand and pulled him forth. Not wishing for him to suffer alone. Not anymore. Not while she breathed.

"Let me in." Yelena whispered to the man.

His grip gently tightened on her wrists, watching as he struggled. Battling himself. Wishing to shove her away, to have Yelena turn her back on this castle, on him, and leave, never to return. But another part of him, the larger part, wished to bring the woman into his arms. To have those ocean eyes look upon him and a smile to fill her lips whenever their gazes met. Dravmir wished to have her. Wished to know her, the soul within, and the beautiful mind trapped in her head. Dravmir wanted Yelena, yearned for her companionship even if it was in the simplest of ways. She had been the warmth within his cold world, the light in his darkness. And he could no longer deny himself. No matter how much he pushed her away, she chased after him, ever the stubborn woman she was. But he admired that about her.

He admired *her.*

Tenderly, Dravmir pulled her closer and he listened as her breath hitched. "You are incredibly stubborn." His voice whispered like soft velvet against her ears.

She smiled and when Dravmir was alone later, he would immortalize it on canvas, capturing this moment. "Stubbornness seems to pay off, doesn't it?"

And for the first time, in decades, Dravmir *truly* smiled.

Yelena stared, as if mesmerized. Her eyes widening as if in shock. The Count had released his hold on her wrists and Yelena reached for him. And this time, he did not retreat into the shadows. This time, he would not allow his fear to consume to him. Yelena's fingertips grazed the skin of his cold cheek, her warmth teasing him as her fingers lightly traced over his immortal skin. She traced over the sharpened edge of his cheekbone, down along his jawline. Exploring the man before her and Dravmir watched. Seeing the curious wonder within her eyes. Sparkling like an ocean beneath the golden light of the sun. Her fingers drifted toward his lips, tracing along them, finding that they were not made of stone but soft skin. His breath licked at the tips of her fingers.

As Yelena explored the plains of his face, her fingers dancing across his cheek, she remembered how it had burned before her eyes. How the sun had slowly eaten away at his immortal flesh. Burning it until darkened embers drifted along the air, fluttering to the ground like ash. But now, not a trace of it could be found. No scar, no wound. His skin was smooth and unmarred as if he had never basked in the light of the sun. As if the sunlight had never graced a monster. But the man before her now, was no monster. The Count had never been.

Yelena's palm caressed Dravmir's cheek, her warmth spilling over his skin and slipping beneath the surface, down into his heart. The ice that encased it began to thaw and melt at her touch. A river of warmth flooded into his being, spilling over his soul, and bringing it to life once more. Where the cold, harshness of winter had taken root, Yelena's summer had thawed that eternal winter and unearthed it. Dravmir had not felt this since his first bride. Had never thought he would feel such a thing again. But here this miraculous woman stood, gifting him with a piece of her warmth, igniting his soul on fire once more.

Tenderly, the Count traced his fingers from the crook of her elbow to her wrist. His hand laying atop hers before pulling it away, feathering his lips into her palm. Heat scorched through Yelena's veins at the simple kiss. So featherlight she had hardly felt it, but that warmth was undeniable. Those red eyes held hers as his breath traced over her palm, placing another kiss upon her skin. Dravmir brought her hand back to his cheek, resting it against his cold flesh. The Count closed his eyes and pressed her palm against his skin, leaning into her warmth, wishing to never forget the feel of it against his cursed being. He felt her pulse beat against his cheek, feeling the blood coursing through her veins. So delicate mortal flesh was but that made her something tangible to this world. Each beat of her racing heart was a reminder that Yelena was here, in this castle, with him.

Yelena stroked her thumb across his cheek, causing him to open his eyes to find her smiling at him. "There you are." Her voice was a sweet caress to his ears.

"Here I am." He rasped. "Apologies for making you wait so long. I allowed my fear to consume what was left of my soul."

Though she smiled, her gaze hardened. "Swear to me, that you shall not cage this man again."

Dravmir lowered her hand from his face, keeping a tender but firm hold upon it as he lowered to his knees before her. Recreating that moment between them in the throne room. He looked up at her, "I swear to you now, Yelena, that my heart will remain uncaged." He squeezed her hand gently, "Only you hold the key to it now. For eternity." Dravmir pressed a kiss to the back of her hand, "And now that you have my heart, what do you wish to do with it?"

Yelena met his gaze as she said, "I wish to know you, Dravmir."

"And what do you wish to know?"

Yelena smiled as she said, *"Everything."*

CHAPTER TWELVE

Painting and Portraits

THERE WAS A LIGHTNESS in Yelena's step as she trotted back to her chambers. Finally, Dravmir had set his soul free. No longer binding it to the cage he crafted within his soul. Gifting Yelena the key to its cage and setting it free to the world. It was a tormented soul, full of agony and heartache, but Yelena had sworn to be tender with it. To learn every ache and woe that riddled his poor soul. As Yelena traversed the halls of the castle, she was unaware of the stalking shadow that crept in her steps. It grew ever closer, waiting to pounce.

When Yelena stood before the doors to her chambers, she reached for the knobs, but something latched onto her shoulder. A gasp erected from her lips as pain laced through her skin, cutting deep into her flesh, and freeing the blood trapped within her being. Yelena was whirled around and forced against the stone wall, the back of her head cracking against the unforgiving stones. The breath was knocked from her lungs, her body ached, and her shoulder wept.

But all that pain was left forgotten as she beheld the monster before her.

Drezca pinned Yelena against the wall, her nails puncturing into her shoulder, seeping ever deeper, drawing forth that tempting crimson. But it seemed to be all but forgotten to Drezca as it painted her fingers in red. Her fiery eyes burning in flames so ravenous Yelena could feel their heat scorching her. Drezca's beautifully immortal face was twisted so hideously in hatred. Her lips curling as she bared her teeth, snarls escaping the woman. Her fiery tresses a disarray, a lone strand dangling between her eyes. Yelena's heart beat so loudly it was like thunder against her ears, and she could have sworn it echoed down the halls.

"YOU'VE TAINTED HIM!" Her voice was a snarled shout.

Another cry of pain erupted from Yelena as Drezca forced her nails deeper.

"Do you think that you, a mortal, are worthy of the Count?" Drezca's eyes narrowed into slits. *"You are* nothing. *And you will always be nothing."*

Shadows crept into Yelena's vision. Darkening around the edges and Drezca's face soon became a blur of three. Hardly able to focus on any of the faces before her. Her mind had grown groggy, her body becoming limp. Warmth trickled down her shoulder and stained the front of her gown. Yelena could hardly hold her head up as the blood drained from her being. The world around her was blackening, Drezca's face slipping into the shadows as they coiled around her. Yelena could no longer hold her eyes open, her knees buckling beneath her, but Drezca's nails kept her pinned to the wall. Her mortal weight nothing within the grasp of an immortal.

"You mortals are useless. Weak. Frail." Drezca's words were muffled as if they had fallen into the watery depths of a well and she shouted beneath the water.

Yelena was slipping away. Her skin becoming tinged in cold. Paling as if Death had already greeted her. Plucking the soul from her mortal flesh and carrying it far away. When her eyes sealed shut, and she began to drift away, a shriek rattled her ears. A scream freed itself from Yelena's lips as Drezca's nails were torn from her shoulder. Slicing her skin deeper. Once she was freed from Drezca's grasp, her weight became too much for her numb legs to bare and she slid down the wall. Falling into a set of strong arms. Yelena opened her eyes a crack enough to find the blurred face of Danika before her. Her head lolled to the side and she found that Daria had slung Drezca against the wall. The stones had been cracked; dust had tainted the air. Drezca rose onto her feet with a snarl but Daria became a blur of shadows to Yelena's eyes. And when she blinked, she found Daria had caught Drezca by the throat and hefted her into the air, holding her against the broken stones.

"Have you gone mad, Drezca?" Daria's voice had grown into a growl.

A snarl escaped the woman, "She has no right to him. She is a *mortal*."

Daria narrowed her eyes, "You'd do good to tame your jealousy, Drezca. Or I shall tame it for you *forever.* Do you understand me?"

Drezca did not answer and the ravenous flames within her eyes burned brighter. Daria dropped the woman back to her feet and stepped aside. "Leave. *Now.* I do not want to see you near Yelena's chambers again."

The woman flicked her eyes to the limp body within Danika's arms, a smirk curling on her lips as she turned on her heel and stepped into the writhing shadows. Daria strode toward Danika as she stood, cradling Yelena close. The woman had slipped into unconsciousness, blood staining the frontside of her gown and dripped down to the cold floor below. Daria gently reached toward Yelena; the woman's cheek was cold beneath her immortal touch. Brushing away the strands of hair from her face, she gently tucked them behind Yelena's ear. Daria lifted her gaze to meet with Danika's. Not a word was shared between them as they swept inside Yelena's chambers and the doors closed behind them.

∞ ∞ ∞

Yelena faded in and out of her dreams. Stepping into the world for brief moments. She was in the arms of Danika and then darkness became her. When she stirred again, she was in the warm water of a bath. Danika and Daria gently washing away the blood from her skin, the water tinged in a pinky haze. Then darkness lay its claim on her once more. When she woke again, Yelena found herself gently tucked into the comfort of her bed. The sheets wrapped around her. The room was blurry, and her head was light. Rubbing her eyes, she blinked through the haze until the room came into focus.

Sitting up, pain laced through her shoulder and a gasp escaped her lips. Flicking her gaze down, she found bruises blooming across the pale skin of her shoulder. Gently, she traced her fingers over the stitching in the wounds left behind from Drezca's nails. Yelena did not remember Danika or Daria stitching the wounds but much from that moment had been lost, a blurred haze to her mind. A flash of Drezca's snarling face flickered in her thoughts and Yelena's hand flinched away from the wounds. Drezca had made it known she did not much favor Yelena's presence but what had provoked such an attack?

"You're awake. How are you feeling?" Daria's voice sounded from across the room.

Yelena cast her gaze to the doors to find the woman standing there, holding a small tray with a kettle, lone cup, and a small jar. "Sore."

Daria nodded and stepped into the room, setting the tray down on a bedside table. Pouring a cup of steaming tea, she handed it to Yelena. "Here, drink this."

"Thank you." Yelena sipped on the warm liquid, feeling as it warmed her soul. "Did you stitch my wounds?"

"Danika did. She is better at such things." Daria plucked the small jar from the tray and popped the lid. She dipped her fingers into the clear balm. "This will ease your pain and dissolve the stitches over time."

"When I see Danika again, I'll be sure to thank her for stitching me." Yelena met the woman's gaze as Daria tenderly applied the cool balm, "And thank you. If you hadn't of come along, I fear of what might have become of me." A shiver coursed down the length of her spine.

A sigh escaped Daria and she cast her gaze to the windows. Staring out into the dark night beyond the castle. "I have never seen her act in such a way. I shall admit, it frightened me."

"What caused her to attack me? What have I done to her?"

Those red eyes snapped back to Yelena, "What she did, is not your fault. It is inexcusable what she's done. I'll be having a word with the Count."

Yelena's gaze lowered into the brown liquid, "What will he do to her?"

"I'm not sure. But what she did cannot go unpunished."

She traced a finger over the rim of the porcelain cup, "Don't tell him."

Daria blinked, "Pardon?"

Yelena met her gaze, "Don't tell him. It'll make her resent me more if he punishes her because of me. Please, Daria, don't."

The frown upon her lips hardened, "Yelena, I don't think-"

"*Please.*" Yelena reached out and grasped ahold of Daria's hand, squeezing it.

For a moment, her gaze flicked down to their clasped hands and a sigh escaped her. "Alright. I won't tell him. But Danika and I shall be keeping a close watch on you from now on."

Yelena nodded, "Thank you."

Daria patted her hand. "Of course. Now, get some rest."

With those parting words, Daria strode from the bedroom and closed the doors behind her. Yelena finished her tea and settled back into the warmth of the bedsheets. And when sleep claimed her, she found nightmares had waited in her dreamland. A lioness prowled through the waiting shadows, stalking Yelena through the forest. And when all was quiet, Drezca leapt forth and claimed her prey. Yelena's screams became a distant echo across the land.

∞ ∞ ∞

When Yelena was freed from the clutches of the beast, the sweet smell of glazed cinnamon biscuits wafted into her room. Instantly, her eyes opened, and she tossed away the sheets, lured by the delectable scent. Swinging open the doors she found Daria and Danika within the main chamber and a tray of silver domes waiting for her on the table. With a smile, she skipped toward the couch and nestled down on the cushions. Moving aside the domes, she devoured the breakfast. Her tongue tantalized by the sweet biscuits. Soft and buttery with dashes of sugar and cinnamon.

Memories stirred within the depths of her mind. Of early mornings just as the sun crested the horizon and the sweet smell of biscuits lured Danna and Yelena from their dreams. Yelena would burst into her sister's room and jump atop the bed, shaking her sister awake, all too eager to devour the sweet biscuits that waited them. Danna would laugh and shove Yelena away and the two would hurriedly make their way down the stairs. Times were much simpler then and Yelena yearned for those moments. But they were now gone, passing between her fingers as she reached for them.

When the food was gone, Yelena cast her gaze back to the women and found Daria smiling. A twinkle within those cursed eyes. Yelena raised a brow, "What is it? Is there food on my face?"

Daria chuckled, "No, dear. The Count wishes us to escort you to him. He has something planned for you."

Her heart fluttered within her chest. Eagerly she stood from the couch and begun to ready herself. Danika selected a dress from the wardrobe. A simple yet beautiful gown. It was crafted from a soft lilac fabric. The neckline was modest, and the sleeves reached to her elbows before splitting and fluttered down at her sides in rippling lilac waves. They made sure the dress covered her ruined shoulder. Danika and Daria had begun work on her hair. Brushing the tangles from her silvery tresses. Parting it down the center of her head, Daria took one side and Danika took the other. The women pulled the front pieces back and began to weave them into separate braids that met in the back and wove them together. Daria came to stand before her and gently tugged some strands loose to frame either side of her face.

Standing back, Daria admired their work and smiled. "Beautiful."

Danika came to stand at her side and offered the smallest smile.

"Thank you, both of you." Yelena held Danika's gaze, "And I must thank you, for stitching my wounds."

Danika nodded her head, "Of course."

"Now, come along, the Count awaits." Daria said.

∞ ∞ ∞

Daria and Danika led Yelena through the winding halls of the castle. Passing through doorways and rounding sharp corners. The shadows danced within the crevices, reaching out to the souls that passed them by. Their cold tendrils winding around their ankles, as if wishing to tug them back into the darkness with them. As they strode through the shadows, they found themselves before tall wooden doors. Daria cast a smile over her shoulder as she opened them. A familiar room was revealed to Yelena. Reminding her of when the Count had painted her portrait. Together they strolled across the room and up the winding stairs to the second floor. When they rounded the top, a large door was before them. Danika stepped aside as Daria opened it, stepping to the other side.

A light gasp escaped Yelena's lips as she beheld the sight laid before her. A circular room with polished floors and walls decorated in paintings waited for her. Yelena felt a pull into the room, mesmerized, she stepped forth. Daria quietly closed the doors behind her, but she was none the wiser. Her eyes beheld each of the paintings, skipping from one to another. Wishing she could gaze upon them all at once. Yelena strode toward the center of the room, slowly turning on her heel to look upon each portrait. Every canvas was painted in such vibrant colors. Distant lands lay before her eyes. Lands she had only dreamed of where now just within reach. Lands crafted from sand and others of snow lingered trapped within frames upon the walls. Others were of vast forests and distant jungles. But one of them had truly captured her interest. Yelena had been drawn to a land that lay next to the sea. Waves rippled and foamed upon the sandy shore. And just passed the shore, tall grass of emerald swayed in a gentle breeze. Cottony clouds lay against a cerulean sky. The sun was tucked in the corner of the painting and its golden rays glistened atop the rising waves.

As Yelena strolled toward it, she was unaware of the watchful gaze upon her. The Count stood in the darkest corner of the chamber lurking at the bottom of the stairs that wound to the final floor of the tower, watching his bride as she gazed upon the paintings that surrounded her and transported her to other worlds. There was such a fascination within those crystalline eyes, admiration. Lovingly, her fingers caressed the painting, tracing over the lolling waves of the sea. Dravmir did not miss the slight wince within Yelena's eyes as if lifting her arm caused her pain. Her fingers fell away from the painting and clasped her hands before her once more. As she spun on her heel to drift toward the next canvas, those alluring eyes met with his. And for a moment, neither moved. Their gazes holding and it seemed as if the world had grown quiet and still.

Dravmir moved first, stepping forth from the shadows and standing before his bride. "Do you like my paintings?"

Yelena's gaze slid passed the Count and marveled at the canvases hung all around them. Surrounded by worlds far different from their own. "They're beautiful, Dravmir."

The smallest smile quirked at the corners of his lips, feeling so foreign to his mouth. His muscles forgetting the feeling, almost struggling. "I'm glad you think so."

Yelena met his gaze again, "Daria said you had something planned for me."

He nodded, "I do." Stepping aside, he flicked his hand into the air. From the shadows in the corner came forth two easels, two canvases, paints, and brushes. The shadows carried them along dark, ripping waves and set them within the center of the room. "I wish for us to paint together. I know you do not enjoy being trapped within these walls so I had Daria bring you to this room that can offer you the sun when I cannot."

Yelena's heart sang with warmth and a smile found itself upon her lips. "Don't you see, Dravmir? You did bring me the sun. You brought me to these beautiful lands." Her eyes drifted back to the painting, "And you brought me the sea." There was a softness to her voice, as if her words sighed blissfully from her pale lips.

Yelena's eyes had grown distant, imagining herself standing before those turquoise waves. Her bare feet sinking into the warmth of the sand as it gritted between her toes. The cool water of the sea washing against the shore and foaming atop her feet. If she closed her eyes, she could almost smell the salty tang within the air, could feel the sea breeze whispering against her ears and tousling her white tresses. Seagulls squawked somewhere in the distance, dancing within the clouds and basking in the golden rays of the sun. When Yelena opened her eyes, the scenery dissolved and once more stood within the chamber with the Count standing before her. Those red eyes curious as they watched her.

Tearing her gaze from his, she approached the easels, "Shall we?"

Dravmir strode toward the easels and took the apron that hung on the back of Yelena's. "This shall keep your dress from getting ruined. May I?"

Yelena nodded her head and faced her back to him. The air stilled around them as the Count stood behind her. Yelena held in a breath as he brought the apron around her waist. His fingers grazing across her dress as he secured the apron and tied it into a knot that rested against her back. She could have sworn his hands lingered for a moment on the knot before he stepped away and draped an apron around his narrow waist. Facing him, she found the Count standing beside his easel. Dravmir gathered his raven tresses and bound them into a low ponytail that swept down his back. A lone strand of hair dangled at the side of his face. Yelena watched as he rolled the sleeves of his blouse to his elbows. Admiring the pale length of his arms and the veins that slightly rippled to the surface. There was an immense difference to the man before her. The first night she came to this castle, she dreaded this new life. Despised the monster that she had believed stolen her from her family and bathed in her birth mother's blood.

But then the truth came to light and Yelena had come to care for the man. For the soul that had been lost within Dravmir's depths. He was never a monster, but a man broken – almost beyond repair. But his cracks were mending, fitting together once more, and warmth returned to his cold heart. When he turned those piercing eyes upon her, there was a lightness within them and a smile upon his lips. Within his hands, he held a paintbrush in each. At the simple sight of him, she could not help but return that smile. Closing the distance between them, she took the offered brush from his hand. Her fingers touching his for a breath before she stepped toward her easel. The cold touch of him lingered upon her skin.

"What are we painting?" She asked.

Dravmir dipped his brush into one of the paints, "Anything you desire."

Dipping her brush into a paint, she brought the brush to the canvas. "I shall warn you now, I was not gifted with an artistic hand."

A chuckled laugh escaped the Count, and it was a lovely sound. As if the life had returned to his immortal being. Facing the blank canvas before her, Yelena began to paint a world she had crafted within her mind. A violet sky with cottony clouds filled the top portion and faded to a deep blue with a splattering of white blots for stars. Yelena was no artist, but she enjoyed bringing to life a world she had only once imagined. Now, it could be birthed into this world, allowing another soul to see what had been trapped within her mind. Cleaning the paint from her brush, she dipped into another color and swept turquoise waves across one half of the bottom of the canvas. Her world was nearly complete. Soon, a snowy forest came to life, set before the gentle sea. A flurry of snowflakes drifted along a breeze and danced atop the lolling waves. While Yelena painted, splatters of color freckled the apron and her hands. Mindlessly, she swiped her fingers across her cheek, brushing aside a strand of hair, leaving a streak of purple upon her skin.

Stepping back, she admired her work. Though it seemed a child of four had gotten ahold of paints and smeared an array of colors across the blank canvas. But to Yelena, it was a perfect representation of the worlds she crafted. Oddly beautiful with a touch of gentle chaos. The imagination of a child, seeing the world through their eyes and the vibrant colors that surrounded them before they grew into adulthood and the world became dull and grey. Yelena had retained the sight of youth and carried with her into adulthood. Never wishing for the world to darken, always searching for the vibrance of life around her.

There was a whisper of air as the Count stood behind Yelena, peering over her shoulder, and admiring her work. "What is it?" He asked, his tone light with curiosity.

Yelena smiled at her painting, "A world I've imagined. I visit it often when I daydream."

"It's wonderful." He said.

"I wished to share a piece of me with you since you brought the world to me." She cast her gaze around at the paintings.

"Thank you for sharing your world with me, Yelena. When it dries, I shall hang here so it may join the others."

When she faced him, she found Dravmir smiling down at her. The warmth within his gaze was enough to make her heart flutter. The tenderness within his smile touched her soul. His eyes flicked down to her cheek, and a light chuckle escaped him. "There is paint on her cheek, allow me."

Yelena's breath stilled as he reached for her. His thumb swiping away the purple stain on her cheek. And though his skin was cold, warmth blazed from his touch. The palm of his hand formed around her cheek, cradling her face within his hand. And for a moment, the two held gazes and Yelena wondered if Dravmir could hear the thundering of her heart as it pounded against its cage. Warmth swelled within her soul as she leaned into his gentle touch, smiling at the man before her.

His eyes shifted, guilt swelling to the surface as if pain had unleashed itself upon the man. "It was never your duty to repair what was broken in me, Yelena. I shall be forever in your debt."

She held his gaze as she said, "I know."

His thumb stroked her cheek, "Then why?"

Her hand traced up the length of his arm before sliding her hand atop his, "Because I saw a man drowning in despair and I wanted to reach out, take ahold of his hand, and bring him into the light."

"I shall spend the rest of eternity showing you, my gratitude. For reaching out your hand." Dravmir smiled before his hand fell from her cheek. Yelena's skin yearned for the tenderness of his touch once more.

Freeing her gaze from his, her eyes wandered toward the canvas that lurked behind him. "May I see your painting?"

There was a slight hesitation in his eyes as they flicked toward his painting, but he stepped aside. His gaze did not find hers as she stepped around him, he did not follow. Yelena stood before his canvas and a light breath escaped her as she clutched a hand above her heart. Before her was a perfectly rendered portrait of Yelena as she painted. A moment of time captured upon canvas. There was a gentle smile upon her pale lips, a softness within her eyes as she painted her world. Her white hair spilled down her back, a few strands dangling down either side of her face. And upon her cheek, a purple blot could be found. Her delicate hand splattered in splotches of paint as she held the old brush.

Whispered footfalls approached Yelena but she could not tear her gaze from the portrait. "You painted me." She rasped.

Dravmir nodded, "Do you like it?"

Yelena had lost her voice, words clogging her throat. It was beautiful. He had even painted the room around her, his paintings hanging within the background while she worked. "I do." Her eyes finally met with his, "Why did you paint me?"

Dravmir cast his attention to the worlds around them, "I once thought that my muse had been the lands in this world. That there was beauty in such bleakness, painting them allowed me to escape my sorrows for a moment as I lost myself in distant lands. But now, you have become my muse, Yelena. The lands could only numb the agony until the paintings were done and the pain would return. But you, you brought life into my soul once more. You brought warmth to my frozen heart. Painting you was only fitting. A gift to you for the kindness you've shown me when I was not so kind to you."

Yelena stepped toward the man. The vulnerability he displayed yanked at her heartstrings. "You may have been cold and at times I disdained your existence, I understand now. You had faced a pain I shall never truly fathom. You endured something many have not. You wished to protect me and yourself from that fate again." Dravmir finally met her gaze, "But I wish to know, why now? Why not unmask yourself to the brides before me?"

His gaze softened as he reached for her, caressing a strand of her hair before tucking it behind her ear. "Because I wish to break this cycle, much like you. I have faced enough death and I do not want it to befall you as it has the others. I had buried myself deep within my regrets and burdens and you pulled me from that darkness. And now, I shall make it my purpose to protect you. I swear to you now, Yelena, that you shall not face the same fate as my former brides have. I will not fail again."

There were no words that came to her. Instead, she gently took ahold of his hand and pressed it to her cheek. Closing her eyes, Yelena pressed a kiss into his palm before cradling it to her cheek once more. Cold and warmth bloomed across her skin at his touch. "Thank you, Dravmir. For this. For the painting. For everything."

The Count smiled, "Of course. Now, allow me to escort you to your chambers."

As they left the room, Yelena cast a glance over her shoulder upon the lands. A smile forming on her lips as she followed Dravmir through the halls.

∞ ∞ ∞

When they approached her chambers, the Count opened a door for Yelena and stepped aside. Sweeping passed him, she halted at the threshold. Her eyes drifted toward the fireplace, the flames steadily crackling, as if welcoming her back as they waved in a fiery dance. Yelena flicked her gaze to the empty space above the mantel. Where a faint outline of dust marked where a portrait once rested.

"What used to hang there?" She asked.

And though she did not face him, Yelena knew his gaze followed hers to the wall. A weary sigh escaped him as he spoke, "It was a portrait of Annika and I."

His first bride.

Yelena should have known, and guilt swam within her stomach. Facing him, she lowered her head to him, "I'm sorry."

"It's alright." Dravmir stepped back into the hall, a hand on the door handle. "May I ask, what happened to your arm?"

Panic nipped at Yelena as she met his gaze. One of his brows were raised as he studied her. Breaking free from his eyes, she said, "I took a tumble the other night. I'm quite alright, just clumsy."

Dravmir did not seem to believe her but he merely nodded his head. "Goodnight, Yelena."

"Goodnight, Dravmir." And she was thankful he did not question her further.

Then the door closed.

Yelena's shoulder throbbed in answer.

∞ ∞ ∞

The Count lingered there at her door after it closed. His fingers still clutching the knob. Dravmir knew Yelena was lying but he did not wish to force the truth from her. He knew he did not deserve her entire trust. So, he stepped back and fell into the reaching arms of the shadows. Dravmir wandered down the stairs but he paid no mind to his surroundings. His body leading him while his thoughts drifted far away. Retreating to the tower where a room of distant lands waited. Falling into the memory of Yelena admiring his works. Wonder sparked within those crystalline eyes. As if the ember of life itself blazed within her soul, as if she was the caretaker of mortality. Her tender warmth kindling it.

Dravmir had watched Yelena as she painted, none the wiser of his gaze. Her eyes had grown distant, and a smile caressed her lips. Her hand was not smooth and graceful while she worked but quick and abrasive. As if she feared if she did not paint fast enough, the image would be lost to her. The portrait was a beautiful blend of chaos and wonder. A rendering of her mind and the worlds she crafted within her thoughts. Flitting about those worlds while she dreamed with her eyes open.

The Count stumbled from his thoughts when he found himself within the throne room. His feet had halted in the center, facing him to the thrones that seemed so far out of reach. A faint sliver of moonlight poured into the room from the broken window, dousing the pale throne in a pearlescent glow. Leaving his throne to the darkness where it belonged. Dravmir strode toward them and ascended the stairs. He stood before the pale throne, his hand reaching toward it, his fingers grazing the cold stone leaving trails within the layer of dust.

Dravmir's ears flickered with the sound of rasped footsteps. "There is a light to you I have not seen in many years." Daria's voice carried through the room. "Yelena has ignited something in your heart."

His fingers lingered on the armrest for a moment before they fell away. "And I fear of what shall become of my heart if fate wraps its greedy hands around her soul."

Daria ascended the stairs and stood behind the Count. Her hand coming to a rest upon his shoulder, "It won't."

Dravmir found himself wishing to argue but allowed the words to die in his throat as he swallowed down his fears. He merely nodded, saying nothing. Daria gave a gentle squeeze to his shoulder before releasing her hold on him and vanishing from the room.

"I won't lose another bride." The words resounded through the room as if a spell had been cast. Ringing out with finality.

CHAPTER THIRTEEN

Daydreaming

T HE NIGHTS HAD come and went, like a fleeting dream. Yelena waking each moonrise expecting the Count to return to his cold mask. To conceal the man he was and step into the man he believed he deserved to be; a monster. But each night he greeted Yelena with warmth and the two of them would wander the castle halls together. Strolling through the long corridors as casual conversation echoed around them. Dravmir smiled often now, listening to every story that spilled from Yelena's eager lips. Telling about her childhood and times spent with her family. He could see that yearning within her eyes, the agony of being apart from her family and it shredded at his heart.

The two found themselves traversing along the paths in the rose garden. Yelena's stories had become a whispered murmur as they fell from her lips and her gaze became distant. Dravmir noticed the vacant but dreaming look within her eyes. That small spark in those crystalline irises all too telling that Yelena had wandered into a land of her own making. Dravmir felt a tinge of loneliness, wishing to follow after her into the beautiful worlds her mind crafted. His thoughts drifted toward her painting in the tower, now hanging with the other worlds he had painted. He could envision her frolicking through the tall grass as it swayed around her in emerald waves. Could hear the phantom of her laughter echoing across the ocean as it lapped at her bare feet.

When Yelena came forth, she turned her gaze upon him. "Apologies, I often drift away without realizing."

But he merely smiled, "It's quite alright." The two came to a halt before a rose bush, his eyes flicked toward the flowers that were dwindling away as winter crept into their land. Dravmir remembered the night he had brought his bride to this garden. Remembered how she pricked her finger on a thorn, how he grasped ahold of her weeping hand and tasted her blood. Unable to resist that sweet call as it pled to his ears. The monster within him demanding he quench its thirst.

Banishing the memory from his thoughts, he faced Yelena, "You know my passion for painting, but I have yet to know any of your passions. Tell me of one."

She smiled with a shrug of her shoulders, "I often like to craft worlds of my own making and wander within them." She tapped a finger to her temple and winked, "Up here."

Dravmir's gaze softened, "Tell me more about these worlds."

Yelena turned her gaze ahead and a wistful smile caressed her lips. "They're hard to put into words, admittedly. But they're unlike our world. In my lands I soar through clouds against violet skies. I swim into the depths of turquoise waves as if I've grown gills. The worlds shift to my liking, transforming at a simple thought."

"Have you ever been to the sea? There is one close to the village."

At the mention of it, a darkness flickered within Yelena's eyes and her smile faltered. She shook her head, "No. We do not leave the safety of our gates too often. The farthest I've ever gone is to the stream to collect water."

Dravmir had not known. He knew the village thought of him as a monster but did not know the depth of their fears. Only thinking they never left at night, feeling safer within the light of day. But even the sun did not grant them comfort. "I'm sorry." He said.

"It is not your fault, Dravmir." Seeing the guilt within his eyes, Yelena wished to shift the conversation. And she realized she did not know much of her birth mother. "Dravmir, may I ask something?"

"You may ask me anything."

Yelena fiddled with her fingers, "What was my mother like?"

At the mention of his former bride, Dravmir's eyes grew distant. Traveling back into the past of his memories, digging up treasured times. A soft smile caressed his lips. "Your mother was not gifted with an artistic touch, much like you." The two shared a laugh. "But she often spent her time with me while I painted. Sitting quietly while she watched. I did not speak with her much, often cold to her as I had been to you. But she was a gentle soul and a lovely woman." Dravmir turned his gaze to Yelena and without thinking, reached toward her and cradled a strand of her hair. "You remind me much of her. But more stubborn." He smiled.

Yelena watched as he gently twirled a silvery strand of her hair around his finger. "Thank you, for telling me of her."

Dravmir's gaze had darkened then, and Yelena felt a pang of guilt lace through her chest. Watching as his eyes drifted deeper into long lost memories. Turmoil bubbled to the surface, burning within those red irises. His hand fell from her hair and slipped toward her cheek, cradling it. As if to reassure himself that Yelena truly stood before him, that she was no ghost here to torment his existence. Tenderly his thumb stroked her cheek.

Yelena reached a hand toward his and pressed her palm to the back of it, "Dravmir, where are you?" Her voice whispered.

"May I confide in you something I have not confided in anyone?" Even his velvety voice had grown rasped, hardly stepping a foot into this world as he lost himself to his memories.

Yelena nodded her head.

His brows furrowed as if the memory playing within his mind had caused agony to rupture within his heart. "After I found your mother, something shattered within me. Something I had thought was broken beyond repair. I stood before the doors in that castle, covered in her blood for I had carried her back to the village where she belonged. I couldn't bring myself to cleanse her blood from my body for that was my punishment. To bear the weight of her death upon my shoulders." His gaze found hers and Yelena watched as silver lined his eyes. "I failed her, failed you for not being able to save her."

Yelena's lips trembled, "Dravmir..."

But he continued, "I stood before those doors ready to accept my fate. To walk out into the light of day and allow the sun to burn me until there was nothing left to burn. Until even my memory was burned from this world."

And then, a silvery tear spilled.

"I was ready to die. I couldn't bear this pain any longer. I had failed so many brides. I couldn't bear the thought of losing another." Dravmir hung his head, "I couldn't..." A broken rasp escaped him.

Yelena's heart wept as did her eyes, clinging to the hand that rested upon her cheek. A slight tremble shook his hand.

"As I stepped toward those doors and grabbed the handles, something stopped me. As if a voice had whispered into my ears. Telling me to wait." Dravmir lifted his gaze to hers, "And now I know what it had told me to wait for. It was you, Yelena."

Yelena had not realized that tears had spilled down her cheeks. Dravmir's thumb tenderly wiped them away, "If I had of embraced the sun that day, I never would have met you. You became the warmth within my cold existence, and I shall be forever grateful to you, to fate. And I don't think I can ever repay you. For your stubbornness to break through my barriers and melt the ice within my soul. *Thank you.*"

Yelena could not find the words to say. Dravmir had confided in her one of his darkest moments. Something he had never shared with anyone before her. The gratitude she felt for this man was unmatched. That he trusted in her enough, felt secure enough with her to share something so heartbreaking. Her heart wept with sorrow but beat with warmth. Words had all but left her. As Dravmir's hand fell from her face, she reached out to him and wrapped the man within her embrace, pulling him close. Nestling her head into his chest, the scent of a burning fire and a forest after a rain tinged her nose. Dravmir gently brought his arms around her, tightening around her small frame. One of his hands came to rest at the back of her head as he held her close. His chin resting atop the crown of her head.

"Thank you," she whispered through broken sobs, "thank you for sharing that with me." Yelena's hands clutched the back of his tunic, "I'm glad you are here, Dravmir."

Dravmir pressed his lips to the crown of her head before pulling back from the embrace. Her hands resting upon his chest where her tears dampened his tunic. Dravmir's hands lay upon her waist as he peered down into the depths of her eyes. As Yelena held his gaze, something shifted between them. As if the air had let out a breath as it danced around them. Dravmir had opened himself to Yelena, allowing her into the darkest parts of his soul. Into his deepest secrets. There was no more hiding. He stood before her, bearing his soul to her. Sharing the burdens that weighed upon his shoulders. And Yelena found herself wishing to truly know Dravmir. All of him. His past, his mortal years, his touch. He was uncharted land to her, and she wished to explore him.

"I wish to know you, Dravmir." She finally spoke. "All of you."

He pulled her closer, "All of me is yours." His hands slipped to her back. His fingertips tracing down the length of her spine. "From now until my immortal heart turns to ash."

Yelena's had slid toward the center of his chest as her other fell to his and grasped ahold of it. Placing it against her own heart, she held his gaze. "Mine is yours till it ceases its beat."

Dravmir felt the beat of Yelena's heart beneath his fingertips. So mortal and precious was the life that resided within this woman before him. Dravmir vowed that he would not lose her to fate. He would tear the world apart if it dared lay a hand against her. He would face the Gods themselves and slaughter them where they stood. He had realized that this woman had captured his heart and soul in ways he never thought possible. Not since the first bride. Not since Annika. And perhaps even more so. He could have sworn his heart beat around Yelena, as if she poured life into it once more. Dravmir's hands left her body to cradle her cheeks. Holding the world within the palms of his hands.

His world.

Yelena merely watched him, as if waiting. And Dravmir could no longer resist. With their bodies close and his hands upon her cheeks, he lowered his head. Only halting when their lips were a breath apart. He searched her eyes for any flicker of rejection but found none. Only a deep yearning before those beautiful eyes fluttered closed and she waited for the embrace of his kiss. A smile found itself upon his mouth before he too, allowed his eyes to close and pressed his lips to hers. That warmth that kindled within his being exploded into a ravenous heat that scorched his soul. And he welcomed the burn for it did not pain him but brought him to life. A sigh escaped Yelena as she gave herself over to Dravmir, to the kiss. Her body relaxing against his as she brought her arms around his neck and pulled him closer. His raven hair spilling over her arms in silky waves.

Yelena was inexperienced when it came to such things but Dravmir did not seem to mind. Guiding her lips in gentle movements. She had spent her life drifting into her mind and daydreaming, hardly paying attention to the world around her. The men within her village not even a passing thought within her mind. His hand came to cradle her back, splaying his fingers across her and gripping at her dress. Yelena's hand mindlessly wandered into his tresses, tangling within her fingers. A satisfied sound moaned against her lips from Dravmir. Nearing a growl that gently rumbled across her mouth. There was a beast that lurked within the man that held her. But not the kind to slay her where she stood and bathe in her blood. No, it was the kind that would ravage her body and cloud her mind in bliss as it took her.

And Yelena would gladly give herself over to it.

To him.

Dravmir gently coaxed her lips open as his tongue slipped inside, searching for hers. They danced between their open mouths, gasps of breath escaping them. Hardly able to contain themselves. There was a spark in Yelena she had not felt before. Dravmir igniting a desire that was hidden deep within her depths, bringing it forth into the light. Heat flushed her cheeks as it spilled to her core, the fires trickling down to her womanhood. Her body seemed to cry out for his, wishing to feel his coldly smooth skin against her flustered being. Wishing to have him tame the fires that swelled in her core.

When Yelena felt as though the flames would devour her entire, Dravmir's lips drifted from hers. As if he could hear the voice of her body calling to her, he smiled as he said, "Another night, Yelena. And I shall make you mine." Turning his head, he reached for the arm that was draped over his shoulder. His fingertips tracing up her flustered skin, causing gooseflesh to rise along her arm. Tenderly wrapping his fingers around her wrist, he lifted her arm and pressed a kiss onto her skin, leaving a trail down to her elbow. "And it shall be a night you shall never forget." There was a growl to his words, a promise.

A thrill danced along Yelena's spine; a slight tremble racked her legs. "And what if I did forget?"

Dravmir smirked, "Than I shall remind you."

Yelena's cheeks flushed a deeper shade of crimson and Dravmir chuckled. "Come, I'll escort you back to your chambers."

Looping her arm through his, the two left the rose garden behind them.

∞ ∞ ∞

When they arrived at her chambers, they found Daria and Danika waiting within. Dravmir grasped ahold of Yelena's hand and pressed a kiss to the back of it, bidding her a farewell till the next night. Yelena watched him vanish into the shadows of the hall and stepped into her chambers, closing the doors. Facing the two waiting women, she found a tray of food waiting for her. As Yelena approached the couch, she found a wide smile upon Daria's face and a faint one tugging at the corners of Danika's lips. Yelena dipped her head to hide the flush of her cheeks but there was no hiding the kiss Dravmir had left upon her hand.

Yelena removed the domes from her food and dug into the feast. She hardly tasted it as she scarfed it down, unaware of how hungry she was. With a sigh, she leaned back and found Daria's watching eyes, patiently waiting. Danika standing at her side quietly. And for a moment, her gaze searched for a woman of fiery hair. Her shoulder throbbed in memory of that night. How Drezca had become unhinged and untamed. The lioness cornering its prey. Pain laced through Yelena's shoulder at the memory as if Drezca's nails were still burrowed into her flesh. Absentmindedly her hand drifted to her shoulder and lingered there.

"Where's Drezca?" Yelena asked.

Daria and Danika exchanged weary glances. "We have not seen her ourselves." Danika said.

"Perhaps she needs some time. We had thought Drezca's feelings for the Count had faded with time after he did not recuperate them." Daria's brow pinched, "but it seems as though some still linger."

A pang of guilt tinged Yelena's heart. "I didn't know."

There was a slight whisper of air as Daria crossed the small distance between them. Gently, she reached out and slipped her fingers beneath Yelena's chin, tilting her head up. "That guilt is something you should not bear. The Count chose you. If Drezca has a problem with that, then that is her burden to bear. Not yours."

Yelena chewed her lip and nodded her head. Daria offered a sincere smile before her fingers fell away. "Now, why don't you tell us about your night with the Count."

Heat flushed Yelena's cheeks again as memories bubbled to the surface of her thoughts. "We took a stroll around the castle and the rose garden." Yelena did not utter a whisper of Dravmir's confession. Of his darkest secret, keeping it locked within her heart. As she sifted through their shared moments, the memory of their kiss burned bright. She could still feel the touch of his lips against her own. Yelena rested a hand against her thundering heart. Racing at the memory of her body pressed against his, how his arms embraced her, how his tongue had danced with hers.

A light laugh escaped Daria, "Judging by the flush of your cheeks more than a stroll happened. But I won't pester you on the details. Now, I'm sure you're ready for a hot bath, I'll fetch a servant."

"Thank you, Daria."

The two women approached the doors, "Of course." And vanished into the halls.

∞ ∞ ∞

As promised, a servant came to Yelena's chambers and filled her bath with steaming, jasmine scented water. Thanking the servant, they bowed their head and hurried from the room, leaving Yelena alone. The water caressed her skin, softening it with its warmth. The jasmine scent clinging to her pores and tresses. Yelena's hand drifted toward her shoulder, her damp fingertips tracing over the stitching. As promised, they were steadily dissolving as her wound healed, thanks to the balm Daria had applied to it. A prickle of unease trembled down the length of her spine. It worried Yelena that she had not caught sight of the fiery haired woman. Had not heard a whisper of her shadows. Unease turned into fear as Yelena allowed her mind to wander to darker thoughts. Perhaps Drezca was hiding away somewhere deep within the castle, waiting for the perfect moment to strike.

Banishing the thought, Yelena stood from the bath and dried herself off, slipping into a white robe of silk. Her damp feet padded against the cool marble of the floors in her chamber, approaching the glass doors that led out onto the balcony. As they opened, a chilling breeze swept passed Yelena, nipping at her damp skin. The nights were growing ever colder as winter crept closer. Within the passing days, it would fully encase their world in blankets of snow. The land turning from a barren land of dying trees to ice and layers of white. Capturing the land around them in a frozen prison. Yelena hugged her arms around herself as she stepped toward the railing. Her gaze drifting through the forest toward her village. From here, she could see the smallest glimpse of the gates and her heart ached. Her family would be sound asleep within their beds. Tucked warmly within the quilts her mother knitted. And here Yelena stood, a creature of night. Never resting till the sun crested the world. And when she slept, her family woke and began their day.

A sigh escaped her lips as she leaned against the railing. Yelena had drifted far away, diving into the depths of her memories. The warmth of them had slowly begun to fade, their voices becoming muffled to her ears, and their faces became a haze. Was her mind truly so weak as to forget her family so soon? Or where her memories just being cruel? Mocking Yelena, stealing away any trace of the ones she loved. The bitterness of tears clogged her throat and burned behind her eyes. Within her heart, Yelena knew she would see them again but each day away from them caused the fissure within her heart to deepen. Splitting it apart until pain laced through her chest, unable to bear the agony. Alone within her chambers, Yelena fell to her knees, clutching at her heart as tears spilled down her cheeks. She wept when she was alone, crying her pain into the world until the rivers ran dry. Gathering the shards of her shattered heart, she put herself together once more before any could see.

With a sigh, Yelena tore her gaze from the gates of her village and stepped back from the railing. As she turned her back to the night, a chill touched her spine. Gooseflesh rose on her arms as a low growl rumbled through the silence of the forest. Yelena cast a glance over her shoulder and peered into the shadows that lingered far below. And there, within the darkness, she caught a flash of a glowing gaze. Death lurked just beyond the castle, waiting for her to step forth from the safety of its stone walls. Eagerly waiting to have a drink of her blood. Her legs had begun to shake, hardly able to stand upright. Yelena did not break her gaze from the werewolf as she retreated into the safety of her chambers, slamming the glass doors shut. The sound ringing out within her room, the hinges groaning from the force. Grasping the curtains, she hurriedly closed them, concealing herself from the night.

Yelena pressed her back against the cold stones of the wall and slid down it. Sitting on the floor with her knees curled to her chest. She leaned her head back and closed her eyes, taking deep, steady breaths to calm her thundering heart. Taming the fear that threatened to claim to her. Yelena was a mortal living with immortals, with death lurking all around her. And she begun to wonder if she would truly live through this. If she could ever break this vicious cycle. Or if a beast would claim the heart within her chest, wrenching it free and bathing in her spilled blood.

Before she could drown the tears that swelled, they burst forth like a dam rupturing. Yelena had been strong, she still was, but even strong people could reach their limits. Could cry their fears into the world. That did not make them any less. That did not make them weak. Yelena was scared. Scared of whatever fate waited for her in the end. If all of this had been a waste. If helping Dravmir become his true self had been for nothing. He would return to that cold man, never again allow himself to feel a shred of emotion. He would become a phantom forevermore. Yelena allowed herself to shatter, to feel the fear she had been suppressing. She cried for her family, cried for the pain that Drezca had inflicted on her, and cried for the Count. For she could not save him. Could not protect him from the loss of another bride.

Broken sounds escaped Yelena's lips as the tears burned her cheeks in a feverish heat. She had curled her arms around her knees and pressed her forehead to them. Her hair curtaining around her and shielding her from the world. Yelena had not heard the voice that had called to her, had not heard the doors open, or the rushed sounds of shadows and footsteps approach her. She had only felt the tender embrace of strong arms coming around her and she did not fight them. Allowing Dravmir to pull her into him and nestle her into his lap. Gently he rocked her, his hand soothing through her damp tresses. Yelena clung to him, her hands curling into his loose blouse as she wept her tears onto him. Dravmir said nothing, allowing her to feel what she must. Offering her comfort.

When her sobs had quietened and her body had ceased its trembling, Yelena lifted her head from his chest, meeting his gaze. There was such a softness to his features, worry within his eyes. His hand came up and brushed away her dampened hair. His touch gentle with care. "My dear," His voice was draped in a velvety softness, "why do you cry?"

Yelena leaned into his palm, her eyes closing as she breathed in his scent. The slight smell of roses lingered upon his skin. "I'm scared, Dravmir. I'm so scared." Her words were broken and whispered as she revealed her fear to him.

And for a moment, when she opened her eyes, she could see the same fear plaguing him. But he shook his head, "I swore to you that I would make it my duty to protect you. *Nothing* shall happen to you, Yelena. Not while I'm near." And then, a fissure of pain cracked through his irises. As if he had made a decision that wrought agony upon him. "I'm taking you home."

The air stilled.

Yelena gaped at him. "What?"

"I'm taking you back to the village."

For a fleeting moment, warmth pounded within her heart. She would be with her family again. She would sit with them at the table and devour the dinner Danna had cooked. Laughter would echo around them untamed. All would be right once again. But as quickly as that warmth filled her, it had left. Yelena would be leaving this castle behind her. She would leave behind this other family she has come to know. Daria, Danika, and Charlotte would be gone to her, becoming nothing more than passing memories. And then Dravmir. Yelena had not realized that this castle had become a home to her. But what was apparent were the feelings that had bloomed within her heart. The seeds that took nesting within her soul.

"I won't leave you." She spoke.

Dravmir's brows furrowed, a slight quiver to them. "You must."

But Yelena would not waver, "You once told me that the village elders would cast me out as they have done to a bride before. When they discover I've returned, they will cast me out those gates. And what then? Shall you wait there each night until they decide to rid me from the village? Shall you wait there while beasts roam the darkness wishing to slaughter you?"

The Count remained silent.

"Here I stay, Dravmir."

He stroked his thumb tenderly against her cheek, "You're a strong woman, Yelena. You possess a strength I wish I had."

A faint smile touched her lips, "An immortal being wishing for the strength of a mortal?"

His smile matched hers, "Wishing for the strength of a resilient heart and soul."

Yelena tenderly wrapped her fingers around his wrist and pulled his hand from her face. Lifting it to her mouth, she pressed a kiss into the palm of his hand. "You are stronger than you realize, Dravmir."

Gently, he gathered Yelena into his arms and rose from the ground. "Let's get you to bed."

And Yelena did not protest, resting her head against his shoulder as he carried her into the bedchamber. Laying her down into the plushness of the bed, he tucked the silky sheets around her. As he turned his back to leave,

Yelena reached out and grasped ahold of his hand. "Will you stay with me tonight?"

His eyes met with hers, "If you wish it of me."

Yelena nodded her head. The bed moaned softly as Dravmir lay atop it. She had pulled back the sheets, offering for the Count to lay beside her. When he was nestled down, the sheet came over him. Dravmir slipped an arm beneath her head as Yelena cuddled closer to the man, draping his other arm around her. Securing her in his comforting embrace. She nuzzled her head against his chest and Dravmir rested his chin atop the crown of her hair. As her eyes closed, he traced soothing patterns into her back. His fingertips creating pathways of warmth along her skin, searing through the silk of her robe. Wrapped within his arms, Yelena drifted into a land of dreams. Of violet skies and turquoise waves with Dravmir at her side.

While sleep became her, the Count remained awake. Staring out the glass pane of the windows. The silver moonlight penetrating the grey haze of the clouds. Soon he would have to leave her as the sun woke. And he dreaded for when that time came for when he was with her, he knew peace. The steady beats of her heart were like the gentle rhythm to a melody. Serenading him. Reminding the Count that he had not lost his bride. That this was no dream. And perhaps they truly could break this wicked cycle.

A light groan escaped Yelena and she turned to lay on her back, her face still faced to him. A smile touched his lips as he stared into her sleeping face. Her white hair was splayed around her like liquid starlight, illuminated by the moonbeams that poured into the chamber. Delicately, he stroked strands of hair from her face. His fingertips tracing over the high bones of her cheeks. And it was here within this room that Dravmir realized the feeling that had swelled within his chest. A word he had once thought cursed.

Love.

But was he truly deserving of such a precious thing? Did he truly deserve this woman before him? This light that had walked into his life, this woman that had brought warmth to his once frozen soul. Dravmir vowed to protect her no matter the cost, whatever they faced.

Even if it meant laying down his immortal soul.

"Anything for her."

CHAPTER FOURTEEN

A Whispered Prayer

THE AFTERNOON RAYS of the sun had finally stirred Yelena from her slumber. Breaking through the thick clouds and blessing the world. A groan escaped her as she rubbed the weariness from her eyes, feeling sluggish. Casting a glance to the emptiness of the bed beside her, pang tugged at her heart. Sometime within the night Dravmir had slipped away, hiding from the light of the day. Yelena rested her head against the rumpled sheets where his body had laid. The shape of him still pressed into the bed. Her fingers curled into the sheets, remembering the night they shared together. Dravmir had been vulnerable with her and now she had been with him.

Tossing away the sheets, Yelena readied for the night. The sun steadily set below the horizon and the shadows crept forth to claim their world. For a moment she stalled at the doors to her bedchamber. Her gaze drifted toward the paneling of windows that crafted a wall. The night stared back at the young woman. Yelena would have never guessed that this would be her future. That this was the grand adventure she had been yearning for all her life. She had been tossed into a world of shadows and immortals. Thrown to the beasts. And though her heart had once cried for the familiarity of the village, this castle had become her home. The night becoming her day. Little by little, Yelena had admitted to this routine. Sleeping while the sun woke and waking when the moon rose. There was a serenity about the night, a quietness as if the world had fallen fast asleep. Yelena spent much of her time while she was alone standing upon that balcony, gazing toward the cloudy sky, seeking the stars that were hidden through the haze.

Though her time outside always came to a quick end when a growl resounded through the darkness and Yelena would slip back inside her chambers, sealing the doors. A thought that she been suppressing stirred in her mind. Her nails curled into the wood of the door. Could she truly shed her mortal flesh? If the option were given to her, would she accept it? If Dravmir asked her that question now as he did her first night, what would she say? Yelena had once said she would never accept such a curse, to step into the flesh of a monster. But now she knew the Count was no monster, that Daria, Danika, and Charlotte were not. They held mortality within their hearts. But the same could not be said for Drezca. Yelena's unease had swollen within her stomach, sickening her. Something dark waited for her along the path ahead. But she would face it with her chin held high.

∞ ∞ ∞

As always, Daria and Danika came to Yelena's chambers, keeping her company while she ate. But her mind had drifted far away, hardly tasting the food she shoveled into her mouth. Her thoughts were a whirlwind of emotions.

Wondering what it would feel like to bear the skin of an immortal. Would she succumb to that thirst for blood, would she steal the life of an innocent being driven by the madness of the call? A flicker of Yelena drenched in blood danced through her mind. Her white tresses stained in crimson, her eyes glowing that cursed red, and a wicked smile of fangs filled her face. The image was something that nightmares would conjure to torment her sleep. But she knew that she would never become that. And that was only if, she were given the offer to change. And only if, she accepted it.

"Yelena?" Daria's voice stirred her from her daydreaming.

Yelena did not avert her gaze from the crackling flames, her chin rested within the palm of her hand. "May I ask you both something?"

"Of course, dear."

"Would you wish for me to change into what you are?"

Silence settled around them. Only the crackling flames echoed around.

When Yelena tore her gaze from the fire, she found Danika stepping forth. "The gift of immortality is a heavy burden to bear." She spoke. "Are you truly prepared to shed your mortal flesh? To never grow old and experience life for what is has to offer? To outlive those, you love? Are you ready to accept such a fate?"

Yelena lowered her gaze, "I-I don't know..."

A gentle hand came to rest atop her own that was draped over her knee. Yelena lifted her eyes to meet Danika's once more. There was a sincerity there within the woman's irises, "I do not say this to hurt you, Yelena. But so, you know the burden of immortality and what you must leave behind when you accept this change." Danika gave her hand a gentle squeeze, "But if you're asking how we'd feel then know this; we shall have you no matter if you bear the skin of a mortal or immortal."

Daria stood at Danika's side, "You are part of our family."

Warmth kindled like a fire in Yelena's heart; to be given the gift of two families. "Thank you." She smiled.

∞ ∞ ∞

When the sun had laid to rest, sinking below the horizon, Yelena ventured forth into the castle. Daria and Danika had insisted on escorting her about, but Yelena ensured them she would be fine. While she wandered about, the feel of watching eyes followed her trail. Living within a castle of immortals quickly adjusted Yelena to them. Sensing when they were near, her skin bristling as if in warning. She said nothing to the women as they stalked through the shadows behind her. Paying them no mind as her thoughts began to drift. The windows throughout the castle had their curtains drawn back, allowing the night to creep within the stone walls. The pale moonlight filtering in. Yelena halted before a window, raising her hand into the beam of moonlight before her. Her pale skin seeming to illuminate.

If she chose to become immortal, this would be the only light she would ever know. Never to step beneath the sun's warmth again. Trapped within the life of night and shadows. She once thought of that as a curse. Being trapped within the darkness, never to see the light of day again. But that was not true. For night held a light all on its own. Silvery in serenity and blackened in tranquility.

The world was within Yelena's grasp, able to traverse the night while others slept, and the noise of the village faded into silence. The chirps of insects became a harmony within the night. Serenading the woman that looked down upon the world from her balcony each night. The darkness had become her light. Coming alive when the moon graced the sky and the stars twinkled against that inky blackness. Yelena had spent much of her time stargazing when the clouds weren't as thick.

As Yelena touched the moonlight, another presence lurked within the hall, watching her. When she finally tumbled forth from her thoughts, her gaze met with one of crimson and her skin bristled as Drezca stepped forth into a patch of silvery light. Yelena's hand fell from the air and rested at her side. Behind her, Daria and Danika moved to step forth, their steps echoing within the hall. But Yelena held out her arm, stopping them. They stilled behind her, watching Drezca with close eyes as the woman strode toward Yelena. A sway to her hips and a feral grin upon her lips. Drezca placed a hand upon her hip as she stood before Yelena and twirled a curly strand of hair around her finger. Yelena did not cower before the woman, merely matching her gaze. Drezca's grin widened.

Her gaze drifted down to Yelena's shoulder, "How's the wound, mortal? Healed yet? I know for your kind it takes some time."

She rolled her shoulder in answer, "Better than ever."

"So, I see." Drezca met her gaze again, "Allow me to apologize for how I acted. It was truly beastly of me and I swear it won't happen again. I know how fragile you mortals are."

Yelena blinked in disbelief. Her mouth gaping slightly in shock. But she was not so foolish to believe Drezca's hollow apology. There was a glint within those eyes and in the way her smirk curled venomously. Drezca was not sorry, and she never would be. It had merely been a warning.

This was not the end,

but merely the beginning.

Yelena offered a smile, "Thank you, Drezca. I tend to forget that *some* of your kind cannot tame their beastliness."

Drezca's smirk faltered, and a flicker of rage ignited within her eyes, but she quickly masked it, returning the bitter smile. "Yes, how truly monstrous we are." Casting her gaze passed Yelena, she addressed the two women lurking within the shadows. "Daria, Danika, always good to see you both."

The women stepped forth and stood by either side of Yelena. Daria narrowed her gaze upon Drezca, "And to you."

Where there was warmth and closeness was now replaced with bitterness and distance. When Yelena first arrived here the women were inseparable but with time, Drezca pulled away from them. And guilt rang out in Yelena for it was her blame for the friction created between them. Walls had been erected and it seemed there was no hope of bringing them down.

Drezca held Daria's gaze for a moment before she flicked it to Danika. The woman remained unmoving, her face set like stone. "I believe our ways part here."

And she did not just mean that they would travel to separate ends of the castle, but that the bond they once had shared dissipated within the air. For they had chosen a mortal over Drezca.

"It seems they do." Danika spoke.

Her voice echoing down the hall.

Drezca flinched as if she had been slapped. Danika had once clung to her but now stood apart from the woman. Yelena could see the pain in Drezca's eyes. Daria may have stung Drezca, but Danika shattered her. Something shifted in Drezca, in the way her eyes turned to ice and her lips pressed flatly together.

They had provoked the beast.

Drezca did not give a parting nod as she turned on her heel and vanished through a doorway. Yelena stared after the woman long after she had gone. Guilt swelled so high it threatened to drown her. Clogging her throat and choking her. If she had never come to this castle those women never would have fallen apart. There never would have been walls erected between them. They never would have chosen a mortal over their family. Yelena had not realized that she was crying till Danika stood in her vision. Tenderly the woman reached out and brushed away her shed tears.

"Why these tears?" She asked.

Yelena chewed her lip, "It's my fault."

"What is, dear?" Daria asked as she stood beside Danika.

Yelena shook her head, "For Drezca turning her back to you both. I'm sorry."

"Listen here," The sternness within Daria's voice rattled Yelena, "none of that is your burden to bear." A light sigh escaped the woman as she turned her gaze to the window, "We have known for quite some time, that this would come. We've been preparing for it, though we never wished for it to happen. We can only hope that Drezca shall come to her senses soon."

"She is no longer the woman we once knew." There was pain within Danika's voice as she spoke the unbearable truth aloud.

Daria took to Yelena's side and slipped her arm through the crook of her elbow. "Come, let's get those tears washed away."

Danika stood on the other side of Yelena, "You have nothing to fear while we are here."

Yelena dabbed at her tears, "Thank you, for all you've done for me."

Daria gave her arm a gentle pat and the three drifted through the halls.

∞ ∞ ∞

When they returned to Yelena's chambers, a servant was fetched to bring steaming tea for her. They vanished and returned in a matter of moments, carrying a silver tray with a lone kettle, cup, and a small dish of sugar cubes. Setting it atop the table, they bowed their head to Yelena and parted from the chamber swiftly, the doors closing quietly behind them. Yelena grabbed the warm handle and poured the steaming, brown liquid into the cup. Taking a few sugar cubes, she dropped them into the tea and leaned back into the couch, nestled before the crackling fire. She savored the warmth leaking from the porcelain cup and filling her palms. Closing her eyes, she lifted the tea to her lips and took a sip. Warmth spread through her being as it cascaded down her throat and into her belly, nesting like an ember in her pits, keeping her steadily warm.

Yelena had her fill of three more cups before a sigh escaped her lips, her belly swollen with tea. Daria and Danika bid her a goodnight before they swept from her chambers in a swarm of shadows and the doors creaked behind them. Changing into a sleeping gown and weaving her tresses together, Yelena strode into her bedchamber and climbed atop the plush mattress, nestling into the soft sheets. Laying on her side and tucking her hands beneath her cheek, Yelena tumbled into her dreams bathed in the pale light of the moon. But sweetness did not wait for her in her dreamland. Darkness lurked and it struck out once she stumbled into sleep.

A fiery beast lurked in the crevices of her dreams, stalking Yelena throughout her travels through the immense fog. Gooseflesh prickled along her arms as unease crept upon her. Yelena's blood ran cold when the sultry sound of mocking laughter echoed all around. Dancing along the frozen air. Yelena spun, her white hair rippling along the air like silvery waves. Her pale gown swishing at her ankles as her bare feet danced upon the chilling earth. The heart within her chest leapt and rattled the bars of its cage, wishing to break free. Yelena spun in each direction the laughter resounded from until the world blurred and her mind grew dizzy. As she stopped and stood in place, she found movement before her within the wisping shadows.

A silhouette stepped forth and fear truly struck Yelena's heart as she beheld Drezca. Her feline body bare to the world and bathed in crimson as if she had bathed in the blood of innocents. Her fiery tresses were a curled mess of tangles that swept passed her waist. A grin curled upon her lips and blood trickled from the corners, dribbling down her chin to her throat. Drezca lifted her arm, her forearm dripping in fresh blood. From the tips of her lengthened nails down her slender fingers, spilling upon the earth beneath her. Those burning eyes of crimson met with Yelena's and Drezca's grin widened. To Yelena's horror, she watched as the woman brought her bloodied hand to her mouth and watched as Drezca flicked her tongue out and tasted of the gore that stained her immortal flesh.

Drezca flashed her sharpened teeth in a grin, *"Run."*

And Yelena did not wait a moment longer. Spinning on her heel she bounded into the thick shadows with Drezca's laughter chasing after her. Though she knew it was futile to run, fear nipped at her heels, urging her faster. But the beast caught up with Yelena easily. A yelp escaped Yelena's lips as her scalp set aflame, her hair screeching in protest as she was dragged back. Losing her footing, Yelena fell to the ground on her back as Drezca dragged her along. She wrapped her hands around the roots of her hair and thrashed her legs, her screams echoing around and returning to her ears in mockery. When they returned to the small clearing, Drezca released her hold on Yelena's hair. Relieving her scalp for a moment before the woman stood over her.

Yelena was trapped with no hope of escape. She stared death in the face and knew it by name. Drezca sat upon Yelena's stomach and leaned close to her face, smiling like a feral feline. Yelena flinched away as the woman's hand came close to her face. So tenderly she stroked away the hairs that clung to the sweat of Yelena's neck. Her dampened fingertips tracing over the length of her pale skin, leaving trails of crimson. Yelena's breath stilled as Drezca traveled the expanse of her chest, coming to a halt just above her heart.

"This shall make a grand treat after I've drained every drop of blood from your veins." Drezca leaned down and her breath traced along the edge of Yelena's ear, "Dravmir was mine long before you strode into that castle and he shall be mine long after your dead."

Before Yelena could utter a word of a response, pain seared within her neck as Drezca plunged her fangs through her flesh. She felt as the blood was syphoned from her veins, feeling each pull as it filled Drezca's being. No matter how much Yelena thrashed against Drezca's hold, the monster did not budge. She could feel the smile on the woman's lips as she drained the blood from Yelena's body. Her vision begun to blur, the world becoming a grey mixture around her. Her mind was slipping, and her heart was losing its rhythmic beat. Yelena was dying. Death was sweeping in to claim her soul.

She did not know when Drezca had ceased her drinking but a forced gasp escaped Yelena's lips as pain seared through her chest. Her vision cleared for a moment to see a smiling beast staring down upon her with its hand plunged through her heart. With a turn of Drezca's wrist, she wretched the beating muscle from Yelena's chest. Before she faded into oblivion, she watched as Drezca lifted her heart to her lips and stole a bite from it as if it were an apple.

Yelena jolted from the dream as if a hand had reached into her consciousness and pulled her out. She sat up on her bed, her hands feeling across the expanse of her chest. Her heart remained within and it had only been a nightmare. But her heart did not calm so easily, roaring against her ears as she tried desperately to calm her breathing. Wiping the back of her hand across her brow, it came away dampened in a sheen of sweat. Shaking her head, she banished the lingering tendrils of the dream to the back of her mind and tossed away the sheets. Sleep would evade Yelena for some time, and she wished to escape the confines of her chambers. She knew Daria and Danika would be lurking close, so she felt secure enough to wander through the castle. Yelena had not a thought in mind as to where she was going, she was simply allowing her feet to guide her.

All was quiet within the stone walls, not a murmur could be heard echoing around. Yelena drifted about, through winding corridors and towering stairs until she found herself within one of the towers on the second floor. She was once again faced with the beautiful portraits Dravmir had painted of distant lands. As her eyes flitted from each painting, one had caused them to halt. A sky of violet above a sea of turquoise waves hung before Yelena. Her world stared back at her. Dravmir had kept his promise, allowing her land to join the others, creating their own world. Warmth kindled in her heart as a smile grew upon her lips.

As she made her way to the winding staircase that crept up the wall, she stalled at the base of the stairs. Hanging upon the wall beside Yelena, was the portrait Dravmir had painted of her while she mindlessly crafted her world upon canvas. Heat flushed her cheeks as she turned her eyes away from the portrait, her smile widening. Casting her gaze ahead, her sight traveled up the winding stairs that crawled up the rounded wall. Taking that first step up,

Yelena began her ascent to the next floor of the tower. Curiosity tugging her along as it grasped ahold of her hand. The polished railing was cool against her fingertips as they traced along it. Her feet softly sounded upon each step until she reached the final one and found herself standing before two, tall doors.

There was a pull within her chest, as if a string had been tied around her heart and the holder of the other end tugged from the other side of those doors. Reaching for the handles, she turned them and pulled open the doors. A light groan echoed down the stairs and a grand room was unveiled to Yelena. A crimson carpet adorned much of the polished marble flooring. A large bed was set upon a dais with curtains that matched the carpet draped down either side of it, spilling atop the stairs that rounded all around the dais. As her gaze drifted passed the wall of windows, she found a lone silhouette stood before a roaring fire in a grand fireplace. The mouth of the hearth stood taller than the Count. The light of the flames danced off the man, creating a wicked show of shadows cast over his form. When those crimson eyes met with hers Yelena found them afire in a burning glow. It was startling yet beautiful all at once.

Warmth crept along her cheeks when she realized that his torso was bare and loose, black trousers hung low at his narrow waist. His raven hair spilled down the length of his back like liquid night. Yelena quickly averted her gaze and bowed her head. "Apologies. I wasn't aware this was your chamber."

"It's alright, come in."

Yelena stepped into his chamber, the carpet plush against her bare feet. With a subtle flick of his wrist, the doors closed behind her. Yelena met his gaze and he greeted her with a smile, beckoning her to the fire. He swept his hand toward the red velvet cushioned chairs, offering for her to take a seat. Yelena nestled down onto the thick cushion. The warmth of the fire doused her in its comforting embrace. Dravmir did not move from where he stood, merely turning his body to face her though his gaze returned to the crackling flames.

"Apologies, I don't tend to keep wines or any such things in my chamber seeing as my kind does not partake in mortal substances."

Yelena smiled, "It is the thought that counts, so thank you."

A light chuckle escaped him, "If you wish, I can fetch a drink for you."

"No, no. Don't trouble yourself, I'm quite alright."

Dravmir nodded, "If you insist. Now, what brings you to my chambers?"

Her smile faltered then, and she averted her gaze to the flames, "Trouble sleeping, I suppose. My mind tends to be restless at times."

"I understand that all too well, I'm afraid." There was a solemn expression riddling the Count's face. A weariness stirring within his eyes. "Though we do not require sleep, it is one of few mortal traits we harbor. It has been too long since I've slept."

"Why have you not?"

"The nightmares wait."

Yelena tore her gaze from the fire but Dravmir's remained fixated, his brows furrowing. "I have known those myself." Her skin prickled as the memory of Drezca devouring her heart flickered within her mind.

The Count freed himself from the flames and took a seat in the other chair beside Yelena. "Are there any lingering curiosities that riddle your mind?"

As if answering his question, two thrones appeared within her thoughts. "The thrones. Did you once rule the land here? The village?"

There was a darkness within his eyes then. Dravmir rested his elbow upon the arm of the chair, his hand lingering close to his mouth as he rubbed his fingers together. "My kind once populated these lands and I ruled them with Annika by my side. Hundreds of vampires thrived here within these mountains and forest." His lips thinned, "But as the werewolves grew in number as well, there was much bloodshed and many of my people fled. All that remain of us are within these walls."

"Do you think the others will ever return?"

Dravmir somberly shook his head, "No."

Yelena reached across the space between them, her fingertips grazing his arm. "I'm sorry, Dravmir."

For a moment, his gaze flicked to her hand. Lowering his arm, he took her hand into his palm and gently began to trace patterns on her skin with his other hand. "Such remorse for my kind. A pure and true heart you have, Yelena." Dravmir turned her hand over, palm up, wrist exposed. Tenderly he traced the tip of his finger across the pale skin of her wrist.

His simple touch set afire beneath her skin. His fingers stoking it as they tenderly traced over the faint veins within her wrist. She cursed her thundering heart and prayed that her quickened pulse did not give her away. Though it was futile trying to tame the heat within her cheeks. And when Dravmir lifted her wrist to his lips an inferno scorched her soul as a kiss was pressed to her skin.

"There is no need to feel embarrassed."

The fire in her cheeks swelled. "You can tell?"

A soft chuckle escaped him as he lowered her hand from his lips but kept a gentle hold upon it, returning to tracing patterns on her skin. "There is a difference within the heartbeat. I have always been profoundly well at reading people, even when I was a mortal man."

"What were your mortal years like?" Her voice was soft amongst the crackling sounds of the flames.

The corner of his lip pulled into a faint smile of reminiscence. "I was quite the stubborn child, as my mother would tell me. But she loved me most ardently, my father as well. I longed for adventure. Setting off on quests I conjured in my young mind. Traversing the small thicket of forest outside our cottage in search of the grand dire wolf clan. Grabbing a stick, I imagined it to be a sword and cleaved the leader of the clan's head from its body. I plucked a rock and claimed my prize as the wolf's head."

Yelena smiled, "Quite the brave young man you were."

Dravmir chuckled, "I surely thought so." And then his laughter faded, "Soon enough my bravery turned into foolishness." His finger stilled its tracing on the back of her hand as his gaze drifted toward the fire. "When I was a man grown, I set off on an adventure into the mountains. I had heard tale of a monster that resided in the belly of the mountains and I wished for the victory of slaying the creature by my own hand. But it was he who had slayed my very soul. His sweetened words lured me into his trap. Speaking promise of immortal life and fathomless strength. And being the adventure seeking man I was, wishing to live a life of it, I accepted the offer. I did not know how cursed I truly would be until it was too late."

Dravmir's hand slipped from hers, setting it down upon the arm of the chair. His raven hair spilled down to curtain his face, shielding Yelena from his grief. Yelena's heart called out to him and she stood from her chair. Dravmir did not look up at her as he continued, "I remember the pain I felt when I first tried to step into the sun's light, how my screams echoed around me as if they were mocking me."

When Yelena reached for him, his hands grasped her wrists, stopping her. He held them gently, but she felt the tremble in his hands. "That monster that I met taught me how to feed on mortals and for a long time, I drowned myself in their blood alongside him."

"What stopped you?" She rasped.

"One day, it was as if I woke from a nightmare. I had. I was covered in the blood of mortals, my belly full of it. And I finally decided that I had had enough, I did not want to live that sort of life. So, I fled the mountains and traveled during the nights, hiding in caves during the day. And then, I came upon this castle, abandoned to time, and claimed it as my own. And though I did not wish to live the life I had once lived with that creature, taming the thirst was never easy."

His words slowly became more broken and rasped as his tale continued. Yelena lowered to her knees before him, his hands still cradling her wrists.

"Oftentimes a lone soul would wander forth from the village and I could not resist the call of their blood. The one thing that monster never told me was that once a mortal was bitten by a vampire and enough life beat within their hearts, then they too would become what I am. I couldn't bear to bring so many lives to an end after I fed, leaving them in pools of their own blood in the forest, hoping they would survive. But they would wake and come to this castle as a creature of night. Soon enough, our population grew as they began to turn people as well and then came the werewolves. Rivals to our kind, nature trying to right the wrongs I had done. They killed many of my people and in turn, I slaughtered them. My first bride was offered during such bloodshed and she died. The wars came to an end, but the battles still lurked – as they do now."

Dravmir's grip finally loosened, and Yelena slipped her hands passed his curtain of hair and cradled his cheeks. But still, he did not gaze upon her.

"It is by my own fault my brides have been killed. I never slaughtered an innocent soul from that village, but I turned them into what I am. The village believing them dead and soon enough began sending brides as peace offerings. If I had never accepted that monster's offer, if I had never come here and turned so many others, the werewolves would have never sought us out. *It is all my fault.*"

Warmth spilled over Yelena's eyes and trickled down her cheeks, "Dravmir, it is not your fault."

It was then he finally met her gaze and she found silver streams glistening upon his cheeks. "Cause and effect. If I had never of come here, never turned all those people into a monster then the wolves would never have felt threatened, never would have fought for this territory." Dravmir's lips trembled as another set of tears crested within his eyes, "I was responsible for the attacks, for cursing people, but never did I kill any soul from that village and yet each death that came, found itself upon my shoulders. For I brought the plague of vampires to this land. To the werewolves. To *your* people."

The cool touch of his tears spilled over Yelena's hands. She had thought she knew most of his aches, but he had unearthed another layer of sorrow. Dravmir was never a monster but a man who merely wished for adventure and got more than he had bargained for. Led astray by a monster who lived in darkness and drowned in the blood of mortals. But he had found his path, freed himself from the clutches of such wickedness. Realized the monster he was becoming and feared it, fled from it. He had fought it, against the thirst.

Yelena tilted his head up, his eyes finding hers once more. Gently, her thumbs brushed away his shedding tears. "You hold such a weight upon your soul for things that are out of your grasp, Dravmir. Do you not see the strength you have? The purity your heart harbors? You foresaw the monster that you would become, and you turned against it. You fought that thirst."

Dravmir shook his head in her palms, "I still partook in the blood of innocents, slaughtered their lives as if they were nothing. I was a beast. I do not deserve such kindness. Not from anyone. And especially not from you, Yelena."

"You may have been a monster once, Dravmir, but that is not who you are now."

A breath escaped him as he leaned into the warmth of her palms, "How could you sit there and not be disgusted by me? My actions? How you can you bear to touch me when my skin is tainted in my sins?" His brows furrowed as he closed his eyes, a lone tear freeing itself upon his cheek. *"How?"*

How could you possibly care for a beast such as I?

His thoughts whispered.

It seemed no matter what words whispered forth from her lips, they did not penetrate his barriers of guilt. Allowing her heart to guide her, Yelena rose from her knees, gaining his interest. His eyes curious as they watched her. Keeping her hands upon his cheeks, Yelena leaned down, lowering her head to his. Dravmir did not move, becoming a statue in her grasp. He dared not move as her breath danced across his lips. She held his gaze, searching for any rejection lingering in those red irises. What she found instead, was that same yearning she felt burning inside her reflected in his eyes. Warmth pooled in her chest and belly as her eyes fluttered closed and she pressed her lips to Dravmir's.

Heat burst throughout her veins as their lips locked. Dravmir relaxed and reached for the woman, his hands gripping her hips. Yelena closed the distance between them as she crawled into his lap, straddling him. The passion that burned in her very being was nearly overwhelming, having never felt this sort of intensity before. Dravmir's hand traced up the length of her spine and found itself cradling the back of her head, his fingers gathering her tresses. A softened sound escaped Yelena as his other hand slid down her hip and gripped it. Her body flushed as she pressed herself against him. Her nipples hardening and a wave of embarrassment washed over, knowing that Dravmir felt them against his chest.

He broke their kiss long enough to say, "Do not be embarrassed." And his lips met hers once more.

Yelena's hands slid from his cheeks, one tangling itself in his raven tresses, and the other tracing down his chest until her palm flattened above his immortal heart. She relinquished herself to her heart, allowing it to guide her limbs and control them like a puppeteer. Her body growing a mind of its own as it began to grind against the Count. A pleasured growl rumbled against her fingertips as it resounded in his chest. The sound stirred the warmth that brewed between her legs. A gasp escaped her lips as she felt his hardened need grow beneath her. Dravmir's grip on her hip trembled as if he could hardly contain himself. Their lips parted as Dravmir's mouth trailed the expanse of her neck. Kissing her soft and flushed skin. Yelena leaned her head back, a heavy breath leaving her as that burning need swelled to an unbearable suspense.

Dravmir's hands slid to her back, steadying her as his lips trailed down to her chest, pressing a kiss to her thundering heart. A shudder trembled down her spine as Dravmir's teeth traced across the plunged neckline of her sleep gown, nipping it, and tugging the fabric down to expose her breasts to the world. They were tinged in blush, her nipples hardened. Dravmir placed a kiss atop each breast before taking a nipple into his mouth, suckling upon it. A gasped cry escaped her lips as he tenderly nibbled on it, his tongue flicking at mercilessly. The pleasure that burst in Yelena caused her body to tremble against him. Her hands grasped at the man, her fingers wrapping around his bicep while her other hand wound into his hair. Yelena's body had never known such touch, such affection. The passion that surged through her was mind-numbing yet welcomed. Wishing to indulge herself in the fires of pleasure that swelled in her core. Dravmir fondled her breast as his lips moved to the other, giving it the same attention.

Yelena could hardly contain herself, her voice echoing around the room as she moved against his hardness. Heat swelled in her core and spilled out, soaking her sleep gown, and dampening his trousers. Her pleasure vanished as mortification claimed her. Dravmir's lips left her breasts to gaze upon her but Yelena allowed her tresses to curtain her face, shielding herself from his heavy eyes. She had wished to vanish from this room, from this world. Gently, his hand brushed aside her hair and yet, she still could not bring herself to meet his gaze.

"My Yelena," His voice was velvety and tender to her ears, "it is a natural response to arousal. It is nothing to be embarrassed by." Dravmir braced his hands against her back and pulled her closer, causing her to finally meet his eyes, "And I find it quite arousing."

Dravmir kissed her neck as one of his hands slid down her back to cradle her backside in his palm. "I-I've never..." Her words were breathless as the pleasure returned, claiming her mind, giving herself over to it. Becoming a slave to passion. Yielding her body to him.

Dravmir lifted his head and cradled her cheek, stroking his thumb against her flushed skin. "I swear to be gentle with you and if you wish for me to stop, then I shall. No questions asked. If you wish to lay with me tonight, the choice is yours, Yelena."

She took in a breath and leaned into his palm. Steadying her nerves, she steeled her gaze. "I want you, Dravmir. Tonight, and always."

"Then I am yours."

"As I'm yours." She spoke.

There was a spark within those red eyes as she proclaimed those words. So simple to any other listening ears but profound to theirs. Claiming one another and no other. He was hers and she was his. Dravmir held Yelena as he stood from the chair, her legs wrapping around him as he carried her to the large bed. The mattress let out a soft sigh as Dravmir lay Yelena down. For a moment, the two held one another's eyes as if neither of them could believe this was more than a dream. Yelena's hands palmed his cheeks and smiled. So brilliant and pure that Dravmir could have sworn his heart beat for the first time in centuries. Happiness truly blossomed in his heart and soul, tilled by the gentle hands of this woman as she tended to the soil in his garden. Coaxing the once dead flowers to bloom once more, thawing the winter that once claimed him.

Dravmir returned the smile and feathered his lips against hers. The two soon becoming lost within the bliss of each other. Dravmir was careful to be delicate with her, her mortal flesh easily bruised if he did not control his strength if he did not lose control of himself. His hands roamed the expanse of her body. Coaxing the gown from her limbs and tossing it aside. Yelena's hands tugged at the hem of his trousers, urging them down. Her eagerness matched his own. Neither of them capable of containing their arousal. But Dravmir grasped ahold of her hands and lifted them above her head. Their kiss never broke, and Yelena did not protest against his hold, lifting her leg and caging him to her. The sweetest of moans escaped her moist lips as Dravmir teased her wetness. Grinding his hips into her, the bulge of his erection tempting the heat in her core. His trousers becoming damp from the sweetness that poured from her. Arousing the beast within him. The temptation tantalizing. His mind becoming a haze of thoughts as he gave himself entirely to Yelena. And she gave herself to him.

Dravmir's lips ventured from hers and traveled down the pale length of her body. Leaving a fiery trail of kisses upon her skin as he ventured further. Dravmir came to her womanhood, a silvery thatch of hair sprouted like a garden. He flicked his eyes up to find hers watching him and with a grin, he began to pleasure her. Yelena's head fell back onto the bed as a gasping moan escaped her lips. Her hips were restless against his mouth as he drank in her sweetness, his tongue slipping inside her and stoking that fiery pleasure in her core. The feel of her fingers in his air aroused Dravmir as they burrowed into his tresses. Unable to contain herself as she gave over to that pleasure.

Yelena's eyes burst open as an orgasm captured her body. She shuddered against Dravmir as a river poured forth and cascaded down his throat like a waterfall. Her legs quivered as he rose from her womanhood, his lips glistening in her arousal. Her chest rose and fell as heavy breaths escaped her. And there was no denying that spark in her crystalline eyes. That passion, that desire, that burned so fiercely. Yelena reached for him as he crawled atop her, her hands capturing his face and dragging him down to her. Their lips crashed together in a feverish need. A shudder coursed down Yelena's spine as Dravmir's hardened need brushed against that sensitive spot. Her wetness soaking the trousers he wore, and Yelena wished she could tear the damned fabric apart and feel him against her.

In her.

The thoughts that swarmed Yelena's mind startled her for she had never experienced such a burning passion before. That yearning for another. But she wished to burn in this moment, in him. She wanted Dravmir, every inch of him. From his soul to his heart to that hardened need that swelled against her. As if he could read her mind, one of his hands gingerly traced down the length of her body before it found itself near her womanhood. A gasp escaped Yelena's lips against his as he began to massage that tender spot, the one that would send her mind and body teetering over the edge. Yelena opened her legs to him, spreading herself so he may enter. One of his fingers slid between her dampened lips and teased her opening before slipping inside, causing a moan to escape Yelena. There was a slight tinge of pain, but she hardly paid it any mind. Another moan escaped Yelena as another finger slid inside. Dravmir moved them gently at first, almost as if he were teasing her, but then they moved so fiercely her back arched from the bed as the pleasure overcame her and she burst once more, coating his hand. Breathless gasps escaped Yelena as her back fell into the mattress once more.

Dravmir merely smiled at her as he lifted his glistening fingers to his mouth and tasted of her. Warmth stirred in her belly as she watched him clean his fingers of her arousal. Dravmir then leaned over her and braced a hand beside her head on the bed and cradled her cheek in his other. His thumb gently stroked her skin.

"Are you ready?" His voice was a low rasp, velvety and sweet to her ears.

Yelena swallowed and nodded her head, "I am."

"If it becomes too much, tell me."

"I will."

Dravmir pressed his lips to hers before he lifted from the bed and finally removed his trousers. A dark thatch of hair loomed above his hardened need. Yelena admired the girth of him and feared it all at once. Their eyes held and she knew he would stop if the pain was too much. She trusted him. She gave a subtle nod of her head and Dravmir positioned himself between her legs. A small sound escaped her as the tip of his cock brushed against her opening. Dravmir hesitated, seeming ready to pull away from her but she reached for him. Her hands finding his cheeks, bringing him down to her. Dravmir held her eyes and she smiled at him, nodding her head. She was ready. As he began to slide inside her, Yelena brought his face down to hers, sealing her lips over his. Yelena did not wish for him to see the pain in her eyes, did not wish for him to feel guilty for any ache she felt. Her eyes closed as she kissed him. Tingles of pain sparked through her as Dravmir began to fill her. A rupture of pain singed her core and a gasp freed itself from her throat. It was then that Yelena knew, Dravmir was fully inside of her.

Delicately, his fingertips traced over her cheek, brushing aside a strand of hair, and tucking it behind her ear. "Are you alright, Yelena?"

"I am." She spoke breathless.

And before he could speak, she pressed her lips to his and Dravmir surrendered himself to her and to that passion. It was slow at first, easing himself into her before pulling back and filling her once more. The two soon learned the rhythm of one another. Their bodies seeming to mold against each other, fitting as if they were pieces of a puzzle. The pain became a numb sensation and then pleasure overcame Yelena's being. Her core sweltering in need. Dravmir's pace had quickened, feverishly thrusting inside of her faster and faster. Her hips rocking against him as her moans filled the air. Dravmir could hardly contain himself, one of his hands rested above her head. His fingers curled fiercely into the sheets, threatening to the shred them to pieces as he thrusted into Yelena faster. He nestled his head into the nape of her neck, nipping at her skin, careful not to break the surface and spill her blood. Her pulse thundered against his lips as her heart raced in her chest. Yelena's sweetened sounds echoed in his ears and stoked his pleasure.

The feel of Yelena's nails raking down the length of his back caused a growl to rumble in his chest. *"Yelena..."* His voice rasped, a growl coating his words.

And she cried out the sweetest of sounds. One that spoke his name upon her moist lips. Her voice a symphony of moans as their bodies became one. The feel of her swollen breasts pressed against his chest coaxed him over the edge. Her hardened nipples teasing him. Pleasure claimed his body as a shudder trembled down his spine. A grunted moan echoed from Dravmir's throat as he spilled his seed into Yelena. And since he was no mortal man, it would never take root in her womb. Dravmir lifted his head from her neck, noticing the bites he left on her pale skin, he had been careful not to pierce her flesh with his fangs.

When he met her gaze, he found such warmth kindling within those crystalline eyes. A tender smile written upon her lips. "How are you, my bride?" His fingers stroked her cheek.

She reached for him and tucked his hair behind his ear, "Marvelous."

A soft chuckle escaped Dravmir, "And I shall say the same." He grasped ahold of her hand and pressed a kiss into her palm, "Allow me to fetch you a washcloth."

With a swift motion, Dravmir hurried from the chamber in a blur but returned before Yelena could miss him. He strode forth from the doorway across the room, hidden in the shadows, holding a washcloth. Yelena scooted to the end of the bed, seating herself on the edge of it, her feet dangling in the air. Dravmir knelt before her and gently coaxed her legs open, and it was then she noticed the smearing of blood between her thighs. She dared a glance at Dravmir's manhood and found blood had stained him. Panic scorched her chest and mortification flushed her cheeks. Gently, Dravmir placed his hand on her knee, drawing her eyes to his.

"Does it hurt?" There was pain in his voice, his eyes brimming in agony.

Yelena shook her head, "No, I'm alright." She dared a glance over her shoulder and found darkened spots in the bedsheets. Guilt swelled in her as she faced Dravmir again, "I-I'm terribly sorry about the sheets."

"My bride, there is no need to apologize. It happens during a woman's first time." Dravmir was tender as he began to wash away the lingering blood that clung to her skin.

"Does it bother you? The blood?" She asked as she watched his hand wipe at her thighs.

He merely shook his head, "No. Not anymore."

Yelena cast her gaze down into the palms of her hands, a curiosity stirring in her mind and a hint of fear. "Dravmir, may I ask you something?"

"You may always ask me something, Yelena."

She cleared her throat, "Would you still have me if I decided to remain mortal?" Yelena hated that warmth brewed behind her eyes, readying herself for the rejection she may face.

Dravmir set aside the washcloth after he had cleaned himself and grasped her hands, but she could not bring herself to look into his eyes. Fearing what she would find. Dravmir lifted a hand, reaching for her. His fingers slid beneath her chin and tilted her head up, meeting her worried eyes. "Yelena, no matter what you choose, I shall always have you. You are my bride." His hand lowered from her chin as he lifted hers to his lips and pressed a kiss to her knuckles. "I will worship you until the end of time, Yelena."

His voice was so gentle as he spoke her name. It was like a whispered prayer from his lips, as if it were meant for the Gods' ears to hear. It was an oath to them, to her. The ultimate promise. A declaration of his devotion to her whether she was mortal or choose to walk at his side as an immortal. He would have her. And she would have him. As silver begun to line her eyes, she tossed her arms around him and clung to him. For a moment, they sat there wrapped within one another's embrace. Yelena had never felt more at home than she did in Dravmir's arms. Her place was here, in this castle, with him. The grand adventure she had been seeking all those years unraveled before her. This was what she had been seeking and she would follow this path until her mortal heart ceased its beat. And perhaps long after then.

Dravmir gathered Yelena in his arms and lifted her onto the bed. Once he laid her down and the bed sighed as he lay next to her, Yelena rested her head upon his chest. Her arm draped across his stomach. Dravmir had pulled the blanket over her bare form and begun tracing patterns on her back. His cold fingers trailing down the length of her spine and up again. Yelena allowed her eyes to close and fell into the deep pits of sleep. Allowing it to claim her as she tumbled into a land of dreams wrapped in Dravmir's arms.

Fast asleep, Dravmir gently pressed a kiss to the crown of her head. "Sweetest of dreams, my love." His voice murmured.

And though Yelena was fast asleep, his words had whispered through her ears and echoed across her violet skies. She smiled, *And to you, my Count.*

Yelena's dreams were the sweetest they had ever been.

CHAPTER FIFTEEN

The Kiss of Death

YELENA SLEPT WHILE the sun greeted the world. Pouring its golden light upon every spec of life it could find. But it did not penetrate the stones of the castle nor the thick drapes that concealed the sun's harmful rays. Yelena had been captured within the warmth of her dreams, by the sun that brightened her land and skies. And here within her dreams, Dravmir walked at her side beneath the golden light of the sun, unburnt. Basking in those dazzling rays as they stood before the turquoise waves of the ocean, lapping at their bare feet, and foaming upon the sand. Yelena could taste the salt that tinged the air and filled her lungs and she happily breathed it in. The breeze from the sea tousled their tresses, trailing them along the gentle wind in dark and light wisps. It was so serene here, Yelena wishing to never leave this dream behind her. But she knew the Count waited for her in the waking world.

When her eyes opened, she found a crimson gaze upon her. Dravmir lay on his side, his head nestled in his palm. Those raven tresses tousled from sleep and spilled over one shoulder, sweeping across the bedsheets between them. Dravmir merely smiled as his other hand continued to brush through her silvery tresses. Yelena turned over on her side and tucked a hand beneath her cheek, reaching the other toward him and tracing her fingertips down the center of his chest. This was far better than any dream her mind could conjure. Within the waking world, Dravmir was tangible. Where as in her dreams, he felt too light, no weight to ground him. But here, now, he was solid against her fingers. He was here, with her and her smile widened.

"How long have you been awake?" Her voice was groggy from the lingering traces of sleep.

"Since nightfall." He answered.

"Why didn't you wake me?"

Dravmir brushed her hair behind her ear, "You looked too peaceful to disturb so I waited till you woke."

"Such a gentleman." Yelena closed the distance between them, her hand reaching up to cradle his cheek.

With a smile, Dravmir leaned down and feathered a kiss to her lips. "I'm sure you're famished; I shall fetch a servant to bring you some food and have a bath drawn for you."

He kissed her once more before he slid from the bed, gathered his trousers from the floor and quickly slipped into them. Dravmir vanished through the doors and returned moments later. Yelena had grabbed her discarded nightgown from the floor and dressed herself in the wrinkled fabric. Dravmir crossed the room and stood before her, his hands tenderly grasping her waist and drawing her close. Her hands came to rest upon his bare chest as she beamed at him.

"The food shall be brought to your chambers; a servant is drawing a bath for you as we speak."

"Thank you, Dravmir."

He leaned down and pressed a kiss to her forehead, "Anything for my bride."

∞ ∞ ∞

Dravmir had swept Yelena off her feet and carried her through the castle swiftly, the shadows gathering and writhing all around them, blurring the edges of her vision with darkness. When they stood before her chamber doors, Dravmir opened them and carried her over the threshold before setting her upon her feet. The Count kissed her, wrapping her tenderly within his embrace before he left her chambers. The doors closed behind him and he had taken the warmth with him, leaving a hollow feeling within Yelena's chest. Her hand clutched above her heart as she realized the emotions that wakened within her. Yelena was a stranger to romance, never knowing its name. But coming to this castle, it had greeted her unexpectedly but welcomed it now. Allowing her heart to feel what it must, guiding Yelena to the Count.

Turning her back to the doors, she found a silver tray of food waiting, as promised. As she nestled down and readied to eat, there were knocks upon her doors. "Come in." She called, removing the silver dome from her tray.

Daria and Danika strode into the room, smiles upon their faces as they stood before the fire. "Good evening, Yelena." Daria spoke.

"Good evening to you both." And she dug into the gravy and biscuits that steamed upon the porcelain plate before her.

Yelena kept her gaze down, knowing why both women strutted into her chambers smiling. Her cheeks flushed with warmth as she kept herself distracted with the food. Slowly nibbling at it and taking slow drinks of the crisp water. But she could not drag this out forever, her plate becoming bare and her glass running dry. Yelena gathered herself and lifted her head, facing the women that seemed to eagerly await the details of her shared night with the Count. Their gazes became too heavy, and she flicked hers to the writhing flames in the fireplace.

"Apologies, Yelena. It's just been so long since we've seen Dravmir so... *happy.* It's truly infectious." Daria said.

"It has been too long since he last smiled." Danika added. "He does it often now."

Warmth simmered in her heart as she smiled to the flames. "He is a wonderful man."

"And you are a wonderful woman, Yelena." Daria said. "There is a warmth to the castle that has not been here in many years."

"You have brought an end to our eternal winter." Danika added.

Yelena shook her head, "I'm just a mortal, I haven't done much."

Daria closed the distance between them and tilted Yelena's head up, "Do not undermine yourself, Yelena. Mortal or not, you can do extraordinary things."

"Thank you, Daria." She smiled.

And she smiled back, "Always, dear."

∞ ∞ ∞

A servant had to be summoned to heat the water in Yelena's bath. Pouring a bucket into the cooled bath. Yelena thanked the servant and they hurried away, closing the door, and leaving her alone. The nightgown pooled around her feet and she lifted one foot into the tub, dipping a toe in to test the water. Perfect. Yelena eased her body into the bath and relaxed her aching limbs. Resting her head against the back, she closed her eyes, taking in deep breaths. The scent of lavender filled her senses. The warm water helped unwind her muscles. Her legs still throbbed slightly when she walked, and she wondered how long until her body grew accustomed to love making. At the thought, a wave of warmth flushed her being. Memories began to surface, of bodies intertwined. Heavy breaths and gasping names moaning from dampened lips.

That night was something that felt like a dream and Yelena found it hard to believe that it had been reality, that it was not something her mind had conjured to mock her. Her hand drifted toward her lips, her fingers tracing over them, remembering the feel of Dravmir's lips pressed to hers. Then her fingers traced down to her neck, remembering how tenderly he had nipped at her skin. Careful not to pierce her mortal flesh. Dravmir had been so delicate with her, as if he feared breaking her. Were mortals truly so fragile? Or were immortals all too powerful? A sigh escaped her as she sat up in the bath, curling her knees to her chest and wrapping her arms around them.

Would Dravmir truly have her if she chose to remain mortal? Yelena lifted her hands and stared into her palms. But did she truly wish to remain mortal or was the call of immortality beginning to entice her? With a sigh, Yelena shook her head and stood from the water. She was in desperate need of a space to clear her thoughts and consider the paths laid before her. And there was one room within the castle that would offer such.

Charlotte.

∞ ∞ ∞

Comfort and warmth greeted Yelena once those doors opened and golden light spilled over her, as if the sun had been captured within this room. Charlotte bustled about while Yelena lounged on the couch, watching the woman sort through piles of fabrics. Charlotte muttered to herself about how some of the colors were absolutely atrocious. Yelena could not help but smile as she watched the woman dance around, seeming crazed as she organized her fabrics. There was a pile of discarded pieces, small cuts and trimmings left forgotten.

Yelena propped an elbow on the arm of the couch and rested her chin in her palm, "Where do you acquire all these fabrics?"

Charlotte grabbed a large piece of material. "Dravmir conducts business with the village." She folded the sequined fabric, "That's how we have food to feed you, since we don't indulge in such things."

Yelena supposed she guessed as such but to know Dravmir had been in contact with the village, caused an ache to form. She missed her family dearly and hoped that one day soon, she would see them again. "How does it work?"

Charlotte flitted to the large expanse of shelved fabrics and tucked the folded piece neatly in a shelf atop others. "A group of servants and Dravmir go to the village gates with a cart and the village elders fill it with whatever needs he requests. And then they hurry back here before the werewolves can attack."

"Does he pay them?"

Charlotte returned to the pile of fabrics, "Of course. When he found this castle, its riches had also been left to dust. There's plenty here for centuries." Charlotte grabbed a wooden box and flipped up the silver latch. She bent over and gathered the trimmings into the box. "I've found many of these fabrics within the forgotten rooms here in this castle, the ones that lurk just below us. Though I wouldn't recommend going down there, it's quite dirty and you'd ruin your gowns." A sigh escaped her, "I mistakenly ventured down there in a white dress, I never could get the stains out of that beautiful fabric."

A light laugh escaped Yelena and Charlotte joined her as she continued along with the fabric sorting. Yelena began to drift away watching Charlotte. The woman becoming a blur of shadows. Allowing her eyes to close, she lost herself within the serenity of the room, the warmth and comfort it offered her. Clearing her mind and easing the thoughts that raced about. Yelena could see two clear paths before her as she eased through the fog of her mind. One was made of the earth, tree roots rippled through the dirt. She took notice of the trees that lined the path. The ones at the beginning bloomed with life, rich emerald leaves sprouted from the branches. But as the trees continued, they began to whither one by one as death claimed them. The path that led to her mortality. The beautiful stages of life set before her. From youth to old age. Yelena could not help but wonder how old age would warp her soft skin. How her face would wrinkle with time. And she knew at the end of this path, her family would be waiting.

She cast her gaze to the other path. This one was crafted of cobblestone. Smoothed rocks laid out before her and she knew what waited at the end of this path. Immortality and the castle with Dravmir waiting upon the stairs with his hand outreached to her. And standing around him was her other family, those she had come to know during her stay at the castle. Those she had come to care for deeply. Yelena could picture herself, frozen in time. Her skin never touched by age. Wrinkles would never crease her eyes, laugh lines to show the joy throughout her life would never form. She would be eternally youthful on the outside but age within as the years passed her by. And then, that dreaded thought whispered through her mind. Would she be driven mad by the thirst for blood? Would she be able to resist, or would she fall victim to its call and drown in the blood of innocents?

Yelena was stuck at that fork in her path. Torn between both lives that waited for her. Each one pulling at her heart, tempting her forth. As she made to step forth, a knocking sounded and brought Yelena forth from her thoughts. Charlotte flitted toward the doors and opened them, and Yelena felt her heart drop into her stomach. Standing at the threshold was Drezca. Those piercing eyes found hers instantly and a smile curled poisonously upon her lips. Yelena swallowed down her fear and steeled her gaze, keeping her chin high. Drezca seemed to smirk.

"Needing something stitched?" Charlotte asked.

Drezca flicked her gaze to the woman, "No. Dravmir sent me to fetch Yelena." Her eyes met Yelena's again. "He has a surprise for you."

Yelena wished he had sent Daria or Danika. But she stood from the couch and smoothed out the wrinkles in her dress. Clasping her hands before her, she approached the doors. "Then let's not keep him waiting." She said.

Drezca arched a brow, "Yes, let's not."

"Thank you for having me, Charlotte." Yelena said as she crossed the threshold.

Charlotte smiled, "Of course, you're welcome anytime."

And then, the doors closed.

Drezca towered over Yelena, "Shall we?"

Yelena matched her gaze, "We shall."

Drezca closed the distance between them, causing Yelena to stumble back into the doors. "But I must carry you if we wish to be there quickly. Since you mortals are quite slow."

Before Yelena could protest, Drezca swept her into her arms and the hallway became a blur of shadows as Drezca carried her through the castle. Yelena sealed her eyes. The blurring world caused her stomach to churn. Reluctantly, she clung to Drezca as the woman hurried through the castle and into the night. A chill shuddered her body as the cold air embraced her. The wind roared against her ears and whipped her tresses about, snagging them. But if she listened closer, she could have sworn the wind was whispering warnings. And fear churned sickly within her stomach. It was then that a third path opened before her and it was one that led to her death.

The air shifted and the taste of salt touched Yelena's tongue. "Where are you taking me?" She demanded.

"Don't worry, little moral, your surprise will arrive soon enough."

And Yelena knew what her surprise was.

What waited for her.

Death.

The sound of crashing waves greeted Yelena's ears; the pungent smell of salt filled her lungs as she breathed it in. The world began to clear as the shadows faded away and the wind ceased its roaring in her ears. Before them, the earth halted at a cliff's edge, the sea lurking just below. Hollowing as if the waves tried desperately to reach up and grasp the two women and drag them down into its depths. Drezca carried Yelena to the edge and dropped her as if she were nothing. A rush of air escaped her lips as her back smacked into the ground. Drezca merely smirked at Yelena as she scrambled to her feet. As she looked into those red eyes, Yelena saw Drezca's true intentions. Death lurked within those cursed irises and she would revel in Yelena's blood. She had been a fool to follow Drezca from that room, but would she have snatched her anyways? Carried her far away before Charlotte could stop her?

Yelena was powerless against the immortal before her. Cruelly reminding Yelena how mortal she was. But she would not allow Drezca the pleasure of her fear. Yelena straightened her spine and narrowed her gaze. Drezca seemed to admire her strength but she could see mockery dancing within the curve of her lips. Drezca stole a step closer, and Yelena retreated one back. The edge of the cliff coming dangerously close. A few more stolen steps and Yelena would tumble down into the ravenous waves below and be swallowed by the ocean she had yearned to see for so many years. She would soon be in the belly of it. Thunder roared overhead; lightening crackled across the sky. A light shower of rain began to drench the world, the wind stirring it about. It was as if the world was mourning the loss of Yelena's life before it ever left her veins.

"Why are you doing this, Drezca?" Her voice hardly rose above the sound of the thundering clouds.

"In my mortal years I was to be wed to the man I loved." There was a shift within her eyes, her smile faltering as she tumbled into the rage of her memories. "But my cousin stole him from me. I fled into the forest heartbroken by those I loved most. But then, Dravmir found me, and I saw no other except him. I pled for him to change me and so, he did." Her lips curled back as a snarl formed, "I thought I was to be his, but he held no interest in me. And then, those foolish elders sent a mortal woman to his doorstep and he became enraptured with her."

For a moment, Yelena felt sorrow for Drezca. That sort of betrayal buried hatred deep within one's soul. Her trust had been destroyed by those she loved, and Yelena could not imagine the agony she felt. "You hold a grudge against me for something that others have done to you. Tell me, Drezca, how does that help your pain?"

Those crimson eyes snapped back to her, "Killing you will free Dravmir from the chains of you. From your foolish love and he shall be mine." Her smirk returned and she stalked forth, urging Yelena closer to the edge, "Allow me to confess my greatest sins before you perish." Pleasure dripped in her voice for she had been proud of the sins she committed.

Yelena gasped as her foot met the edge of the cliff, nearly toppling over into the waiting waves. "What are they?" Yelena wished to draw this out, to distract Drezca long enough that Dravmir would go searching for her. Yelena prayed to the Gods that he would find her before it was too late.

Drezca reached out and Yelena flinched as the woman coiled a strand of silvery hair around her finger. "I murdered his brides." She met Yelena's gaze, "I murdered your mother."

The breath was stolen from her lungs.

Her mind reared.

"W-What?"

She laughed, "I make their deaths seem like those beasts mauled his brides, but it was me all those years, all those decades. You mortals had a fondness for running away, making it all too easy to fabricate lies surrounding your deaths."

"Then why do the werewolves hate your kind so much? Why do villagers turn up mutilated at our gates?"

Drezca released the strand of hair and reached for Yelena's face. She stiffened beneath her touch as her fingers grazed across her cheek. "They hate our kind for intruding on their land, but I ensure they keep their hatred burning bright. I go out and hunt the smallest beast I can find and slaughter it, leaving it to be found in a mess of limbs and blood. The beasts mostly hate me, trying to hunt me down. But they're never fast enough." She smiled, amused with herself. "As for the mortals, I fed on them. Any who stumbled forth through those gates at night fell victim at my feet. And once I had drank my fill, I tore them apart."

Yelena's stomach churned, "All this death for a man that doesn't love you?"

And Yelena regretted those words as soon as they escaped her lips. A fiery rage simmered within Drezca's eyes. *"He has been blinded and poisoned by you mortals."*

Yelena made to back away but there was nowhere to flee. She dared a glance behind her and found jagged rocks waiting at the bottom of the cliff, the waves sprayed against them. And it was then she knew that time had run out. The paths she once saw vanished, swallowed by the shadows that crept forth, leaving only one. And it led to death. A lone tear shed from her eye, rolling down her cheek before falling to the sea below. Yelena would never see her family again. Dravmir would shatter and return to that cold man he once was. She had not known their time together had been limited. But she was thankful for the time they shared. She only wished she could tell him that.

When she faced Drezca again, a sharpened pain seared across her chest. As if flames had been unleashed upon her and simmered within her veins. Warmth trickled from the wounds and spilled down her pale gown, staining it in her blood. Four gashes cut across her chest and pierced her left breast. A scream ripped through her throat, threatening to shred her voice apart. Drezca stood before her, laughing at her pain. Her hand soaked in her blood, trickling down her arm. Her pale skin like a canvas and Yelena's blood had been the paint.

Yelena gathered her breath, "I-I never told Dravmir what you did to me." Her hands pressed to her wounds, desperately trying to cease the blood pour.

Desperately trying to find any sort of remorse in the woman before her. Any shred of kindness if any still lingered in her immortal heart. If there was any mortality in the woman.

Drezca tilted her head, "How foolish on your part."

Yelena had been wrong.

A fool.

Pain laced through her shoulder as Drezca plunged her nails into her flesh once more. Darkened blots began to fill her vision. The world becoming a blur around her. Fog crept into her thoughts, her mind teetering over the edge much like her feet were. Yelena grasped ahold of the woman's wrists, but her strength was wavering. Survival urged her to fight but how could she? Drezca was an immortal with the strength of centuries at her side. There was no chance as death crept ever closer. Waiting and watching for Yelena to tumble over the edge and plunge to the sharp rocks that waited below.

Drezca pulled Yelena close, her lips tracing over her ear as she said, "I would drain the blood from your veins but that would give me away." She wretched her hand free and a shriek escaped Yelena.

"Why..." She panted through the pain.

Drezca smiled, "Because," and she braced a hand against Yelena's chest, "the beasts are the ones that killed you."

And shoved.

Yelena's screams echoed across the raging waves. Her gaze locked with Drezca's as she plummeted through the air, the wind roaring against her ears. The woman smiled over the cliff's edge, watching Yelena's downfall into

Death's waiting arms. Tears flooded from her eyes as the faces of her family blurred before her eyes. She had forgotten her pain as she lost herself in the memories of them. Their laughter echoed through her mind as they all sat together for one last meal. Prepared by her sister's gentle hands. Her mother and father lovingly teasing her about her daydreaming. And the last face to greet her before she met with Death was Dravmir's. A final tear shed into the world as she closed her eyes and accepted her fate. The path of her death had reached its end.

There was a sharp crack in her spine as her body collided into the rocks. Warmth spilled and matted into her hair on the back of her head. And somehow, the fall had not killed her, not yet. Her final moments would be spent in agony. And she could have sworn she heard Drezca's laughter over the rain. She felt the droplets pelt her face but nothing more. Her body was numb from the neck down. All she felt was the throbbing ache in the back of her skull. Her final moments she would spend feeling nothing and everything all at once. How cruel. The waves sprayed at her body, washing away the blood only for it to spill forth once more. Salt tasted on her lips and tongue, trickling into her nose, and burning her throat as the waves crashed against the rocks once more.

Would she drown or bleed to death?

Time would only tell.

Yelena had wished for a grand adventure but never wished for such an unpleasant end. Her adventure had hardly begun before it was ripped from her grasp, dangled before her in mockery before it was snatched back as she reached out for it. Causing her to stumble over the edge and fall into the darkness that lurked. Yelena wanted to laugh at her own irony. How long had she yearned to see the sea with her own eyes? And now she had, in the cruelest of ways. She lay dying and crippled as the waves jolted her body in icy splashes.

"*Danna...*" She rasped.

"*Mother... father...*" She chanted like a prayer.

"*Dravmir...*" She wept.

There was a rustle within the wind.

She could have sworn her body was moved.

Perhaps the God of Death had come to fetch her.

And then,

"I'm here, my love."

Yelena wanted to laugh. How cruel could fate be? How unhinged had her mind become from the blood loss? It teased her with his voice, with a promise to live. How utterly cruel fate could be. Yelena indulged herself in the illusion. If her final moments were of Dravmir then she could pass from this world in a state of bliss. She would lose herself within the velvety music of his voice.

"*Dravmir...*" Her throat burned as she called his name to the wind.

"I'm here, Yelena. I'm here." His voice was not musical like she wished to imagine. Instead, it was wrought in agony.

This was wrong. If she were to spend her final moments lost in the illusion of him, she wanted for him to sound blissful. Yelena forced her eyes open. Everything was a blur but his face. Seeming so clear that surely this was a dream. Yelena wanted to reach for that perfect face, to palm it within her hand. But her arm refused to listen. Laying limply beside her. Utterly useless. The waves crashed against the rocks again, this time reaching far enough that the cold water jolted Yelena's mind as it soaked her. She blinked again, with more clarity and she realized that this was no dying fever dream. Dravmir had truly come for her but was he too late? She did not care. If she could spend her final moments with him in his arms, she did not care.

"You came." She croaked with a forced smile, her lips feeling heavy.

Dravmir's hand brushed away the dampened hair that clung to her face, "I shall always come for you, Yelena."

And it was then that a second path had formed. The shadows creeping away and revealing a cobblestone pathway. This one did not lead toward death but toward her future. Toward Dravmir.

"I do not wish to die." She spoke.

"And you won't." Dravmir's fingers traced over her neck. "There will be pain, but it shall not last long, I swear it."

Yelena closed her eyes, ready to embrace the gift of immortality.

For it had never been a curse and she knew that now.

Dravmir's lips feathered a kiss to her skin, *"Forever."* He declared as he pierced her flesh.

The kiss of death.

A gasp escaped her as fires erupted beneath her flesh. It was sweet agony. Flames had charred her blood as it rippled through her veins, scorching every inch of mortality that clung to her bones. Burning it away in a feverish heat. She wanted to lose herself in those flames, to dance amongst them. But the bliss of the warmth did not last long as the fires truly began to burn her soul.

Transforming her fragile body into something unbreakable. So easily she had forfeited her mortality. But that did not mean it would shed from her heart. She would grasp ahold of it and keep it deep within her soul, cradling it like a newborn babe. Yelena would not lose sight of herself, of her past. She would become mortal and immortal all in one body. An inferno ruptured throughout her being and a scream escaped her lips as it burned her from the inside out. Yelena did not know if Dravmir still bit her or if he had stopped. She only felt that searing pain as it branded her soul.

The burning spread to her eyes and she mourned the loss of the oceans she once held captive within her irises. Now replaced with pools of blood. Her spine snapped into place like some sort of wicked puzzle piecing together. She felt as her skin wove itself together once more, mending the wounds Drezca had wrought on her body. Another shriek echoed through the world. Her mouth felt as though a fire had been set within the roots of her teeth. Something was pushing its way through as if she were a newborn babe growing her first set of teeth. Warmth pooled in her mouth as two of her teeth were forced from her gums and something sharp pierced its way through.

Fangs.

The cold splash of the waves tamed the heat that ravaged her flesh, but the heat would only blister hotter as the chill faded. Soon her screams faded into the distance, carried away by the sea and the heat had simmered down to embers before nothing remained of it. And when she opened her eyes, she saw with a new clarity. Seeing every detail of Dravmir's face that had been blurred to her mortal eyes. Seeing each streak within his irises and every strand of hair upon his head, she could count the lashes that framed those piercing eyes. She could see every raindrop that cascaded down his raven tresses. And Yelena saw the glistening tears that had swelled. And when she willed her arm to move, it did. Lifting from the rocks, she reached for the man she would spend eternity with and cradled his cheek in her palm.

"Forever." She smiled.

Relief flooded Dravmir's face as he cradled Yelena in his arms, holding her close as he buried his face in the nape of her neck. "I thought I had lost you." His voice had grown strained.

His arms tightened around her and she wrapped her own around him. Clinging to him to reassure him and herself that she was alive. That he had not lost her, and she had not lost him. Her hands curled into the damp fabric of his shirt, nearly ripping it. Dravmir held her with equal longing, seeming reluctant to let her go and perhaps he never would. The rain steadily poured on them, drizzling upon the world but neither cared. Basking in the reality that they had not lost each other. When they pulled back, Yelena held his face within her hands. Her thumbs stroking away the raindrops that trickled down his face. Dravmir reached up and placed his hands over hers.

Yelena smiled, "It seems I'm too stubborn die."

A chuckle escaped Dravmir, "It seems so, my love."

"How did you find me?"

"I went to find you and Charlotte told me that you left with Drezca. That she had said I sent her to fetch you. I followed your scent and then I heard your screams." He shook his head, "I'm so terribly sorry. If only I had done something. If I had gotten here faster..."

"You came. And that's all that matters." She spoke.

His thumbs tenderly stroked her hands. "Now, it seems we have a punishment to deal out."

Yelena was never the vengeful sort but after learning the truth, Yelena wished to avenge each of Dravmir's brides. To avenge her mother. "There's much I need to tell you."

Dravmir kept ahold of her hands while he stood, bringing her with him. "Tell me everything along the way." Then, he swept her into his arms and the shadows claimed them.

There would be time to teach Yelena the ways of vampires but for now, there was a fiery haired monster that needed to be slain.

∞ ∞ ∞

Along the way, Yelena told Dravmir everything that Drezca had confessed. From the murders of his brides to the killings of the werewolves. That it had been Drezca all along. That it was she that was coated in the blood of so many innocent lives. Yelena could see the guilt swelling with Dravmir's eyes and she knew the thoughts that would be whispering through his mind.

Why did he not see it all these years?

If he had of loved her, then all those women would never have died.

The werewolves would not be so blood thirsty against the vampires.

All this death, all this blood, was on his hands.

Yelena wanted nothing more than to take him in her arms and comfort him, but the castle came into sight. Dravmir lowered to the ground before the doors, the shadows falling away. Before he set Yelena down on her feet, his eyes shifted through the darkness lurking behind the trees. And then he stiffened, his hand going to Yelena's back and bringing her close. When she was mortal, she would not have heard the silent footsteps prowling the forest but now, they were clear. She followed the sound and found glowing eyes watching them from the shadows. Her skin bristled as she remembered the sight of the creature that had chased her. More footsteps approached and more eyes glowed at them from the darkness. The werewolves did not stalk further, as if waiting. Watching. Drezca was the true one they had been hunting for and Yelena wondered if they had heard the woman's confession. If they knew now, that Dravmir had never ordered her to kill the creatures.

The werewolves remained where they were and Dravmir urged Yelena forth, keeping his hand on the small of her back. They ascended the stairs and stood before the looming doors. "Stay here." He rasped.

Yelena nodded her head.

Dravmir cast a glance over his shoulder, toward the creatures. And there they remained, merely watching as if curious to see how this would play at. If they would see justice served against the one who had killed those of their kind. Facing the doors, Dravmir opened one, leaving Yelena hidden by the other. And then, he stalked forth into the shadows of the castle. There was a trudge in his steps, and he hung his head, his shoulders slumped. Dravmir appeared as though he were mourning, lost within the haze of loss and heartache. It pained

Yelena to see him in such away, even if he was acting. For she knew that he had felt this sort of agony before. Felt it in a hundred different ways with each bride he had lost. And Yelena had nearly been one of them. The heart that had been mended had almost been broken beyond repair.

Dravmir stole four steps into the castle before three silhouettes emerged from the shadows and appeared before him. Daria, Danika, and Drezca all stood together. He took note of the worry and swelling fear within the first two women's eyes. But Drezca, there was nothing. As if she were fighting the smirk that wished to form upon her lips. Dravmir's dampened tresses spilled over his shoulders to shadow his face in a veil of darkness. His shoes left wet prints upon the carpet, droplets of water cascaded from his being and spilled upon the floor. The front of his being was drenched in Yelena's blood from cradling her broken mortal form. Crimson tinged his lips from where he saved her. But to them, it would be a failed attempt. Dravmir looked every bit the mourning lover. The three women stalked closer, as if waiting to catch him, seeing how his knees were beginning to buckle beneath him. Dravmir hung his head and slowly shook it. The whimpered cries of Daria and Danika greeted his ears, but nothing escaped Drezca. She was proud of what she had accomplished.

But little did she know that her dark secrets had been spilled to the world.

Dravmir lifted his head to meet her gaze and stalked forth. Daria and Danika had fallen back into the shadows, weeping their sorrows quietly shielded by the darkness. It was then that Drezca smiled victoriously. At long last she believed that he finally had come to her. That he would have her. But Drezca could never be more wrong. For his heart belonged to Yelena and no other for the rest of his days. Dravmir wished to wish to claw that damned smirk off those poisoned lips of hers but her punishment would come soon enough.

Drezca opened her arms to him and stepped into her embrace, his skin crawling as her arms wrapped around him like a vice. "I always knew you'd come to me, my darling." Her voice purred into his ear.

Dravmir's arms hung loosely at his sides. "Tell me," he finally spoke, "why you did it."

Drezca stiffened.

Slowly, her arms fell from him as she took a step back from Dravmir. "What do you mean?"

Dravmir's eyes narrowed then, "Tell me why you killed Yelena."

Gasps sounded from the darkness beside them.

Panic flashed within Drezca's eyes, "I don't know what you're talking about. That foolish mortal fled back to her family and those *beasts* mauled her."

Dravmir merely shook his head as he stepped aside. "No, they didn't, Drezca."

Her brows knitted together as she watched him.

Then, footsteps whispered into the throne room as Yelena stepped around the door and strode into the castle. It was then that fear truly seized Drezca, and the color faded from her face. Drezca's eyes shifted between Yelena and Dravmir, as if she were seeing a phantom. Searching for signs that he too, was seeing the woman that approached them. To Drezca, Yelena appeared like the ghosts of the past brides. Each of them formed into one being before her eyes. Each coming to claim their vengeance.

Yelena stood before the woman and now she, was the one smiling. "Hello, Drezca."

"But how? I killed you!" Her voice shrieked throughout the room.

"No," Yelena stepped forth, "you only thought you had."

Drezca backed away into the shadows but two silhouettes stepped forth, blocking her path so she could not flee. Daria and Danika narrowed their gazes upon the woman before them. There was pain and betrayal pouring from their beings. That Drezca had been the one to murder the brides that they once held dear to their hearts, had once taken care of. And that the woman they had claimed as family, had been the murderer amongst them. A rush of wind blew into the room and Drezca's eyes widened as she caught the scent of the creatures that lurked in waiting just beyond those doors. There would be no fleeing. No escape. Drezca had been caught and now, her punishment would greet her.

Drezca eyed everyone around her, and defeat flickered in her eyes. "So, what shall my grand punishment be, my dear Count?"

Dravmir flicked his eyes to Yelena, "That is for my bride to decide."

Yelena cast a glance behind her and found that the werewolves had stalked forth, towering on their hind legs. Their teeth were bared, snarling. Ready to claim their prey and drown in blood. And when she met Drezca's gaze again, she saw her fate laid out before her. Drezca had become nothing but a statue, frozen in fear as it paralyzed her being. All those centuries of lying and murder had finally caught up to her and now, she would pay the price.

Drezca narrowed her gaze at Dravmir, "If only you had loved me, none of your precious mortals would have died. All this is *your* fault. All their deaths are on *your* shoulders, Dravmir."

The shadows crept forth and swirled around Yelena as she closed the distance between her and Drezca. Rage had scorned her being as Drezca's words resounded through the room and Dravmir flinched at them. She reached out and grasped ahold of Drezca's throat, lifting her from the ground and silencing her. The power Yelena felt rippling through her being was intoxicating. Drezca kicked her feet in the air, thrashing in Yelena's hold. Daria and Danika stalked closer, Dravmir coming up to Yelena's side. There would be no escaping for Drezca. She had reached the end of her blood-soaked path. Yelena whirled around and allowed the shadows to swallow them as they sped across the room to the doors. Yelena thrust her arm forth, summoning the air, remembering how Dravmir told her that vampires can summon things that were not of the living. The other door burst open, cracking against the stone wall. And there at the bottom of the stairs, the werewolves waited. And Yelena could have sworn they smiled.

"This is your punishment." Yelena said.

Drezca cast her gaze upon the creatures and tears swelled within her eyes. "Please..." She pled.

"The brides before me pled for their lives. *I pled for my life.*" Yelena said, "And you showed no mercy."

Drezca met her eyes.

"And I shall not."

And then, Yelena tossed Drezca to the wolves.

Screams reverberated through the night as the creatures lunged and snatched Drezca from the air, dragging her down to the earth. Their teeth piercing her immortal flesh. As Yelena turned her head away, Dravmir appeared at her side and brought her close. His arms embracing her as she buried her face in his chest. But nothing could silence the shrieks that filled her ears as the wolves claimed their vengeance on the vampire. The sounds of their snapping teeth would find their way into Yelena's dreams, always reminding her of the life she punished. Yelena forced herself to glance upon the scene and found the creatures dragging Drezca into the shadows. The woman thrashed and cried out but to no avail. The wolves vanished into the darkness, leaving one behind. The creature met Dravmir's eyes, and their gazes held. Subtly, it inclined its head to the Count and Dravmir did the same. The werewolf turned and stalked forth into the trees and it was then that Drezca's screams had been silenced forever.

CHAPTER SIXTEEN

Eternity Together

T HE WEEKS FOLLOWING Drezca's death, Yelena found herself haunted by
the ghost of Drezca. Her screams rattling her dreams. Drezca would not be
forgotten, refusing to rest. Reminding Yelena that Drezca was dead by her
hands. And Yelena could not help but wonder if Dravmir was suffering the
same. Yelena had stopped sleeping, remembering how Dravmir said immortals
did not need it. But she missed the vibrant dreams that once waited for her.
Missed the violet skies and turquoise waves. One day, she would be able to visit
them again. One day. But for now, she spent her waking hours with Dravmir.
Spending nights wrapped within one another's embrace. Losing themselves
within the lust and pleasure of each other.

Other nights she would spend with Daria and Danika. Wondering the castle
halls or venturing through the garden. The roses had long since withered as
winter fully graced the world. Blanketing it in layers of snow and ice.
Crystalizing the dead flowers and hedges. The snow crunched beneath the trio's
feet as they wandered the frozen pathways. The icy air nipped at Yelena's flesh,
but it did not pierce it. She hardly felt the bite of the cold as she wandered the

world barefoot. Exploring the limitations of her immortal form. Everything was new to her; it was as if the world around her had been unveiled. Seeing it with new eyes, shedding her mortal vision. And then, the thing she feared most, the thirst. It burned her throat, her tongue feeling like a weight within her mouth. It was like a whisper in the back of her mind, tempting her to feed. To go hunt and claim a mortal life. To drown herself within the warmth of their blood. To drink that sweet crimson that flowed through their veins. She had been assured that it would pass with time. That she would not die if she never quenched that burning thirst.

And Dravmir swore that when Yelena felt confident enough, she would see her family. She only need to tame that thirst. He had been gentle as he explained to her that she would not be able to contain herself. Once a mortal crossed her path, she would smell the blood that pumped in their heart and it would drive her into a frenzy. And there would be no stopping her. Yelena's heart ached. She missed her family more than she could put into words. She yearned to be in the arms of her mother and father. To hold her sister in her arms. Her heart broke that she would never be able to taste Danna's cooking again. To indulge herself in the sweet and savory meals. Dravmir said that mortal foods would taste ashen upon her tongue and her stomach would heave it up.

A sigh escaped Yelena's lips as she stopped on the path and reached for a frozen rose. The thorns incased in ice. She ran her fingers over the prickled edges and her skin was left unmarred. The night she pricked her finger felt like decades ago now. So much had happened since then. Since Dravmir had tasted of her blood and fled from the garden. It all felt like some sort of dream. Perhaps it had been. Perhaps she did die the night Drezca shoved her over the cliff's edge. Perhaps Dravmir had been a second too late and she died in his arms and she now was in her own afterlife. Her hand fell from the frozen flower and she faced the two women at her side.

She met Danika's gaze and remembered how Daria had once told her that Danika and her mother had been close. "Danika, how close were you and my mother? Daria told me that you two had been close."

Danika cast her gaze to Daria for a moment, "Sadly, I'm afraid she's mistaken. Though I spent much time escorting her about the castle and the garden, I did not truly speak with her."

Yelena's shoulders slumped slightly as she nodded her head. "Apologies."

Danika closed the distance between them and placed a hand on her shoulder, "I shall not make that mistake again." She gave a gentle squeeze before her hand fell away, "But your mother did speak of you quite often, Yelena. She loved you dearly."

Yelena nodded her head and offered a smile, "Thank you, Danika. To both of you for watching over my mother."

Daria smiled, "Of course."

Yelena's mood shifted as Drezca's face flickered in her mind. "How are you? Both of you? I know each of you loved Drezca a great deal."

A long sigh escaped Daria, "We did love Drezca, but she was not the same woman we once knew."

"Perhaps we never truly knew her." Danika spoke.

Daria nodded. "We should have taken notice sooner. Seeing how vile she was becoming to the brides, how rude. And how much she pined for Dravmir's affection. We should have known but we were blinded by our love."

"It is not your blame to carry, neither of you. Drezca choose her path."

"Indeed, she did." Daria's voice had become hushed.

"But now, we move forward upon our own paths." Danika added.

Yelena smiled, "And now we do, together."

Daria smiled in return, "Together."

The fire crackled steadily. Yelena watched the dancing flames as if they were putting on a show for her. Her mind began to wander as if often did. But it was not to her own worlds, it was to that night. Where the sky cried its sorrow upon the world and a mortal woman stood at a cliff's edge with a monster stalking ever closer. The waves below crashed against the jagged rocks that waited to pierce the mortal woman's fragile flesh and claim her life. There had been pain and blood and then the wind roared against her ears as she plummeted through the open air. There had been a crack in the most vital part of her back as her body collided with the rocks. Pain seared through her skull and warmth trickled and matted into her hair. But then came the horrible truth, her body lay still. And though she urged it, it did not obey. Her spine had been severed and she was left to die there alone. All she felt was the icy jolt of the waves as it splashed against her face. Salt burned her lips and parched her throat. Her vision had begun to blacken as the world blurred. Death lurked in the shadows and waited.

Yelena had tried to process the few weeks that felt like an eternity. Her mortal life had come to a quick end and stepped into the flesh of an immortal. In truth, Yelena was not entirely ready to leave her mortal body behind. Though it was silly, she wanted to have at least one more dinner with her family. Seated around the table and indulging in Danna's cooking. And now, she would never taste her sister's food again. Her eyes drifted down to her hands, rested atop her knees that leaned against the arm of the chair. Lifting a hand, she traced over the smooth skin of her other. Never would they know age. To wrinkle with time, to become crooked. Never would she know how it felt to grow old, to bear children if she ever wished for any. Dravmir had told her that vampires could not birth children. Though it did not truly bother her, there was a sorrow that lingered. To never have the option if she ever did wish it.

Yelena had thought she would have time, so much time, before she walked that path to immortality. But she never knew how limited the days had become. She had meant what she said in Dravmir's arms. *Forever.* They would have eternity together. She had only wished that it would have been under different circumstances. That she had not been broken and dying in his arms. Had not been struggling to keep her grasp on this world. Her heart slowing its beat. She had only wished that Dravmir did not have to have that memory of her burned into his thoughts forever. If there had been a choice, Yelena would have waited a few years from now. Would have wished to be in the privacy of her chambers or Dravmir's while he gave her the gift of immortality. But there was a comforting thought that crossed her mind, that they had broken that vicious cycle. No other brides would die. The agony was over and this castle, Dravmir, would know peace.

Yelena's ears flickered at the sound of the room doors opening. Light footsteps approached the chair she was seated on. Fingertips traced over her bare shoulder causing a smile to caress her lips. Tilting her head back, she found Dravmir's gaze. He smiled to her before he leaned down and feathered a kiss to her lips. Yelena could spend hours, days, becoming lost within him. In his kiss. Giving her body entirely over to him while they tangled beneath the sheets.

Dravmir's lips left hers, his mouth lingering a breath away from hers. Gently, he tucked her hair behind her ear. "How are you, my love?"

"Still coming to terms, I suppose."

A grave expression twisted his face as he nodded his head. "I'm sorry."

Yelena palmed his cheek within her hand. A sigh escaped him as he went to his knees, pressing his cheek into her palm. "I already know what you're thinking and stop that nonsense."

His hand rested atop hers, a light chuckle escaping him. "You read my mind too well, Yelena."

She stroked her thumb across his smooth skin. "You are too easy to read."

"I cannot say the same for you." His eyes met with hers, "How are you, truly?"

A sigh escaped her then, "You'll think I'm silly."

"Never."

Yelena's gaze drifted to the flames, "I wish I could have eaten one last dinner with my family. My sister made the best meals, I'll miss them."

Dravmir moved her hand to his lips and pressed a kiss to her palm, "That's not silly, my love. My mother used to make these caramel treats when I was a young boy, I have long since forgotten their taste. I would love nothing more than to eat one, one last time."

A tender smile found itself on Yelena's lips, "Look at us, mourning over food."

"Yes, how silly we are." He laughed into her palm.

Hearing his laugh reminded Yelena of her first days in the castle. How cold and bitter Dravmir had been. Never smiling, never laughing. And now, he did it often and it was the most beautiful sound she had ever heard. Warmth kindled in her soul knowing that she would always be able to hear such a treasured sound and she would cherish it till the end of her days. Cherish him entirely. Yelena shifted in the chair and slid to the ground before him. Dravmir watched her closely as she took his face in her hands. Closing her eyes, she brought him close and pressed her lips to his. Yelena relaxed her body against his as Dravmir's arms came around her. One of his hands palming the back of her head while the other remained on the small of her back. The world around them melted away and it was only them in this moment, in this room.

A whimper escaped Yelena's mouth as Dravmir's lips left hers. For a moment he stared into her eyes, into the changed irises that no longer held the oceans he once loved. But now reflected her immortality. Forever he would be by her side.

"I love you." His velvety voice whispered into the world.

Yelena could hardly give the words voice, her throat becoming choked as she swallowed back her tears. "I love you, Dravmir."

The brightest smile she had ever seen filled Dravmir's face. As if relief and ardent love had surged through him and filled his soul. Dravmir's lips found hers with more urgency. Kissing her as if he had never kissed her before. As if he had been holding himself back when she was mortal. Only this time, she was not so fragile. So breakable. But now Yelena was crafted from the stones of immortality. And Dravmir would no longer hold back. He fully unleashed himself upon Yelena and she eagerly gave herself over to him. The fires of passion scorched through their beings and a growl escaped Dravmir as he hoisted Yelena into his arms. Her legs wound around him as he carried her over to the bed, their lips never parting. Feverishly claiming one another. Yelena did not know when their clothes had been shredded from their bodies but all she felt was him. His skin against hers. His hands roamed the plains of her body, touching every inch of her and leaving a trail of heat in his wake. Her body becoming scorched in his inferno.

Dravmir's lips parted from hers, traveling down the expanse of her neck to her chest. Placing a kiss to each breast before venturing further. Yelena spread her legs to him and Dravmir indulged himself in her wet need. Stoking it and calling it forth, causing the dam to erupt and burst forth, flooding down his throat as he swallowed her river. Yelena's voice echoed all around them. Dravmir's tongue coaxed that fiery passion in her being. Stirring her arousal. Her back arched as another wave scorned her. Growls rumbled against her womanhood as Dravmir devoured her. She could hardly contain herself, writhing against his lips. Her fingers tangling within his tresses as she cried out.

When Dravmir rose from her hips, there was a spark in those crimson eyes. His desire burning brightly and hers echoed it. Dravmir crawled atop her and his dampened lips met with hers. Yelena tasted herself upon his mouth, his tongue, as their lips sealed. Gasps escaped them as they lost themselves within one another. Dravmir's hardness brushed against her womanhood and she moaned. Pleading for him to enter her and he answered her cries. A gasped moan escaped Yelena and Dravmir swallowed the sound as he kissed her. Dravmir thrusted inside her mercilessly. Her body burst as pleasure consumed her mind. Her body rocking against his. Her back arched from the bed and Dravmir slid an arm around her, holding her close as he braced his other hand above her head. Yelena clung to Dravmir, her nails breaking his skin as they raked down the length of his back. Growls of pleasure rumbled against Yelena's chest. Her nipples hardening more at the sound, becoming sore.

A grunted moan escaped Dravmir as he released himself. But he was far from finished. "Turn over." His voice rasped against her ear.

Warmth flared within Yelena and she happily obliged. Dravmir slid out of her and she turned on her knees, resting her elbows on the bed. The mattress sunk as Dravmir positioned himself between her legs, spreading them further apart. Yelena bit back a moan, chewing her lip, as his hardened need rubbed against her wetness. His hands grasped ahold of her hips and he shoved himself inside her, forcing that moan forth from her throat. Dravmir pounded himself in her feverishly and her nails curled into the bedsheets, shredding them. Groans escaped Dravmir as his fingers curled into the skin of her hips. Dravmir was no longer gentle, and Yelena did not wish him to be. Not while the fires that scorched her felt so good, reveling, and basking in the heat of their shared pleasure.

But now, Yelena wished to reign in control.

It was her turn, to pleasure him.

As if sensing her desire, Dravmir had ceased his thrusting. Yelena whirled to face him, blurred in shadows, and grasped ahold of Dravmir. Flipping them so that Dravmir lay on his back, beneath her. A sly grin crossed her lips as she straddled him, hovering above his cock that glistened in her arousal. There was a feral-ness within Dravmir's eyes, as if a beast stared back at her. But she did not fear it for a beast had been wakened within her as well. Yelena braced a hand against Dravmir's chest and lowered herself onto his hardened need. She tipped her head back as a burst of heat flooded her being and she began rocking her hips against him.

The bed creaked and groaned beneath their bodies. Dravmir's hands gripped her hips and she rocked faster with a feverish heat. Her need spilling over him. Dravmir tilted his head back, his teeth clenched as if he could hardly contain himself. Reigning control over the beast that ravaged him from the inside. His hands roamed to her breasts and fondled them. His fingers pinching the hardened peaks of her nipples causing her moans to grow louder. And then, as if he could no longer tame the beast, his hands gripped her hips once more. Yelena met his gaze and then, he began to thrust his hips, pounding inside her.

Her mouth gaped open as fastened breaths escaped her lips. She braced her hands on his chest as he thrusted inside her again and again.

Though she was now immortal, her strength was waning. One last, screaming moan echoed from her lips. His name resounding through the room and her name followed as he called it out. Yelena crumpled against him, falling into his arms as they caught her and held her to his chest. Yelena rested a hand upon his chest, and she felt as he began to trace soothing circles on her back. A light kiss was pressed to the crown of her head before Dravmir rested his chin down on her hair. She could never truly put into words the bliss and peace she felt. Not just within moments like these but any moment she shared with Dravmir. With Daria and Danika. This was her forever.

Yelena lifted her head as her hands slid down either side of his chest and she lifted herself up, staring into his eyes. Dravmir reached up and took her cheek within his palm. "What is it, my love?"

She smiled, "Just thinking."

"About what?"

She sat up on his stomach, one of her hands pressed to the back of his as her other held his wrist, leaning into his touch. "About this – all of this. Us. Forever."

His thumb tenderly stroked her cheek, "Eternity together."

"*Together.*"

∞ ∞ ∞

The winter air whispered against Yelena's ears, its icy fingers stroking her tresses. Ice tinged the wind as it nipped at her cheeks, her bare shoulders. Snow coated the ground, blanketing the crooked branches of the trees. Encasing them in eternal winter till spring graced the world and brought warmth with it. Snow crunched beneath Yelena's feet as she stepped down the stairs of the castle. Her pale, lavender dress trailing behind her in a river of silk. She closed her eyes and breathed in the icy air. Tasting winter upon her tongue. The wind swept by again, tousling the ends of her long sleeves, causing them to ripple like the currents in an ocean. There was the faintest hint of salt in the air. Something her mortal senses never plucked from the wind.

Behind her, footsteps whispered upon the snow. Dravmir took his place by her side. Watching her. The serenity he found on her face was utterly beautiful. She had found peace within her newfound immortal life, but he knew there was something missing. Her family. He saw it in her eyes when her mind wandered. He saw it in the way she spoke about them. That yearning in her voice. But he knew it was not safe for Yelena to walk amongst the village, near so many mortals. Their beating hearts would be all too tempting to her. He knew that all too well from his earlier years. How he could hear the blood pumping through their veins, roaring against his ears. And each time, he could not stop himself. He would forever be haunted by those memories and he did not wish for his bride to suffer the same. Did not wish for her to fall into those darkened pits of despair if she ever harmed her family.

Dravmir reached out and stroked her cheek with the backs of his fingers. A light sound escaped her, and she leaned into his faint touch. "Are you ready, my love?"

Her eyes flicked open, and a smile wrote itself upon her lips, "Always."

"Would you like a head start?" He teased.

A snort escaped her, "I can beat you without one."

Dravmir grinned, "Are you so sure about that?"

She flicked her gaze to him, "Try your best to keep up."

And then, Yelena was a blur of shadows as she darted into the trees. Laughter echoed from Dravmir as she chased after his bride. For a moment, the world seemed to slow around them as he watched her. Her stride was graceful as if she had been immortal for years and not mere weeks. Those white tresses danced along the wind, swaying from side to side. A wide, dazzling smile danced on her lips as laughter escaped her. There was such a glimmer in those now, crimson irises. And Dravmir had come to realize that they were like the softened petals of roses that bloomed when spring brought life to them once more, melting away the icy winter that caged them. Her lavender dress rippled along the air behind her like waves. Often catching the snarled branches of trees but it never slowed his bride. Her stride even and steady as she leapt over unearthed roots.

It had been too long since Dravmir could enjoy runs such as these. Hiding away within his castle while the werewolves lurked in waiting to claim his life. But peace had finally brought itself between their kinds. No longer living in fear. The beasts still roamed the forest, but they never attacked, merely watching before retreating into the shadows. Catching glimpses of glowing eyes watching in the darkness. Since Drezca's death, they never again attacked. Guilt laced through Dravmir, feeling so blind. If only he had of known. Had pieced it together. He never wished to believe that someone he had once trusted had betrayed him in the cruelest of ways. Had claimed the lives of werewolves to stoke their hatred. How she claimed the lives of his brides and placed the blame on those creatures. He could not change the past, no matter how much he wished it. He could only face the future. And Yelena was there on that path, waiting at the end with her hand outstretched to him and smile upon her face. And he could see her seated upon that pearlescent throne – if the vampires ever returned to this land – she would rule at his side.

Dravmir returned to the world to find her running ahead of him. She cast a glance over her shoulder and smiled. And he knew, there was nowhere else he wished to be than with her. By her side forever.

Together.

EPILOGUE

THE NIGHTS CAME AND WENT, as did the years, and the time had finally arrived. Yelena stood before the castle doors; eagerness clawed beneath her immortal flesh. She had spent the years repressing that endless thirst. That craving that seemed to never sleep. But she had conquered it, tamed the beast within. Never feasting upon mortal blood. No longer did it burn her throat, her tongue no longer a weight in her mouth. Yelena had embraced her immortal body, taken control over it. Taking in a breath, Yelena was ready. It was time, she could not wait a moment longer for tonight, she would see her family again.

Dravmir stood at her side, "Are you ready?" He asked.

She nodded eagerly.

He did not make her wait a moment more for she had waited too long. Shadows stirred around them as they darted into the night. Winding through the trees as they bounded through the forest. Yelena's mind was a whirlwind, hardly focusing on the world around her. Her gaze was locked ahead, searching for the faintest sign of the village gates. And when they burst forth from the forest, there they stood. Yelena did not cast a glance behind her, knowing that Dravmir was right on her heels. She dashed toward the gates and soared into the air over them. The cobblestones groaned beneath her feet as she landed with force, dropping the shadows away too eagerly. And before her was the village. It had been too long since she stepped foot through those gates. Not since she was chosen as Dravmir's bride those years ago, carried through them into the darkness beyond.

Dravmir came up to her side and took her hand in his. Yelena met his gaze, and he offered a smile. She would not do this alone. He would be by her side. Focusing ahead, she kept a firm hold on his hand as the shadows crept forth and they darted through the cobblestone streets of the village. She knew the paths all too well, able to walk them blindfolded. And then, a familiar house crept into her vision and she halted. There it stood. Her home. Memories swelled and stirred within her mind. And she could have sworn she heard the phantom laughter of her family echoing around them. Yelena could not wait a second more and she dashed toward the small door. She did not bother knocking as she grasped ahold of the knob and turned it. The door's creak was so loud it could have woken the dead. The world all too silent around them.

And then, she crossed the threshold.

Before she could even take in the familiar surroundings, gasps filled the air and her head snapped up. And there they sat around the table. Her family. The scent of cabbage and spiced onion tinged the air. For a long moment, Yelena stood in that small doorway, holding the eyes of her family. It felt like a dream. She never thought she would truly see them again and here they sat, just within reach. And yet, she could not urge her body to move, frozen. Danna was the first to stand. Her beautiful sister. Her dark hair pulled back into bun that dangled loosely atop her head. A smearing of flower coated her forehead and dark wisps of hair framed her face. Danna rounded the table. Taking slow steps at first as if she could hardly believe Yelena stood before her. And when reality came crashing down on them, choked sobs escaped Danna and she crossed the distance between them and tossed her arms around her sister. The two laughed as they cried, clinging desperately to one another. The sound of kitchen chairs screeching on the floor pierced their ears as Yelena's parents tumbled forth and hugged their lost daughter. Relishing in this reunion.

Yelena clung to her family, breathing in their scents. So distinguished now. She could smell the blood in their veins, could hear their thundering hearts but the thirst did not tempt her. Did not scorch her throat. Danna smelled of spices and vegetables. Her mother smelled of a garden and her father was doused in hints of cologne and musk. Yelena gave one last squeeze to her family before pulling back to look into their faces. She saw the shock in their eyes as they realized the change in her eyes. And the realization of what their daughter had become. Yelena had readied herself for the fear, for the rejection, but she found none. There was only that relief and unconditional love in their eyes.

Her mother's hand touched her cheek, her father touched her other. And Yelena had not realized how aged her parents were. How mortal they were, and her heart ached. She could see every fine wrinkle on their faces. Saw how their cheeks had begun to sag. Saw the slight tremble in her parents' hands as they reached for her. There were fine strands of silver hair atop her mother's head. Yelena knew she would have to face their deaths but seeing them now broke her heart knowing the inevitable to come.

The creaking of floorboards echoed in the silence as Dravmir stood in the doorway behind Yelena. For a moment, fear widened her family's eyes as they gaped at the man behind their daughter. But Yelena only smiled, nodding her head. Dravmir placed a tender hand upon her shoulder and bowed his head to her family. Confusion danced within their eyes as they shifted between the two. Yelena's hand rested upon his as she stepped back into him. Danna was the first to smile, seeing the trust between the two. And the love that burned so fiercely within Dravmir's eyes and how it reflected the same in Yelena's.

"We have much to talk about." Yelena said.

The group gathered around the kitchen table. Yelena took her seat, feeling so at home. Finally, everything was perfect in her world. Dravmir stood behind her, his hand still on her shoulder as she began to tell their tale.

My Other Works:

CREATURES

SHADOWS AND NIGHT

(CHILDREN OF DARK)

BLOOD AND NIGHT

(CHILDREN OF DARK)

DEATH AND NIGHT

(CHILDREN OF DARK)

HER DARK DESIRES

A TALE OF TWO PACKS

THE CIRCUS OF SHADOWS

ASSASSINATION OF THE HEART

GOLDEN HEARTS AND SILVER KEYS

Made in the USA
Middletown, DE
01 January 2022